THE CITY ON THE OUTSKIRTS

Chapter 1

Darkness swallows everything in front, behind lies a bright safe garden, it isn't a place Vincent recalls & yet is somehow familiar, but there is something pushing him relentlessly towards the unknown hidden in the gloom. This has been a recurring dream for years with no variation or explanation. As Vincent slowly gains focus as the fog of sleep falls away, he hears the familiar white noise of another rainy day gently tapping on the window like a beat to a distant song. Vincent lived in a small apartment, an apartment that had come to him by strange circumstances, a lawyer contacted him on his seventeenth birthday informing him of the death of an aunt he had never known.

The apartment building had two floors, the top being split into two separate dwellings, the other inhabited by Mr Devon, a curmudgeon of a man who maintained the abode such as it was. The whole ground floor was occupied by a strange little woman who just went by Dot, she was always smiling to herself as if she was constantly being amused by something others weren't aware of. Vincents days bled into one another as the weeks fold over into months. He closed his door, Mr

Devon glared down at him from the ladder he was
aloft changing a globe that always seemed to be
out at the top of the stairs, as he passed Dot's door
it sprung open & Dot already mid-sentence asked,
"Oh yes, hmm, Vince, will you remember to pick up
my order from the corner store?"
Vincent Smiled & remarked,
"Of course, Dotty, every Monday, I'll remember"
Dot broke eye contact & shuffled back inside
continuing her musing too the unseen.

Despite the cold rain the streets bustled with people
under umbrellas & hoods, so much so that the
three large men standing on the corner didn't
register although as he passed a cold shiver ran
through his body & his heartbeat quickened not
noticing their eyes tracked him as he continued
down the road. Vincent arrived at the small book
store nestled in amongst the shiny new store fronts,
it was aged, the paint cracked revelling colours of
previous incarnations underneath. The key was
large & had a swirling pattern inlayed into top. The
lock snapped as it released with a satisfying thud.
The large door opened to the chime of a small
brass bell which accented his arrival. The store was
not organised with any real rhyme or reason he
could understand & the rows of books somehow
seemed to extend higher & further than possible.
The owner Arthur Mack was a quiet man, but when
he did speak, he chose his words carefully. The
day they met Arthur had said,

"Words have hidden power & should be respected,
not taken at face value"

It always amazed Vincent that every day when he
arrived there was a newly acquired pile of books on
the counter even though the stores customers were
few & far between, but somehow books appeared
to come & go with some regularity. He picked up
the books wrapped neatly in brown paper tied with
thick rough string that tore at his fingers. The smell
of the leather & the common scent of old
parchment familiar & calming to him as he
unwrapped the bundle. The books seemed to have
no category that he could ascertain, so he had a
shelf to the right of the counter with a small sign
that simply read "New Acquisitions", he slid the
books into the slots left by books that must've been
sold by Arthur he had concluded. In the back of the
store was a small makeshift kitchen with a small
bar fridge, a cupboard with four mugs, not one a
match to another, three small plates & a random
selection of biscuits in a tin that had been added to
over time. Below was a draw containing the most
random assortment of cutlery obtained from diners
& restaurants along with some little trinkets that
always seem to find their way into those draws.
Vincent made himself a mug of the tea from the
small silver tin that sat on the bench since Arthur
had forbidden coffee in the store,
"Horrible bitter muck" he called it,
Vincent picked through the biscuit tin searching for
a hidden tasty treat, but only finding plain oatmeal,

he stacked a few on the same chipped plate he had
chosen on his first day & every day following &
made his way back to the register. Sitting down on
the stool he put his morning tea on the frayed mat
that protected the top of the tarnished glass case &
opened the book he had left there the previous
evening, finding his place marked with an ornate
wooden bookmark that had been a gift a few years
ago from Dot for the birthday. She had chosen one
for him since he didn't know his real one,
"Everyone deserves one day a year" she told him.
He had read many of the books in the store over
the years but in truth only a tiny fraction of those
that filled the shelves. Vincent had been on a
historical kick of late, fascinated by civilisations &
societies lost to the ages, he pictured himself living
in these foreign places, dreaming that he belonged
somewhere other than the mundane world he had
found himself in.
He reached out to grab the last biscuit without
looking up from his current distraction, a book on
the myths of the Norse people & his hand only
found an empty plate, before he could even look
up, he heard a crunch & an inquisitive chirpy voice
asks,
"Whatcha reading"?
Vincent fell back off the stool he was perched on,
startled he yelped in a high pitch that left him
somewhat embarrassed.
"Shit, where did you come from?"
Stood in front of the counter a spritely looking
individual clad in a deep green hooded long coat

secured with long belts that lashed across his athletic build. The coat reached to his knees where it met black leather boots that were fastened with buckles & braided laces.

"Yuck, these aren't very tasty at all" he said playfully,

"Disins usually have better snacks"

Vincent stood up & realised that not only had he not seen the stranger come up to the counter, nor did he didn't hear the bell chime as he entered. He walked over to the door opening it & to his surprise the bell chimed, as he began to turn back to question the stranger he heard a second voice, a grizzled & ill temped mutter

"Yeah it's this one, its right here in my ledger"

Vincent's eyes searched the room for the source of the voice only to see a small creature come into focus sitting on the edge of one of the bookshelves, shocked & with his mouth a gasp he stared trying to make some sense of his situation. The creature had a large round face with big dome style eyes which had two sets of pupils, one large in the centre & a smaller set at the bottom near the lid. Its clothes had pockets up & down each side with tarnished golden chains webbing into the pockets from a central leather sash which ran down his middle, his feet were claws, akin to some kind of bird of prey but with coarse black hairs rather than feathers.

"Are you going to tell me what the hell is going on?" another voice scaredly questioned,

Vincent turned to see a young woman standing in
the corner looking terrified, she lunged & dashed
for the door, she had barely made it three steps
before a large hand appeared & grabbed her by the
back of the neck lifting her off the ground &
stopping her advance.
"They're always so skittish when the Faige still has
them"
Growled the voice from shadows,
"You know it's to keep them safe" replied the impish
stranger,
Who was now behind the counter flicking through
the book Vincent had been reading,
"I don't know why we need the Falaichte anyway"
Growled the unseen creature that still cloaked in
shadow had placed the trembling girl back on the
ground but still had a grip on her,
"Yes, you do"
Replied the small creature atop the bookshelf with
a very stern look.
Vincent terrified & unable to comprehend what was
taking place in the sanctuary he had become most
comfortable in could only muster the words to ask
timidly,
"wha..what is the Falaichte?"
"Ah, Good question!"
The impish individual exclaimed with a smile
"See they're not all so slow Sikes"
The creature in the shadow growled disapprovingly.
"Simply put, The Falaichte are hidden weapons"
 "& the faige?"
Vincent queried, his curiosity overriding his fear.

"Why don't you take this one, Sapere" the Imp
suggested.
The small creature narrowed his gaze as the smile
on the Imps face spread to reveal teeth that came
to a point.
"The Faige is what has hidden & protected you for
all these years" sighed Sapere.
"We had better get moving Nadaur" Sikes said,
With a deepness to its growl that you could feel
through the floor.
"Right! we've got a few more to pick up before the
day is done" said the Imp,
bounding over the counter with little effort.

All at once Sapere blurred & vanished, Sikes pulled
the young woman into the shadow. Vincent looked
up & in an instant Nadaur was in front of him, he
crossed his arms grasping Vincent shoulders with
opposite hands giving another toothy grin. The floor
seemed to disappear & Vincent felt the sensation of
the drop of a rollercoaster, he fell & his stomach
remained above, in a blink they were in a
completely different place. Vincent's face turned a
pale white as he heard the girl being sick mixed
with sobs,
"You'll get the hang of it" Nadaur chirped,
Slapping Vincent on the back.
They appeared to be in a small cobblestone village,
standing on a bridge that crossed a gentle stream.
A concerned look fell across Sapere's face as he
pulled one chain from the many pockets that criss
crossed his coat to obtain a book at the end & then

another & another, flicking ferociously through the pages,
"This isn't right, we've been Drifted…Sikes get out here!"
Out of a shadow a large brown hairy beast came bounding forward, the size of a small car, with yellow eyes & a mouth that reached back far into its cheeks full of teeth that extended forward as they gnashed. On its head were two horns which curved to points above its eye line. Nadaur opened his stance crouching as he surveyed the area, on his arms black blades had protruded from his elbow ending at the knuckles of his hand in a razor edge. Vincent shocked saw that his eyes had also become a vibrant blue with a slight vapour emanating from them as he the scanned the area,
"There!" he yelled,
Pointing into the darkness,
Vincent tracked his eye line & saw a large black shape moving smoothly amongst the trees, as his eyes focused, he could see that this huge beast resembled a black wolf but the black seemed to fall into itself like staring into some type of deep void, a black abyss.
"It's a bainly wolf" said Sikes,
With more concern in his voice than was comfortable.
"I've got him" grinned Nadaur,
Looking wilder than he had previously.
"No" Sapere stated,
With an authority that immediately snapped Nadaur out of his aggressive state,

"It's come for the Disins, we must get them back,
Sikes you make a wall while we get them out of
here" ordered Sapere
Sikes leapt easily over the group putting himself in
between the beast & its prey, Sapere & Nadaur
moved next to Vincent & the almost catatonic girl,
"We have to make sure of our passage this time"
Sapere urgently said,
He retrieved a silver orb from the end of one of the
chains.
"Oh I hate using the Dyrr orb, it always gives me
the worst headache" Nadaur groaned,
"I think that's the least of your worries" replied
Sapere, In a judgmental tone,
"Sikes get ready, here we go" Sapere announced,
Sapere twisted the sphere & pulled the two halves
apart, a bright light shone from inside the
mechanism. The Wolf snarled & Fired forward at a
truly startling speed, the girl out of some basic
instinct grasped Vincent's hand & squeezed with a
force that took him by surprise, Vincent was
transfixed by the deep black of the wolf, his mind
had become trapped, mesmerised by the viscous
black of its form, He hadn't even realised that they
had all started the glow with a pale white hue, Sikes
moved forward to engage the wildness that came
for them,
"Stay Close" Sapere yelled.
As the wolf flew forward Sikes chambered his
massive club of an arm, claws longer than the
fingers on you hand sprung into place, he loaded
up with his entire weight & swung catching the

beast in its side with a deafening swack, the black void of an animal flew across into the trees, shattering trunks & branches as it tumbled out of control sending splinted wood out with an explosive force. The orb snapped back into place & everyone bathed in the hue was instantly enveloped by the orb with then disappeared with a mighty crack of energy.
A tall being stepped from the shadow of the forest, his face concealed by a black hood
"Interesting" he stated as the mighty wolf found its place at his side.

In a large room with a domed ceiling there was a much larger mirror image of the orb Sapere had used to whisk the group away from the imminent danger, it began to glow with the same white hue. The other inhabitants of the room upon seeing this back away & shield their eyes as the light intensifies. A slender muscled Imp raised her eyes from her conversation, with a crack of energy, the sound amplified & bounced off the walls of the room in a deafening echo. Nadaur, Sikes & Sapere appear in the flash shaken but unhurt. Vincent & the young woman still grasping hands are lying unconscious at their feet,
"Ugggh it gets worse every time" Sikes grumbled
"Look at the size of you" Sapere snapped rubbing his head,
"For someone so intimidating you certainly do complain a lot"

Nadaur Laughed at the petty conflict of his compatriots when he was tackled to the ground by the Imp girl who had come flying across the room with the silent stealth of a big cat. Nadaur shocked looked into her big green eyes & gasped,
"Nyah, you almost took my head off!"
She Planted a big kiss on him, but as she pulled away, she grasped his face with both hands & examined his eyes closely. A faint blue ring remained around his light grey eyes that Nyah recognized, she moved her doll like face framed with a black pixie cut in till there button noses met & whispered
"Are you alright?"
"Yeah, I'm doing better" Nadaur replied with a reassuring tone,
"Ok" Nyah replied,
Stealing another kiss, she grabbed him by the lapels easily lifting him to his feet.
Sapere called over two people dressed in matching uniforms & ordered them to take the two unconscious strangers to the dorms. They lifted them throwing them over their shoulders with relative ease & left down one of the many corridors leading off from the room.
"I have to go & look into why a Bainly was sent to intercept us & who pulled us of course" Sapere said with obvious concern in his voice,
Mumbling to himself as he disappeared down one of the dark hallways.
"I'm hungry, gonna get something to eat?"
"You're always hungry Sikes" Nyah Playfully teased

As she jumped up onto Sikes' back & hugged him,
her arms struggling to reach around the width of his
furry back,
"Where are you off to" inquired Nadaur,
He noticed a group of people getting ready off to
the side. Nyah now sitting quite comfortably cross
legged on Sikes broad shoulder looked down
"We've Gotta go & retrieve the wayward golden
child again"
With that she stood up & with a slight shrug Sikes
she was propelled high into the air, with elegance &
grace she flipped & twisted till she landed behind
Nadaur threw her arms around his shoulders &
kissed him on the cheek,
"I'll see you later" she said,
As she turned to leave, she gave Sikes a little wink.
Nyah picked up her jacket & as she zipped up the
form fitting black leather, she nodded toward the
three individuals gearing up,
"You scallywags ready?"
A blonde with prominent shoulders looked up &
sighed as she picked her claw like nails with the
point of a red bladed dagger,
"What's the problem Tallie?, you fought to be part
of the elite & you've more than earned your place"
"I don't like being a babysitter to a spoiled little shit
who only cares about himself & what he can get
from people" interrupted Tallie
"I know you joined up for the action, you were bred
for it after all, but sometimes boring is a good thing.
You good Faucon, Dabn?" Nyah asked.

A large thick beast of a creature turned & with a
relaxed casualness
"Yup, let's go get this pain in the arse"
Nyah looked up to Faucon, she crouched above
them balancing effortlessly on a small outcrop on
the wall, with perfect precision she jumped &
landed directly in front of Nyah toe to toe, Nyah
smiled but didn't flinch.
"Off we go then" Faucon spouted in a sing-songy
way.
The Elite armed with an assortment of weaponry
stood in a square & Nyah gave the command,
"Tallie, if you would"
They all grabbed the arm of the person to their left
& Tallie read a passage inscribed on the inside of
her right forearm causing it to glow red, on the floor
a shadow spread from her feet engulfing them all.
In an instant they were on a rooftop in a busy city,
the cold night was still but the low thud of bass
could be heard. With a skip Faucon popped up onto
the edge of the building crouching, her eyes had
lost all colour as her pupils expanded.
"Two out front…wait make that three"
She closed her eyes & whispered something under
her breath, when she opened her eyes, the black
had switched to a vibrant purple, the three men
took on a sickly greenish yellow aura "They're
Alimanas"
"Great where there's three there's bound to be
more" Dabn added in a huff

"They are nothing to be scared of anyone of us can take out ten of them without breaking stride" Tallie said impatiently

"We aren't here for a fight Tallie, we are here for The Regents son, we'll go in through the roof" Nyah ordered.

They all stepped up onto the ledge & as easy as jumping over a puddle they silently cleared the 50 feet between buildings. A skylight flashed & pulsed with the lights within, they took up positions on all sides,

"Faucon, you got him?" queried Nyah

"Yup, back left, but he's not alone"

"Ok, Tallie & I will go down & get him you two stay up here & keep watch"

Dabn made a slight grumble,

"I know you don't like splitting up the team but you'd cause a riot in there" Nyah said, patting him on the chest.

Nyah & Tallie moved to the back side of the building there was a window on the second floor. Tallie jumped from the roof turning & catching the windowsill in one motion, she slipped a knife under the lock & silently entered into the room. Nyah followed as she approached the door, she could see the shadows cast by someone's feet at the crack at the base of the door. Nyah took out a yellow gem set in an intricate silver frame from a pouch on her hip, when it made contact with the door the pattern spun & there was a solid thunk, she opened the door gently revealing a large man, unconscious but attached to the door. Nyah

grabbed the man as Tallie removed the gem as she
did the man slumped into Nyah's arms, although he
was much larger than her, she carried him easily &
tossed him into a closet. They found themselves on
a catwalk above a dark dance floor, the sea of
people moving in rhythm with the strobing lights &
bass lead electronic tunes that filled the building
like a pulse. Tallie gestured with her eyes to a slim
pale man sitting in a secluded back corner of the
club, his area was clad in layers of black curtains
that dampened the music. The two women moved
across the dancefloor camouflaged by the oblivious
dancing mass. Tallie split off as Nyah continued her
approach to the restricted section. There was
another impressively large individual blocking the
entrance,
"Private party sweetheart" he said,
In a low register placing his hand on her shoulder to
prevent her advance,
Making eye contact with the slim man, who met her
gaze with an arrogant smile, she shifted her weight
slightly & struck the bouncer in the side with such
force he immediately crumpled & passed out from
shock. Nyah held the large man with one hand &
dropped him onto a chair to the side. Four other
men shifted in their seats but just as they were
about to get up Pfft,Pfft,Pfft,Pfft four sharp noises &
they fell back into their respective seats. Tallie
moved out of the shadows created by the curtains
placing her hands on the slim man's shoulders,
Nyah walked through the men who had turned a

grey colour & were most definitely dead, leaned in close,
"You're more trouble than you're worth Cocker" she said.
"You can't tell me what to do, you work for me" he replied dismissively.
Tallie gripped his shoulders so aggressively it caused him to wince in pain.
"We work for The Regent, not you, you spoilt little shit!" Tallie snapped.
Nyah looked up to the skylight & flicked her pupils to the back of the building, Faucon & Dabn moved to meet them, But as Nyah was leaving she noticed a figure in the curtains hidden by the shadows she moved closer & the shape disappeared into the black. They moved through a backdoor & into the alley behind, the night air was crisp & cold enough for them to see their breath. Tallie pulled back her sleeve & was just about to activate the travelling enchantment when she was struck with a bottle,
"Alimanas!" shouted Faucon,
She spun around using the force of the turn to propel handfuls of razor sharp quills which embed into the faces of the advancing foes causing them to fall to the ground writhing in agony. Dabn turned to see more slinking down the alley, to his left was a large dumpster, he pushed it to the middle of the alley & with a swift kick sent it sailing down the alley collecting the sleazy creatures as it went. Nyah grabbed Tallie,
"Are you good?"

"No, I'm Pissed that one of those snivelling pricks
snuck up on me"
Rubbing her head she spoke the words & they
disappeared, whisked into the shadows.

<u>Chapter 2</u>

The gentle familiar sound of rain coaxed Vincent
into consciousness, he lay in bed listening to the
soothing patter, all of a sudden remembered the
previous day & his eyes opened wide as he sat bolt
upright, SMACK, his head stopped cold by a low
ceiling. Laying there rubbing the bump that was
forming quickly on his forehead he realised this bed
was actually a carved out divet in a large wall. The
bed was dressed in remarkably soft bedding it was
warm & very comfortable.
"Well good morning" a calming voice said,
"We were wondering when you would join the land
of the living"
Vincent scanned the room for the owner of this
relaxing tone. Sitting to his left was a petite older
woman who was comforting the mysterious girl
from the previous day,
"My name is Halcyon & this young lady is Kayla"
Kayla looked up at Vincent but was too shy to
speak, Vincent opened his mouth about to ask
"Where are we & what's going on?" Halcyon said
with a relaxed smile
Vincent shut his mouth & nodded
"Yes, it can be a bit much to fathom at first, we shall
start with the basics, this is Comhchoteann
Oberom, Oberom for short, it's a melting pot where
people can try to find the truth of themselves. We
have all come here because we're searching for

something that we've been unable to find anywhere
else"
"We didn't come here, we were kidnapped"
interjected Vincent
"You were brought here for your own safety" calmly
stated Halcyon
"Safety, what do you mean, I was perfectly safe"
"Really, lately have you been experiencing cold
shivers through your body, a quickening of the
heart & a sense of dread?" Halcyon queried
"That's just anxiety, it's not something magical" said
Vincent
"No, that's the Faige. It not only cloaks you from
danger, but when danger is close it puts you into a
state of readiness, heightens your senses & makes
you more aware of your surroundings, it also sends
a chime back to Oberom, that's how we knew you
were in danger"
"You keep saying Danger, in danger from what?"
Kayla asked timidly
"Not everyone looking for those hidden by the faige
wants to help them, some want to use them as
weapons. After all you were hidden for a reason"
said Halcyon
"But there's time for this later, are you two hungry?"
Vincent & Kayla realised it had been hours since
they had last eaten & nodded.

They walked through the door & saw that they were
at the base of a tall tower that climbed high into the
sky. Balconies crisscrossed the inner edges draped
with vines, many colours of leaves & flowers

adorned the walls. The air was clean & crisp with a lovey blend of the scents of the many flowers. The whole place moved with a life. There were creatures everywhere, huge lumbering beasts that had flowers & vines intermingled into their shaggy hair that hair had become home to a microcosm of life. Tiny sprites flying around them landing & then taking flight because of a shake from the great beasts.

The ground level bustled with an assortment of interesting varieties of beings all moving through the streets with an ebb & flow of the waves in a distant ocean. Kayla stuck close to Halcyons side but Vincent amazed with this beautiful place wondered, gazing around at the many wonders. One of the great beasts brushed against the hanging vines & a cloud of sprites took flight filling the air with an iridescent shimmer, one of the sprites flew down, Vincent held out his finger the tiny creature landed on the tip virtually weightless it sat down its wings folding around it like a shimmering coat. Kayla looked in wonder at the delicate creature a small smile on her face for the first time,

"What is it?" she asked,

"It's a Rasp" answered Halcyon,

"They're very pretty, But they…"

At that moment the tiny creature bit the tip of his finger,

"Bite!"

Vincent squealed with a high pitched yelp, which caused Kayla to burst out laughing. Halcyon smiled

as Vincent slightly embarrassed sucked his finger
tip. Kayla felt something brush against her leg
looking down she saw a perfectly white cat, but as
it made contact with her its fur strobed with many
different colours, she bent down to pat it.
"Ah yes, sometimes animals from other worlds find
their way here too, it looks like this one has been
catching Rasps for dinner, sometimes things have
an effect on you that is hard to foresee" Halcyon
said,
The cat startled by something ran off like a shot,
Vincent walked forward not looking where he was
going & was bowled over, he looked up to see a
man wearing a very elegant outfit. A white flowing
jacket that reached almost to the ground that
sparkled in the light over a matching pale grey shirt
& pants embroidered with golden thread that
moved on its own within the garment, finished with
slip on shoes that despite the less than clean
streets somehow stayed virgin white,
"I'm so sorry" Vincent exclaimed
"Yes, I would hope so. Halcyon, who are these
two?" said the man curtly
"Just a couple of new Disin arrivals sir, I was just
taking them for something to eat"
The man narrowed his gaze,
"Hmmm" he replied with obvious contempt,
Four creatures with coarse black hair that was
slicked down with some sort of viscous substance
all hunched over & dressed in the very same drab
brown hooded outfits came from behind pushing
Vincent out of the way. The man flicked his thinning

long hair over his shoulder pointed his nose in the
air and started off with the others slinking closely
behind.
"That was The Regent" said Halcyon,
With a mocking nature underlying her tone,
"Now let's get you two some food, follow me" she
said,
Shuffling off down a corridor.

The halls were cut into a stonelike substance that
on closer inspection had a grain akin to wood.
Pictures of beautifully rendered landscapes &
gathered creatures cover the walls all woven
together with carved vines flowing from one
painting to the next, although the level of
craftsmanship was so fine it seemed impossible
that it was created by any tool known to Vincent or
Kayla,
"It's beautiful" Kayla remarked,
"Stories & tales of what came before" Halcyon
replied,
"So, they would have you believe" muttered a
grizzled old goblin,
Under its breath as it hobbled past,
Halcyon glared at him & he turned & glared right
back at her.

Halcyon led them into a large room on one side a
large table filled with plates, platters, bowls & big
dishes all full to spilling point with a huge
assortment of delicious smelling food. In the middle
of the room was three long tables carved from a

black stone, each had long benches either side. At
the end of the room there were massive windows
through which light streamed in catching on all the
little particles in the air illuminating them in ribbons
of light that reached out like fingers into the room.
Kaylas eyes widened she had never seen anything
like it before,
"We can just have whatever we want?" she asked
timidly
"Of Course, my love," Halcyon replied.
They approached the bountiful banquet & began to
fill their plates with all manner of scrumptious
treats, each morsel looked more delicious than the
last, sections filled with cakes, cookies, Pies adored
with icings & toppings that made them look even
more inviting, next to many variations of frozen
desserts all with the freshest looking fruit, many of
which they did not recognize that glistened with
sweet syrups. Followed by a huge assortment of
dark & light cut meat all trimmed of the fat, next to
roasts glistening glazes, herbs & gravies that sent a
beautiful warming scent into the air. The last portion
of the selection was mouthwatering bevy of
vegetables all roasted & ordained with sprigs of
herbs & spices.
With full plates they found seats together at the end
of the table close to the window which looked out
on an open grassy area sprinkled with wild flowers,
the idyllic setting contained by a rim of tightly
grouped trees. As Kayla & Vincent began to eat,
they found that the food although extremely yummy

& satiating it didn't leave them feeling overly full,
Kayla looked curiously at Halcyon
"I'm surprised I'm not feeling sick, I've eaten so
much"
"The food in our realm has been prepared so that
you can enjoy all you want & your body will only
absorb what it needs, the rest with freely dissolve
away" Halcyon explained,
"Although there is a vast market for treats obtained
outside these walls".

Sapere looked in the arched door as he was
moving swiftly down the corridor, spotting the trio
he broke stride turned & approached as fast as his
tiny legs would allow.
"I've been looking for these two everywhere" he
said in a flustered state
"Well, we were right here" Halcyon cheekily replied,
smiling at his annoyance,
He collected himself & moved around beside her to
try to get some level of privacy,
"These two were being tracked by a Bainly wolf"
Halcyon's face immediately lost the cheeky grin, it
being replaced with a look of real concern,
"The Kanti?" she said with trepidation
"I fear so"
"Why are they after them?" she asked
"I do not know, but it can't be anything good, we
were also pulled of course when we were shadow
sailing last night & we had to use the orb to get
back"

"No wonder these two were in such a bad way, you know the orbs wreak havoc on Disins, but it sounds like you had little choice" said Halcyon
"We need to get them down to my library & remove their faige if we have any chance of finding out their true purpose" Sapere said,
Halcyon looked concerned.
"I know it's dangerous but I don't see another opinion, do you?" he asked
"No, but I wish I did" she replied.
Halcyon turned to Vincent & Kayla who had overheard enough of their conversation that they both had a renewed look of fear in their eyes,
"I'm not going to lie to you, it is concerning but it is the best way for us to keep you safe & there is no one I trust more than Sapere" she said,
Calmly enough to allay some of their fear, but not all.
Sapere turned & began to rush out of the room the others followed closely behind, he weaved in & out of the people & creatures that occupied the halls, turning left & right, going up & down stairways that dropped into deep chasms & climbed high till almost out of sight. Sapere finally stopped in front of a door. The frame of which was only slightly above his wrinkled face, he looked back to see Vincent, Kayla & Halcyon still trying to catch up all huffing & puffing at the exertion. He reached into one of his pockets & produced a small brass block, in which were many keys of various size all fastened by a pin that ran through the top of the keys. He pressed one of the many latches on the

top of the block causing one of the keys to come springing out, Sapere slid the key into the lock & the door proceed to grow by first height then width & breadth. When it finally settled the door had now doubled in size.

"Um, I don't think that was the right key" Halcyon said,

Standing next to the door that barely came past her waist

"Yes, Yes I know" Sapere snapped,

Folding the key back in & looking at the side of the block which had all kinds of numbers & calculations inscribed in the brass. He turned it over & over again & the inscriptions changed again & again, Sapere audibly mumbling to himself trying to figure out the calculations.

"No, not that, maybe, well, um, yes here this should work"

He released another key, strangely it was much larger than the block it had sprung forth from. He brought the key closer to the lock & it expanded to accommodate the larger dimensions of the key. It slid into the lock with a dense thunk & he had to use both hands to turn it. The door began to grow & change again the wood creaking & cracking as it was forced into the new configuration. Once it was finally at rest Sapere reached out & turned the large brass handle that was in the shape of the head of a large bird of prey that had stayed in the same position as it was on the original small door. With a prolonged creak the door slowly swung open revealing a room filled top to bottom with books,

papers & all manner of scrolls & tapestries. On the
walls hung large portraits depicting battles,
gatherings & coronations from long ago. All
covered in dust & web thicker than spiders would
leave.
"Don't touch anything, I have a system" he said,
Rummaging from pile to pile.
"It's obviously not a cleaning system" said Halcyon,
With as much seriousness as she could muster,
causing a giggle from Kayla & an annoyed grumble
from Sapere as though it was an ongoing joke.
Vincent felt very at home among the piles of books.
The smells unlocking a sense memory that relaxed
& slightly saddened him, making him wonder if he
would ever see his old shop again.
Sapere opening book after book scanning small
passages reading them out loud in a muffled
grumble. Vincent noticed that he was using the two
different sets of pupils depending on what he was
reading. Some of the books had tiny text around &
inter mingled throughout the paragraphs that just
looked like patterns or some kind of artistic border.
When Sapere turned the books to read these
hidden texts his eyes focused with the small pupils
at the bottom of his eyes.
"Don't you know where the removal texts are?"
inquired Halcyon.
"Having some things hidden keeps us all safe"
Sapere replied.
Halcyon responded with an understanding nod.
"To find these particular texts is always quite
difficult, but that is by design, they change

locations, so the steps to reach that destination is also always different. There are patterns in the passages that lead you along a path if you know how to interpret & decipher their trickery, it's not straightforward, but sometimes a little effort & skill can keep dangerous things out of the reach of people whom it shouldn't be freely available to"
As he read a small inscription at the bottom left corner of an impressive tapestry depicting a man all in black standing in front of an ancient ruin with the bodies of fallen soldiers & beasts littering the ground,
"Ah ahh!" he proclaimed,
Closed his eyes & whispered a short phrase,
As he did a chime could be heard coming from the piles of books. Kayla looked down & noticed that the book also had a pale light emanating from within its pages,
"There!" she said,
Pointing towards the strangely energetic volume.
"Oh good, if you would be so kind"
Sapere gestured for her to retrieve the book for him.
Vincent picked up the books that obscured the book in question & Kayla lifted the heavy leather bound book, which was a great deal heavier than it had any right to be given its dimensions.
"The resistance you feel is another safety precaution, I mean it would be quite hard to run away with, don't you think?. Over here on the desk if you wouldn't mind" He directed.

With a mighty heave she hoisted the book onto the desk, it landed with a loud thump. A plume of dust was sent into the air causing them all to cough. They all gathered around as Sapere opened the book bound in a thick leather substance & held together with brass plates down the spine of the book. On the cover was a few worn titles that were too faded to read & a symbol that seemed to change forms depending on the angle on which you viewed it. He turned the pages a few at a time until he came to the illuminated page. The shimmer on the page now dissipating making the words easier to read.

"First we need to identify the level of the Faige that was used on you two" Halcyon said,

"There are many different varieties & many different reasons for their use"

Sapere gestured for Kayla to come forward, she looked down at the page, it was not laid out as a normal book, its passages scrolled around the page in circles, forward, back, up & down.

"Focus on the page as a whole, is there anything that stands out?" Sapere asked.

Kayla stepped back to get a better view of the page & as the words lost focus the patterns began to form a shape

"Um..a Bird…it kinda looks like an eagle or a falcon" she said.

"Oh it's the Rapace, isn't that interesting" Halcyon said

"You next Vincent"

He walked up & although looking at the same page
the text were triangular, sharp shapes & as he
relaxed his eyes An image almost leapt of the
page,
"It's a Wolf!" he exclaimed
"That's the Blaidd" Sapere said,
With a little trepidation,
"Ok, now we know the type of Faige we have to
unlock, this is your area Halcyon"
"Thank you, we will need to go to my conservatory,
I have what we will need, follow me" she said.
Vincent & Kayla follow trying to get their heads
around how their lives have taken a rather
unexpected turn in the last few days,
"How are you doing with all this?" Vincent asked,
"I was terrified at first but the more time I spend
here it somehow feels right. I never really found my
place in my day to day life, but here it doesn't feel
like such a struggle, if that makes any sense" She
answers.
"Yes, I know what you mean, there's something
about this place, like a part of me recognises it"
They rounded yet another corner and they came to
a long hall, at the end a pinpoint of light. Walking
towards it the light grows, the stone walls now have
little artwork but have become covered in vines
stretching out from what now is an apparent exit.
Stepping through the round arch style door the light
is almost blinding, it takes a few seconds for their
eyes to adjust. They've stepped out into a beautiful
garden. Everywhere they looked is another strange
& beautiful plant, all manner of trees, flowers &

vines climbing high creating a canopy among the treetops. There was an abundance of life there too, small flying insect like creatures' flit from plant to plant. Kayla hears a rustle at her feet, peering into the undergrowth a small purple lizard scurries out into the light chasing a quick little iridescent beetle, the lizard extends its neck triple its normal length & snatches the tasty morsel, making eye contact with Kayla as its neck returns to its previous position it turns & disappears into the dreamlike oasis.
"Keep up, it's over here" Halcyon announces.
She stops in front of a large wall completely covered end to end with vines, thick enough you can barely see the wall at all. Vincent & Kayla stare in amazement as Halcyon reaches into her pocket deeper & deeper until her arm is past the elbow.
"I know it's here somewhere, I used it this morning" she says, rummaging around.
"Here hold this" she says,
Pulling a tangled mass of chains & lockets out of the pocket & handing it to Sapere who seems slightly bemused,
"Whose messy now?" he says, with a chirp in his voice,
Halcyon grimaces but nods in agreement
"Ahha! here we are"
She pulls a tarnished old brass spray bottle from her pocket,
"Stand back a little dear, the effects of this on people can be…a little unpredictable" she says looking at Kayla.

The group steps back as Halcyon sprays a couple
of squirts using an outstretched arm then quickly
stepping back into line with the others. The
shimmering spay lands on the leaves of the vines
causing them to rustle & retract revealing a round
wooden door previously hidden.
The wood was worn, weather beaten & had cracks
that had been repaired many times over the years.
Halcyon reached into her shirt & pulled out a
braided ribbon fashioned into a makeshift lanyard,
on its end a carved wooden circle encased in a ring
of metal around the perimeter, in the centre of the
door is a round hole inlaid with the same metal that
binds the key, placing it into its mirror image there
is an audible thunk, turning the key one way then
the other in a well learned combination the door
releases & swings open with a loud creak that
causes all the surrounding creatures hiding in the
undergrowth to scurry away in a frenzy of activity.
Kayla & Vincent enter the strange little nook, they
see that it is quite a bit larger than outward
appearances implied, not to mention the ceiling had
a huge skylight letting in the golden sunshine.
There were plants everywhere in pots & preserved
in jars that lined the shelves that ran the length of
the walls & even growing out of any crack they
could find their way through. In the centre of the
room was a large wooden table, the top was strewn
with all manner of scientific instruments well worn
after years of use,
"Kayla sweetheart we shall start with you, come
over here & take a seat"

Kayla nervously sat down in a tattered leather chair
that had a heavy metal frame which cracked as the
put her weight on it. Halcyon attached a sliver vice
to the end of the table & cranked down on the four
screws securing it to the heavy table top. By
pressing down on a lever at the end of the device it
opened like a flower revealing a padded cradle.
”Your left hand, if you would” she said.
Kayla laid her arm into the device & it closed tight,
Halcyon looked her in the eyes & said in a calming
tone,
”I know it's scary but I will be as quick as I can.
Now to unlock your Faige, it's a tricky process,
think if it as a lock made of twine that has been
knitted into a specific pattern, what we need to do is
move certain threads to release the lock, the
difficulty lies in that if you pull the wrong thread the
lock will change configuration & you have to start all
over again, luckily we also have these" she said,
Placing a small jar of red powder with an outline of
a bird of prey on it & a pair of goggles that are
adorned with all kinds of lenses, switches & dials
on the bench.
”These will help me to navigate the lock & make it
somewhat safer”.
“Will it hurt?” Kayla asks, obviously afraid.
“No, it won't hurt, but it is a little uncomfortable. You
will feel some pulling & your temperature will rise,
but I will be as quick as I can be" Halcyon replied.
“Here, you can watch what I'm doing on this”
Halcyon pulled up a square frame that was
attached to the end of the table & manoeuvred it to

in front of Kayla, then retrieving a long braided cable that was coiled around the bottom & plugged it into the googles & as she did the empty frame flashed to life with an incredibly crisp image being sent from the goggles.

Halcyon took the red powder & with a tiny set of measuring spoons, she checked her notes twice & added a precise amount to a glass of water that was sitting on the table stirring it in,

"This might not taste the best but it is necessary" she said,

Handing the glass to Kayla.

"Down in one" she said

Kayla taped the glass on the table & took it like a shot which made Vincent smile in approval & just like a shot her face contorted in disgust as the vile taste became apparent.

"Yuck, you weren't kidding" she said sticking out her tongue.

Kayla felt a shiver go through her body from the tips of her toes to the top of her head, followed by a wave of warmth. Kayla noticed her arm had glowing lines criss crossing & running from the elbow down her forearm ending at the tips of her fingers. The lines all blurred together, Halcyon pulled the goggles down flicking one of the sets of lenses into place, they all looked to the screen which showed there were thousands of microscopic threads woven into an intricate lattice of light. Halcyon opened a small case containing a set of tools. The tools had a metal handle & each was tipped with a filament that was so fine it was almost invisible to the naked eye.

"You see the inflection of red on this thread" she said,

Pointing it out on the screen,

"That's our starting point, we shall activate that point & it should lead us to the next" she said, With enough confidence that put Kayla at ease.

As she pressed the tool against Kayla's skin it pierced with little force & no pain. Looking at the screen she could see that at the very tip of the tool there was an incredibly tiny hook which Halcyon used to separate the thread & pull it slightly off centre revealing another red point deeper into the lock. Halcyon attached the tool to a small arm that jutted out from the side of the cradle securing it in place. Taking another tool she hooked the second level & by doing so two more red treads became visible.

"Here's where it gets a little more difficult" Halcyon said,

leaning in to get a closer look.

"It is definitely an art rather than a straight forward path" Sapere chimed in,

Using both hands she hooked the two threads pulling them in opposite directions, the threads became blindingly bright & then melted into nothingness,

"Got it!" Halcyon yelled in celebration.

"Is that it? I don't feel any different," said Kayla

"We have unlocked your Faige, but one of the reasons using the Faige as a protection is so

successful is that it wipes all memory, that also means whatever personal skills it was also suppressing have laid dormant for many years & atrophied, you will need to discover, learn to use & train to strengthen them, which can be a trying process for some" Halcyon explained.
Halcyon released her from the clamp,
"Ok Vincent your up" Halcyon said,
Walking over to a safe in the corner of the room,
"You were a Blaidd right, I don't think I've done a Blaidd removal in over two hundred years, around the…"
She stopped herself & looked over at Sapere who had a serious look spreading across his face.
"Around the?" Vincent probed
"It's not important right now, it just means that your Faige is a little trickier that's all" she said trying to redirect him.
Halcyon returned to her seat with a tiny black tin with the imprint of a wolf foot pad stamped into its top. She took a few grains of the contents & added it to a glass of water that Sapere had placed on the table.
"Bottoms up I guess" he said,
Taking it like a shot in the same fashion as Kayla had,
"Jezze that's awful" he sputtered.
The threads began to become visible but unlike Kaylas they weren't a lattice of white light these had a black outline with a glowing red line running through their centre. Halcyon did not just jump straight in as she had with Kayla, she examined the

complex entanglement searching for a way in
flipping back & forth with the lenses on the goggles
& using the screen to get a more detailed look,
"What's that?" Kayla asked,
Pointing to a small orange point almost
indistinguishable from the red.
"Great eyes" Halcyon praised
"She must have Contre sight" said Sapere
"What's that? Asked Kayla
"It's the ability to see things that others are unable
or unwilling to"
Halcyon carefully hooked the tiny inconsistency
causing the black to take over the red making it
even more difficult to see where to go next.
"Ah so not a pull" she said
Gently twisting the tool ever so slightly one of the
deeper threads pulsed so insignificantly that if she
weren't paying such close attention, it would be
easy to miss. Keeping her eyes fixed on the thread
she asked,
"Sapere, can you hand me the pick on the far left of
the case? the one with the two ends"
Sapere gently laid the tool into her palm being very
sure not to bump her, she had only just made
contact with the filament & a second then a third
pulsed
"Kayla come around this side & hold these two very
still"
Kayla took a deep breath & took control of the tools
with the tips of her fingers using all her
concentration to keep them steady. Beads of sweat
were running down Vincent's face

"I'm getting really hot!" he said in a minor panic.
"Just a little more, I've almost got it" Halcyon replied
The stress & heat emanating from Vincent was
making her sweat as well, trying to maintain her
focus she slipped the hooks under the two threads
& …nothing, there was no visible reaction.
"Did I miss it? I didn't see anything" Sapere said.
"Shhh, let me think!" she responded sharply.
Just at that moment a bead of sweat rolled down
the lens of the googles hung from the tip of her
nose for a second then fell landing in the middle of
Vincent's palm, Halcyons eyes widened as she
noticed that the drop had formed a natural
magnifying lens & that precise spot had a virtually
invisible spot of red, she slowly picked up a tool
with a point so fine that you could only just see it
when it hit the light.
"No one breath"
She closed her eyes & steadied herself, then with a
supreme control & confidence began towards her
objective. The millisecond she made contact with
the point All the threads released & so did
everyone's breath, just as they were all finding their
way back to a calm baseline Vincent grunted in
pain, his skin changed from his normal tone to jet
black then pure white then a deep red. Kayla
terrified looked to Sapere & Halcyon for some kind
of reassurance but was shocked to see that they
looked just as frightened as she did. Vincent let out
a otherworldly deep howl that rattled all the jars on
the shelves & his eyes lost all colour, then as
suddenly as it started he regained all his colour &

seemed quite unaffected "What the hell was that?!"
exclaimed Kayla
"Truthfully I'm not sure, although I've had very little
experience with the Blaidd Faige, so normal is
relative" Halcyon said,
Releasing Vincent from the clamp.
"How do you feel" Sapere inquired,
"Drained & sore, like I've been up for three days &
I've been working out the whole time" breathed
Vincent.
"Hmmm, I'll have to look into this, why don't you
take them out into the garden to relax for a while"
Sapere said,
To Halcyon over his shoulder as he left the room.
"Yes, what a lovely idea"
Halcyon led the two bewildered & tired newcomers
out into the beautiful garden taking a seat on the
ground, she beckoned for them to join her. Vincent
Sat down while Kayla lay on her back looking up at
the sky, Vincent seeing this also lay back, they both
silently going over the events that had taken place
trying to make some kind of sense of it.

<u>Chapter 3</u>

Nyah, Tallie, Faucon & Dabn emerged from the shadow in the same room they had left, Tallie still with a tight grip on the back of Cocker's neck despite his struggle.
"Let me go you glorified bodyguard" Cocker squealed
"You just wait until my father hears about this, you could have killed me"
"Who do you think sent us to retrieve you, you spoilt entitled little shit" Tallie snapped,
Squeezing his neck even tighter.
"It's alright, you can let him go now Tallie" Nyah said calmly.
Tallie released her grip, Cocker wiped the blood from his neck where Tallies claws had penetrated the skin.
"You've made me bleed!" he whined.
"I can get some more out of you if you wanna keep this up " she said,
Getting right in his face.
Cocker turned & quickly skulked of into the darkness,
"You'll regret this!" he shouted,
But only when he was far out of Tallie's reach.
"You shouldn't antagonise him like that, you know he's just going to make life difficult for you" Nyah said,
As gently as she could.

"Oh screw him, he needs to be put in his place now
& then"
"You said it, that whiney little punk is more trouble
than he's worth" added Dabn,
Putting his arms around their shoulders.
"Ok, you've both got a point, but was it completely
necessary to kill those four Alimanas at the club?
You know they hold a grudge" asked Nyah.
"I'm a warrior, I saw danger & I just reacted, was it
overkill, maybe but I'd rather have a bunch of
Alimana mad at me than have you get hurt" she
said,
Giving Nyah a bump with her shoulder.
Nyah turns giving her kiss on the cheek,
"I just worry about you, you know it's different now,
this is a different kind of battle than were used to,
there's all kinds of politics involved"
"Yuck I hate politics" Adds Faucon
Eliciting a laugh from the entire group as they split
up.
Nadaur & Sikes enter from one of the many halls.
"Hey, you're back, that didn't take too long" Nadaur
says happily.
"I'll bet it felt like it did Ha Ha" Sikes added laughing
"Did that little toad give you any grief?"
"Not really Sikes, he's more of an annoyance than
anything else"
"Cause if he did, I'm happy to eat him for you" he
says,
Leaning & giving her a cuddle.
"What are you two up to?"
"We're just going to get something to eat"

"Really, Sikes you just ate you can't possibly still be hungry" complains Nadaur
"What, that little snack? It was barely a morsel," he said with a grin.
"Excuse me Miss Nyah" said an unseen voice,
Nyah turned around to see that one of the Regents lackeys had slinked up behind her.
"Can we help you?" Nadaur asked with an impatient look.
"The Regent has asked for a personal debrief about his son"
"I'll bet he has" snorted Sikes,
He lent in to Nyah's ear,
"I can eat him too"
Nyah smiled, patting Sikes on his giant head, messing up his wild hair more than it already was.
"I'll see you two later" she said,
Walking away, closely followed by The Regents underling.
"I hate that she has to deal with that lecherous old fool"
"I know you do Nadaur but she's far more than a match for him" Sikes said reassuringly.

Nyah walked up to a large door, much different than the others that lined the hall, this one's design was much more garish & over done with little subtlety.
"I'll be fine from here, you can go"
"Yes, milady" the strange little creature said, scurrying off down the hall.

Nyah placed her hand on the large golden knocker
& paused, closed her eyes & took a deep breath to
centre herself, then knocking three times the heavy
thuds reverberating & echoing down the halls.
"Come!"
A voice announced from within.
Nyah pushed the door & entered the massive room.
She walked down the pure white rug that ran the
entire length of the middle of the room, she passed
all manner of bejewelled & ornate objects all
propped up on pedestals as an obvious display of
wealth that did little to impress her.
The Regent sat at the end of the room in a chair
that dwarfed him, he looks like a child paying at
being an adult thought Nyah. He was examining a
long sword, not the type of weapon that had any
place on the field of battle more like the type that
the rich keep on display to make believe that they
have some kind of warrior's heritage. He glanced
up & upon seeing Nyah striding down the room
leapt from his chair rushing down to meet her.
"Nyah my sweet, I'm so happy to see you, what do
you think of my latest acquisition?" He asked as he
waved the sword about in a foolish attempt to
impress her.
"It's…very shiny" she said,
As it was all she could think of.
"Come, come sit down" he beckoned,
Placing his hand at the small of her back. To which
it took everything in her not to take that sword &
remove that offending hand at the wrist. He sat
down & she purposely went to sit in the chair on the

other side of the table to have as much distance between them as possible, but he gestured to the chair to his right.
"You'll be more comfortable here"
She hesitantly sat down & he leaned in closer than was comfortable for her,
"So, what was my son doing this time?"
"He was at a club run by the Alimana, we had no choice but to engage with a few of them & there were some casualties on their side"
"Oh no you weren't hurt I hope"
"No, but I think there was something else going on"
"Just more of his youthful shenanigans I'd wager, don't give it another thought. I will reprimand him have no doubt about that" he said,
With a lack of conviction that left her less than convinced.
"If there's nothing else" she said,
In an attempt to hasten the end to their meeting.
"I was hoping you would join me at the dinner tonight that I am hosting tonight?"
"I'm sorry but I've already made plans to have dinner with my & Nadaur's units, we get such little time to spend together outside missions"
"Of course, of course it's a must to keep up team morale"
Nyah was halfway down the room when The Regent called after her,
"Give Nadaur my best"
In an obvious false pleasantry.
She flung her hand into the air as an acknowledgement as she slipped out of the room.

The Regent walked slowly back to his chair, a foul
look grew on his face.
"You really can't do anything right can you waste of
space" he said,
Looking to see Cocker standing at the bar on the
side of the room fixing a drink,
"She didn't see anything, I don't know why you
keep that bitch around anyway"
The Regent walked up & snatched the glass &
smashed it on the wall,
"You wonder why I don't intrust you with more
important business, You can't even set up a
meeting covertly"
"You sent her in there, not me" he challenged,
The Regent pushed him up against the bar with the
sword to his throat,
"Because you were seen by everyone!, I told you to
meet in a secure place not the club with your
Alimana scum friends"
The Regent regained his composure,
"You have to be smarter than that, with what's at
stake"
"You haven't told me, I'm ready to be more
involved"
The Regent placed the sword back into its cradle
on the wall, completely disregarding what his son
had said, pausing at the door to say,
"Clean up that glass before you leave"
Closing the door behind him.
Cocker scoffs & reaches over behind the bar
grabbing a bottle of green liquid crossing the room
while swigging from the bottle, he presses a book

on the shelf releasing a latch causing a hidden door
disguised as a wall to open & disappears though
into the dark as the door automatically closes.

Nyah walked trying to clear her head, not paying
attention & without really meaning to found herself
in the beautiful garden outside Halcyon's
Conservatory. Sitting in the grass picking at the
loose thread on the knee of her pants she went
over what had happened in her head trying to rid
herself of the sense of revulsion she had been left
with.
"Is it something I can help you with?" Halcyon
quired from behind her,
"I don't know maybe, I've just got this feeling that
something bad is going on" she said,
Looking up at Halcyon.
"Hmm, Yes I've come across some strange things
myself, let's sit over here on the bench, getting up
from the ground is murder on my knees" she said,
With a smile that comforted Nyah.
They sat on the bench Nyah sitting sideways facing
Halcyon,
"I had two young Falaichte brought to me
yesterday, which in & of itself is somewhat of an
anomaly. One is rare these days but two on the
same night can only mean trouble"
"I can't remember the last time I was sent to escort
a Disin Falaichte let alone two" recounts Nyah.
"Not only that, they were pulled of course travelling
the shadows, which I don't have to tell you is no
mean feat. On top of that when Sapere analysed

the young man Vincents Faige it was a Blaidd
which is beyond rare & the young lady Kayla seems
to have Contre sight which is also quite
remarkable"
"That just adds more questions," Nyah said
furrowing her brow.
"People with Contre sight can see glimpses of
hidden things including past the veil of the shadows
right?"
"I've got Sapere doing some research into it, but I
believe so, why?"
"When I was sent to retrieve Cocker I could've
sworn I saw something slip into the shadows &
disappear but it was much different than when
someone fades into the shadows for travel"
"Hmm, very intriguing, we know so little about the
shadow realm & what we do is mostly hearsay. I
mean we use it for passage for travel & moving
between the worlds, but even how that came about
is a closely guarded secret of The Regents. I've
heard stories of hidden volumes containing the
original texts concerning the calling of portholes,
but in all my years I've never met someone who
has actually encountered them" Halcyon explained.
"Well, I've seen The Regent leave his chamber
through hidden doors but I've never actually seen
where they lead, possibly a secret stash. Faucon's
family used to work very closely with The Regents,
I wonder if she can shed any light on any of this?"
"If you're right we need to move forward carefully
who knows who might be listening in the shadows"

"Didn't you say one of the Disins Faige was a
Blaidd could he have some connection to the bainly
wolves? Nadaur said he, Sapere & Sikes had an
encounter with one the other evening"
"Yes & it was while retrieving the two Disins. The
Blaidd is from a time of darkness & the secrets
surrounding it's cultivation is cloaked in that same
darkness"
"Nyah, you have to come quick" Tallie yelled,
Attempting to catch her breath as she entered the
garden.
"What's going on?" Halcyon asks,
Since Tallie wasn't one to scare easily.
"I don't really know what happened, one of the
gatherer teams left on a supply run but when they
re-emerged from the shadow they were torn apart,
but not like a beast attack they were sliced
precisely & from what I could see the intent was to
cause as much pain & damage as possible while
keeping them alive until their bodies couldn't take it
anymore only then were they killed. I've been in
plenty of vicious battles but honestly this was like
nothing I've ever seen, it was like the evisceration
was the point & was done by a very practised hand"
"I have to go & investigate this, you will talk to
Sapere?" asks Nyah
"Yes, yes my dear go we will regroup later"
Nyah hugs Halcyon & runs off down the hall with
Tallie in tow.

Nadaur & Sikes stand trying to make sense of the carnage, while Sapere & Faucon examine the bodies.

"You see many of these cuts were concentrated in the non lethal areas, they are deep cuts but they have been meticulously butchered to keep them alive, I don't understand why someone would do this" Sapere said,

Baffled & highly disturbed.

"Maybe the carnage is the point, I mean look at us, we're in a state of shock" Faucon suggests.

"Where were they before they came back Sapere?" asked Sikes

"I believe they were at the off world Hilend markets. They went to retrieve the growing stones for The Regents new courtyard"

"As slimy as The Regent is I don't see him having anything to do with this, I mean this is barbaric" Faucon pondered

"We need to get down to those markets & see if anyone saw anything, Sikes & I will go & take a look around" said Nadaur

"We're coming too" Nyah said,

As she & Tallie turned the corner.

"Ok good, honestly, I could use your help, I really don't know what to make of this. Sapere you & Faucon take their remains down to Otto's lab & see if you can get us any incites on to what happened. We will go to the market & see what we can dig up on our end. Arm up you two we don't know what we will be walking into".

Sapere & Faucon move the mass of flesh onto a
laid out piece of cloth then folding in the edges lift it
onto a wooden trolly
"It's shocking that this used to be four people, it's
almost impossible to tell one part from another"
Faucon said,
As the realisation of the incident set in.
Nadaur, Nyah, Tallie & Sikes enter the armoury, the
walls adorned with the weapons of wars past &
present. A monument to pain & death.
Nyah & Tallie open two large chests, secured within
the inner lids an assortment of knives, daggers &
throwing weapons attached to the lid with loops of
leather. Nyah lifts a package of folded black linen
tied at the top with a piece of braided leather, she
opens it revealing a set of leather armour, removing
her clothes & slides the leather pants on, the hard
plates shifting into position by themselves in such a
way as to offer protection but not hamper
movement.
"I love this dragon scale armour, even though it's
hundreds of years old but I'd believe you if you said
it was made yesterday" Tallie says,
Slipping on her jacket that forms to her figure.
Spines jutting from her shoulders & elbows. She
turns & with a smooth motion brings her arm across
her body the bladed tip of her elbow making contact
with the large wooden pillar in the centre of the
room, slicing deeply into the wood with a
smoothness, she may as well have been slicing
nothing but air.

Nadaur slipped on his armour adding small marble like objects to a belt across his front
"You sure you wanna take those?" Sikes askes
"I know using the Imps cradle comes with its own consequences, but I've gone against my better judgement & people died. If it means keeping all of you safe I'm willing to take the risk".
Sikes' armour consists of a set of metal tips that are mounted to the ends of his horns, attached to a metal helmet with three large spikes down the middle & an open form jacket that is comprised of a strap holding two spiked points on his shoulders. Attached to the end are gloves that fit over his massive mitts of hands, completed with hooked claws along the knuckles.
Tallie sheaths two daggers, one on each hip, a small blow pipe along her bicep along with an assortment of barbs & thorns as projectiles on the other arm. Across her body she straps a long curved blade which once in position behind her right shoulder with startling speed she unsheathes the blade spinning slicing through the wooden post & with a little flourish slips the sword back into position.
Nyah slides a dagger into a sheath running horizontally along her belt. She reaches into the chest, wrapped in smooth silk she lifts a short sword she secures at her hips fastening it in front with a beautiful buckle in the shape of a leaf & lashing it to her thigh for security.
"Everyone good to go?" Nyah asks,

Looking over at Nadaur, noticing the Imps cradle she walks over & straightens the belt across his chest.
"We don't know what we're walking into so those might be very necessary, but just be careful, ok"
Nadaur leans in & gives her a kiss,
"I really hope they're not necessary too"
"You two love birds done? can we get moving?"
Tallie teases,
With a cheeky grin.
Just as they are about to call the shadow Sapere came running down the hall fighting to catch his breath,
"I want you to take this with you"
Handing Nadaur the small travelling orb,
"It only works to return, you'll still have to use the shadows to travel there but there's something troubling happening within the shadows that I don't quite understand, you all need to be on high alert"
Nadaur attaches the chain to his belt & places the orb into a small pocket on his jacket
"We will"
"Ugh can we go now?" Tallie complains,
"I've been itching for some action"
The group stand facing each other in a tight circle & Nadaur calls the shadow in an instant they're swallowed into the black. They emerge in a poorly lit car park the little light there is reflecting on the puddles caused by the constant rain.
Nadaur, Nyah & Tallie flip up their hoods to shield them from the rain. Sikes moves forward to an overhang created by the buildings above, the walls

are covered in graffiti. Sikes shakes the rain of his fur,
"Oh, thanks for that buddy" Nadaur says,
Looking at him with a slight amusement,
Nyah turns to Tallie who walks to the wall, she takes a small amulet from around her neck & holds it up to the wall. A purple glow illuminates the graffiti causing three symbols hidden within the chaos to become brighter than the rest. Tallie places her hand on a symbol sliding it down to a central position then the second, once the third snaps into place the wall to their left grinds open, revealing a bustling market full floor to ceiling with stalls using every inch of available real estate.
The stalls were contained only by a path that weaved between them. All manner of strange creatures filled the space, all shouting over the other trying to be heard.
"Keep your wits about you, I grew up going to places like this they will rob you blind & worse if you let them" Tallie explained
"You better take point then" Nyah suggested.
They all follow closely behind, as they move between the stalls, they hear the calls of,
"Hey, you there, over here I've got the strongest Imp berries, really high quality stuff"
"Blades I've got Blades, you look like someone who would appreciate a hexicron dagger"
"Not interested" Nyah says,
Pushing past as the shopkeepers who try to corral them into their stores.

”Up here, this is where the gatherer team was supposed to be” said Tallie

A round fat little creature with beady little eyes behind round glasses that were attached to the sides of its head with pins driven into the sides of its head as it did not have any ears.

“What can I help you with today? I just got in some nice cablah root, its top quality, best you'll find in the market” it said boastfully.

“Just some information”

“Ah Information, pricey, very pricey”

Tallie quickly grabbed it by the shirt front bringing it close to her face,

“I've got a bargain for you, either you are helpful or I'll have my lovely friend Sikes here bite your limbs off one at a time until you decide to be forthcoming”

“Hehe ok, ok sounds like a deal, what exactly do you wanna know?”

“There was a gatherer team down here this morning, what can you tell me?”

“Yes, yes, they came to pick up an order for the Regent, they took it & that's it”

“He's lying” Tallie says

“How do you know?” Nyah queries

“Because he didn't mention payment, all these things care about is coin”

Sikes snarls & bares his teeth in an impressively scary display,

“Eeek! ok, ok no need for that” the creature cries quivering

“I saw them in some sort of conflict with a group of Alimana”

"Alimana again, they were there with Cocker too"
Nyah recalls.
"But they're just muscle, they aren't smart enough
to come up with a plan, they just work for scraps.
Where did you see them exactly?"
"Over by the exit to the black tunnels"
Tallie releases her grip & Nyah tosses it a few
coins.
"This seems like a trap" Sikes says
"I agree Sikes, but what choice do we have, a lead
is a lead" Nadaur says with a shrug.
"I hate the black tunnels, the Alimanas are such
feral creatures & their dominion over the tunnels
has made them a disgusting place" Tallie
complained,
Shaking her head.

As they approach the entrance to the tunnels, they
are spotted by two Alimana standing guard who
immediately turn tail & disappear into the darkness.
"Quick we can't lose them" Nyah yells,
Sprinting forward at an impressive speed.
The entrance to the tunnels is a large chasm that
leads into the purest black, within a few feet you
lose all sense of direction. Nadaur grabs three
marbles from his belt and tosses one to each Nyah
& Tallie.
"You good Sikes?" He calls
"Yeah, I grew up in caves like this, my eyes
acclimate almost instantly".
Holding the marbles in their hands the swirling
green patten of the marbles is almost alive as it

twists & turns, they crush it in their fist releasing a green vapour, which almost with a presence of purpose floats up forcing its way into their eyes "Ouch! shit I forgot how much these Imp sight stones hurt" says Nyah,
Wincing & rubbing her eyes. Still running forward, she opens her eyes that now have turned a vibrant green with the vapours emitting from them leaving trails in the darkness. Their vision now heightened to level they can easily spring from stone to stone. The smell of the tunnels alone is terrible but following close after the Alimanas is making breathing more difficult.
"The Alimanas are just out of sight, but we're gaining on them" Tallie calls.
"No killing Tallie, we need them alive" Nyah says, Eliciting a groan from Tallie.
Nyah & Nadaur turn a corner & there is a huge drop of twenty metres or more, they both jump out, Nyah instinctively reaches out for Nadaur's hand finding it as he flings a small tethered blade from his sleeve that sails through the air until it makes contact with the ceiling. Once it finds its target it automatically splits into four points securing its seat, the two then slide gracefully down, releasing the tether to retract before they reach the ground allowing them to keep sprinting without missing a step. Tallie runs up the wall flipping backward & landing on Skies back,
Sikes on all fours running at a gallop,
"Hold on tight T" he bellows
As he leaps out landing on the wall his long claws dig into the wall giving him enough grip to run down

the wall with Tallie grinning ear to ear on his back.
They smoothly make it to the ground where Tallie
dismounts by simply releasing her grip & letting
Sikes move out from beneath her landing mid stride
& not missing a beat.
Nyah & Nadaur are just ahead completely focused
on the chase when from one of the side tunnels a
lash fires from the darkness silently snatching
Tallie, yanking her off into the abyss unnoticed by
the others.
Tallie is flung into a wall with such force it knocks
the wind out of her & leaves her seeing stars. A
kick comes from one side then another, as she
braces to protect herself as best she can while she
regains her senses, she slides a red bladed dagger
from her boot & when the next blow comes, she
grabs the assailants leg inserting the blade at the
calf slicing up until she hit the knee causing them to
let out a high pitched scream. Looking up Tallie
realised she was in a room filled with Alimana, the
largest of them who was still holding the whip that
had snagged her in the first place. He darted in
quickly lifting her up by the throat slamming her
against the wall, he inched his face closer his skin
pitted by all manner of poxes. His sickly yellow
eyes darted around her face. Tallie gasped for
breath not only was she being strangled but the
stench of being in such close proximity to the large
Alimana was making breathing almost impossible.
"It was her?" He asked in a high pitched tone,
His voice as revolving as the rest of him.
"Yes, yes, yes" a chorus of voices replied.

"You think you can just kill us & there will be no repercussions? think again you little mongrel, I'm going to enjoy taking you apart piece by piece".
As he leaned in, two Alimanas flew across the room, their faces driven into the stone with such power that they're obliterated & fell to the floor in a heap.
"You've got exactly one second to get your hands off her!" a deep voice growled,
As he sent a bunch more flying into walls upon fully entering the room.
"Skies!" Tallie struggled to say.
The leader of the group turned his head startled, this was all Tallie needed, grabbing him by the wrist close to her throat she pulled a blade from the sheath on her hip bringing it up slicing through his bicep to the bone, the tendons all severed he could no longer hold on to her, he screamed in pain.
"If you are going to do something, do it don't talk about it" she said,
Swiftly driving the knife through his throat & out the back severing his spine.
Skies was in full beast mode, his teeth & claws tearing through the Alimanas leaving them piled around the room. The remaining scurrying off down into the dark wailing & screeching.
Sikes regained his control.
"Are you ok T? He asked, moving towards her,
She ran up & gave him a big hug.
"I got your back, luckily their screams travel"
"You good big guy?"
His wild aggression shocking her slightly.

"Yeah, but we gotta catch up to Nyah & Nadaur,
Let's go"
The two bolt off down the tunnel.
"Sikes & Tallie aren't behind us anymore" Nyah
remarked looking around,
Nadaur's singular focus of catching the Alimana
that were just within his grasp. He flung the
tethered blade catching the two fleeing combatants
around the legs causing them to fall in writhing
mass. Nyah looking back notices Sikes & Tallie in
the distance running up out of the dark of the
tunnel. Nadaur flexes his arm causing the blade to
spring from his forearm, gripping one of the
Alimana by the collar he slams him against the wall
pressing the blade into his neck, while Nyah keeps
a close eye on the other.
"What do you know about a gatherer team that was
killed after coming here earlier today?" He asked
menacingly.
"We don't know anything about anything, get your
hands off me" said the Alimana with an
unconvincing bluster.
"Check um" Nadaur said, gesturing to Nyah,
Nyah flipped the grounded Alimana over & started
to check through his pockets
"Hey, hey what do you think you're doing you don't
have the right to…"
Just then Nyah felt something stashed in a hidden
pocket at the small of his back causing him to cut
his sentence short.
"What's this?" she asked pulling it from its hiding
place

"I don't know, I just found it is all".
She unwrapped the item. It was a Regents seal, a very ornate circular disk both sides covered in jewels & engraved in the centre is the crest of The Regent of their region.
"Where did you get that!" Nadaur yells
Pressing the blade into his neck until his putid yellow blood starts to flow.
"I swear, I found it" he whimpers
"Where exactly?"
Tallie & Sikes run up & join their compatriots. Nyah looks up at Tallie, her shaggy blonde hair matted down with sweat & grime.
"What happened to you two?"
"We got ambushed by a bunch of these pricks" Tallie snaps,
Pointing to the Alimana,
The Alimana being held against the wall grins a slimy smile causing Tallie to give him a short sharp punch to the jaw leaving him spitting out teeth.
"You think this is amusing?" Tallie questions.
Nyah looks up at the Alimana being pinned to the wall & notices he has his hand in his pocket
"What's that?"
"Just calling some friends" he cackles.
Out of the darkness a deep growl then another, even with the Imp sight it's impossible to see what created the spine chilling sound, all they can make out is movement in the darkness.
"Sikes you see anything?" Nadaur shouts.
Sikes moves around to the front, narrowing his eyes in an attempt to focus, the two large shapes

moved forward with a smooth elegance that Sikes
had seen before.
"Oh shit it's Two bainly wolves!" Sikes said quite
alarmed
Lowering his huge head so his horns were at the
ready & crouching into a battle stance.
"Alimana's have never had any connection to bainly
wolves, how did you call them!" Nyah yells,
Picking up the floored opponent holding him
against the wall.
The Alimanas share a glance, quickly the Alimana
being held by Nadaur spits a mouthful of his vile
blood into their faces causing Nyah & Nadaur to
recoil, the stench burned their eyes,
"You foul creatures!" Nyah exclaimed,
As she rubbed her eyes struggling to regain her
sight.
The two Alimanas ran off down the tunnel towards
the Bainly wolves that are stalking ever forward.
Cackling in the excitement of escaping their
captors, looking back not paying attention they turn
realising they are a mere three feet in front of the
massive beasts, they attempt to move to the side &
let them pass but in a moment of teeth & claws they
are ripped to shreds & left in a broken mass on the
tunnel floor.
The two terrifying hunters now in a state of
bloodlust take off at a truly frightening speed. Nyah
with shrug of her shoulder flicks her sword, which
when she looks the blade now has symbols in a
language that she has never seen before into her
hand. Tallie pulls her two flame red daggers holding

them pointed to the ground with her thumb on the end of the scales for stability. Nadaur widened his stance flexing harder causing the blades along his forearms to extend slightly past his fists & elbows, he grabs another marble of the imps cradle a bright fiery orange colour crushing it causing his muscles to grow & densen.

One of the Wolf hits Sikes head on with an astonishing crash the two of the tumble down the tunnel, Nadaur & Nyah only just managing to avoid the mass of muscle, claws & teeth gnashing as it passed them. The second wolf lunges at Nadaur he is only just able to bring his arm up the wolf biting down on his forearm its long jagged teeth piercing clean through to the other side,

"Ahhh shit!" Nadaur grimaces,

Trying to push forward forcing the blade into the mouth of the snarling beast. Tallie turns as Sikes tumbles past striking at the wolf with his mighty clublike paws, the wolf ends up on top with Sikes pinned to the ground. The wolves drooling teeth right in his furry face. All of a sudden, the wolf cried out, Sikes looked up to see Tallie on the back of the monstrous beast stabbing over & over again into its sides causing oil black blood to pour from it. Sikes reached around grabbing Tallie & with his strong back legs catapulted the wolf past Nyah & Nadaur into the darkness.

The wolf still tearing into Nadaur's arm pushes him against the wall where from his left Nyah moves in & in one fluid motion spins slicing the wolf the length of its body, the wolf lets out a deafening howl

which reverberates down the tunnel & releases its grip on Nadaur's mangled arm turning its attention to Nyah, she crouches low to the ground & the wolf comes at her its tooth filled mouth extended wide, the cuts Nadaur's weapon left in the corners of its mouth tearing further into its face. She pushes off with her powerful legs, the sword outstretched she drives it deep into the roof of the animals' mouth & extending out the top of its head piecing its brain, the wolf falls silent to the ground. Nyah stops & takes a breath as the danger has passed, just then the other wolf spilling blood, making a last ditch effort & a frightful noise flies through the air towards her, she pivots on her front foot moving her back foot to the side & as the wounded beast comes into range she brings down her blade severing the head of the wolf sending it bouncing down the tunnel.
"Fucking hell is everyone whole?" Tallie asks looking around,
"I think I might need some attention" says Nadaur, Nyah snaps out of the fog of battle upon hearing this running to his side, His arm is losing a lot of blood,
"There's something wrong, this wound doesn't feel right" Nadaur says,
Stoic yet slightly panicked.
Nyah & Tallie lift him up,
"We need to go Sikes!"
Sikes checking the remains of the fallen wolves' notices shadows forming around the bodies, as the two merge together the instant before the

disembodied head disappears the eye moves
staring directly at him & then it's gone.
"Sikes!" Nyah yells,
He bounds up the tunnel to their side.
"They just melted into the shadows & I don't think
they were dead"
"We'll figure it out later, we need to get him to
Sapere, use the Orb. I've a feeling the shadows are
no longer safe," Nyah says.
Tallie fishes it from Nadaur's pocket she twists the
two halves & the bright light fills the darkness they
shield their eyes she snaps it together & they
vanish.

<u>Chapter 4</u>

Kayla & Vincent sit in a corner of the cavernous room containing the larger orb trying to stay out of the way of all the strange creatures passing through.

"It kinda reminds me of catching the train to work, everyone rushing around completely in their own worlds" she said

"It's all so strange yet somehow familiar at the same time, don't you feel?"

"Yes I get what you mean & I don't feel out of place & I always sorta feel out of place" adds Vincent.

Kayla sees something bright out of the corner of her eye, she turns to look as the light continues to get brighter & brighter.

"What do you think that is?

"What exactly? there's so many strange things around here"

"That bright light, can't you see it is almost blinding" she asks, covering her eyes.

"Light. No, I don't see a light"

Just then there was a loud crack & Nadaur, Nyah, Tallie & Sikes appear.

"Tallie get Sapere!" Nyah yells,

Sending Tallie sprinting off down the hallway.

Vincent & Kayla run up to see Nadaur pale, blood covering him & Nyah as she cradles him trying to

keep him awake. Kayla turns hugging onto Sikes arm.
"What happened?" Vincent asks.
Sikes just looks at him,
"He'll be fine" he replies,
With all the conviction he can muster.
Sapere comes flying down the hall carried in the talons of a huge bird that drops him & continues down the hall, he hits the ground rolls & pops up & sprints the last little bit as fast as he is able.
"Nyah what happened?"
"He was bitten by a bainly wolf" she says,
Tears now streaming down her face,
Sapere picks up his arm examining the wounds,
"It looks like there's something mixed in with his blood"
"He cut the wolf in its mouth as he was getting bitten" Nyah explained
"Some sort of blood poisoning I'd wager. We know so little about the wolves & where they come from but I recall reading something about this while I was researching. We need to get him outside" He says,
Blowing a whistle that was hanging around his neck, the huge bird flies back into the room, Nyah tosses him & Sapere into the air the bird catching them,
"Halcyon's observatory he yells & the bird circles the room speeding off down a different hallway followed immediately by Nyah, Sikes, Kayla & Vincent.

At the end of the hall is Halcyon's garden, they hurry through her door. Her roof is a crystal dome split into sections by long ribbons of silver.
"Over here!" Sapere yells, pointing to a table off to the side of the room.
Above the table was long cylindrical tube with all manner of dials & levers near its base. The bird placed Nadaur on the table with much more finesse than its size would suggest. Sapere jumping down to a small platform alongside the table, he was furiously moving the levers into position while checking the dials when the others came running into the room.
"What does it do?" Nyah asks in a panic.
"Halcyon uses this device to study the effects of different spectrums of light on her plants,
Hold his arm here, do not let it move no matter what happens" he said,
Pointing to a marked portion of the table.
"This is going to really hurt" he says,
Looking at Nyah.
She nods, gritting her teeth.
Sapere pulls the lever at the bottom of the tube, opening a cover to expose a lens from which a powerful white light is forcefully focused onto his arm. Nyah cries out in pain as the light burns the skin from her hands.
"Keep it right there we need the light to completely clean out the wound" Sapere instructs.
As he looks through thick goggles that shield his eyes, he can see the black blood of the wolf being burnt away. He watches for the last remnants of the

toxic infection to be cleansed from his friend's arm
he then shuts the lens.
The colour begins to return to Nadaur's face & his
breathing becomes less laboured, Nyah gasps not
for her pain but for the relief that her love was safe.
"Sikes, can you find Halcyon?, she will need to use
some of her growing's to dress their wounds".
Sikes lifts the still unconscious Nadaur, while Kayla
& Vincent assist Nyah.

Sitting in the garden outside Halcyon's nook,
Halcyon very tenderly wraps Nyah's injured hands.
"These bandages have been infused with the sap
of the mugwump tree, it's the most powerful
antibacterial & regenerative potion I've discovered
in my many years" Halcyon educated.
"What exactly happened?" she asks.
Nyah is not paying attention, she's transfixed on
Nadaur lying in the gently swaying grass, still
unconscious bathed in the beautiful sunlight that
spills into the garden.
"Sweetheart?" She prompts to break Nyah's
concentration.
"Oh sorry, somehow the Alimana were given the
ability to summon the wolves, but they had no
control over them"
"Interesting, Sikes said that after I dispatched them,
they passed into the shadows & even though I had
decapitated one of the wolves it wasn't dead"
"The Bainly wolves are a mystery & we know even
less about the world of the shadows, so it is
possible that the wolves originate there. Sapere

has been doing research into this so hopefully any
information can help jolt him in the right direction of
inquiry".
"Thank goodness he was, I don't know what I would
do without Nadaur"
"None of that now, he's going to be fine. How does
that feel sweetheart?"
"Incredible" she says,
Looking in amazement at her bandaged hands,
"I can barely feel any pain"
"There are many secrets in the natural worlds & we
are only just scratching the surface of how powerful
things like plants can be"
"Cocker!" Nyah jumped up.
"Excuse me?" Halcyon inquired.
"Cocker, that snivelling little shit, he's always
hanging around with Alimana planning & scheming.
Nothing not even his father is going to save him this
time, if he had something to do with what's going
on" Nyah says furiously.
"Well, you need to let your hands heal for a little
while before you go tearing his head off"
"I'll take Tallie, she'll enjoy beating the truth out of
him"
"Take Sikes too just to be on the safe side, I love
Tallie but sometimes that girl is scarier than Sikes &
he's a huge monster"
The shock of this statement breaks Nyah's anger
causing her to Laugh,
"You are not wrong".
"Ahh here they are" Halcyon says.

Nyah looks over her shoulder to see a young elf with long black hair wearing more layers than seems necessary, topped with a black coat that is slightly too big, so much so it hides her hands & drags on the ground as she walks. Next to her is a ball of muscle, bone growths protruding from his knuckles & the points of his elbows. He is covered by a ultra fine coat of hair that sticks out from his knee length grey overcoat.

"Hi Miss, I heard you were look'n for us" says the girl in a sing-songy fashion.

"Yes Luma, I need you & Rava to help me acclimatise two new arrivals"

"Hello Nyah" they both say in unintentional unison that makes them both blush.

"Hello you two, you staying out of trouble?"

"Oh definitely" Luma answers with a cheeky smile.

"How's Nadaur?" Rava asks,

Looking at him lying in the grass.

"He'll be fine" Halcyon interjects,

Trying to keep Nyah's attention off him, if only for a second.

"I'll see you later sweetheart, you two follow me"

Luma waves goodbye to Nyah, her little hand lost in the sleeve of her jacket.

"So who are these newbies Miss?" Rava asks

"Two rather interesting Disins, they've had their faiges removed but they've not had an introduction to our world, so I'm counting on you two to show them some of the fun to be had, within reason of course & stay out of the forest ruins, I know you like to hang around there but it's not safe, Ok?"

"Yes, ok miss" they replied with little conviction.
Halcyon leads them down the long hallway to the dorms. Vincent & Kayla are sitting on the bunk like bed chatting having just woken up.
"Oh good you two are up, I'd like you to meet some friends of mine"
Kayla & Vincent jump to their feet, both a little unsure how to behave.
"Kayla, Vincent this is Luma & Rava, they're going to show you around & try to get you two a bit more acclimated to your new surroundings. Have fun" she says,
Already halfway out the door.
Luma without provocation walks forward giving first Kayla then Vincent a big hug.
"So when did you get here?" Luma probes.
"Um, well we got here a few days ago" Kayla answers cautiously.
"Oh were you the ones who encountered the Bainly wolf with Nadaur?"
"Yeah, it was not fun" Vincent replied.
"Wow, I've only ever heard stories, it's extremely rare to see one especially in your world" says Luma.
"Well then, how about something to eat, I've only eaten twice today & I'm starving"
"It's only the morning, Rava, I'll never understand where you put it all, how about you two wanna get a snack or something?"
"I could go for something," says Vincent.
"So where have you been in the city?" Luma inquires

"You'll get used to Luma she's very noisy"
"I prefer to think of myself as inquisitive Rava" she corrects
"Um we've been to the dining hall, Halcyon's garden, Sapere's workshop & that room with the giant orb thingy" Kayla explains.
"Oh cool you've barely scratched the surface, let's grab a few snacks then we'll go have some fun" says Luma happily.

They walk into the dining hall, the long tables full with people. The chattering voices echo across the walls.
"Rava grab a few Sqire cakes"
Luma turns,
"They are not really cakes, they grow on the Sqire bush but they taste so good & they're velvety soft once you get through the peal & we'll need some fire spring water, it's great for when you need a little energy"
"It comes from a spring up in the mountains, they say the energy comes from residual magic in the stones it's filtered through left over from the troll wars" Rava adds.
Just then a piece of fruit sales passed Luma's head.
"Ooo just missed" A voice laughs.
A tall slim boy walks up, dressed in a grey outfit well crafted but a little overworn, all the edges & seams so meticulously finished it kept a strict structure even when he was walking.

"Do that again Urchon & I'll throw you across this
room" Rava growled,
Putting himself between them.
"Oh don't get so protective I'm just playing around &
who might you be?" he replied with a scoff.
"This is Kayla & Vincent & we were just leaving"
Luma says.
"Kayla, Hmm Well maybe you'd like to come & eat
with us?"
"No, I'm pretty sure that's the last thing I could
possibly want"
The joy of tormenting disappears from his eyes,
Kayla smiles believing she has bested him at his
own game.
"What are you four up to?" Growled a voice from
behind.
Kayla spins around to see Sikes standing there in
all his menacing glory.
Realising her mistake.
"Oh Hi, Sikes, Luma & Rava were just about to take
us on a tour, do you wanna come?"
"Ah ok, No thank you I'm gonna grab a little
something to eat" he said,
Making constant eye contact with Urchon, causing
him to scuttle off back to his table
"You guys have fun" Sikes said,
Already distracted by all the tasty treats.
"You know Sikes?" a wide eyed Luma asked.
"Yes he was one of the people that brought us
here" said Vincent
"He's really quite sweet" Kayla adds,

"Although when I first saw him I'm not ashamed to
say I was quite terrified".
"Where do you think we should go first, Rava?"
"Um, how about the Highaster Tree?"
"Yes that's as good a place as anywhere" Luma
says leading them out of the room.
"Why was that guy messing with you?" Kayla
askes.
"Oh my family is on the elvish council & he claims
his are a part of the High Regents court in the
capital, but it's commonly known that that is a lie"
Luma says,
With more than a hint of scepticism.
"Not to mention he hangs around with Cocker,
which makes him think he can do whatever he
wants & he can get away with it" says Rava.
"Who's Cocker?" Vincent asks.
"He's the son of The Regent, but since his wife left,
he treats him like any other of his lackeys".

The hall comes to an end with a beautiful arch
made from vines latticed together to form a natural
pattern that flows into intricate shapes that mirror
each other. They step out into a monumental
courtyard at its centre a monolithic tree extending
high into the sky. The tree sits on top of a lush
grassy hill speckled with people & creatures
reading & running about playing games. The roots
had spread out creating large ridges with holes
intermittently scattered around.
Kayla looked up in awe as she had never seen
anything like it, the sheer size dwarfing any trees

she had encountered before. Looking up into the
branches she notices something small & furry
darting about from branch to branch.
"They're Sabians, they used to be raced but that
was outlawed many years ago" says Luma.
"This is the Highaster Tree & as the story goes
thousands of years ago the Highaster tribe used
the secrecy of trees canopy to plain a rebellion
against the trolls who wanted to pave over the all
the grasslands surrounding the city"
"Well I'm glad they didn't, this place is really
beautiful" interjected Vincent.
"Just watch out for those Barker burrows, it's easy
to break your ankle if you're not paying attention"
"Barkers?" asked Kayla.
"Oh, Barkers are a round tunnelling animal that are
solid as a rock but can move really quickly. They
roll themselves into a ball to speed around their
massive warren of tunnels they've built
underground".
Vincent sees a group of people playing with a huge
dog-like animal. Its hair is so long that with every
movement & change in direction of its mass its hair
takes a second to catch up.
"That's an Ikeanove, they may look a little silly but
they make excellent pets" Rava says,
He whistles to get the animals attention.
The beast runs towards them in a mass of hair &
limbs, the closer it gets Vincent starts to realise to
true size of the animal, it rears up & knocks him to
the ground its massive face inches from his. Its
mouth was not a snout like a regular dog but a wide

horizontal grin full of jagged teeth. Just as Vincent was starting to panic a long slobbery forked tongue slid from its mouth slapping him in the face like a wet sheet. Rava grabbed the Ikeanove giving Vincent a chance to get back to his feet.
"Can I pat it?" Kayla asked somewhat timidly.
"Yes, they may look mean but Ikeanove's are just big softies, aren't you" Luma says Smooshing his face around.
Kayla reaches out stroking the playful beast.
"I never could resist petting a dog" she said with a big smile on her face.
The Ikeanove runs off bouncing over the roots of the giant tree.
"Where should we go next?" Rava askes with a wry grin.
"How about we go for a walk in the Reverie Forest" Luma suggests.
"Ok lead the way" Kayla says following.
They walked to the top of the hill, standing at the base of the tree. The sheer scope blew Vincent's mind.
"How old is this tree?" he asked.
"No one really knows, but it was here long before the city & hopefully it will be here long after" answers Luma.
Kayla looks down from the hill to a dreamlike meadow full of long grass & dozens of different species of wild flowers.
"It's so pretty" she says
"Isn't it, I love coming here. Halcyon has been teaching me about phytomedicine, it's really

interesting, although you have to be very careful
cuz there seems to be as many plants that can be
used for harm as there is to help & they often look
very similar" Luma says.
"I like Cylatom pollen, it's such a rush" says Rava.
"Cyla… what" Vincent asks
"Cylatom pollen is an extract from the Cylatom
flower, there are many strains that all have slightly
varying effects but it's essentially a medicine that
has become recreational & it's very safe as long as
you stay away from the speckled varieties" Luma
explains.
Each step though the long grass causes eruptions
of the tiny sprites they had seen in the city.
"This is where they live naturally, but lots of them
move to the city on the backs of Whalmera, those
huge beasts that roam around the city, they use to
live out here in the Reverie Forest but some left
because they absorb toxins in the air as
sustenance & there's much more in the city causing
them to grow much larger" explains Luma.

In front of them is a wall of trees that run in either
direction as far as the eye can see. The edge of the
forest is remarkably straight as if the trees made a
choice to stop there.
"Come on" Rava says,
Forcing his way through the undergrowth.
"It's a bit of a chore but it gets easier the deeper
you go & it's well worth it".
Kayla pushes back the entangled plant life that acts
as a barrier, as she is released, she looks around,

the forest is not a dark or foreboding place at all, the light bleeds through the canopy creating shards of light that spill onto the ground illuminating pools of water that have gathered on the moss covered floor & in the bows of the trees.
Everywhere they look there's life, from tiny multi coloured lizards that dart into hollows as soon as they are spotted. Large butterflies with wings split into segments that seem to dance through the air.
Kayla, fascinated spots a small furry animal clinging to the side of a tree, she makes eye contact with the curious little creature it blinks its dome like black eyes & disappears up the tree in an instant.
"Are there any dangerous animals in the forest?" Vincent askes.
"Well the Cybra can be very dangerous, lethal in fact, but they are also very solitary & don't particularly like people much so seeing them is very rare" says Rava.
Luma picks a dainty white flower & hands it to Kayla.
"Here blow on this"
Kayla gently blows the petals which begin to spin & as they do an otherworldly tune emanates from the flower that floats off to dance among the trees.
"It's a Siren Silatant, they use their song to attract sprites & other insects to pollinate when the wind blows"
"It's really lovely," says Kayla.
In a moment the dense forest opens into a clearing where the ruins of a large stone structure remain.
Luma climbs the rock with ease perching on the

edge gesturing to Kayla to follow. Kayla cautiously
finds foot & hand holds, slowly climbing to sit next
to Luma. From the top she can see deep into the
forest the light dancing among the trees.
"I needed this, the last few days have been a lot"
she says,
Taking her first calm breath in days.
"It reminds me of going for bush walks as a child"
reminisces Kayla
"Yes, the whole thing with Nadaur must've been a
shock, I wonder what happened?" wonders Luma.
"I hope I never see one of those wolves again"
Kayla adds.
Rava pops his head over a wall,
"There's definitely something weird going on, Bainly
wolf attacks are impossibly rare".
Kayla looks down & something catches her eye on
one of the partial walls. It is a faint illuminated
outline.
"What's that?"
"What?" Luma asks
"That light over there on the wall"
"I don't see anything" Luma replies,
Grabbing Kayla squashing her face against hers in
an attempt to gain the same vantage point.
"Is this like in the orb room?" Vincent askes,
With a twinge of fear in his voice.
"What did you see in the Orb room?" Rava askes.
"Before Nadaur & the others returned I saw a bright
light coming from where they appeared, but Vincent
couldn't see it. Do you think it has something to do

with that Contre sight thing that Sapere spoke
about?"
"You have the Contre sight?, I've only heard about
it in stories" Luma says,
Excitedly jumping around on the rocky outcrops.
They jump down to investigate, Kayla runs her
hand around the edge of the seam of light,
"I need something to pry it open"
"Here" Vincent says, pulling a folding knife from his
pocket & opening it.
She runs the knife in the hidden edge removing
many years of dirt & moss. Slipping the knife into
the gap she attempts to force the compartment
open but to no avail.
"Hmm maybe there's some kinda lock" Guesses
Luma.
"Kayla stops to examine the door, looking closely
she can see very faint markings that have been
covered by stone over the years.
"I can see something, they kinda look like shapes"
"What kinda shapes?" Luma asks.
Kayla uses the knife to scrape away some of the
stone.
"Um, I think this is a tree" she says, scraping away
more to reveal the other symbols.
"There's a tree, some stars, a moon, a road, a boat,
a sun, a door, a cat, a fish & a house"
"It must be some kind of code" suggests Vincent.
"It could be an ancient Imp cryptogram. From what I
remember the pattern the symbols need to be
placed in make some kind of sense to do with the
natural world" Luma recounts.

"Huh, ok well the sun comes before the moon"
Kayla says, placing her finger on the sun, it shines
a bright blue reacting to her touch.
"Oh that's cool!" she exclaimed,
Moving the moon into the next position.
"Oh how about the moon is at night & so are the
stars, try that" Vincent says.
Kayla nods moving the stars across into place.
"But what's next, none of these symbols fit, let's
start over" says Kayla.
"I don't know a lot about these, only what I've read
in books, but the Imps made these locks so they
were difficult but if you put your mind to it not
impossible" Luma explains.
"How about a tree grows because it gets light from
the sun" Rava says hopefully.
"Sounds reasonable" Kayla says,
Moving the tree into the first position, followed by
the sun.
"Well the moon follows the sun" Kayla says, sliding
it into place.
"What I said about the stars still tracks, right?"
Vincent says
"Yes that still works" she says moving them into
place
"We just need three more"
"What do we have left?" Rava asks.
"We've got a road, a boat, a door, a cat, a fish & a
house" Kayla says looking at the symbols.
They all walk around mumbling to themselves.
"Cat, fish, house, road & boat"

"Hey, in our world people use the stars to plot a
path & a path is kinda like a road" Vincent
suggests.
"Yes, the Imps use the stars to navigate too," Luma
adds.
Kayla moves the road & says
"Oh if you're going somewhere your destination
could be a house"
"& houses have doors!" Luma excitedly yells.
"Then the cat & the fish are pretty obvious" Kayla
adds.
"& you use a boat to catch a fish"
Kayla moves the last symbol into place causing
them to chime & pulse with light three times. The
four step back unsure of what to expect. The door
splits into many segments each moving out in
different directions until they all come to rest at the
edge of the secret compartment, Kayla moves
forward looking in the dark hole.
"What's in it? " Vincent asked.
Kayla extends her hand into the dark,
"Ouch! something bit me" she shrieks,
Pulling her hand quickly back.
Luma pulls a necklace from inside her shirt, on its
end hangs a pretty little gem, she holds it up in front
of her mouth & blows which causes the gem to
luminous lighting up the darkness. "That's handy"
says Vincent.
Kayla holding her bleeding hand peers into the
opening, laying on the stone is a beautiful silver
bracelet in the shape of a serpent.

"I don't understand, what bit me" she says moving
closer.
"Look" Rava says,
Pointing to the mouth of the snake, there was blood
dripping from the serpent's fangs.
"Wait!" Luma cries,
But it's too late the bracelet leaps from its resting
place dust flying everywhere they all shield their
eyes & when they look back the bracelet is gone.
"Where'd it go?" Rava askes looking around at the
ground.
"Um, it's here" says Kayla, Holding out her arm.
The bracelet had attached itself to her wrist, the tail
of the snake grasped in its mouth. Kayla pulls at it
but the snake bites down harder.
"What the fuck is this thing?" she says panicked,
"You'll have to ask Nyah, she's the expert, but I
think it's an Impish Blood tie & once the blood has
paired with the object it's impossible to remove,
sometimes even after death that's why it hasn't
been used for hundreds of years" explained Luma.
"We should be getting back" Says Rava
"If Halcyon finds out we brought them out here
we're gonna be cleaning her specimen jars for the
foreseeable future".

A cold wind blows through the trees, a few tiny
drops of rain start splashing off the leaves,
"We'd better get a move on" Luma says,
Taking off her long coat then the second layer a
hooded jacket handing it to Kayla.
"This should keep you pretty dry"

"What about me?" Vincent askes,
Rava reaches up snapping a huge leaf from one of
the trees,
"Hear ya go" he says,
Handing it to him.
Vincent holds the leaf by the stem, its domelike
shape acting as a natural umbrella
"Wow, very cool".
By the time they make it to the outer edge of the
forest the downpour has become torrential.
Standing under the sparse protection of the canopy
looking at the massive storm hammering down the
long grass the wind whipping the water around, it
catches Vincents makeshift umbrella sending it
sailing off into the sky.
"This is amazing, I love a big storm" Vincent said,
Turning his face into the air, feeling the rain.
"Me too, there's something cleansing about a
storm" adds Kayla.
"We really need to get inside before the fire
lightning starts" says Luma with some haste.
"Fire lightning?"
"When the clouds get this close together, they rub
causing sparks that can sometimes catch &
become Fire lightning" Rava explains
"Rava you go first to clear a path & you two where
he goes, you stay in his wake".
They all get ready.
"Ok Go!"
Rava takes off laying the grass flat behind him
creating a path.

Kayla, Vincent & Luma following as closely as they can, suddenly overhead a massive bang that makes them all jump.
"Nearly there. Don't stop under the tree, it's not safe" Luma yells pointing to the arch.
As they pass the tree, Luma puts her foot down a Barker hole, she lets out a cry as she hits the ground.
Vincent turns back asking,
"Are you right?"
"No, I've hurt my ankle"
Vincent grabs her around the waist as she puts her arm around his shoulder. They start to move down the hill. Standing under the safety of the arch Kayla looks up, in the black clouds flashes of orange light dance across the sky.
"It's very pretty"
"Most really dangerous things are" Rava says.
Vincent & Luma join them.
"Ah ouch, I've definitely done something bad" she says,
The pain obvious in her voice, looking down at her already swollen ankle.
"We've gotta take her to the infirmary, follow me" Rava gestures,
Walking off down the hall.
Kayla moves to the other side of Luma giving her another shoulder to lean on.
"Shouldn't we take her to Halcyon?" Kayla asks.
"It's not that serious, the old Doc should set her right" Rava says,
Turning the corner.

A large white arch at its apex a carving of a snake
wrapped around a flower. The room has three walls
made of stone & one made from panes of glass
held together by weathered metal beams. Through
the glass you can see a small courtyard garden
with benches forming a circle around its perimeter.
The rain sheets on the glass splashing on the stone
path. There are beds scattered around the room all
at weird angles to one another.
In the corner a large apothecary cupboard stands
against the wall.
"Ah what have you done this time, playing around
in the forest ruins again Hmm" a voice questions
from a darkened room lit by candles strewn about
their wax dripping making shapes hanging from
every shelf.
"No of course not, I just put my foot in a Barker hole
as we were running from the storm".
A man neither tall or short, fat nor all that skinny
walked from the darkness, around his neck were
many pairs of glasses all attached to chains. His
feet & legs were much larger than a man of his
stature should have. He put one of the pairs of
glasses on to examine Luma. Kayla noticed his
ears were pointed & stuck straight out from the side
of his head filled with tufts of white hair,
"It's impolite to stare young lady" he said,
Peering over the top of his glasses at her.
"I'm so sorry" Kayla said,
Turning bright red.

"She's new here & she's never met an Amalgum
like you before" Luma offers as an excuse.
"I do have a name you cheeky little Elf. Hello my
dear my name is Ottomire Olaphlopson, but my
friends call me Otto & So shall you" he said,
His words pleasant, yet his face still stuck in a
scowl.
"What do your enemies call you?" Rava asked with
a mischievous grin.
"I have none, well not any more, they all seemed to
pass away from very mysterious & terribly painful
medical conditions…oh what's that on your face
there Rava, it looks like it might be a medical
mystery Hmm" he said with a glint in his eye.
Rava went very pale & quiet.
"So let's take a gander, hop up on the table missy"
he directed,
Planting himself on a wheeled stool spinning round
& shuttling himself across the room with one push
of his enormous feet.
Lifting her leg with tremendous care, examining her
ankle switching glasses once then again. "Ah ok,
it's going to have to come off" He said,
With as much authority as he could muster,
looking up to see the tears in Luma's eyes.
"Oh no my dear, sorry bad doctor joke, you'll be
fine I think I've got…" He paused
pushing off & going flying across the room to the
cabinet, he opens & rummages through one draw
then another & each time he pushes in one another
pops open.
"I've got a system" he yells

"It's just not a very good one" he continued under his breath.

"Yes, here we go the sap from a constrictor Phylaimun. In nature it squeezes trees to death but in the right dose it also will contract your injured ankle back to its original state. Only issue is it is quite foul, but you're a big girl I'm sure you can handle it, stick out your tongue".

Luma sticks out her tongue & to Kayla & Vincents surprise it is purple as if she had been sucking on a purple candy.

He pulls the stopper from the bottle & fishes around in his pocket retrieving a fine glass tube, he places one end into the bottle filling it with a few drops then placing his thumb over the end, he places it over her outstretched tongue.

"Just two drops should suffice" he says,

Dropping one then another.

"Hold it in your mouth for ten seconds then swallow" he says.

As the seconds tick by, the look on her face gets more & more disturbed, until finally Otto gives her permission.

"Ok swallow".

She gulps it down sticking out her tongue,

"Yuck!" she screeches

"Oh did I say ten seconds I meant one, well that's what you get for lying about the ruins" he says with a knowing look.

"How does that feel now?"

Luma reaches down pulling up her pants to see the swelling shrinking back to normal before her eyes.

"It might be a little tender but you should be fine to
walk around. Was there anything else?" he asks
looking down at Kayla's wrist & the small trace of
blood on her hand. Luma's jacket all but concealing
the bracelet. Otto begins switching his glasses
again & looking closer. Kayla hurriedly shoves her
hand into the jacket's pocket.
"No, I think we're all good now, thank you very
much Otto" Luma says quickly.
"Oh you are very welcome my dear" he says,
Still looking at Kayla's obscured wrist.
"On your way then" he says,
Pushing the stool & rolling off & disappearing into
the darkness with only the glint of the candle light in
his eyes giving away that he is still studying them.

Chapter 5

Nyah lies sleeping soundly in the dark, next to her a sleepless Nadaur climbs from the bed that hangs suspended from the ceiling, he reaches out with his hand to slow the sway of the bed as to not awaken his sleeping love.

Strolling out into the cosy living room of their small but homey sanctuary he opens a carved wooden box that sits on a round glass top table next to a very slouchy but comfy couch.

Opening the box sends a pungent aroma out into the crisp night air, he removes one of the hand rolled joints, he places it to his lips, turning the box on its side there is an engraved image of a flame with an intricate series of circles next to it, he places his finger on top of the symbol causing the flame to jump from the carving into life, placing the tip in he takes a few puffs, the burning ember on its tip glows with deep soothing blue mixed with hints of orange.

Returning the box to the table he walks across the room to a set of bay doors that lead out onto an open balcony with no rail, it's just a platform reaching out into the air. At the tops of the doors are two ornate polls that hold back the hanging vines that cascade from high above like they were curtains.

He sits staring out into the night the speckled lights
of others abodes scattered up the cylindrical shaft
reaching high above & deep into the darkness
below.
Blowing plumes of blue tinted smoke that get
caught by the wind & sent climbing high into the air
till they disappear into nothingness.
Nyah rolls over, her sleeping hand travelling across
the silken sheets to find something that is no longer
there.
The absence wakes her from her slumber looking
around the room she sees the pale blue glow &
smells the smoke wafting on the night air. She gets
up sitting on the edge of the bed as she becomes
more conscious. Stepping down as the bed sways,
she slips one of Nadaur's jumpers on, swimming in
it she pulls the sleeves up enough that her finger
tips can grasp the cuff.
Walking out into the other room to see Nadaur
perched on the edge of the balcony, his legs
dangling into the abyss. She steps out, he looks up,
"Sorry I couldn't sleep & I didn't want to wake you,
you looked so peaceful" he says.
She takes the half finished joint taking a draw &
blowing three rings that float off staying perfectly
together until they finally break & disappear in the
air high above.
"This new mix that Halcyon gave you is much better
than her last, it's much smoother & the sedation
effect is less brutal" she says,
Taking another puff before handing it back to him.
"Are you ok?" she asks

"I just can't seem to get my mind to switch off" he
says,
Knocking the ash from the smouldering end into a
small jar sitting to his left.
"I know that what we do is important & very
necessary, but sometimes I look at the people with
simple lives with a longing for what they have, you
know?"
"If you wanna go live in a small cottage in the hills
I'll be right there with you" she says,
Rubbing her hand across his shoulders.
"I know you would" he says,
Turning & giving her a soft kiss on the lips.
"Unfortunately, I don't think that would solve my
problem, I fear it would just give me more time to
dwell on the mistakes of the past".
Nyah takes another drag letting the smoke trail
from her mouth.
"Is your arm feeling better?"
"Yes" he says,
Pulling back the bandage.
"Soon it will just be another scar, to add to the
stories of battles long past".
The marks where the mighty wolf sank his teeth
into Nadaur's arm are defined slashes, a testament
to the tremendous sharpness of the wolf's fangs.
"How is your new position as High guard for The
Regent going?"
"Aside from his lecherous advances, it's not at all
what I expected. When we were on a team
together, we were the elite, the tip of the spear, but
now I just seem to be doing babysitting jobs & I

kinda miss the action, but I know that is just the
view from the outside cuz when we were in the
middle of it the pressure & danger was too much,
does that make sense?".
Nadaur pops his jaw sending a much poorer
example of a smoke ring than Nyah had.
"You really need to teach me how to do that"
"It's pure skill" she says with a smile.
"Yes, I completely understand. When I feel the
sudden rush of adrenaline when the battle is
imminent my mind goes straight back to those days
& I miss it too, but we both knew it was only a
matter of time until one of both of us would be
another nameless casualty in the dark & neither
one of us could have lived without the other".
Nyah lays her head on his shoulder.
"Maybe we just need a hobby" she says,
Causing them both to laugh which crashed through
the silence of the night.
They both take one final draw then Nadaur presses
the ember out into the jar.
"Let's go back to bed, I think I can sleep now"
"Yes, remind me to complement Halcyon on that
Hybrid strain, she has really outdone herself with
that one, I love it" praises Nyah.
With a lovely warmth & calm running through their
bodies they begin to walk back into their bedroom
when all of a sudden Nadaur grasps his arm in
pain, pulling back the bandage the mark left by the
beast is pulling as if it were trying to escape from
his skin.

"Ahh shit this hurts, it seems to be pulling me somewhere".
They both throw on a pair of pants & the long jackets that hang by the door & move out into the hallway.
Nadaur stands at the intersection of four hallways.
"Are you sure you're, ok?" Nyah askes concerned.
"It's more of a burning in the muscle, but it's literally pulling me almost off my feet" he says, Gritting his teeth.
He stops & holds his arm across his body allowing the wound to lead, his feet sliding across the stone floors drawn on by an unseen force.
"It looks like we are headed for the dorms" says Nyah,
Following closely at his side.
They turn a corner leading to the hall where the dorms are separated into rooms of two. Halfway down the corridor a shape moving in the darkness, Nyah & Nadaur's instincts take over as they move to either side of the hallway blocking the escape.
A deep growl reverberates down the hallway & upon it reaching his ears,
"It can't be"
"What is it?" Nyah asks
"I think it's a Bainly wolf!"
Nadaur Flexes his arms & the blades extend from his forearms causing him extreme pain on his injured arm. Nyah looks around seeing a large wooden chair against the wall she flips it onto its side & with one swift kick she breaks the legs from the chair for a makeshift weapon.

The two move in sync criss crossing down the hall
as the dark shape stalks toward them. The beast
breaks into a run, gnashing its lethal teeth. Nadaur
runs at the encroaching threat closely followed by
Nyah the wolf takes flight towards him, Nadaur
jumps up planting on foot on the wall spinning & at
the same time removing his long overcoat.
The wolf now feet from him sailing through the air in
a single minded attack. Nadaur spreads the coat
throwing it over the massive head of the thrashing
animal & vaulting off its head landing on its back
holding the jacket tight around its neck covering its
entire head, its claw striking out in every direction
catching Nadaur on the shoulder with a glancing
blow that tears the skin.
Nyah now in a full sprint dives forward landing with
her knuckles on the stone floor still holding the two
pieces of broken wood & with incredible grace
pushes off using the momentum to propel her high
into the air, always with one eye on her target.
Nadaur instinctively knowing where she is grips the
thrashing vicious creature as tight as he is able.
Nyah completes the flip by bringing the two
splintered ends of the wood with all her might
impaling the wolf in either side of its head,
continuing all the way down until the points embed
themselves into the floor sending Black blood &
splinters flying.
The animal lays silent on the cold ground, Nyah &
Nadaur still gripping tight to their points of attack,
their breath heavy as the adrenaline courses
through their bodies.

Nyah looks at the black abyss of the wolf's body, the darkness falling into itself in an almost hypnotic lack of anything.

"Are you good?" Nadaur asks

"Nyah!"

She snaps back to reality.

"Oh sorry, I lost myself for a second there, yeah I'm good, what the hell was that?" she asks, Her big eyes wide open.

"I don't know, but something weird is going on. I've gone my entire life only hearing about Bainly Wolves in tales & I've encountered Four in such a short time".

Nyah tears a patch from her pants placing it gently on his wounded shoulder to stem the flow of blood. As they stand looking down at the corpse of the fallen beast, they notice a thin line of shadow extending from its long tail creeping off down the hall mixing in with the darkness. Nadaur looks around seeing a lamp sitting on a table a few feet away, grabbing the light he holds it high in the air to cast as much light into the darkness as possible. The dark gives way to the light but the shadow trailing from the wolf is unaffected & continues moving off down the hall having a mind of its own. The two of them were so focused on the mystical shadow that was behaving in such a mysterious fashion they were startled when the two stakes the Nyah had driven into the skull of the wolf fell to the ground with a bang. The shadow now seemed to be moving the inert creature down the hall, dragging it toward some unknown goal.

Nyah retrieves her makeshift weapons, tossing one of them to Nadaur. The beast begins to move with greater speed, its blackness sliding down the halls like oil.

"Look!" Nyah says,

"The shadow is leading into that dorm room"

The two move quickly but with caution arriving at the door of the dorm just in time to see the wolf disappear under the door jam. Nadaur places his hand on the long handle of the door making eye contact with Nyah in a nonverbal communication of intent, she readies herself taking a tight grip on the blood soaked wood. As he quickly but quietly as he can opens the door illuminating the darkness with the lamp.

He sees Kayla sound asleep in one bunk, the other is Vincent he is tossing & turning as if in the clutches of a terrifying dream, they look down to see the shadow now leads into his bed disappearing under the covers. The carcass of the wolf now melting into the shadow as it moves further into the room.

Nadaur moves to the end of Vincent's bed, gently taking hold of the bedding pulling it down to the base of the bed. Nyah lets out a gasp as the shadow is consuming Vincent's body, his skin taking on the same appearance of the unending black of the wolf.

Maybe it was the light or the presence of somebody else in the room, but Vincent wakes with a start & at the very moment of him regaining consciousness the last of the shadow disappears into him leaving

him shocked looking up at Nyah & Nadaur with similarly stunted looks on their faces.
"Wha... What the hell's going on?" he yells, Waking Kayla who peers out from her bed.
"I really don't know, but what I do know is we need to get you to Halcyon's light chamber until we can figure it out, I'll take him you go & get Sapere & possibly Otto, Nyah".
Nyah sprints from the room as Nadaur directs Vincent through the doorway.
"What should I do?" Kayla asks
"Do you know anyone here yet?" Nadaur asks.
"Yes I've got a couple of friends"
"You go find them & stay there, but don't tell them about what happened here" he says sternly.
"I don't know what happened here" she quietly says to herself.

Nadaur with a tight grip on the collar of Vincent shirt move through the halls with a pace that denotes the danger, almost lifting his off his feet as they dart around the few inhabitants out in the dead of night.
Turning down the corridor to Halcyons home, Nadaur using the tarnished metal knocker in the shape of a cascading vine pounds on the door sending echoes down the dark hall.
The door opens with a loud creaking that cuts through the silence intercut by Vincent's heavy breathing.
"Who the hell is banging on my door at such an insane hour?" She asks,

Very annoyed, rubbing her eyes to displace the
sleep.
She looks up & her demeanour is immediately
altered by the intense looks on her friend's face.
"What Has happened?"
"We need to get him into your light chamber that
Sapere used to heal me from the wolf's bite!"
Nadaur says,
With a cadence that informs her of the urgency of
his request.
"Let us go!" she says,
Taking off down the tunnel without even closing her
door behind her & at a quite impressive pace for
someone of her years.
Her long thin nightgown flapping behind her as she
makes the final turn into her garden bathed in the
light of the moon. The night flowers all open
soaking up the delicate light.
Nyah Runs down the hallway closely followed by
Sapere & Otto, Sapere seated on a small single
wheeled device as he would have no chance to
keep up on foot.
"Another wolf you say?" Otto says,
"How intriguing"
"It's not intriguing you nihilist, it's dangerous"
snapped Sapere angrily.
"There has never been a sighting of a Bainly wolf in
any city in my lifetime, what could have prompted
such an aggressive escalation?" he queries,
whizzing around the corner with incredible balance
& skill.

Nyah enters the garden to see Halcyon opening the
door to her Observatory.
"Up on the table young man" she says to Vincent,
Who is looking sufficiently freaked out by this point.
"Can someone please tell me what the fuck is going
on?" he yells
"As soon as I figure it out, ok, try to stay calm
sweetheart" she says,
Placing a pair of goggles on him to protect his eyes
from the light.
Halcyon lifts the huge array into position above the
table pushing levers & turning wheels while
checking the myriad of dials that cover the device.
Finally opening the lens at the focal point
illuminating Vincent in the concentrated light.
"So what exactly happened?" Halcyon asks.
Nadaur starts to explain while Otto takes the
temporary bandage from his shoulder, taking a
small vial of pink powder from his pocket he
sprinkles it into the wound which causes Nadaur to
wince in pain, as the powder fizzes it creates a
scab like covering on the wound.
"Wait so the wolf's bite alerted you to its presence?"
Sapere asks,
Pacing around the room chewing on the tip of one
of his many pairs of spectacles.
"Yes, but once the wolf was dispatched it retreated
into its host, is that normal?" Nyah asked.
"We know so little about the Blainly wolves that
what's normal is a very thin line" Halcyon replies
with a shrug.
"What do you mean host?" Vincent says in a panic,

"I've got one of those black wolves in me?"
Seeing his panic becoming worse Halcyon takes a
small silver bulb from the shelf squeezing it over
Vincent releasing a puff of yellow particles into the
air over Vincent's face, the cloud then with the
appearance of intention disappears into his nose &
mouth rendering him unconscious instantly.
"Why did you do that?" Otto exclaims,
"It's obvious the boy doesn't know what is
happening to him & there is nothing to be gained by
traumatising him further" Halcyon answers,
Looking sternly at Otto as he turns away grumbling
to himself.
"There doesn't seem to be any reaction" Nyah
says,
Looking over Vincent.
"When we removed his Faige, his skin did flash jet
black…"
"So this is your fault" interrupts Otto.
"I've removed thousands of Faiges over the years &
I've never seen a reaction like it, I do not believe it
was anything that I did, although I cannot be
definite" she says reassuringly.
"Remember his Faige was the Blaidd, which is
represented by the wolf & was originally used to
contain a force either too great or dangerous to be
left unchecked" Sapere recounts.
"But its connection to these ethereal wolves is
unknown".

Vincent wakes but lays on the table listening to the
conversation discussing his predicament as if he

weren't even in the room, but just as he was about
to open his mouth to voice his fear a hand landed
on his shoulder.
"How are you doing with all this?" A calm voice
asked,
It was Halcyon.
"Try not to worry" Sapere says,
"We are going to figure this out".
This inclusion made him feel measurably better,
"Do you remember what your dream was about?"
Nadaur asks.
"Dream?" Vincent asks, looking confused.
"When we found you, you seemed to be in the
throes of a nightmare" Nyah adds,
"No, I'm sorry but I have no memory of it" he says,
Shaking his head.
"Nadaur, do you feel anything from the wound
being in close proximity to Vincent?" Sapere asks.
"No, not a thing" he says,
Pacing his arm on Vincent's chest.
"Let me try a different spectrum of light" Halcyon
suggests,
Sliding a large lever from the side of the light
chamber.
"This will cycle through the many different forms of
light this chamber is able to display".
The lever slowly moves around the circular device
clicking into place every few seconds changing the
colour of light being emanated onto Vincent's body.
The colours change from blue to red then green
with no visible response from the mysterious
inhabitant.

"Hmm wait a moment…Shadow" Halcyon said,
Quickly running off into one of the many back
rooms.
A flurry of activity followed, banging and things
falling over. She emerged dust & cobwebs clinging
to her as she darted into the next room then
another.
"Where did I put it?"
Her voice can be heard from out of sight.
She returns into the main room scanning around
with her eyes,
"Ah ha" she says,
Spotting a barely noticeable glint high on a shelf off
to the side of the room.
Pulling an extremely long and rickety ladder from
against the wall sending a shower of dust
cascading down. Otto moves over to hold the
ladder at the base.
"Are you sure this thing is safe?" he says with a
snigger.
"This ladder is made from the Bayawa tree & is
incredibly strong, it's older than you & a great deal
more reliable" she retorts,
As she ascends into the rafters.
Halcyon arrives at the item releasing it is just out of
reach, leaning from the side of the ladder reaching
out with her fingertips.
"Nearly got it"
She pulls a book which the object is on top of
causing it to fall, the black lens tumbles through the
air,
"Shit!" Halcyon shouts

Nyah darts across the room like a shot diving &
catching the fragile disk at a full out stretched dive,
sliding into the shelves with a thump.
"Thank you my dear" Halcyon says graciously,
descending the ladder.
"I've only got the one of those & to be perfectly
honest I've not got the slightest idea where I
obtained it".
Nyah pops back to her feet.
"What is it?" she asks
"From what we can ascertain the wolves seem to
have some sort of attachment to the shadows" she
says,
"So, what are shadows?"
"The absence of light" Nyah answers slightly
unsure.
"Very good, so what this lens is supposed to do is
use the light to cast a shadow, if it works, to be fair
I've never actually had a reason to use it before".
Halcyon pulls a lever which closes a cover over the
end of the huge telescopic device so she can
exchange the lens.
"Nyah can you help me over here" She asks,
Holding open the spring loaded shutter with both
hands.
"I need you to take the lens out that's in there &
replace it with the shadow lens, while I hold it open,
ok?".
Nyah slides the thick oval piece of crystal out of the
slot, handing it backwards to Nadaur who moved
instinctively because he knew she would need
somewhere to offload it. The black crystal was not

an oval but a jagged multi edged shape, she lay it
into the opening but the side caught on the
mechanism halfway in,
"It's stuck" she said,
"Keep trying sweetheart, I'm sure it will fit" Halcyon
said,
Noticeably struggling herself to keep the lever
pulled back.
Nyah took the lens out looking into the recess, she
noticed a small bar sticking out that was preventing
it from simply sliding into place, so placing the lens
at an acute angle she muscled it in & then moved it
into the correct position with a satisfying snap.
"I've got it" she said excitedly.
"I knew you could, sometimes you just have to look
at things from a new perspective" Halcyon said,
Releasing the lever.
"I'm not too shy to admit I wasn't sure how long I
could've held that for" she said,
Wiping a bead of sweat from her brow.
Halcyon looked over at Nyah & Nadaur, then
behind them to a wall filled with all manner of
edged weapons she used to prune her plants,
Nadaur casually moved back while Nyah shifted in
to block Vincent's eyeline, crossing her arms
behind her as Nadaur picked up two long daggers
from the wide array to choose from. He concealed
them both behind his back slipping one into Nyah's
hands as he stood beside her.
Halcyon seeing them in position out of the corner of
her eye,

"Ok Vincent my dear, I'm going to attach these restraints just to make sure you don't move during the procedure, all right?"
Vincent nods in agreement, a tear wells up in his eye & he shuts them tight, but it is unseen due to the goggles.
Halcyon pulls the lever & opens the shutter & as soon as she does Vincent & the table disappear into darkness, yet the rest of the room remains well lit.
It is not only the lack of light, or a common shadow, the more they look into the darkness the darkness opens up in their minds spreading out more & more.
"It's like looking into the ocean at night, it's nothing but you just have the feeling it's much deeper than you could possibly imagine" Sapere says, Struggling to look away.
"I don't like this, turn it off!" Otto yells, Moving toward the lever, but as he does, he trips falling out of control into the middle of the shadow. Nadaur reaches out grabbing the tail of his jacket while his whole top half is consumed by the darkness.
"I can't pull him out, something has got a hold of him!" he yells,
Nyah grabs Nadaur's belt & begins to pull, both of them are pulling with all their strength. Nadaur has slipped from his original position down to his knees & both he & Nyah are losing traction & starting to slide across the floor.
"Help!" Nyah cries,

"I can't hold him"
Halcyon is frantically trying to close the shutter,
"It's stuck, something is holding it open, I can't get it
closed!" she yells.
Sapere pulls a crystal from one of his pockets,
blowing on it the crystal begins to emit a blinding
bright light. The crystal's light meets the darkness
but it doesn't just disappear it actively seems to
have enough substance that it is battling with the
light.
Sapere moves closer, using all the force he can
bring to bear against the challenging abyss.
Halcyon looks around to see a large book just
within reach, grabbing it she pounds on the lever
once, twice then on the third the lever moves & the
shutter snaps closed
"What's going on, the shadow is still here?" Nadaur
yells.
Nyah looks over at him, he nods as he already
knows what she is about to do, he plants his feet,
grabbing Otto's other leg as Nyah grabs the crystal
from Sapere & with all her strength drives it into the
heart of the darkness.
The pitch black fragments sliding off into every dark
corner like a broken mirror.
Otto falls to the floor as soon as his head emerges
from the black his blood curdling scream fills the
room.
He had been screaming this whole time but they
were unable to hear him, it wasn't just an absence
of light it was an absence of everything.

As he lays trembling on the floor Sapere goes over
to examine him, rolling him over. What he sees
drains all the colour from his face.
Otto had large gashes that run from his forehead
down his face continuing down his torso, the
wounds gape wide open, but there is no blood, not
a drop even on his shredded clothing.
"He's in shock" Sapere says
"We need to get him back to his surgery" he says.
Halcyon jumps down & runs over to the shelf taking
down a small ceramic jar, she pours the entire
contents into a large brass syringe. She runs over
kneeling down beside him.
"Hold his head!" she yells to Sapere.
She inserts the tips of the syringe up his nose
slowly pushing the plunger. She gives him a little,
then a little more but to no avail. Eventually she
empties the entire contents & he falls limp.
She stops frozen for a moment believing him dead,
then a shallow breath then another. The rest of
them then begin to breathe again too, they have
been holding their breaths in terror.
"What the hell could have done that to him?"
Sapere yells
"What the hell is going on?" Vincent screams,
Attempting to sit up, completely oblivious & still
attached to the table.
Halcyon undoes his restraints.
"Is that wise? We have no idea what is going on, or
what role he plays" Nadaur questions.
"I agree, but I don't believe he is any more in the
loop than we are" she says, gesturing to

Vincent.
Nadaur looks into Vincent's eyes
terrified young man.
"These wounds, there's somethin
them" Sapere says,
Looking inquisitively at his uncon
"It must've been the wolf" Halcyo
"No, the wolf's wounds are much
more viscous" Nadaur says,
Pulling back his bandages to rev
his arm & shoulder.
"These are more precise; they h
intent to cause pain & terror" he
"The gathering party!" says Nyal
"Yes, that's where I've seen it be
same precise wounds inflicted o
practised hand.
It's as if the carnage is the point
they can endure before the fatal
Halcyon lifts Otto onto a wheele
"I'll take him to his surgery. You
back to his dorm & keep him the
protection until we find out what
she says,
Looking him in the eye.
Vincent nods, hopping down fro
following them from the room.
"I'll go & research to try & make
of this" Sapere says hurrying ou

Chapter 6

Kayla travels down the immense halls, running the
vents over & over in her head trying to make
sense of it all.
Sticking her head in the dining hall which is all but
empty as it is the middle of the night after all.
Sorting through her conversations with Luma &
Rava to try to pinpoint where she might find them.
Rounding a corner at great speed she runs directly
into Sikes with a thump.
She begins to fall backward but is caught by the
outstretched giant furry arm of Sikes. He steadies
her on her feet.
"Whoa Missy, where are you headed in such a
hurry?" he growled,
in his best non terrifying tone.
"Oh, Sikes, I'm so sorry, I was just trying to find
Luma & Rava, I've had rather a strange night".
"Really, ok, well at this time of night they're
probably in their home or hanging out down at the
balconies overhanging the main hall. They like to sit
up there smoking & watching all the people moving
around below. Here I'll walk with you, I cannot
seem to sleep well of late, so I just end up
wandering the halls trying to get my brain to shut
up".

Kayla looked up at this giant beast, amazed at how
sweet he was despite the terrifying nature of some
of their previous encounters.
"So what has you so disturbed?" he asks,
Even at a low volume the rumble of his voice
passes straight through her.
As the move slowly down the halls Kayla begins to
explain,
"Well, to be completely honest I'm not exactly sure.
I was just woken up by Nyah & Nadaur in our room.
They seemed quite concerned about something to
do with Vincent & sent me away for safety,
apparently"
"If those two are on the case I have great faith that
they will not stop until they figure it out, they're a
very tenacious duo" he says,
In a way that calms Kayla.
At the base of a grand set of stairs Sikes knocks on
a small door in the corner of the room waiting for a
moment then opening the door.
"Nope they're not in there, where else did I say they
might be? I get forgetful when I've not been
sleeping well" he says,
Rubbing his head at the base of his long horns.
"Um you mentioned a balcony" Kayla answers,
Becoming more comfortable with him.
"Ah yes righto, that's this way" he says,
Rubbing her on the head, which made her smile
because of his appearance, it made her think of
petting a dog but in reverse.

She walked close by him as they travelled through the dimly lit halls that seemed to travel out in every direction.

His larger size now becoming a source of comfort rather than fear.

"How big is this city? These hallways seem to stretch out forever" she asks,

Becoming more chatty.

"This is nothing, some of the capitals dwarf this place, but between you & me I prefer to live somewhere close to a nice forest, they tend to cut them down around the bigger cities which I think is a real shame, sometimes you need to be able to go for a walk in nature don't you think?"

"Yes, Luma & Rava took me for a walk out in the forest. It was really beautiful".

Stepping out into the great hall, the open roof showing the sparkling stars above.

Sikes looks up to a balcony high on the wall off to the side, he spots two pairs of legs dangling over the edge plumes of colourful smoke billowing from the elevated position rise into the air.

"Yup, there they are" he says,

Pointing upward with his huge clawed finger,

"We'll take the lift, this way, I just can't deal with all the stairs tonight" he says with a tired huff.

He leads her across the huge expansive room that even in the dead of night is still surprisingly active with a myriad of creatures moving around, ducking off down halls left & right.

"I don't know how some of them function" he says,

"Apparently goblins only sleep for a month every fifty years & they're fine, meanwhile when I have fragmented sleep like I've been experiencing lately I'm a mess. My mind gets all fuzzy"
Without even meaning to, Kayla blurts out,
"Well at least it matches the rest of you"
Completely embarrassed she fixes her eyes to the ground, going bright red, until she hears a bellowing laugh come from the beast.
"You're not wrong," he laughs,
Continuing to chuckle to himself.
In the wall is an ornate gilded lift, as she moved closer Kayla could see that it looked to be grown rather than constructed.
"It was created for The Regent by the Elves, they have the ability to essentially program the golden builders' vine into any conceivable shape & once it's taken its final form it's solidified into a structure that's much stronger than most equivalent building materials" Sikes explains.
Kayla looks nodding up in awe at Sikes' obvious intelligence.
Sikes stops in front of the doors, the Vines of the door untangled themselves allowing the door to smoothly & silently open.
"On ya hop" He says,
Placing his hand on her shoulder completely dwarfing her & making her feel very small. The second they were both situated in the centre of the lift it takes off moving at an incredible pace, yet as Kayla held onto Sikes arm for stability, she noticed

the inertia of the speed they were travelling was not felt by the two as they hurtled skyward.
"You didn't push a button" She says,
Trying to regain focus as the floors zipped past the doors.
"No, these use Elvin telepathy to take you to the desired floor, it's a little hit & miss in my opinion, sometimes It'll take you to where it thinks you need to go" Sikes explained.
The lift stopped instantly & even without the movement being felt Kaylas stomach felt as though it were in her chest. Stepping off onto one of the higher levels the lift took off like a shot as soon as the doors closed.
Kayla walked to the edge peering over, the true height of her new location giving her a start, she stumbled back again being caught by a casually placed arm of Sikes.
"Careful now, over this way let's see if we can't find those two scallywags" he said,
Sikes walked along the lofty atrium, he guided her to an arched opening in the wall, looking out she saw Luma & Rava chatting sitting precariously on the edge of the balcony that extended out into the open space.
"Hey you two!" Sikes bellowed,
Making them both jump & Almost sending Rava toppling off the edge.
"Not funny Sikes!" he yelled
"It was pretty funny," Luma said,
Laughing at how pale Rava had gone.

"You two don't mind looking after Kayla for a little while?"
"Ooo yes please" Luma replied,
"Come on pull up some stone".
Kayla looked up at Sikes furry face, almost amazed that she had ever been scared of him.
"Thank you, Sikes," she said,
Giving him a big hug.
"You're welcome sweetheart" he said,
The deep rumble of his voice sending vibrations through her entire body, she watched as he walked off down the hall.
"So, what's the go?" asked Rava.
"I really don't know" replied Kayla,
"I was woken up to Nyah & Nadaur in our room & there must've been something to do with Vincent because they hustled him off"
"Really? There's definitely been something going on. The Shadow travel has been suspended across the board & The Regent has been receiving lots of Ether correspondence from the capitals "
"Ether correspondence?" Kayla asks
"The Ether is the way that The Regents can communicate over long distances.
Access is highly restricted but one of The Regents lackeys Holmont has a giant crush on Luma so he let it slip" Rava explains.
"Shut up!" Luma says,
Punching him in the arm turning bright red.
"We're just friends" she continues
"Have you discovered anything about your new bracelet?" she asks.

Kayla pulls back her sleeve revealing the snake like adornment on her wrist.
"No, other than look really cool it hasn't done anything"
"Shh" says Rava,
Gesturing for them to come closer.
The three lay on their bellies looking down to the level below.
"My father thinks he knows everything, he never even takes my ideas seriously" A whiny voice complains.
"What about the Alimana, can't we use them to help move the goods?" Another asks.
"No, they're pissed because I won't get them into the city to kill Tallie"
"That bitch is going to ruin everything"
"Don't you ever speak that way about her!" the voice angrily yells,
Grabbing the other person by the neck & hanging them over the edge.
"It's Cocker & Stinal" Whispers Luma.
"Why don't you move them out using the secret passages that run from your fathers chamber?"
"Because I'm yet to completely map them all out & it's far too easy to lose your way if you're not familiar. I only know the way to the Highaster Tree exit by heart, but it's so hard to get into the tunnels because my father has upped his security since The Regents council has been contacting him daily via the Ether over the trouble with the Shadow travel"

"Wasn't your father on the original expedition that
discovered how to access the shadow realm? man,
if we had access to that we could move anything
we wanted" Stinal muses.
"I've been trying for years to discover the secret.
I'm sure he has something hidden down in those
tunnels, but if you're there without some kind of
map you'll get lost down there forever" Cocker
explains.
Rava shifts his position knocking the still
smouldering remains of their joint sailing off the
edge like a beacon in the night air.
"Hey you snooping little shits!" Cocker yells,
Pointing up at them.
"You two get them, I've gotta get out of here" he
orders.
Stinal & Urchon look up to see them scurry back
from the edge.
"We've gotta get outta here!" Luma says,
With obvious concern.
The trio run to the lift only to see it pop open, Stinal
& Urchon stepping forward.
"No one to protect you this time" says Urchon
pushing Rava.
Stinal produces a long thin blade from a sheath
concealed on his back.
"& who might you be?" he questions,
Pointing the blades tip at Kayla.
"Get them back to the edge, we'll make it look like
an accident, they just fell off the balcony" Urchon
suggests.

"All three of them, use your head no one is going to
believe that" Stinal chastises,
Smacking his brother in the back of the head".
"We'll do them & stash their bodies up here until we
can get rid of them" He schemes,
Lunging forward at Kayla,
She brings her arms up in front of her to protect
herself but her arm is propelled forward by some
unseen force. Looking down she realises the
Impish bracelet is now completely engulfing her
hand in a gilded gauntlet, smooth & gleaming. The
gauntlet trusts her hand with a strength she does
not possess. Moments before it made contact with
Stinal's cheek, small barbed spikes form on the
glassy smooth knuckles of the gauntlet piercing his
face, shattering his cheek bone & tearing chunks of
flesh as it followed through.
Stinal went tumbling across the hall coming to rest
against the wall unconscious but alive.
Upon seeing his injured brother Urchon picked up
the knife that lay at his feet, lunging forward with an
outstretched arm attempting to keep his head &
body out of Kayla's reach.
Kayla completely terrified at what she had
apparently done stood frozen in shock but again as
the attacker's blade came closer her body seemed
to move on its own as if it was being puppetired by
a skilled combatant, pivoting on her front foot she
effortlessly stepped aside, as Urchon's momentum
drove him forward the gauntlet again fired up at
starling speed, a singular slim stiletto blade
extended from the central knuckle.

The point slicing cleanly through the meat, bone &
cartilage of his elbow.
Urchon let out a high pitched scream. The blade
began to retract, thorn like barbs grew from the side
of the blade like the stem of a rose completely
destroying his elbow as they went.
Luma grabbed Kayla by the shirt, her eyes shut
tight in fear.
"Come on, we've gotta get out of here!" she urges,
Pulling the terrified girl into the lift to join the
awaiting Rava.
"What the hell was that?!" Rava yells,
Looking down to where the weapon once was.
Kayla raises her arm to see no signs of the
gauntlet, it had completely disappeared, no blood,
nothing, only the serpent remained sitting snugly
around her wrist.
"I knew there was a reason the Imps council
outlawed the use of blood tie weapons, but I never
imagined anything like this, that was wild" says
Luma,
With a look of excitement.
"I need to get this thing off me" Kayla says,
Pulling at the bracelet in a panic.
"Let's take her to Halcyon, she'll know what to do.
Try to breathe Kayla, if you didn't find that thing,
we'd all be dead right now" he says,
With a comforting look that has little effect on the
panic stricken Kayla.

Halcyon leans over the observation table, she
sprinkles grey dust into the bloodless wounds
covering Otto's unresponsive body.
"Here this should see you right" she says,
Putting on her glasses & moving in for a closer
look. She watches the microscopic particles knitting
together, stitching together the wound as they go.
"I'm not loving you colour" she mumbles to herself,
Pushing off & using his chair to sail across the
room towards his apothecary cabinet.
"I can see why he enjoys this" she says,
With a smile, whizzing across the room with ease.
Upon opening the cabinet she is struck by the
beautifully organised medicines, all categorised,
labelled & sectioned into helpful little groupings
making her slightly embarrassed of the state of her
atrium.
"Now let's see" she says,
Running her finger across the labels
"Ah ha, here we go Otto, haematology. Let's see"
She searches through the unfamiliar terms finding a
small vial, the label full of unfamiliar words but on
the front is a picture of a drop of blood with a plus
sign, then two drops of blood.
She takes it down from the shelf turning it over to
find
'For best results administer two drops under the
tongue to the patient suffering from blood loss'
She rolls back across the room, unscrewing the top
of the vial, squeezing the rubber tip to take a few
drops into the pipette, then opening his mouth.

After administering the required dose, she sits back
as the colour begins to return to his face. She dabs
the blood with a cloth as it trickles from his closing
wounds.
"Miss!" Luma calls,
Running into the room followed by Kayla & Rava
"We need your help! "
"Calm down & tell me what's going on, what kind of
trouble have you three gotten into?"
"It wasn't their fault" Kayla says,
Stepping forward.
"It wasn't your fault either" Rava adds
"Ok now that we've established that it isn't
anybody's fault can you tell me what exactly
Happened?"
Kayla walks up to her with her arm outstretched
pulling back her sleeve to reveal the serpent
adorning her wrist.
"Oh my " Halcyon exclaims,
Reaching out her hand to take a closer look.
"No!" Kayla yelled
"Don't touch it, it's not safe" she cries,
Pulling her arm away.
"It's ok my dear, you won't hurt me, let me see" she
says,
In a reassuringly calm tone.
Kayla places her hand in hers.
Halcyon gently pulls back her sleeve & begins to
examine the bracelet.
"Hmm, it appears to be very old Impish
workmanship, where did you say you found this?"
She asks,

Looking up at her with a more serious look.
Kayla looks back at Luma not wanting to get her
new friends in trouble.
"It's ok Kayla" Luma assures.
"I found it in the forest"
"In the old ruins" adds Luma
"This is precisely why you were told not to hang
around there, it's not safe" she says, somewhat
exhaustedly.
"It took control of my body & made me do some
violent things" Kayla says,
With a tear rolling down her face.
"Rava could you be a dear & run & find Nyah, she
should be down at the dorms with Nadaur"
"Of course, miss" he replies,
Running out of the room.
"Nyah's family is very knowledgeable about the
Impish weapons of the forgotten wars, I'm sure she
will be able to shed some light on your newly
acquired accessory" she says,
Looking up at Kayla calmly enough that it reassures
& relaxes her.

Nyah & Nadaur stand outside Vincent's dorm room
leaning against the wall.
"There seems to be something going on yet I just
can't quite make sense of it" Nyah says, Looking at
the door to Vincent's room.
"I have faith that you will, I'm more concerned about
the incursions into the city, someone is testing our
defences & that is never a good sign. It's very

difficult to fight an enemy that you don't know what their goal is" Says Nadaur.
Vincent sits on his bunk trying to keep his eyes open. He's not had a good night's sleep in a week & is feeling decidedly more drained than usual.
He stares at the two standing outside his room wondering, are they his protectors or his jailers. He moves to the back of the bunk leaning his back against the wall resting his tired head on his knees, closing his eyes just for a second.
"They are your captures" a soft voice whispers.
"Ever since you arrived here things have not been right, what aren't they telling you" The words bounce around inside his head.
He's not quite sure if it's his inner monologue or something else.
Nyah looks into the room, they had both become distracted with their conversation.
Vincent's whole bunk had become consumed, lost in the shadows & they were reaching out into the otherwise well lit room.
"Look!" she exclaimed,
Nadaur Pulled a gem from around his neck blowing on it to illuminate it, tossing it into the growing darkness.
The gem creates a small sliver of light to where Vincents foot is just visible. Nyah takes off her belt that unravels into a long whip with barbed hooks at the tip & with a flick of her wrist she sends it with incredible speed into the darkness wrapping around Vincents exposed ankle. She pulls with all her might & Vincent emerges up to his waist from the

gloom, but then something pulls back dragging her across the stone floor.

Nadaur grabs a table pushing it against the door frame just in the nick of time as Nyah stops her ingress by bracing her leg against the tabletop, Nadaur grabs her around the waist placing both feet on either sides of the door frame, with them both pulling with all their might Vincents progress in either direction has been halted, yet the barbed tip of the whip is cutting ever deeper into the flesh of his leg tearing the skin down to the bone spilling his blood all over the floor.

"We're gonna lose him" Nyah cries.

Just then Rava bounds around the corner, seeing the struggle he increases his speed taking up position behind them he reaches around both Nyah & Nadaur wrapping his massive arm around the thick end of the tether.

"One, Two, Three!" he shouts

The three give their all, Vincent emerges from the shadow wide awake & screaming in pain as not only is the whip cutting into him but something in the dark still has a grip on his left arm.

"One more time" Rava yells

With one giant heave Vincent is completely out of the shadow, but just at the moment his hand leaves the abyss he looks up to see a porcelain white hand with long fingers & nails that tear the flesh from his wrist relinquish their grip leaving him to fly across the room, causing Nyah, Nadaur & Rava to fall back landing in a pile against the wall.

Nyah jumps up running over to Vincent

"Are you all right?" she asks,
Holding his face.
"Not even a little bit!" he yells
"What the fuck is happening to me?"
"We're going to get to the bottom of it & I swear to
you we will keep you safe until then"
Nadaur adds.
Nyah pulls the barbs from the shredded flesh of his
ankle, tearing a length of cloth from his sheets &
binding the wound stemming the blood flow.
"We need to get him to Otto's surgery to get these
wounds cleaned up"
Nyah turns to Rava,
"Thank you, you got here just in the nick of time"
Nadaur nods in agreement, putting his hand on his
shoulder.
"Funnily enough, Halcyon sent me to bring you to
Otto's to help with Kayla" he says.
"Is she alright?" Asked Vincent,
His concern for his friend overrides his pain & fear.
"She's ok, there was just an incident with the
Cocker & some of his lackeys & her bracelet" he
quickly explains.
"You two run ahead, I'll carry Vincent & meet you
there"
"You sure you'll be ok?" Nyah asks
"Yes, go help Kayla" Vincent assures.
Nadaur looks back as they run off down the hall at
high speed,
"Did you see something in the shadow as he was
coming out?" he asks

"Yes, I think I saw a glint of white, what do you think
it was?"
"I don't know but I think we need to fill Sapere in as
soon as possible"
Nyah still at a full sprint lean's across planting a
kiss on his cheek,
"Let's divide & conquer, I'll go to help Halcyon &
Kayla & you go & fill in Sapere"
Nadaur slips across in front of her, giving her a kiss
on the lips as he passes.
"Stay safe" he says
"Show off" she yells,
As he disappears down the hall amused by his
antics.

Kayla sits across from Halcyon, her arm laid on the
table.
Halcyon peers at the strange device attached to the
young woman's wrist through a set of goggles,
switching through lenses & muttering occasionally
to herself at an indistinguishable volume.
"They really suit you Miss" Luma says,
As seriously as she can while sitting alongside.
"You know what, you impudent little elfling, if you
want to be able to continue to pilfer from my
garden, I'd keep your comments to a minimum" she
says,
Grumpily looking up at her, her eyes magnified
multiple times through the lenses.
"You know about that?" Luma replied sheepishly.
"You should just work on the premise that I know
everything" she replies,

With a little glint in her now comically enlarged
eyes.
Nyah comes hurtling into the room stopping with a
perfectly controlled slide bringing her to a halt
inches from Luma who had closed her eyes
expecting to be bowled over by the unexpected
entrance.
Her eyes widened in recognition as she saw the
newly acquired adornment on Kayla's wrist. Quietly
she asked,
"Where in the world did you get that?"
Moving in for a closer look.
"Apparently she came upon it in the old ruins in the
forest"
"It was in a secret hidden door in one of the
crumbling walls" interrupted Luma.
"Hmm, do you mind if I?" Nyah asks,
Looking at Halcyon,
"No, no be my guest" she replies,
Vacating her seat.
Nyah gently lifts up Kayla's wrist turning it over,
"Fascinating I've never actually seen a Maylar
Venet"
"A what?" Blurts out Luma,
Prompting an annoyed look from Halcyon.
"The Maylar Venet were a group of weapons of
great power that was worn by the Impish high
priest. Its rough translation means Driven by
emotion, which is why it was only given to the
priests who were supposed to be pure of heart & in
complete control of their mind, body & soul.
"Ha" snorted Luma,

Upon receiving another angry look from Halcyon
she said,
"Sorry, that was supposed to be an inside Ha"
"No, you're right, it's impossible for anyone to be in
full control of all aspects of themselves as much
became evident soon after.
Some of the priests began committing random acts
of violence often far exceeding the threat or anger
they had experienced "
"So, no one could control it?" asked Kayla
"As the story goes there were a few who truly
bonded with the Maylar Venet causing their control
to become much stronger, but even those in times
of stress, fear or under threat could still find it
difficult to predict its response to the outward
stimulus".
"Could use a little help hear" a familiar voice said,
Entering the room,
It was Vincent being carried on the large back of
Rava.
Rava placed his wounded companion down on the
bed closest to the door collapsing onto a chair in
the corner huffing & puffing.
"You doing all right?" Luma asked,
With a big grin
"I've gotta start doing more exercise," he said in
between pants.
Kayla runs over to Vincent's side seeing the gnarly
gash on his leg turning quite pale.
"What happened?" she said,
Leaning on the edge of the bed to steady herself.

"It's all right, it looks much worse than it is" he says in his most convincing voice.
"We're getting through his whole supply of this today, he's not going to be pleased when he recovers, but then again I've never known him to be particularly pleased about anything really" says Halcyon,
Retrieving the same jar of grey powder from Otto's cabinet sprinkling it into Vincents wounds
"Ouch, that really stings" he yelps
"That's how you know it's working" she says
Patting him scarily close to the gash, which had already stopped bleeding & was healing before their eyes.
Kayla turned to Nyah,
"Is there any way to remove it?" she asks,
Hopefully holding out her arm.
Nyah walks across to her holding her outstretched hand tenderly.
"Once the blood tie has taken effect it is quite impossible to remove"
Kayla's eyes begin to well up,
"But there are tales of Maylar Venet choosing whom they commune with. Long after the they had been removed from the priests, they remained completely inert, becoming little more than trinkets traded by the uninformed, they could pass through the possession of many until they were awakened by someone in need but with no ill intent. The serpent knows your heart" she says leaning in close to Kayla,

"Besides in the impish natural law, if you find
something that has been lost, it was meant to be
yours.

Chapter 7

The Regent sits in his overly extravagant throne staring into the middle distance when a chime rings out filling the room with a vibration that is slightly uncomfortable & burrows its way into his skull.
The Regent tries to ignore the pervasive tone but eventually rises from his chair walking slowly towards the source of his annoyance.
In the corner of the room stands a pedestal, the base although it appears to be crafted from some kind of crisp white metallic substance on closer inspection it is evident that it has actually sprung forth, grown from a circular inlay that has been cut into the hard stone floors of his sanctuary. Laying in the branches is a large copper basin, the branches spread out intertwining around its circumference securing it into place.
The Regent climbs the three small stairs to the elevated platform carved from stone that allows him to see directly into the swirling silver liquid that moves with a kind of strange deliberateness.
He stands for a second taking a deep breath, the chime even more irritating with his closer proximity.
He reaches out with his elongated index finger the long nail manicured to a fine point which presses into the silver pearlescent viscous liquid that at first

does not yield to the pressure but then as the tip of his nail pierces the surface it begins slowly climb up his finger until it has reached his boney knuckle. He actually has to exert some not insignificant force to resist the force now pulling his arm into the bottomless shimmering liquid.

The Regent takes one more breath them closes his eyes, immediately his eyes snap open his whole eyeball now bathed in the same swirling silver abyss of the basin. His consciousness instantly transported space devoid of boundary, there was endless nothing in all directions, there was not even a floor, he was floating in an endless pool yet there was no surface it was all encompassing.

"What do you plan to do to resolve this unfortunate situation?"

A voice appeared from the void, followed by a shape, first of mist & smoke then more tangible but still his edges trailing off eventually becoming one with the environment.

"I'm not entirely sure what the problem is, it's not as though I can reveal the truth behind the shadow realm to any of my underlings, those are your rules" he says impudently.

"Do not forget who you're speaking to! Without the Shadow travel we're cut off from many of our strongholds & I don't have to tell you that if some of our less trustworthy allies discover that fact it won't be long until they begin to make small incursions into our territory, left unchecked it could be catastrophic.

I do not care how you do it, just figure it out or you can be replaced with someone with more viable solutions" scolded the shadowy visage,
Dissolving into the surroundings till he was gone.
The Regent blinked, his connection severed the pearlescence slowly receding from his eyes. He walks to the bar in the corner of the room taking a small vial of liquid from the shelf, using a dropper concealed in the lid he places two drops in each eye. Then pouring himself a large glass of a vibrant green liquid then by adding a splash of an orange liquid the colour shifts to a deep blue.
He takes the glass walking over to the shelves that run the length of the wall running his finger along till he reaches a specific book pushing it in, then another, then another.
An audible click can be heard following each selection, then with the final book into place the books spread open peeling back like an opening flower revealing a dark stairway carved from smooth black stone, spiralling down into unseen depths.
He follows the staircase down passing door after door cut into the wall, none of which have knobs or keyholes or any conceivable way of ingress. He continues until he reaches a long foreboding hallway, the walls smooth like glass but there was no reflection to be found, just an unending darkness that swallowed all light.
At the very end of the hall was a door, bright white light bleeds from the tiny seams of the door.

The Regent approaches the door reaching into his pocket retrieving a small folding knife, pressing the fine point into the flesh of his finger until the blood runs down the untarnished blade. Using his blood, he draws a triangle crossed with another surrounded by five small symbols that when completed disappear into the stone door, as if it gained some sort of nourishment from the offering. The Regent dons a set of goggles with thick onyx lenses. He slips on a long overcoat complete with a hood which covers his entire head. The material is remarkably heavy & does not bend of flow in the way clothing usually would, his outfit is completed with a pair of thick black gloves that take quite a bit of effort to manipulate.
Placing his hand on the door it swings open cleanly & without opposition, a white light that has a weight to it fills the entirety of the halls. The light is so pervasive it moves like water, it finds every single gap or shadow filling them with light.
The Regent steps forward into the light & is completely consumed, the door slams closed behind him returning the halls to darkness.

Tallie & Sikes sit together, Tallie resting against the massive bulk of Sikes sharpening her wide variety of knives & daggers, Sikes pulling pieces of Alimanas skin & blood from the metal plates on his armour. He looks up to see Cocker followed by some of his lackey Stinal & Urchon clutching themselves & looking past the worse for wear.
"What do you think they are up to?" he asked.

Tallie looks up, her gaze caught by Cocker who
sends a smile back that is met with a cold stare.
"Who cares? What I'm wondering is when we're
gonna get some real action.
I'm getting sick of these useless petty squabbles
amongst wealthy people with too much time on
their hands" she replies with annoyance.
"Is that what happened with the Alimana?, you're
one of the people I'd always want by my side in a
conflict but lately you've been even more quick
tempered than usual"
She looks up at the massive beast with a little
smile, understanding his veiled compliment
"I don't know, there seems to be something that is
stirring me up inside, I don't know if it's I'm just
antsy from the transition to The Regents guard or
I'm just not built to be without a conflict" she says,
Checking the edge on her knife by gently running
her finger along the newly sharpened blade.
"I find you always seem to find what you're looking
for in one way or another, so I'd try to enjoy the
calm while you can. Go see Halcyon she can fix
you up with something to relax you" he suggests,
giving her a little nudge that almost lifts her from the
ground.
"Thanks Sikes, not only are you a great pillow
you're also a pretty good friend"
Sikes lifts his giant arm, letting her fall back onto
the floor.
"I show you who's a pillow" he says,
Playfully falling on top of her,
"You're pretty comfy yourself" he laughs,

Letting her up her shaggy blonde hair sticking out in every direction looking up at him as she finally lets out a laugh of her own.

Cocker followed closely by Stinal & Urchon hurry down the corridors to his lair as best as they are able. They arrive at a large door with the handle & a large keyhole on one side, Cocker stops & looks around,
"Can you hurry it up, this really hurts" Urchon complains.
"Keep your mouth shut" Cocker says sharply.
He takes a small key from his pocket, much smaller than the lock on the door, but instead of placing it in the lock he moves over to the middle hinge on the door pressing the head of one of the screws that fasten the hinge, it springs out revealing a small key hole. He inserts the key then turns the handle opening the door, striding in slowly as his two injured underlings hobble into the room collapsing on the long couch in the corner.
"Don't get any blood on my couch!" Cocker yells,
Calling them over to the bench he is standing behind.
He reaches under into one of the compartments retrieving a wooden box that he places on the bench.
"Who's first?" he asks,
Stinal steps forward pushing his younger brother out of the way.
Cocker opens the box which is full of a variety of small vials all thrown together with no real care at

all. He rummages through the assorted mess taking
out what he needs as he finds it.
Stinal sits on one of the four stools that surround
the bench peeling back his hood to give Cocker
access to the gaping wound in his cheek
"How could you let her do this to you, what kind of a
fighter are you?" Cocker scoffs with disdain.
"She wasn't just a random girl, she had this weapon
&..."
"I don't wanna hear any of your excuses Urchon,
you're lucky I don't just hand you off to the Alimana
& let them finish you off" Cocker says,
Cutting him off.
Cocker slides a small silver case across the table
which Stinal immediately grabs prying it open, it is
full of little dark purple ball shaped pills, he takes
two from the tin swallowing them both, almost
instantly his eyelids droop & he slumps against the
bench laying down with his still bleeding wound
now far from his thoughts.
Urchon reaches out to grab the painkiller, but his
hand is swatted away by Cocker.
"You wait your turn, maybe the pain will teach you
to think before you act next time. Urchon shrinks
into himself cradling his badly injured arm.
Cocker takes the two vials that he had placed on
the bench top, he opens the first & tips a thin
covering over the wound, after a moment it flashes
into a bright green flame cauterising the wound &
causing Urchon to jump back.
"These Alimana healing potions are really effective,
but they are incredibly unpleasant" Cocker laughs,

Adding more fear to the already terrified & injured Urchon.
Once the flames die down the skin is charred but the wound has stopped bleeding & is sterilised. Cocker takes the second vial placing a single drop at each corner of the wound, it begins to pucker & all the edges begin to pull together, the wound foams, Cocker takes a rag & wipes the orange substance from his cheek, Stinal is left with some faint scars as the only reminder of the incident.
"Ok now it's your turn"
Urchon takes off his jacket gingerly trying to avoid his mangled elbow as much as possible, but as he reaches out to grab the painkillers Cocker places his hand over the tin,
"What did you mean by She had a weapon, what kind of weapon?"
Urchon grimacing in pain explains about the gauntlet, finally causing Cocker to relinquish the medication, he speedily takes the pills.
Stinal regains consciousness groggy but awake.
Cocker says flippantly,
"You deal with him"
Walking over to the bar & pouring himself a drink.
"I don't think we can deal with them all ourselves, we're gonna need some outside help, we could hire an Alimana hunting party" he suggests gently,
As the flame from the potion flashes.
"How are we supposed to get them into the city genius, you know they are banished & if they get caught there is no guarantee those bastards wont

rat me out to save their own slimy skin" Cocker
rants
"What about if we use the Highaster Tree tunnels &
sneak them in through your fathers' chambers?"
"However, I could sneak them in through the secret
passageway" Cocker muses,
Completely usurping his underlings' idea.
He pours him a drink, leaving it on the bar so he
has to retrieve it himself.
"I have to stay here to head off any inquiries, so
you two will have to go & make a deal with the
Alimana. Do you think you can handle that or
should I find someone else to place my trust in?"
"No, no we can handle it" Stinal insures,
He reaches for the drink, but before he can grab it
Cocker snatches it downing it.
"Well off you go" he says,
Pointing to the door with the empty glass.
"Stinal, if someone is going to take the fall for this
it's not going to be me, I'll let you decide who does"
he says coldly,
Looking over at the still unconscious Urchon laying
on the bench.
He walks into an adjoining room closing the door
behind him.
Stinal slaps Urchon lightly across the face rousing
him. Putting his arm around him they walk
unsteadily from the Cocker's space.

Sapere sits at his desk searching through books &
parchments.

"I know I read something about the inception of the
shadow travel but I can't for the life of me
remember where"
"How long ago was that, it's always just been a
common thing as far back as I can remember"
Nadaur says
"Many thousands of years ago, but it's funny, it
doesn't seem to be in any of my historical records
for that time period, it's almost as if it has been
purposefully removed" Sapere recalls, rubbing his
tired eyes.
"There is one last place I can look" he said,
Shuffling off into the bowels of his library.
A few minutes pass, Nadaur opens one of Sapere's
ancient volumes causing a few pages to fall to the
floor, as he hurriedly picks them up, he is startled,
"Ah ha!" Sapere cries from the darkness,
Nadaur runs down between the rows of books to
find his old friend standing in front of a massive
portrait of a beautiful pale woman flanked by a
snarling wolf.
"Is this it? Nadaur inquires,
Looking puzzled,
"She is very pretty, but how does this help us?"
Sapere reaches into his pocket producing a light
gem blowing on it & illuminating the beautiful
artwork,
"You see it?" he asks,
Looking up at him.
Nadaur furrows his brow looking closely at the
painting, Sapere holds the gem a little higher,
Nadaur notices little glints of light sparkling.

"There's something shining on the painting" he
says.
"Yes, sometimes when you want to hide information
the best place is in plain sight. In ancient times the
scribes knew that some information was too
important to trust to those ruling parties who
wouldn't handle with the reverence it deserved & in
the worst case hide or remove it entirely, so they
made copies & hid them in places they knew would
not be destroyed & also would be accessible to
those who cared enough to seek them out" He
explained,
Rushing back to his desk.
Nadaur turned to follow but was only half way back
when Sapere darted past him back to the painting
clutching an armful of glasses.
He tried one then another,
"No, no, no" he said,
Passing the failures to Nadaur in quick succession,
until finally he stepped back with a gasp,
"What is it, what do you see?" Nadaur asked,
Sapere took off the glasses unfastening a screw
that sat on the bridge of the frame separating the
glasses into two singular magnifying glasses,
placing one over his eye & passing the other to his
confused friend.
Nadaur looked up, closing his uncovered eye &
letting out a gasp of his own.
"Yes, you see"
The painting had completely changed, Nadaur
opened his other eye removing the lens & the
portrait returned to its original state, looking back

through the lens he began to examine the hidden
image.
It was of a long table surrounded by five cloaked
figures, on the table lay five books, the books
appeared to move & change like smoke in the air
shifting back & forth. At the head of the table was a
void, a large black shadow a single pale white arm
extending from out of the darkness laying its hand
on the book that lay in front of it.
Black wolves circled the table. Nadaur looked at the
beasts & as he did, he fell backwards as the wolf
returned his gaze,
"It moved!" He yelled,
Sapere turned to him,
"This painting uses a technique called Medriry, it
means a memory, a captured moment in time.
These things did happen & will continue to happen
as long as this snippet of time remains" he
explained
"What does it mean?" he asks.
Sapere leans in finding the pieces of scripture that
move constantly throughout the painting.
"Do you see the words?"
"Yes" Nadaur said,
Tracking one off the multiple phrases that inhabit
the image,
"The words are ever moving, so as to hide the
knowledge. There are lots of ways to scrub
knowledge from all volumes of a book as long as
you have one copy you can redact all the copies
that exist, but adding a breeze to the words hidden
here keeps them in motion & it's a lot harder to hit a

moving object, especially from a distance" Sapere
said with a little grin.
"The words tell a tale of a bargain struck
between…" he pauses leaning in,
"It's quite difficult to read a constantly moving text,
but I guess knowledge should take a little effort.
The occupance of the dark & the leaders of the
light" Sapere deciphers.
"Do you think that it's referring to the shadows?"
"It is quite possible, hmm, this portion speaks of a
betrayal but it doesn't say whom was the source of
the deception & here it talks about the volumes five,
a means of controlling the portals that allow
passage throughout the darkness"
"We need to find those books, does it give any clue
to their location?" Nadaur asks.
"Unfortunately, not" Sapere replies,
Shaking his head.
As Sapere steps in for a closer look, Nadaur looks
down seeing his friend's feet are completely
engulfed in shadow,
"Sapere!" he yells,
Grabbing by the scruff of the neck lifting him from
the creeping death, just as his feet emerge from the
oily black a long thin pale arm pursued him
snapping closed millimetres from him then recoiling
into the dark with a speed that suggested it itself
was being acted upon by an unseen force.
Nadaur jumped up pulling one of the large curtains
that ran floor to ceiling & tossing it over the painting
causing the shadow to retract back into the
enchanted object.

"Are you all right?" he asked Sapere,
Not hearing a response, turning around to see his
friend white as a sheet with eyes like saucers,
"Sapere!" he yelled,
The sudden shock dissipating, he finally replied,
"Thanks to you I am, another moment & that thing
would have got me. What the hell was it?" Sapere
said, still visibly shaken.
"We saw something like it, Nyah & I. The last time
someone was trapped in the shadows & Nyah said
when she when to retrieve Cocker there appeared
to be someone who disappeared into the shadows"
"Hmm, Cocker you say, well it stands to reason that
The Regent would know something about this, yet I
don't see him volunteering any of that information,
feigning ignorance is his MO when it comes to
anything that could possible jeopardise his
precarious grasp on his little kingdom, but maybe
Cocker would be an easier point of attack"
"Well, he does have a crush on Tallie, we could ask
for her assistance. He might be more inclined to let
something slip if he is distracted by her presence"
"Tallie, you say, you ask her, she scares me"
Sapere admits,
 With a serious expression.
"I think I'll ask Nyah if she wouldn't mind, just
between you & me she kinda scares me too" he
replies with a nervous chuckle.
"Don't mess around with that painting alone, no
matter how curious you become" Nadaur instructs,
With a knowing look,

As he sees Sapere already staring at the cloaked
portrait hanging on the wall.
"OK you have my word" he says, sincerely.
"They might've redacted all references to the
bargain but there may be other threads I can pull
on, I'll come find you if I discover anything"
"I'll do the same"
Nadaur pats him on the shoulder & Sapere trundles
off into one of his many back rooms, as Nadaur
leaves to find Nyah.
With them both out of the room the very bottom
corner of the painting is still slightly uncovered as
the curtain is caught on the frame a tiny patch of
shadow remains a singular unblinking red eye, then
the weight of the fabric causes it to free itself falling
to the floor completely covering the cursed work of
art.

Chapter 8

Kayla stands in the wide open garden outside
Halcyons sanctuary,
"You can do this girl" Luma yells,
From the stone benches where she sits with Rava
& Vincent.
In front of her stands Nyah,
"Now Kayla, the Maylar Venet is somewhat
influenced by your emotional state as much as it is
controlled by you will" Nyah Explains
"My will? but I didn't want it to do those terrible
things" she says,
With a tremor in her voice.
"You must remember that it is a weapon & as such
its purpose is to inflict damage the same as any
other weapon, be it a knife or a sword. Your
intentions might have just been to protect yourself
& get away from those two scumbags, the Maylar
Venet did that but it doesn't know you're not in a
battle scenario, it just fed on your heightened
emotional state & reacted, so what we're going to
try to do is help you find your centre, a place where
you can control your emotional state so that the
Maylar Venet knows the level of hostility your facing
& responds accordingly, hopefully eventually you
will gain full control over its power".
Kayla looks over at her new friends, seeing their
faith in her.

"Ok I'll do my best" she says,
With a little more confidence.
"Good girl" Nyah replies.
Sitting at Nyah's feet is a basket full of small
grapefruit sized fruit that resemble watermelons
with orange stripes, she lifts one throwing it
underarm & quite slowly at Kayla, Kayla in turn
brings the adorned arm up to meet the incoming
projectile, but the bracelet remains inert causing the
fruit to bounce of her arm, then hitting her in the
head splitting the fruit open causing the sweet
sugary juice to explode all over her prompting a
loud laugh from Vincent.
Kayla wiped the bright yellow juice from her face,
her determination now very evident as she
instinctively crouched into a fighting stance
mimicking Nyah.
Nyah noticed how her entire body had tightened up
& become more controlled, she reached into the
basket tossing one of the fruits high into the air.
Kayla's eyes automatically tracked her target, Nyah
leapt impressively high with surprisingly little effort
striking the fruit at the top of its apex sending it
hurtling towards Kayla at a tremendous velocity.
Standing her ground Kayla's arm thrust forward
connecting with the oncoming fruit smashing it into
many pieces sending them flying in all directions,
"Whoo Hoo!" yelled Luma,
Kayla stopped looking down at her hand that was
covered in the bright yellow flesh of the fruit, Nyah
walked across to her,

"Well at least we know you can throw a decent
punch if the occasion calls for it" she says, lifting
her hand & wiping the remanence off her & looking
at the bracelet that is still remaining inactive.
"Maybe this is the wrong approach" Nyah says,
She steps back Yelling shockingly loudly startling
Kayla & firing an expertly placed kick coming at the
side of Kayla's head.
Kayla without a moment to think froze & closed her
eyes but upon feeling the impact on her forearm
she opened her eyes to see the Maylar Venet had
formed a shield that ran from her knuckles to her
elbow wrapping & encompassing her arm.
Kayla immediately looking to Nyah who was smiling
from ear to ear.
"It didn't hurt you, did it?" Kayla asked.
"No, I'm fine, you did great, see there are levels to
any form of combat & learning what is the
appropriate level of force to use against an
opponent is key, learning to block is just as
important as an attack, you wanna try some more?"
Kayla with her confidence growing says,
"Yes, I'm ready",
Settling into her fighting stance.
Nyah comes at her with a variety of attacks at a tiny
percentage of her actual ability.
Kayla able to block the first few attacks, but Nyah
faints with one arm but striking Kayla in the
stomach with the other hand knocking the wind
from her, folding her into a heap on the ground.
Luma, Rava followed by a hobbling Vincent rush
over to her. Nyah looks down to see a big grin on

her face, she reaches down lifting Kayla back to her feet,
"You alright?"
"Yes, I'm all good, I could actually feel it following my will, rather than some sort of automated response" she said,
Looking down at the device with amazement for the first time rather than fear.
"I think that's a good stopping point, I just wanted to help you get your head around the concept that although it's a powerful weapon, you are wielding it, not the other way around. It is only a thing, an object, something to be used & like anything worthwhile sometimes it takes practice. Can you clean up this mess you two?" Nyah says,
Turning to Luma & Rava who were already feasting on the unassailed fruit left in the basket.
"Yeah, all good" Luma says,
With a face covered in the fruits flesh & the juice dripping off her chin.
Nyah smiles resting her hand on Kayla's shoulder, we'll pick this up later, but there's always the training room if you wanna get in a little practice on your own, I'm sure these two miscreants can show you the way"
Looking over her friends who are completely distracted by the tasty treat.
Luma looks up with a big cheesy grin noticing everyone looking at her,
"What?" she asks,
Slightly confused prompting a loud laugh from Kayla & Nyah.

Cocker sits alone at his bar mulling over his
options.
"I can help you. If you would be willing to assist me"
A voice wafts into his ear.
Cocker jumps from his chair in shock, his eyes dart
around the room searching for the origin of the
voice. In the centre of the room a shadow had
formed, yet there is nothing to cast it.
"Who said that?" he calls out,
In a slight panic.
"Who I am is not important, but since you people
seem to be so fixated on your singular identity you
may address me as Galbaial".
"Where are you?"
"My kind dwell in the shadows, this is our home just
as you have yours"
"No, you're lying, no one lives in the shadow realm,
it's just a construct for travel" Cocker scoffs.
"Lies, fed to a starving gullible population to hide
the truth behind stolen power" the voice says, in a
melodious & quite hypnotic tone that floats around
the room.
"What can you do for me?" Cocker asks,
Returning to form quite quickly.
"I can allow you passage to places you wouldn't
believe, hidden places of wondrous things that a
person could use to gain great power & fortune".
Cocker's eyes widened
"& you'll just do this for me, what do you want in
return?"
"We shall discuss that later, first a little gift"

A long pale hand emerges from the shadow placing
a small crystal vial on the floor.
Cocker moves cautiously over picking up the
trinket, moving back quickly to what he perceives
as a safe distance.
He opens the lid, a pungent aroma fills his nostrils,
"Oh, what the hell is that?" he yells,
Averting his face from the vial.
"Scents are more important in a world without light"
Galbaial explains.
Cocker peers into the vial trying his best not to
breathe too deeply, he sees three small seeds each
about the size of a pea.
The seeds are black with vibrant red slashes
across their surface.
"What do they do?" he asked,
His curiosity sufficiently stoked.
"They will afford the consumer a great boost in
strength & speed for a short period of time"
"Short, how long exactly?" Cocker asks rudely.
"The effects are varied, it rather depends on the
recipient, but it should be long enough to complete
a modest task" Galbaial explains.
Cocker is so distracted by the possibilities of this
new found acquaintance stares at the seeds rattling
around in the jar, that as he looks up to inquire
about the possibility of more favours for his service
but shadow had faded from the room.
He takes a small silver case from his pocket, it is
full of a wide assortment of pills, he shakes one of
the gifted seeds into the tin, snapping the lid closed
returning it to his pocket.

Taking the jar containing the remaining two over to
a wall at the side of his lair.
He pushes one stone then another then another,
until the painting of himself swings open revealing a
beautiful ornate safe. He moves the painting flush
against the wall.
On the front of the safe there is an obvious lack of
dials or levers, the only thing aside from the garish
swirls of gold is an oval indent in the centre.
Cocker places his thumb into place, there is a
sharp metallic click, when he removes his thumb a
drop of blood runs down his hand that he wipes
away with a handkerchief pulled from his pocket.
The golden swirls that adorn the front of the safe
slide across the face, like ghostly apparitions until
they finally lock into place with a click the door
opens slowly & smoothly, a testament to the
incredible craftsmanship of the safe.
Cocker places his newly acquired gift into the safe
alongside the many other riches he had squirrelled
away, closing the door & reinstalling the painting,
the stones in the wall all moving back into position.

Halcyon sits in Otto's surgery administering the
latest potion that she had concocted.
"Let's see if this has any effect" she says to herself,
Hopefully having almost exhausted her entire
repertoire of healing potions & poultice.
"I don't see why these are not having any effect"
she mumbled,

All of a sudden Otto cried out leaping from the bed, coming to rest cowering in the corner next to the window.

Upon seeing the bright sunny day outside he made a mad dash through the glass doors almost taking them off their hinges as he manically attempted to flee.

Halcyon followed him out finding him crouched tightly in the middle of the paved courtyard. She walked toward him, the sun at her back her shadow reached out in front of her, causing Otto to freak out screaming, she did not understand his screams accelerating her ingress to attempt to aid her crazed companion.

"What's wrong?" she asked,

With a great deal of concern,

"The shadows, there are things in the shadows" he said trembling,

Then with that he promptly lost consciousness again.

Halcyon picked him up, carrying him back to his bed, but as she placed him gently down his hand fell open, in his palm sat a pendant.

Halcyon picked it up examining it, it was caked in blood so she brought it over to the sink washing the dark black dried blood that took on its original red as it swirled in the water disappearing down the drain. She brought it over to the window to take advantage of the light. The pendant had been torn from a chain the reminisce of which dangled from a ring at the top of the piece.

The pendant itself had on one side the mark of The Regents council but on the other a mark that she was unfamiliar with, it was crossed blades with at its centre a black jewel that the closer she looked pulled her focus deeper in an almost hypnotic way, she blinked multiple times regaining herself. She ran her finger around the circumference of the object feeling a tiny latch hidden amongst the intricate design, she attempted to pry it open but to no avail, wrapping it in a small piece of off cut cloth she pulled from her pocket she shoves it back into her over filled pockets.
"I must take this to Sapere, he'll be sure to know something about this" she said to herself,
She passed one of Otto's assistants in the outer office,
"He awoke for a moment, you'll need to go & sit with him, let me know of any & all changes in his condition" she said,
With authority as she hastily ran from the surgery.

Nyah stands in the warriors training alcove strapping on the thickly padded gloves, pressing the leather around her knuckles conforming the well worn gloves to her hands.
She moves to the centre of the circular room, at her feet is a square with buttons in each corner & one large button at its centre. She presses the top & bottom left buttons then lowering her stance she stamps on the central button causing padded polls to jut from the floor & ceiling. The polls fire across the room a great speed, Nyah dodging in between

them with an elegant grace. She plants her foot on the wall springing off meeting one of the targets as it hurtles across the room at breakneck speed, striking the leather pad with her elbow shattering the wooden base. Then using the impact to pivot she turns to meet another pad driving her knee through the leather sending the splintered wood & leather flying across the room landing with a crash against the wall.
Nyah looks up to see Tallie standing in the doorway,
"You up for some training?" she asks,
Playfully dodging the incoming targets as she moves back to the centre of the room.
Tallie sporting a rare grin moves into the path of the high speed apparatus, skilfully stepping out of the way microsecond before impact.
"I could use a little fun" she says.
Nyah stamps on the central button causing the training exercise to stop,
"Full bore?" she asks,
Looking at the growing smile on Tallie's face,
"Let's see what you've got" Tallie answers,
The grin now replaced by a glint in her eye & an intense look on her face.
Nyah presses all four buttons in a particular order then at a count of three she hits the activation button. The room erupts into a frenzy, posts spring from the floor, ceiling & the walls, whizzing past. The two expertly avoid the flurry of activity.
Tallie plants her foot leaping forward to meet one of the targets with an intense ferocity, the impact of

her strike sending the leather clad wood catapulting across the room taking out two more targets as it went.

"That's three" she crowed.

Nyah looking over at her friend with a smile, it was good to see her enjoying herself, but her own drive for combat & competition burned deeply forcing her to jump into the fray.

She catches two targets simultaneously with both elbows propelling them off in either direction, one crashes against the wall while the other sails past Tallie taking out the target she was about to strike.

"Nice one!" Tallie yells,

As she effortlessly kicks the broken target in mid air.

They both took turns eliminating target after target with unrivalled skill, until only two targets remained. They both steadied themselves, Nyah meeting the first with a shoulder strike but as she turned to meet the second a blade came flying past her head impaling the other target, she turned to see Tallie a laser focused look in her eye.

"Draw again" Nyah laughed,

Which snapped Tallie out of her hyper focused battle state.

"That was great fun, I will beat you one of these days" she announced.

"I have no doubt" Nyah said with a wye smile,

Walking across the room & retrieving Tallie's blade, it takes a great deal of force to remove it from the target. She tosses the blade, Tallie catching it & skilfully returning it to the scabbard on her leg.

"Were you looking for me?" she asked,
The two sit against the wall, Nyah taking a drink
from her bottle then passing it to her friend. Tallie
takes a sip then wipes her mouth,
"I just wanted to let you know that the Alimana have
apparently put out a contract on me & Sikes for
what they perceive as our crimes against their kind"
"Oh really, somehow I don't see that going the way
they expect" Nyah says,
Bumping her shoulder against her friend,
Tallie smiles,
"Yeah, not too bright the old Alimana, although their
numbers can be a problem, I just thought I should
make you aware"
"Thank you for that, do you need any help?"
"Not presently, but I'll keep you apprised of the
situation" she says,
Getting to her feet offering her hand & helping Nyah
to her feet.
Nadaur comes to the door looking at the carnage
around the room,
"Good training session you two? I'm glad I don't
have to reset all of the targets" He laughs,
prompting a small smile from Tallie & Nyah who
both turn to each other,
"Final point!"
They say rushing at a startled Nadaur, he smiles
moving swiftly around the room staying just out of
their reach.
Tallie catches up to him but as she strikes, he
catches her foot sending her tumbling into the
corner, but the moment that his focus was split

Nyah jumped over flipping in the air laying a single
finger on his head as she pirouetted through the air
landing gracefully behind him.
"You two are a dangerous team" he said,
Admiring their skill & timing.
"Sometimes when one of us wins we all win" Tallie
replies
"But I really do prefer it when I win" she adds,
With a cheeky grin.
Nyah spins him around kissing him,
"What are you up to, wanna go a few rounds?" she
asks,
Playfully punching him.
"Whoa, whoa, not right now, I actually came looking
for Tallie"
"If it's about those weasley Alimana, I already know
about the contract"
"Contract?" he quires,
"The contract put out on Sikes & I"
"Oh no, I wasn't aware of that, I was coming to ask
you for a small favour"
"Really, what is it?"
"I was wondering if you would be open to…Um,
feeling out Cocker about what he knows about
those who dwell in the shadows?"
"Agggh, Cocker, I hate that slimy little prick" she
complains,
Rolling her eyes in an almost audible fashion.
"He's always trying to smile at me & it just makes
my skin crawl"
"Wait, what do you mean those who dwell in the
shadows?" Nyah asks.

"Well, according to what Sapere has managed to
figure out, there was a bargain struck between a
group from our world & some individuals who call
the shadow realm home for use of their realm as a
means of transport…"
"The being that disappeared into the shadow at the
nightclub" Nyah interjects,
"Exactly, we were hoping you could use his obvious
infatuation to gain some sort of insight into what
these shadow dwellers are after & who the deal
was made with"
"I guess I can, but if I kill him, it's on you" she says
drily,
Nadaur looks genuinely shocked but Nyah just
laughs, coming to his senses Nadaur remembers,
"Did you know that you can challenge a contract
put out by the Alimana, it's a challenge of combat"
"Great! Sikes & I could clean up a whole room of
those despicable creatures" Tallie boasts.
"I have no doubt, but you should be aware that they
make up arbitrary rules & they always cheat, but if
you win the contract will be lifted. If I were you, I
would take some back up just in case"
"Why don't you ask Faucon & Dabn, I'm sure they
would love a chance to repay you for all the times
you've saved their asses" Nyah suggests.
"Good idea, a few extra eyes couldn't hurt, I'll go
find Sikey" Said Tallie,
As she left the room with a skip in her step that
showed her excitement for the upcoming battle.
"I'll see you two love birds later. " she called back
from the hall.

"Should I have told her about that? I realise that her people are bred for conflict, but she can be a little scary…Don't tell her I said that" Nadaur says wide eyed.
"You don't know the half of it, she is one of the most naturally skilled fighters I've ever known & that is saying something, but I would trust her with my life in an instant. She has a good heart" says Nyah reassuringly.
"What are you up too, got time for a little snack?" she asks,
Raising her eyebrows.
"I just ate…Oh a snack" he says,
Catching her drift,
"I could go for a little something" he says,
Picking her up,
"Maybe some cheeky takeaway" he says,
Laughing as he carries her from the room.

Sapere lays slumped over his desk, the low vibrations of his snoring rattling the pens he has strewn about his desk.
The page in front of him rises & falls with every breath, then suddenly a loud bang on his door causes him to wake with a start, a page still stuck to his tired face. Pulling the paper off his drooly cheek he trundles over to the door in a worse mood than usual.
The knock comes again,
 "Ok, Ok I hear you" he shouts,
Becoming more irritated by the second. He flings open the door,

"What!" he yells,
"I have important things to attend to" he announces,
He looks to see one of The Regents snivelling
helpers standing in his doorway.
"I am so sorry to interrupt you Mr Sapere, but I
must inform you that The Regent would like to seek
your council on a matter of some importance" he
said,
Making as little eye contact as possible, which was
quite difficult seeing as Sapere was at least two
feet shorter than him so he could not look down nor
up.
"Hmmm fine, just allow me to retrieve my jacket &
we shall go" He replied,
With a little glint in his eye happy to make the gofer
squirm. He walked over to his desk taking a small
wooden box from the drawer, slipping it into his
pocket, then taking his jacket off the back of the
chair he strode from the room.
"Well then keep up" he ordered,
To the startled creature shuffling along behind.
Sapere moved down the halls at his usual
impressive pace until he arrived at the door of The
Regent chambers, where he promptly stopped. The
Regents stooge rushed up out of breath & sweating
under his thick robes.
"Well, aren't you going to announce me?" Sapere
said,
With a serious tone but a cheeky grin was barely
visible.

The creature rushed through the door moving right
up to The Regent sitting in his self bought throne
that sat at the end of the room,
"I have Mr Sapere for you Sir"
"Well show him in" The Regent ordered impatiently.
As Sapere was being shown into the room The
Regent stood walking to meet him, which
immediately had Sapere on guard. The Regent
never greeted someone who he thought of as his
lesser in this fashion & that was pretty much
everyone.
"Sapere" he said,
Extending his hand to greet him which only stood to
reinforce Sapere's lack of trust.
"Would you like a drink or something to eat?"
Sapere thought for a second,
"You wouldn't happen to have any of that Elvish
whiskey, would you?" he asked,
To his surprise The Regent replied,
"Of course, my good man, You there, a tumbler of
my finest whiskey for my dear friend Sapere".
This surprised Sapere & confirmed his suspicion
because The Regent was gifted this particular
bottle of Elvish Whiskey on the day of his
ascension to the station of Regent, some two odd
thousand years ago & ever since that day Sapere
had been dying for a taste of the amber liquid. It is
so coveted because the Elves only produce ten
bottles every thousand years & he would never be
afforded a chance to sample it again.
The Regent ushered him over to the small table
surrounded by four tall backed chairs, Sapere

hopped up onto the chair as The Regent sat across
from him. His underling placed the two portions of
the immensely rare liquor on the table.
"That will be all" he said curtly,
Sending the creature scurrying out a side door with
as much haste as he dared.
"What do you know of fallen stars?" The Regent
asked,
Casually but with a serious undertone.
"A fallen star is an extremely rare object as most
burn up either as they fall or before they can be
retrieved, but if the literature is to be believed a still
burning star has a wide range of uses, from an
incredibly powerful energy source to a form of light
that is all consuming"
"& what of moving one?"
"I Do not know, much of my knowledge on the
subject is anecdotal, but from my limited research
you will need something akin to an obsidian box to
contain the power & light of the star, which is a rare
object in its own right" Sapere explains,
As he sips from the glass of highly sought after
liquid.
"What do you think?" The Regent inquires,
Sapere thinks for a second, choosing his words
carefully.
"It is genuinely a singular experience" he said,
Trying to hide his disappointment at the mediocrity
of the converted beverage.
"Thank you so much for the assistance Sapere"
The Regent said,

Standing to let him know their meeting had come to
an end.
Sapere stood leaving half of the unfinished drink on
the table, The Regent walked halfway to the door
then turned,
"You can see yourself out" he said,
As more of a statement than a question &
continued out the side door leaving Sapere to exit
the room alone.

Chapter 9

Kayla stirred in her makeshift bed on Luma &
Ravas couch, she had been invited to come & stay
with them as her own room was a little unsafe.
Luma had made her very comfortable on their deep
fluffy couch that she sinks into & that feels like a
warm hug.
Kayla rolls over opening her eyes only to jump back
as Luma was sitting on the table her big green eyes
blinking as she chowed down on a bowl of
something crunchy,
"You're awake!" she yelled,
Crumbs falling from her mouth with every word.
"You make noises in your sleep, did you know
that?" she asks curiously,
"I've been told" Kayla says,
Sitting up still half asleep.
Attempting to focus her eyes she asked,
"How long have you been sitting there?"
"About half an hour, I don't sleep much, my brain is
difficult to stop"
"Yeah, I know how that goes"
"You want something to eat? I've got a stash of
breakfast cereals, I collect them from your world, I
like the grainy ones, the sugary ones kinda give me
a headache but I love the colourful boxes" Luma
announced with a big smile.

Kayla walks to the counter, seeing her friend's stash of human cereals gave her a twinge of homesickness, but it only lasted for a second.
"Have you spent much time in my world?" she asked,
"Well, travel to & from the other realms is restricted, but there are some sneaky ways around their control, but most of my souvenirs I get from the market, those guys can get you almost anything if the price is right, luckily for me most of the things I find cool are not all that sort after by the hoity toity so I don't have to pay all that much".
Luma had decorated her little sanctuary with a wide array of knick knacks that were scattered all around. Everywhere you looked there was a little toy, picture or plant on every surface something to catch your eye. The plants long tendrils cascaded down from high above giving the whole place a fresh smell.
Kayla made a bowl of cereal, she chose the same simple weet bix that Luma was so happily munching away on,
"Let's go sit out here" Luma invited,
Crumbs falling from her mouth with every syllable. She led her out through two white doors, the paint chipped & cracked, glass windows separated into squares ran the height of the doors. Outside was a small outcrop that resembled a balcony yet it did not have any sort of railing. Luma sat on the edge without a second thought, letting her legs swing over the edge without spilling a drop from her bowl.

Kayla moved cautiously forward standing back from the edge but leaning over to get a glimpse of their height, she was slightly startled to see that they were several stories in the air.
"Have a seat" Luma invited,
Patting the ground beside her.
Kayla gently sat down letting her legs dangle over the edge but still leaning back as she was not as comfortable as her free spirited friend.
"It really is an incredibly place" she said in awe,
Forgetting her precarious position for a moment as she looked out into the vast open space, seeing the vines cascading down from high above as if it were an extension of Luma's apartment.
Luma swipes at one of the small flying pixies that flit around going from flower to flower.
"You've gotta be careful, a bite from a pixie will itch for days & leave you with a very sore bump" Luma explained.
Kayla's eyes followed the tiny flying creatures, sailing through the sky getting caught on the gusts of wind then dropping way back down.
"What do you think about what those guys were talking about the other day?"
Kayla asks,
"Are there many secret tunnels around the city?" she continues.
"There are lots of secret little nooks & passages around the place, but they seemed to be talking about a completely separate set of tunnels that I'm not aware of, but then again there are lots of places around the city that are restricted, so it is difficult to

explore & trust me, I get into a lot of trouble getting caught in places I am not meant to be, I find rules to be more of a guideline rather than an actual law" she says with a cheeky grin
"I was wondering, maybe I can find one of the hidden entrances with my, um what was it called…?"
"The Contre sight" Luma chimed in.
"Yes, I had thought about that but I didn't wanna get you into any trouble, but if you're up for a little adventure I'm all for it" Luma proposed with a hopeful grin.
"Well, it did seem like something was going on in those tunnels that someone should look into"
"Someone, we're someone" Luma said excitedly.
"We should invite Vincent, he seems to be having a rough time with the whole wolf incident" suggests Kayla.
"Yes, a distraction will do him wonders" agrees Luma
"I'll go wake up Rava & we can go & find Vincent" Luma says,
Jumping up close enough to the edge that it makes Kayla's heart skip a beat bouncing in through the doors.

"Hurry up you two" Cocker says,
With his usual lack of patience.
"Ugh, why do we have to come all the way out here into the forest anyway? " complains Urchon.
"Because we want to be away from prying eyes" Stinal reminds,

"Now keep your mouth shut or I'll sew your lips
together" he says,
Prompting a shocked look from Urchon.
The three walk into a small clearing a good
distance from the city walls,
"This should be fine" Cocker announces,
His two subordinates slump against a tree.
"So what's this all about boss?" Stinal asks,
"We're gonna do some…training" he slyly replies,
Throwing two blades onto the ground,
"Pick those up" Cocker ordered,
Walking some distance away, with his back to the
others he fished around in his pocket, finding the
small silver pill case opening it & selecting the red
& black gift that he had been given earlier.
He stares at the vibrant seed in the palm of his
hand then swallows it, he pauses for a second the
seed having no discernible effect, turning around to
his underlings. Then all of a sudden, a bolt of
intense pain shoots through his entire body, it was
as if every fibre of his being was suddenly on fire.
He let out a muffled cry as his jaw was clenched
shut.
As quickly as it had started the pain subsided
leaving him with a feeling of control over his body
that was difficult to fathom. Suddenly he could feel
every cell in his body, from the tips of his fingers to
the tips of his toes. He flexed feeling the new power
coursing through his entire body.
"Are you alright?" Urchon asked timidly
"I feel incredible" he said,

Leaping high into the air landing on a branch of a tree, as he looked down, he couldn't believe that not only had his strength & coordination increased many times but his eye sight & hearing were on another level too, from his position high in the canopy he could hear his lackeys' heartbeats & breathing not to mention the folding of the blades of grass as they shifted their footing. Cocker jumped from the height landing centimetres from their faces "Your eyes boss" Stinal said,
With a hint of concern.
Cocker picked up one of the blades he had tossed on the ground looking into the polished silver of the blade, he was shocked to see that his eyes had taken on the colouring of the seeds, the black bled out into his face with slashes of red bright & vibrant across his eye balls.
He gently tossed the knife into a tree & the blade buried itself all the way to the hilt sending splinters flying.
"Attack me!" he raged,
"NOW!"
Stinal picked up the knife as Urchon attempted to retrieve the blade embedded in the tree to no avail. Stinal moved forward but in the blink of his eye Cocker was behind him, seeing this he tried to spin around, being caught by the arm by Cocker who with the slightest of pressure shattered is arm in multiple places, he fell to the ground screaming in agony, Cocker with a flick of his fingers to his jaw knocked him unconscious.

Urchon showing his lack of intelligence, but a great
loyalty to his brother charged at Cocker who had
become completely engrossed by his new found
power that all he did was throw his hand out to
meet the oncoming foe. As his hand made contact
with him he tore all the muscles & tendons in his
shoulder sending him flying back crashing into the
tree that still had the blade protruding from its trunk.
In the blink of an eye, he was standing at the tree
looking down at the unconscious heap, his twisted
body laying at the base of the tree.
Cocker grabbed the handle of the knife pulling it
free from the tree with almost no effort. Cocker
stood there, his mind swimming with the
possibilities but again a crippling pain consumed
his entire being, unable to stand he fell to his
knees, but as the pain subsided taking this newly
acquired strength & skill, his body was rendered
inert. He had put his body under so much strain
that he had overworked every part of himself
leaving him essentially unable to move & in a great
deal of pain.

Luma, Kayla & Rava walk through the halls toward
Vincent's dorm room.
"Where do you think is the best place to start
looking for the entrance to these hidden tunnels?"
Rava asked.
Luma & Kayla thought for a moment,
"Well, those bozos said that there was an entrance
somewhere around the Highaster tree so I think

that would be as gooda place as any to begin our
search" Luma suggests
"If we are unsuccessful there, we might also wanna
look around The Regents den, cause if anyone
would know about secret tunnels it would be him"
she added.
The happy trio rounded a corner bumping into
Vincent almost sending the whole group tumbling to
the ground.
"There you are, we were just coming to find you"
Kayla said
"Really, I was just coming back from seeing
Halcyon, she was just checking on my healing
process on my ankle"
"How is it?" Kayla asked,
"Almost one hundred percent, it's just a little stiff but
the pain is completely gone"
"That's good, are you up for an adventure?" Luma
asked excitedly.
"What kind of adventure?" he replied,
Being more than a little cautious following his
recent terrifying encounters,
"We're going searching for the hidden tunnels that
we heard about from Cocker & his little minions"
Luma explained
"That doesn't sound too dangerous" He concluded.
"Ok, I'm in" he announced,
Falling into place with his friends.
"So, what do you know about these tunnels, where
do they go?" he asked
"No idea" Luma said happily,
"That's half the fun" she added,

Smiling away, her happiness & free spirit made him relax & surrender to the adventure.
Kayla looked at her friend curious about what had happened in their room, but as she saw his smiling face as he chatted with Luma & Rava she didn't want to sour his mood so she thought she would just concentrate on the adventure that was afoot.
The foursome entered through the immense arch into the beautiful open space of the Highaster tree. It was a lovely sunny day so the grass around the tree was populated by a wide range of the inhabitants of the city enjoying the day.
"So where do you think we should start?" Rava inquired.
"Well, how about we start at the tree then move our way out from there" Kayla suggested
"Sounds great" said Luma,
Locking her arm with Kayla pulling her into a skip. They both skipped up the hill laughing as they went,
"Hey wait for us" the two boys said in unison,
As they ran to catch up with the girls.
"It's enormous!" Kayla exclaimed,
Looking up into the massive canopy of the mighty tree, the trunk was so wide around that it took several minutes to circumnavigate its girth.
"Anything?" Luma asked
"Nothing jumps out at me" Kayla says,
Walking around the base of the tree.
"I don't see Cocker or The Regent climbing down from high in the branches of the tree, so we should take a look around the surrounding area".

As they walk down the hill Rava grabs Vincent by the shirt,
"Watch out bud" he said.
"You almost stepped in a Barker burrow, you've already had enough bad luck with that ankle we don't want any more" He continued
"Thank you" Vincent said,
Jumping over the deep hole.
As Kayla & Luma made it to the edge of the clearing, the trees at the edge of the forest created a dense barricade. The light mostly blocked by the thick canopy yet ribbons of light cut through the overgrowth creating patches of wildflowers in amongst the trees.
The two of them walked through the dreamlike place, Kayla's eyes wide scanning the beautiful area, while Luma was picking assorted flowers holding them in a beautiful natural bouquet which she put up to her nose inhaling resulting in a blissful smile.
"I'm not seeing anything," said Kayla,
Slightly disappointed.
"Don't fret, we have only been looking for a little while & they are secret tunnels after all" reminded Rava.
Luma gave her the bunch of flowers, skipping off among the trees. Kayla sat on a rock watching the free spirit of Luma dance as if in some sort of fairy tale come to life, she was looking around at the streams of light that breach the canopy marvelling at how pretty it all was, when she spotted a different kind of glow, it was warmer, much more

golden in hue on the side of one tree. Transfixed
she began to walk towards it,
"Kayla?" Vincent called,
But she was too distracted, the others followed
along behind. Luma ran up,
"Do you see something?" she asked,
Breaking Kaylas focus.
"Yes, over there, there's a glow on that tree" she
pointed
"Like the one in the ruins?" Rava asked
"Kinda, it's not a white light like that one, this is
more golden, warmer somehow. It's over there" she
said,
Traipsing through the undergrowth.
Kayla stopped beside a tall tree, which didn't seem
out of place but at the same time it did, but to the
rest of the group the difference was
indistinguishable.
"Here" Kayla said,
Pointing to the base of the tree.
Luma circled the tree,
"I don't see anything, do you see any sort of way to
access the tunnels?" she asked.
Kayla looked the tree up & down,
"I don't know" she said
"There's nothing like on the other hidden door, no
symbols or anything"
"What do you see?" asked Vincent
Kayla stood back,
"Um, there's a subtle warm glow emanating from
the base of the trunk, but aside from that I don't see

anything. I'm sorry you guys" she said looking defeated.

Luma sidled up next to giving her a hug,

"Don't be sorry, this is only the beginning of our adventure, you've found something that none of us even had a chance to find & that's an achievement in itself" she said,

Squeezing Kayla until she let a little smile creep across her face.

"So, what do we do now, do we dig or something?" Rava asked.

Kayla looked over at Vincent who was running his hands up & down the trunk of the tree.

"What are you doing?" she asked

"A few years ago, I was obsessed with mystery novels & one of the recurring tropes that a lot of the authors seemed to use was the secret door controlled by a hidden latch or trigger"

"Like Batman & the piano!" shouted Luma.

Kayla & Vincent stopped & stared at Luma who had a big smile across her face,

"How do you know about Batman?" Vincent asked

"Oh, she's obsessed with most things from your world, but one of her favourites is comic books. She collects as many as she can get her hands on"

"They're just so colourful & fun" she exclaimed.

They all can't help but to smile at her childlike infectious joy.

"Yes, like Batman, so look around for some kind of trigger to open the tunnels" Vincent said.

They all took a section of the tree & searching around the surrounding area.

"What exactly are we looking for?" asked Luma,
As she pulled on a branch that snapped hitting her
on the head.
"Um, well in most of the stories it was a book on a
shelf or a candle holder on the wall, so look for
something that is normal but somehow out of place"
Vincent suggested.
Luma & Kayla moved over to the base of the tree,
moving the plants away from the trunk.
"What are these?" Kayla asked,
Pointing to a group of tiny mushrooms.
"Oh, don't touch those! They are the floating death
toadstools, they are extremely poisonous" warned
Luma.
Kayla picked up a stick,
"Maybe they are the trigger, what better than
something that people are unlikely to touch"
"That's good deductive reasoning" Vincent praised.
Kayla pushed on the toadstools but they just
squashed sending colourful spores out into the
forest.
"Oh bugger," she said.
"It was a good idea" said Luma
"Hey what's this!" Luma asked,
Excitedly pulling back a thick fern.
The others gathered around to see what she had
discovered. Luma cleared the area revealing a root
running of the bottom of the tree,
"I don't get it, it's just a root Luma" Rava said,
Scratching his head.
"Yes, but look" she said,
Pointing to the root,

"It's got a footprint on it, how would that have got there under that plant?".
The other three looked closely & sure enough there was a muddy boot print on the large root.
"Well, go ahead," said Vincent
"Really?" asked Luma.
"Yes, of course, you found it it's only fair you get to try it," said Kayla
"EEEEE!" Luma squealed,
Stepping forward quite seriously pushing down on the root.
"Nothing's happening" she said sadly.
"Try pushing a little harder" Vincent suggested.
Luma stood on the root with both feet jumping up & down.
The group heard an audible click. They all began looking around for some type of entrance to these mysterious tunnels.
"Has anyone got anything?" Rava asked,
A resounding,
"No"
Came back from everyone.
"Rava, you stay there, Luma & Kayla look around for some kind of secondary latch" suggested Vincent,
"A lot of times in those stories the door would require more than one point to be triggered so that someone wouldn't accidentally find their way into the secret location"
"That's pretty clever" said Luma.
Kayla walked around the tree & something caught her eye. On one of the knots on the side of the tree

next to the one Luma was standing by was a barely
perceivable warm glow,
"Here!" she cried
"What do you see?" asked Rava,
Investigating the point where Kayla was pointing.
"That knot, in the centre is a tiny point of light, she
pressed it in with the tip of her finger & again a
small click,
"Was that it?" asked Luma,
Looking around for some kind of indication that they
had succeeded, but alas against there was nothing.
"Well, these are definitely buttons of some kind, so
maybe there is a third?" supposed Rava.
Rava stood by the knot in the tree while Kayla
searched around, her eyes peeled & an intense
focus came over her face furrowing her brow.
"You'll give yourself wrinkles screwing your face up
like that" Vincent teased with a chuckle.
Kayla was far too distracted to respond,
"It must be close by" she mumbled to herself,
Moving the undergrowth away with her feet as she
searched.
Then as she pushed a small plant out of the way
she saw a rock lined by the same subtle warm light
by the base of the tree, on the other side from the
original tree.
"I think I've got it" she said excitedly,
Stepping on the stone, once again an audible click,
but as the group looked around in earnest, they
were left unfulfilled.
"Damn, I thought that was it" Kayla said,
Starting to get a little frustrated.

"Hey, in my Batman comic the piano that allowed access to the Bat cave, the keys had to be struck in a certain order to open the clock, maybe we just need to figure out what pattern is required" Luma proposed
"Yes, you're right, often there is some type of sequence to trigger the locking mechanism" added Vincent
"Well, if we assume that the lock was made to be opened by one person the sequence should be a one, two, three style of code" he devised,
Stepping back & looking at his three friends standing by their individual trigger points.
"I guess the easiest would be left, middle right" suggested Kayla,
To which the others nodded in agreement.
"Ok, everyone release their switch" said Kayla,
As she stepped off the rock, then Luma & Rava released theirs.
"All right I'll go first" Kayla said,
Stepping on the rock & again hearing that telltale click,
"Now you Luma" she said,
& Luma jumped on the root until she heard the click,
"Me next" said Rava,
Pressing in the knot, but again nothing.
"Hmm" Vincent said,
Perplexed, rubbing his chin.
"Well, if we think about this logically for a second, Kayla, you said the tree where Luma is standing has the brightest & most noticeable glow, right?"

"Yup" she replied
"& the other two are a lot less prominent, then
maybe the central tree is the main & the other two
are the auxiliary switches" Vincent proposed.
While the others looked at him with confused looks
on their faces.
"Auxiliary?" asked Luma,
Tilting here head to the side in an attempt to
understand.
"Oh sorry, I went through a faze where I was
reading a lot of books on computers & they used
that term a lot, it just means secondary"
"Got ya" Luma said with a wink,
Repeating the word to herself under her breath.
"So how about we try, Rava then Kayla then Luma"
The three stepped off again & retried it in the new
order, but again nothing.
"Ok, well I'll start this time" said Kayla pressing
down on her rock,
"Now me" said Rava pushing in the knot
"My turn" Luma said,
Happily, jumping on the root.
This time there was an obvious difference, the
three stepped back from their respective switches
as a loud whirring noise was coming from the tree
where Luma stood, the sound of gears turning &
pins snapping into place.
The tree lifted slowly as the ground opened up
beneath it.
The four stood in shock as the mechanism went
through its cycle until it finally came to rest,
"Whoa, that was so cool!" said Luma,

Jumping up & down,
She rushed forward to look & see what they had
unearthed.
"Be careful Luma, we don't know what or who is
down there" warned Rava
"She sometimes rushes in without thinking" he
continued.
"Sometimes?" asked Kayla,
With raised eyebrows looking up at him.
"Yeah, all of the times" he said with a sigh.
They all moved forward peering down into the hole,
the top was well camouflage by the foliage around
the tree but just past that a path was cut into stone.
A black pathway of stairs spiralled down into the
darkness.
"It's a tight fit" said Rava,
Being much larger than the others.
"It's just not Rava sized, not many things are" Luma
said,
Giving him a little nudge in the side & a giggle.
Vincent looked around, finding a small rock by his
feet, he walked up to the edge tossing the rock
down into the hole & listening for the sound to
determine the depth of the stairs
"Why did you do that?" interrupted Luma
"Shhh"
The others said as they all leaned in close hearing
the rock skipping down the steep stairs, after a few
moments the sound stopped,
"Jezz, that's a long way down" he said
"Should we go down?" asked Luma,
Creeping ever closer to the entrance.

"No!" Kayla said,
Grabbing her around the waist,
"We don't know what's down there or where it leads
& we don't even have a torch" she explained,
"Plus, we don't know how to get out if this door
closes" added Rava
"Fine" said Luma,
Obviously disappointed,
She stepped up to the edge of the hole looking
down then she turned her head to look at the
others,
"Now that we know how to get in, we can plan the
next part of our adventure"
As she finished talking the tree snapped back into
place in a much faster & more aggressive way than
it had opened, sending Luma tumbling backwards
ending up resting against Rava's legs.
Kayla reached down picking her up,
"That was lucky & now we know that the door only
stays open for a short time before automatically
closing" she said.
Small drops begin finding their way through the
canopy bouncing off the leaves & landing on
Kayla's face.
"We should be getting back before the rain really
starts coming down" said Rava.
Luma goes over to a tree just in front of the opening
to the tunnels, taking a small knife from her pocket,
carving KLRV into the bark,
"Just in case, we don't know how Kayla's Contre
sight works there's no guarantee that she will see

the light a second time, this way we can find our way back" she said,
Finishing up the carving.
"Good thinking" agreed Kayla.
They walked quickly as the rain was becoming heavier, but they were still protected by the forest canopy. Kayla said,
"We should ask Halcyon about the tunnels, maybe she knows more about them, like where they lead or who built them?"
"Maybe we should try to find out all we can by ourselves before we bring it up with anyone" Rava suggests,
"You don't trust Halcyon?"
"It's not that, I'm just a little concerned that she might not let us investigate any more after we fill her in" he explained.
"We could go down to Sapere's library when he's in the dining hall, that guy never misses a meal" suggests Luma.
The rain is coming down at an impressive rate, Luma reaches the edge of the forest first, standing huddled against the trunk of a tall tree. She watches the rain sheeting down over the Highaster tree, its mighty limbs swaying, dancing in the wind. The others catch up with Luma, all gathering together under the tall tree,
"I love storms like this" Vincent said with a big smile,
"Me too" replies Kayla

"There's just something so calming about sitting &
watching the rain & the wind cascade over the
trees"
"& the smell of fresh rain in the air" Vincent adds
"We've gotta make a run for it" Rava says
"Let's run to the Highaster tree cuz there's no
lightening, then we can make it to the city walls"
suggests Luma,
Who was already jogging on the spot.
"Go!" she yelled,
Running as fast as her little legs would carry her.
As they ran up the hill they had to dodge & jump
Barker burrows that had become almost invisible as
they were now completely full of water that spilled
out causing little waterfalls all over the hill.
"Mind you footing" Rava yelled,
As he jumped over one Barker hole only to land
disappearing up to his knee in another, Vincent
coming up behind him held out his hand as he
passed the two grabbing each other's arms above
the wrist locking in to a secure hold, Vincent gave a
great heave pulling the much heavier Rava from
the hole that had enveloped his leg.
The two boys made it to the tree completely
soaked, where Luma & Kayla were waiting for
them,
"You should've minded your footing" Luma said,
With a little smirk,
Rava smiled reaching up & grabbing a branch that
was just above her head giving it a shake sending a
shower of rain that had become trapped on the

leaves down all over Luma to which she let out a
high pitched squeal.
The group watched the pouring rain trying to find a
lull or moment of peace the they could make their
final dash back to the sanctuary of the city walls,
not seeing any coming in the immediate future
Luma says,
"We've gotta make a dash for it".
The four launch out into the large grassed area
between the tree & the city walls laughing as they
run trying not to get completely soaked but to no
avail.
They came to a stop under the large archway,
Rava shaking his huge head eliciting cries from the
others,
"Arh watch it" Luma yells,
Wiping the rain from her face.
"You two can come back to our place to get
cleaned up" Luma offers,
Taking Kayla's arm & in her innocent way skipping
off down the hall with Kayla trying to keep time with
her, being followed by the boys still shaking the rain
from their head & clothes.

Cocker throws his door open, his two badly injured
underlings hobbling along behind.
Cocker moves immediately to the bar, taking a
bottle of vibrant green liquid from behind the bar,
unscrewing the cap with haste, taking a long slug
from the bottle & collapsing in a chair off to the
side.
Stinal carries his brother over to the bar,

"It hurts so bad" Urchon cried
"Give me a second " Stinal said,
Digging out the box of medical potions from behind
the counter.
Rummaging around in the box he finally finds the
painkiller, jamming the syringe into his brother's
arm.
Urchon collapsed onto the bar his pain masked by
the powerful sedative. Stinal gives himself a half
dose so he is still functional. He takes three small
vials from the box, he takes a cartridge from the
box & removes a glass tube from its centre, wincing
in pain he tips a small measure of each of the three
bottles into the glass tube replacing it into the
cartridge. He places the device above his
unconscious brother's injury, pressing the button
that forces the contents into his arm with a woosh.
Urchon's arm slowly begins to move, the bones
resetting as though they were experiencing the
original trauma but in reverse. The bones snapped
back into place tearing the flesh as they found their
place, the skin & muscle knitting itself back together
after the bones reset.
Stinal finished mixing a second dose pressing the
applicator into his badly mangled arm. He paused
for a second pouring himself a shot of a swirling
purple liquid from the box, which on ingestion
drooped his eyelids & left him in a state of twilight
sleep, conscious & aware but highly subdued, he
presses the button & with a woosh the medication
was administered.

His arm violently jerked back & forward as the bones, muscles & tendons found their way back into place, Stinal grunted, even though he was highly sedated the mind bending amount of pain still found its way to his nerve endings sending slices of pain to his brain.

Urchon's shoulder stopped reconfiguring with a final few cracks, like the last few kernels of popcorn, while Stinal had a death grip on the edge of the bar, an intensely aggressive look fell across his face as he looked over at Cocker slumped in the chair sipping his drink.

The moment his arm finished the healing process he charged from behind the bar across the room picking up Cocker from his chair by the collar slamming him against the wall.

Cocker let out a cry of agony as his body was still in a state of overuse that left every muscle in his body in intense pain.

"What the fuck was that!" yelled Stinal,

His arm healed but not one hundred percent he pressed through the pain, lifting Cocker from the ground, his knuckles pressing deeply into his throat.

"You're choking me" Cocker struggled to say, Grabbing the arms of Stinal but he was in no condition to defend himself, besides Stinal was a very capable warrior in his own right & Cocker was never a physical match for him even in his normal state.

"How did you move like that & where did that strength come from?" he questioned,

Pushing his knuckles deeper to accent his point.
"I'll tell you, if you let me go" muttered Cocker,
Through his constricted airway.
Stinal threw him down into the chair taking a seat
next to him, grabbing the bottle that was sitting on
the table taking a swig.
"Well!" He said,
His patience at an end.
Cocker tried to regain his composure,
"I was gifted a means of exhibiting a level of
heightened strength & speed by a new
acquaintance" he said,
Trying to remain as vague as possible.
"Who exactly?" Stinal asked sharply.
Cocker looked at him releasing that he was in no
mood to be toyed with,
"To tell you the truth, I'm not exactly sure. From
what I understood they are a race of beings that
live in the shadow realm"
"What are you talking about, no one lives in the
shadow realm, it's just a means of transport from
one place to another" Stinal says,
Rolling his eyes.
"Yes, I know that's what we've all been told, but I
swear to you, someone from the shadows talked to
me & gave me a red & black seed that they said
would give me great power. That's what I used in
the forest" Cocker said,
Omitting the other two seeds that he had stored
securely in his safe.
"So, let me get this straight, a mysterious being
from the shadows gave you a power boosting seed,

which you then took not knowing what the results
would be & decided to test it out by brutalising my
brother & I, is that about the size of it?"
"Pretty much, yeah" Cocker answered surprisingly
glibly.
Stinal moved forward placing the bottle down on
the table, then in one swift motion cracked Cocker
hard across the face.
Cocker looked up blood flowing from his lip.
"If you ever lay your hands on my brother & I again
you had better make sure I'm dead because if you
don't, I'm coming for your head" Stinal said,
Picking up the bottle & sitting back into his seat.
He sat for a moment while Cocker tended to his
split lip, dabbing it daintily with a hanky.
"Wait, so this being just gave you this incredible
power as, what a gift? what did they want in
return?" he asked
"Yes, he said we could help each other, but they
did not go into specifics, when I turned to ask some
follow up questions the shadow had disappeared.
Stinal sat staring at Cocker in a way that unnerved
him, until his focus was broken by his stirring
brother.
"I'm gonna take Urchon home to recuperate, but we
will continue this conversation later"
He walked across the room picking up his barely
conscious brother carrying him from the room.
Cocker gingerly got to his feet, his movement still
hampered greatly. He shuffled across the room to
the bar, opening a box of joints that rested on the
top of the bar. On the side of the ornate little box

was a small gem, that when he touched the tip of the joint to it burst into flame. He took a few puffs then moved to the back room to lay down. What neither he or Stinal had noticed was the shadow that had filled the corner of the ceiling above where they had been having their conversation, that was now receding into oblivion once again.

Sikes sat in the garden outside Halcyon's lab, revelling in the sunshine & eating a tray piled high with an assortment of cakes & treats.
"Oi" a voice called,
From behind him which made him jump.
It was Tallie, she was doubled over in laughter, Sikes had turned around his shaggy hair on his face covered with cream & icing from the many cakes he had consumed.
Tallie walked over taking a napkin from his tray & wiping the remnants of his snacking from his face.
"Were you looking for me?" he asked,
As she picked the last few crumbs from his fur.
"Yes, I've just found out that the Alimana have levelled a contract on the both of us for that little skirmish we had in the tunnels"
"You're kidding right, they don't have anything better to do with their time & besides they were the ones who started it by attacking you" he said with a huff.
"Well, I did kill four of them previously, but they were advancing on Nyah. What was I supposed to do?"

"You're darn right, if one of your friends is in danger you have every right to protect them with whatever force you deem is necessary, besides they are well known for attacking in large packs for only one target & almost always kill their intended target" Sikes added.

"So, what do you wanna do about it T?"

"Nadaur informed me that a contract put out by the Alimana can be challenged in a sort of trial by combat & in victory we can nullify the contract"

"Is it really worth it? I'm not really too concerned about their abilities. What kind of guarantee do we get that they will actually honour the lifting of said contract, seeing as the many factions of Alimanas don't even agree with each other most of the time" he said,

Standing up & shaking his massive face, sending more crumbs sailing to the ground.

"Hey, watch it you grub!" said Tallie,

Jumping back as the shower of crumbs fall on her head.

Sikes laughs, grabbing her shaking his head over her, which made her laugh a rather rare but becoming more common occurrence.

"You're not wrong but according to Nadaur, who has had a lot more contact with them that if we leave the contract open then any & all Alimana are required by their code of conduct to attack us on sight. However, if we successfully have it lifted the likelihood is that only the faction that first levelled the contract are likely to still hold a grudge" Tallie said,

as she shook the crumbs from her hair,
"He's not wrong, those Alimanas are everywhere in
all the realms, so it would mean we would always
have to be on guard & I don't like to split my focus
like that, especially in a combat environment. All
right how do we go about it?" he asks begrudgingly.
"Well, as much as I dislike him, Cocker has some
sort of association with them & I've been asked to
question him about another matter by Nadaur, So
I'm sure I could have him relay the message that
we intend to challenge".
"Oky Doky, do you want me to accompany you to
go & talk with him?"
"No, I think I'll have more luck getting some viable
info out of him if I go alone"
"Are you sure that will be safe?"
"You're not worried about me, are you big guy?"
"Well, one yes, I always want to keep all my friends
safe, but that's not what I meant. You know I love
how much of a firecracker you are but I know that
little entitled slime ball makes your skin crawl & I'm
not sure you'll be able to resist the urge to cut his
throat if he makes unwanted advances"
Tallie gives him a little bump with her shoulder.
"I'll do my best, but no promises" she says,
With a mischievous little grin.
"I'll let you know what I find out" she says,
As she strides out through the archway.
Sikes looks around then goes right back to finishing
his treats.

Sapere moves rapidly down the hallway, his arms full of parchments & papers that he continuously drops & has to turn around to retrieve, while mumbling to himself.
"But if there are beings, what is stopping them from coming into our world?"
He stops in the middle of the hall, all the other people just walk around him as they are used to his little eccentricities & they realise that whatever he is investigating is likely much more important than they know.
He looks around as he has been walking on auto pilot to see that he is close to his desired destination, he marches off again people jumping out of his way as he flies off down the hallway towards Otto's surgery to find Halcyon.
He comes barging in to the surgery already mid sentence,
"Where did you obtain that shadow crystal lens you used on Vincent?" he demanded.
"Excuse me" Halcyon said,
Looking at him with a displeased expression,
"Would you like to try that again?"
"I'm sorry, I've been working on this for hours & the more I look into it the worse it seems" he says,
As some sort of reasoning for his behaviour.
"What exactly have you discovered?" Halcyon asks calmly.
"From what I've been able to piece together, it seems that someone made a bargain with the shadow dwellers for use of their realm as a means for travel"

"What was the other side of the bargain?" Halcyon asks.

"What do you mean?" Sapere asks.

"Well, you said it was a bargain, so what did the shadow dwellers as you have dubbed them ask for in return?"

"That's a very good point, I've been so focused on who made the deal that I've completely neglected what was their motivating factor in the first place".

"So, what have you discovered?" Halcyon asks, Sitting down at the table in the corner of the room. Sapere joins her saying,

"From what I've gleaned from the available sources, a long time ago there was a meeting of two ruling parties. The shadow dwellers had five books which among other things I'm sure, allowed access to the shadow realm as an instantaneous method of travel, which I assume were gifted to the rulers from the other realms"

"So why exactly have we never encountered any of these shadow beings before now, I mean it's not as if you & I are in the throes of our youth after all"

"I'm not sure, but what I do know is that The Regent has something to do with it" Sapere says, With a furrowed brow.

"What makes you say that?"

"The other day he summoned me to his den to probe me about fallen stars, their life cycle & how to safely move one from one location to another"

"Oh & a fallen star is an incredible source of unyielding light that would eliminate the possibility of a shadow in its aura" Halcyon adds

"Yes, that was my thoughts exactly. How did you know about fallen stars?" Sapere asks, looking over his glasses in surprise.

"My father was obsessed with the idea of finding a fallen star as a gift for my mother, but alas he was never able too, but as a little girl he used to tell me bedtime stories about the ancient wizards that called the stars down from the heavens to boost their powers in times of battle or strife, but those were only stories surly" she reminisced.

"Wow, very interesting, I don't know about the ancient wizards, but I have heard of people finding still burning stars & being consumed by the intensity of the power"

"Where did you find out about all of this?" Halcyon asked,

Pouring herself a drink & gesturing to Sapere as an offer of a beverage.

"Yes please" He replied,

Taking a cup from the side of the table & placing it down in front of her.

"Nadaur & I found a hidden layer concealed under a portrait that I had been given many years ago, by who I do not recall, but that was the source of the only insights I've been able to discover. That's why I came to ask you about the shadow crystal that you have in your possession. I was hoping it would lead us to some sort of insight to who exactly these mysterious shadow dwellers might be, or at least point us in the direction of who were the recipients of those books"

"Or even more pressing, what prompted this
apparent uptake of hostilities rendering the shadow
travel as so unsafe after years of it being benign"
added Halcyon.
Sapere sat sipping his drink nodding in agreement,
"That is why I was wondering, did that crystal come
in some kind of packaging, do you recall anything
about how it came to be in your possession?" he
asked in earnest.
"Well," Halcyon said,
Taking off her glasses & rubbing her eyes,
"I do have quite a few self inflicted holes in my
memory, but if I recall it was in amongst a shipment
I received, from who I know not, it just arrived on
my doorstep on day many years ago, & honestly
I've never had any call for its use until now"
"What else was in that package, do you recall?"
"Unfortunately, those were the years which I had
my apprentices & honestly one of the reasons I
stopped utilising their help because I found it more
difficult to stay on top of my research if I didn't do
the all the research & busy work myself, you'd be
surprised what can trigger a good idea, inspiration
is in the smallest detail, but look who I'm telling"
she said,
tipping her cup in respect to which he returned the
gesture.
"But, yes that is a very good idea, after I finish up
here sorting out Otto's appointments, I will be sure
to go & search through the inventory that arrived
around the time of the crystals first appearance. I
have a vague idea of where to look"

"Thank you, that would be very helpful" Sapere
says,
finishing up his drink,
"Mmmm, that was very tasty"
"I'm glad you liked it, most people won't even give
my slug reduction a chance"
Sapere's face dropped as he looked into the empty
cup.
"I wouldn't have guessed that" he said,
With a little burp.
Halcyon fought the sly smile that was forming in the
corners of her mouth,
"I will get back to you with anything I find. I'll also
contact my father about the fallen stars, I'm not
sure but if he has kept up with his hobby, he might
be able to give us some sort of insight"
Sapere turning progressively greener shouts in
agreement as he hurries from the surgery.

Chapter 10

Nadaur relaxes on the slouchy couch that looks incredibly comfortable placed in the middle of their living quarters. Nyah is moving through the room singing to herself, not an actually song but a lovely gentle sting of notes that float on the air & out through the window & can be heard an impressive distance away seeing as her tone is quite delicate. Nadaur relaxes his eyes closed as the beautifully haunting melody wafts around the room.

Nyah moves around the room tending to the myriad of plant life that she has carefully curated. All manner of flowers, vines & leaves of every colour imaginable hang from baskets & pots on every free surface around the cosy dwelling. It is not only her obvious affinity for the plant life that helps them to thrive & in turn helps her to thrive, but as she floats through the room watering & trimming the foliage her singing seems to have a physical effect on her collection.

Three hard bangs on the door breaks their idyllic afternoon. The force & rudeness of the knock fires Nadaur from his relaxation & across the room opening the door,

"Do not knock on someone's door in that fashion, it might be dangerous" he says,

With a scowl.

Standing at the door is a tall slim Imp in delicate
finery, his nose pointed to the air, he barely even
acknowledging Nadaur, he announces,
"I have a correspondence for the daughter of the
lord high Imp, Miss Nyah"
Nyah walks casually across the room, Nadaur
moves to the side as the messenger drops to one
knee presenting the gilded envelope, holding it high
above his head,
"Is that from your mother?" Nadaur asks,
Nyah takes the letter & says,
"You have done your duty, you may now depart"
Sending the Imp marching down the hall. Nadaur
watches him walk away with some amusement
closing the door,
"Hmm, is that from your mother? He asks again,
Nyah looks up completely distracted by the sudden
arrival of the letter,
"Oh, sorry, yes it would seem so" she said,
Showing him the letter.
Nadaur looked over the envelope, the paper was
thick but also very delicate, at the centre was in red
& gold the great seal of the Imp high council,
Nadaur handed it back to Nyah,
"What do you think she wants?" she asks,
Laying the imposing letter on the small wood &
leather chest that has become their makeshift table
that sits in front of the couch.
"Well, there's only one way to find out" Nadaur
says,
Pushing the letter across the table towards her with
his finger tip.

Nyah takes the small knife from her side that she
had been using to trim the lifeless parts of her
garden away, running it along the top of the
envelope the blade slices smoothly along its seam.
She removes a single page from the envelope
unfolding the crisply folded parchment. A small
silken bag falls to the floor that had been concealed
inside the letter, Nadaur reaches down retrieving
the regal little pouch from the floor holding it out to
Nyah. She looks at him & with a tiny nod she gives
him permission to open it. Nadaur opens the pouch
looking inside then he holds out his hand pouring
the contents onto his palm, four tiny seeds roll from
the bag resting in the lines of the palm his hand,
"What are they?" he asks,
Nyah looks closely,
"Oh my, they look like the seeds of the death
blossom" she says,
With a loving smile.
"Death blossom? that doesn't sound good" he says,
With a look of slight shock.
"No, it's not what you think, when I was a little girl, I
use to walk with my mother in the royal gardens,
apparently my mother says I was obsessed with the
death blossoms & would always run to see them
every time we walked there. I didn't realise that
they were highly poisonous, all I knew was that
they were the prettiest flower I'd ever seen, but they
are incredibly rare & almost impossible to
propagate to produce seeds, it only happens once
or twice every few hundred years".

"Huh interesting, what about the letter, what do you think she wants?" Nadaur asks,
Nyah unfolds the crisp parchment, its colour not a brilliant white but a warm yellowy brown with swirls of light & dark circling throughout the page.
Nadaur sits down giving Nyah her space to read the letter, her eyes track the lines of text written in the beautiful Impish script. Nadaur holding his tongue as long as he can eventually blurts out,
"Well, what is it?"
Looking over at her with interested eyes. Nyah smiles,
"It's mostly about my mum's joy that she was able to finally able to get her hands on some Death blossom seeds, since she has been trying to procure some since I first showed such interest in them as a little one,
"I thought your mum was super high up in the Impish world" says Nadaur.
"Yes, she is highly respected but somethings are just so rare that even for her it has been a multiple decade long search" Nyah explains,
Then her brow furrows & a decidedly more serious look spreads over her face, curiously Nadaur slides closer to try to read over her shoulder but the elegant calligraphy of the letter makes it almost impossible for him to read, seeing as he was not brought up with the refined schooling that Nyah received.
"Hmm" he says,
Hoping to prompt her to explain.

"Oh, sorry this part is about Kayla & her discovery
of one of the lost weapons, specifically the Maylar
Venet"

"I thought you said that the Impish high council
believed that objects like that which were once lost
if you found them it was the way it was supposed to
be?"

"Yeah & that is what my mother brought me up to
believe, but apparently according to what she says
here some of the others that sit on the council have
changed their beliefs through coercion, for a belief
that the lost objects with such great power should
be returned to the Imps to be used for purposes
that benefit the Impish agenda as they see it" Nyah
explained.

"But your mum can't be in favour of that?" he asks.

"No, far from it she vehemently believes in the
whole an object finds its own path, if it's is lost it's
for a reason & if someone, no matter who that
might be either Imp, gnomes, elf or even a human,
that is its rightful place & it isn't for any of us to try
to take it from that individual"

"So, what is her concern about Kayla?" Nadaur
asks,

"Apparently the news of Kayla's discovery of the
bracelet has reached the capitol & some on the
council want to forcefully remove the bracelet from
her so it can be reallocated to someone within the
Impish high guard, so the great power can be used
to protect the Impsh council. So, my mum is just
giving me a little heads up that the possibility of an

attempt to steal the bracelet of even just kidnap
Kayla & the bracelet together is highly possible"
"But Ny, you can't just remove the Maylar Venet, it
is a blood tie so they would have to kill Kayla to
retrieve it, right?"
"Unfortunately, that is correct, my mum will do her
best to keep us updated about any plans she
becomes aware of, but since the only safe way of
conveying her findings is by messenger carried
letter it may be a fractured communication. The
ether is far too easy to listen in on, So we will need
to keep a closer eye on Kayla & her new little
friends, because some of the more sinister
elements of the council may try to use them to
obtain information about Kayla & her routines".
The two of them slump back into their comfortable
couch, Nyah looking into the tiny bag examining the
seeds,
"This simple life is getting really complicated really
quickly, but I still much prefer these kinds of
troubles to those we had during war times" Nadaur
says,
looking over to Nyah who is completely distracted &
didn't hear a word of what he said.

The Regent strides through the halls followed
closely by a few of his little minions, their little legs
moving at a great pace just to keep time with his
elevated stride. A stern look covers his face he is
deep in thought as he walks. Arriving at Cockers
door he pounds on the wooden door leaving marks

in the grain from his many rings, the door flies
open,
"Who do you think you are banging…" he stops,
Mid sentence, seeing that it is his father who
doesn't wait for an invitation to enter, he just
pushes past as soon as the door opens, his
minions left to stand in the hallway outside.
Cocker closes the door taking a deep breath, he
knows his father would not make the journey down
to his abode if it wasn't a serious matter that he
needed to discuss & Cocker wasn't sure that it
wasn't about one of his many schemes that he had
running presently.
The Regent walked directly to the bar finding
Cocker's finest bottle, pouring himself a glass
leaving the bottle on top of the bar without even
replacing the lid.
In silence he walks over to the leather bound chairs
taking a sip then resting his drink on the table.
Cocker takes the seat as far as possible from his
father as his fear of what he is here to discuss
grows with every silent moment that passes.
"How have you been?" The Regent inquires,
Cocker stammers unable to answer, since of all the
questions running through his mind this was
something he was not prepared for,
"Um, I am fine"
He finally manages to get out,
His father always looked serious & controlled but
looking at him now Cocker could see that he was
preoccupied & very concerned about something.

"I have a task for you to undertake" The Regent
said finally,
"It is very time sensitive & I can't trust anyone else
with it".
Cocker moved to the edge of his seat to now be
closer, his father never trusted him with serious
matters, he barely included him at all.
"I need you to pick something up for me but you
might need to take some sort of security with you,
more than just those two you usually associate
with, you might need to hire a few of the Alimanas"
"Of course," said Cocker,
In the most professional voice, he could muster.
"Where do I have to go to procure the item" he
asks,
Trying not to push as he thinks his father may
change his mind at any perceived annoyance on
the part of his son & shut him out once again.
"I need you to go & see the fabricator, take him this
letter it holds all the information & specifications
that the order will need to comply with" The Regent
instructs,
Passing a sealed envelope to Cocker, who
immediately slips it into his inside jacket pocket
without even looking at it because he wants to
prolong the strange but comforting exchange he is
experiencing with his father for the first time in
recent memory.
The Regent finishes his drink,
"That was quite a nice drop" he says,

In a rare example of praise, placing the glass down on the table, getting up from his chair he arrives at the door, he turns,
"Thank you for taking care of this for me" he says,
Before disappearing through the door, closing it behind him.
Cocker sat bemused & dumbfounded at what had just occurred, he couldn't remember a time where his father had spoken to him in such a calm way, not to mention coming to see him rather than just summoning him like he was just another one of his lackey's. This new perceived respect displayed by his father even overruled his instinct to open the letter to see what his father needed so badly.
In a daze he walked across to the bar caring his father's glass running it under the water before replacing it in the stack, another knock at the door breaks his train of thought, thinking it might be his father returned to add something to his task he moved as quickly as he could without making any noise, he didn't want his father to hear any sort of urgency he wanted to remain calm & professional.
He paused at to door for a moment to collect himself, then opening the door but when he looked up it was not his father at all but Tallie, he was almost as shocked as with his father,
"Can I come in?" she asked,
As he was looking at her wide eyed & completely dumbstruck.
"Yes of course" he said,
Moving to the side.

Tallie walks in not noticing his odd demeanour
seeing as most of their interactions involve him
staring at her in an odd fashion,
"Would you like a drink?" Cocker asks,
Not really knowing how to behave his brain was
already overloaded from his interaction with his
father.
"Thank you, yes please" Said Tallie,
Trying to cover her dislike for him with pleasantries.
Cocker's mind is going a mile a minute, he has
been infatuated with Tallie from the first time he
saw her, but he had only just realised that they had
only ever really interacted a handful of times let
alone had an actual conversation. Not to mention
his strange interaction with his father still fresh in
his mind.
He pours her a glass of the very same top shelf
liquor that his father had chosen in a thinly veiled
attempt to impress her.
Tallie takes the glass, she sits down trying to think
of a way to broach the subject of the shadow
dwellers as Nadaur had requested but decides to
address the Alimanas contract first.
"I was hoping you might be able to pass on a
message for me to the Alimana?" she asks,
Cocker stops quite shocked that she had just come
straight out with her request rather than the
subterfuge & double talk that he was used to.
"I will do my best" he said,
In his most agreeable manner,
"What exactly is the issue?" He continues,
Trying to sound as friendly as he can.

"So, here's the thing, for some reason the Alimana have decided to put a contract out on Sikes & I & from what I've been told it is possible to challenge that by a trial by combat, do you know anything about that?" she asks,
Taking a sip of the drink, the tart liquor elicited an involuntary reaction from her face.
"You don't like it?" He asks,
"I have a lot of other things to choose from.
"No, no it's ok, I'm just not used to this sort of thing, my tastes are not very refined" she replies, forcing a smile that he takes as genuine smiling back.
"Well, from what I know a challenge is a viable method of removing a contract, although I must warn you that the Alimana are not the most trustworthy of groups & even though they might agree to your proposal it is highly likely that they will not remain faithful to the rules they themselves set out" he explains.
"Yeah, I've been warned about their lack of scruples, but the alternative is to leave the contract open which from what I understand given the far ranging population of the Alimana is not the safest of ideas"
"Yes, that would be my assessment of the situation as well. I would be happy to reach out for you to at least set up a meeting so you can discuss terms, if that would be helpful?" Cocker offered,
Amazed at how cordial their conversation has been.
"Thank you, that would be great, you will let me know when you have spoken to them?" Tallie asks,

Standing up, she extends her hand in thanks,
Cocker jumps up to shake her hand as they touch
both are acutely aware of his sweaty palms, none
the less he tries to hide it & Tallie pretends not to
notice.
Tallie begins to walk to the door racking her brain
for a way to bring you the other topic that Nadaur
had asked her to question him about. As she walks,
she sees that there is not much light in Cockers
Den,
"You should invest in a few lights in here, brighten
the place up a bit, it's rather gloomy & shadowy in
here" she says,
Looking at him to gauge his response.
Cocker's face goes pale & again his eyes widen.
"Shadows, um yes, I'll definitely look into that" he
says,
Walking ahead at an elevated pace reaching the
door a few steps before her turning the handle &
opening it for her.
Tallie looks over her shoulder as she leaves the
room, Cocker's face still in a state of panic,
"So, I'll wait for you to let me know" she says,
Walking away.
After a few seconds Cocker realises he should
respond,
"Oh, yes I'll get right on it & let you know as soon
as possible" he calls,
Down the hallway after her as she is already
metres away.

Cocker closes the door, believing that something must be on his side as he goes over the two miraculous interactions, he had just experienced.

Halcyon stands in front of one of the tall cabinets in her laboratory tapping her finger on her chin,
"Now where exactly did I put that box?" she says to herself,
Scanning the shelves,
"I'm sure it was somewhere up here" she says,
Sliding the ladder across the shelves climbing high into the rafters.
"Achoo!"
She sneezes at the amount of dust as she moves things to the side searching for the box that contained the crystal.
"Maybe I shouldn't have given Sapere such a hard time about the state of his library" she thinks to herself,
Then out of the corner of her eye she spots a black box with a symbol she recalls, but also doesn't recognise all at once.
Bracing her foot against the shelf, she grips tight to the ladder, pushing off the shelf sliding the ladder with her high atop, sticking her foot out again when she reaches the box to stop her accelerated travel.
"That worked better than I thought," she said,
Amazed by her own ability.
She reaches forward, moving a few jars with contents whose identification escapes even her.
"Ah yes, here it is"

The box was aged, its smooth black surface was not reflective but the light seemed to get lost within it.

"I wonder what this is made of" she thought to herself.

Halcyon tried to lift the box but its weight was much greater than its size would suggest.

"Hmm, maybe the better question is how are you going to get it down?" she said,

Looking down at the runs of the ladder not liking her chances.

Just then there was a knock at her door,

"You Hoo Halcyon"

Luma's voice came through the door.

Halcyon looks at the box, releasing she will need some help to retrieve it,

"Coming" she calls,

As she climbs down from the ladder.

Luma, Kayla, Vincent & Rava stand outside the door hearing the snaps of the lock just before the door opens.

"Hey Miss we've found something that we would like to ask you about" Luma says,

So excitedly she barely waits for the door to open.

"Ok Luma, but first could one of you strong young people help me retrieve something from a high shelf?"

"Of course," says Luma,

Stepping forward.

"I know you are a strong little elf but maybe Rava or Vincent would oblige" Halcyon says.

A grumpy look falls across Luma's face but Kayla
puts her arm around her shoulder giving her a little
hug, which quickly brings a smile back to her face.
"So, where's this heavy thing?" she asks.
"Over here" says Halcyon,
Leading the group down one of the many rows of
shelves that populate her laboratory.
"At the top of this ladder there is a black box which I
need you to retrieve for me, if you would be so
kind"
Rava walked up to the ladder, his size dwarfing it
as he put his large hands on the runs, he began to
climb higher Vincent grabs the base of the ladder to
stabilise it as it had already started to move
sideways on the track that helped it move along the
shelves,
"I got you" he called,
Up to Rava,
Who looked down & from the expression on his
face it was quite obvious that he was not feeling the
most confident in his skills on the ascent.
Finally, he reached the top, looking around and
seeing the box at the back of the shelf,
"Is it this one?" he pointed,
Halcyon took a few steps back standing on her
tiptoes so she could see,
"Yes, that's the one" she called back.
"But be careful, it is surprisingly heavy, much
heavier than it looks"
"I think I should be fine"
He smiles back down to her.

He looks at the reasonably small dimensions of the
box, he reaches out grasping one of the metal
handles that stick out from the sides, but when he
pulls with as much force as he thinks will be
sufficient the box doesn't even budge.
"Jeez Miss, what the hell do you have in here?" he
asks
"You just be careful Rava I don't want you to hurt,
either yourself or my property" she replies cheekily.
"You sure you've got me?" he asks,
Looking down to Vincent.
"Yup, I'm good down here" he calls back,
Readjusting his grip on the side of the ladder &
widening his stance for stability.
Rava hooks one of his legs around the outside of
the ladder so he is more secure & he can get a little
more leverage grabbing the box by both handles
this time sliding it forward a little at a time.
A loud grinding noise can be heard by everyone,
"Miss is this, ok? I don't wanna mess up your
shelves" he asks,
Looking at the deep grooves the box is leaving in
the thick wood.
"Yes, don't even worry about it honey, you just be
safe up there"
Halcyon grabs Kayla & Luma by the shoulders
pulling them back away from the obvious danger
that they both seem slightly oblivious too.
Rava pulls the box right up to the edge of the shelf
stopping as even with his great strength he is a little
unsure if he can get the remarkably heavy object
down the ladder safely, he unhooks his leg.

"You've got this!" Luma calls,
Up to him being as optimistic as ever.
He braces himself & with a great heave he lifts the
box from the shelf, letting it rest on the third top run
of the ladder. The true weight of the box now
completely apparent to him he yells down,
"I don't think I can get down with it!"
Halcyon, hearing the fear in his voice, immediately
yells,
"Just put it back, I figure something else out, be
careful!"
But just then a loud crack, the box shatters the thick
hardwood of the ladders run, falling at a great pace
smashing all the runs as it went.
Vincent looked up just in time to see the box
barrelling down towards him, left with no time to get
out of the way he closed his eyes, but the box
doesn't hit him, instead he heard Kayla scream
then a loud impact then a second. He opened his
eyes gingerly to see a golden shield above his
head that had been driven deep into the wood of
the set of shelves, looking down to see the box
right next to his left foot. It had landed with such an
impact that it had smashed the stone floor leaving a
huge hole & yet the box seemed completely
unmarked.
Vincent turned around to see that Kayla had her
arm extended with the Maylar Venet converted into
a shield that reached forward protecting him but
also backwards driving itself into the floor to brace
the impact, he could see that Kayla still had her
eyes shut tight.

"Whoa that was intense" said Luma,
Breaking the silence,
To which Halcyon gave her a clip over her pointy
little ears.
"Kayla sweetheart, are you ok?" she asked,
As Kayla opened her eyes the Maylar Venet
retracted back to its innocuous form of the bracelet.
"Wow that was close I thought I was a goner there
for a second thank you so much" Vincent said to
Kayla,
Running up & giving her a big hug in gratitude. He
could feel her heart was still going a mile a minute
her eyes were wide as dinner plates, then he felt
another person join the hug, it was Luma they both
looked at her in shock,
"What, I needed a hug too" she said,
With big eyes & a little smile,
Which broke the tension enough that Kayla began
to relax.
"UM…Help!"
A panicked cry came from high above. The group
looked up to see Rava clinging to one of the struts
of the ladder like a cat up a tree, the other stut had
completely broken away & there weren't any of the
runs of the ladder left for him to climb down.
"Rava" Halcyon said,
In a very calm but authoritarian tone,
"Reach one of your feet out & find one of the
shelves" she instructed.
He reached out blindly fishing around with his toes
for a solid footing,
"A little lower" Luma directed,

To which he discovered a solid shelf just within
reach & once he had the first foothold, he was able
to use the shelves to slide down the strut all the
way to the floor where he was greeted by Luma
with a big hug.
"What? I told you I like hugs," she said,
Responding to the others' looks.
"What the hell is that thing made of? It must weigh
more than I do" Rava said,
Looking at the black box embedded in the stone
floor
"I'm not sure" Halcyon answered,
Examining the box & rubbing her chin.
"Vincent, grab a side, let's get it up on the bench for
Miss" Rava said
"No, boys don't hurt yourselves" Halcyon pleads.
"It's ok Miss, I was able to lift it off the shelf onto the
ladder. I think if it's the both of us we should be
fine"
"Wait a second" said Kayla,
Looking around, finding a thick piece of wood,
"Can I use this?" she asked,
Looking at Halcyon.
"Yes of course dear"
"Ok, here's my plan, you two lift up the box by the
handles, then I'll slide this underneath & Luma & I
will help from either side holding the wood, Ok?"
"Good plan," Luma says,
Jumping into position around the other side of the
box just happy to be involved.
The boys grab the box by the handles lifting it up off
the ground with a great heave, Kayla carrying the

piece of wood passes it under the box to Luma on
the other side they bring the wood up to take some
of the weight of the box, then the four shuffle
across the floor towards the sturdy bench in the
middle of the room where Kayla & Vincent had had
their Faiges removed.
Halcyon runs ahead pushing the random knick
knacks out of the way as the four move closer, now
visibly struggling under the weight.
"On three" says Vincent
"One, Two, Three" they all count,
With a final mighty heave, they use all their might to
hoist the mysterious box onto the table, which lands
with a loud thud & a lot of creaking from the bench.
"Well, that was easy" says Luma,
Collapsing onto the floor.
"Thank you all so much" Halcyon says in
appreciation,
Moving closer to examine the box.
She takes a small blade that is lying on the bench
to try & get a sample of the material, but as soon as
she puts pressure on the tool the blade snaps,
"Hmm" she says,
Looking at the broken tool.
"I'll bet it's obsidian" says Luma,
From the floor,
Halcyon turns, looking at her surprised by her
knowledge.
"Obsidian?"
"Yup, my uncle was a very skilled metal fabricator
whose speciality was the manipulation of rare
metals. He used to do work for all the big houses,

the elves, dwarves & even the giants, but he
stopped taking commissions from the giants, he
said it was too labour intensive working on the
massive projects" she explained.
"Ah Huh, Ok good to know, what else do you know
about Obsidian?" replied,
A shocked Halcyon.
"Um, from what I can remember, its creation is
highly volatile involving manipulations of volcanic
situations.
Its glass like appearance is great for crafting,
although it can be altered to have an increased
weight & strength by putting it through some fairly
dangerous & secret processes, that my uncle
learned while travelling the realms as a younger
man discovering the secret techniques of the
accent artisans of the many different cultures.
He would only teach them to a very select few, he
tried to teach me but I was a bit too flighty for him, I
couldn't sit still, but I did pick up a few things here &
there.
I remember he told me that obsidian was perfect for
blocking anything from one side to the other, for
example if you made a box like the one you have
here once something is put inside it with the proper
techniques applied to the material it is pretty much
impossible to find out what the box contains short
of opening it & looking inside, it blocks all known
ways of gleaming content" Luma explained
"What was in your box?" Vincent asked

"This was the box that contained the shadow lens that saved your life, although I can't quite recall where I procured it from" she said,
Staring at the shiny black box.
"What about those symbols?" asked Vincent
"Symbols? I only see one on the front under the latch, which looks to be of Elvin design"
"But there are Symbols on every side" he said,
Walking around the bench.
"What exactly do you see?" Halcyon asked.
"Vincent stared closely into the deep black of the box & the deeper he looked the deeper he felt himself falling, like he was over tired & he was falling asleep for microseconds at a time.
A blank look fell over his face as the swirling symbols danced & changed in the deep black of the obsidian.
"Vincent!" snapped Kayla,
As she saw his entire arm had become bathed in the very same black shadow, but he did not respond.
Luma jumped up covering his eyes as Halcyon took off her jacket tossing it over the box.
Vincent took a moment then said,
"Um, what are you doing Luma?"
As he pulled her hand away from his eyes looking down at her as she clung to him.
"You're alright?" she asked tentatively,
"Yes, I'm fine" he said,
Looking around at the others shocked faces.
"Something happened again, didn't it?" he asked,
Looking over to Kayla.

"You were being absorbed by the shadow again,
"The Wolf?" he asked,
In a hushed tone as not to give it any more
purchase in the real world.
"Have a seat over here" Halcyon said,
Pulling out a chair from her work table against the
wall,
"What did you see?" she probed.
"I don't know, it was like a dream, blue smoke like
symbols swimming in a sea of pure black, they
morphed & changed, but they made a strange kind
of sense, but now the further I get from them the
less & less I recall of their shapes & meanings,
what I did know of them is completely gone from
my mind"
"Interesting," said Halcyon,
Looking over at the covered box on her bench,
"I want you four to promise me that you will stay
around the city, I don't want you to be wandering
outside in the forest or the ruins, there's something
happening within the shadows that is becoming
more troublesome & we can't protect you from the
unknown & there is to many places for the shadows
to form in the forest.so promise me" she said,
Looking each of them in the eye one by one.
"Of course, Miss" Luma said,
In her most convincing voice, that was still rather
unconvincing, made even less so by the
mischievous glint in her eye.
"I've got to go & consult Sapere about what I've
discovered" she said,

As she started to walk towards the door she turned back,
"Oh wait, didn't you want to show me something?" she paused to ask.
"Oh, never mind" says Luma,
"I, well we were just wondering if you would like us to take you or Nyah out to the place in the ruins where we found Kayla's fancy new adornment, but as you said it's not safe to be out in the woods it can wait"
"Yes, yes it can wait until we have a handle on this current predicament" Halcyon continues over opening the door,
Standing by the open door waiting for her young helpers to exit then closing the door locking it behind her,
"Thank you for your help" she calls back,
Over her shoulder as she disappears down the hallway.
"Why didn't you tell her about the secret passage?" Vincent asks.
"Because dumb dumb, if we tell them about it, they will have it guarded & we won't be able to get anywhere near it" says Luma.

The chime of the Ether rings out through the Regents quarters. He stands, casually walking across the room in no particular hurry to be talked down to by the other Regents on the high council. They may think they out rank him because of the small station of his city but without his assistance they would have a much harder time ruling, seeing

as they don't want to do any of the work
themselves, they just try to push the tasks off onto
him.
He steps up to the platform placing his finger into
the ether which stops the ringing as his finger
breaks the ripples circling out from the centre of the
basin.
"How dare you keep us waiting"
The regal voice chastises from the swirling liquid,
"My apologies, I was attending to our dilemma" The
Regent replied,
With barely veiled contempt.
"What have you put into place to solve our issue?
we really need the shadow travel up & running
again without delay. Our supply routes have been
cut on both sides by the trolls & the ogres & without
access to the shadow realm we have no way of
replenishing our supplies" The High Regent said
impatiently.
"I have put My plan into motion & I hope to have my
end of this inconvenience taken care of presently,
but I needn't remind you that my copy is not the
only thing holding them at bay, there are four other
volumes to take into account" The Regent reminds.
"Don't you worry about the other volumes, you just
address the task we've assigned to you!" Snaps
The High Regent severing the connection.
"Old entitled fools, they have no idea how close to
oblivion their way of life truly is" says The Regent
as he walks back to his throne & taking a large swig
from his glass.

"Why are we doing this again?" ask's Urchon.
"I told you, Cocker has found something that
affords him a great advantage, but as we've seen
by now, he's constantly squandered his other
advantages, so he's unlikely to use it to its highest
potential, so we're going to take it for ourselves"
Stinal explains, with a lack of patience.
"But how do you know he has more of those seeds
that gave him such an incredible boost"
"Because, he made such a big point to say that he
had only been given one to try, I've learned after
being around him for years how to tell when he's
lying & he was most definitely lying"
"But if we don't know where his supply of these
miraculous seeds come from how are we supposed
to obtain more if we take his remaining supply?"
Stinal stops,
"Huh, you're right, we need to figure out who his
new friends are that are bestowing him with these
powerful new abilities"
"How about we put a larklen in his den? We can
hide one up on the top of his shelves he would
never even think to look up there & it will relay
everything that happens in there to us" Urchon
suggests.
"You know what, that is actually a really good idea,
you go down to the market & pick one up, here's
more than enough" Stinal says,
Handing him a handful of gems.
Stinal grabs Urchon by the arm swinging him
around & looking directly into his eyes,

"Make sure you go to Marrious, I don't trust some of those others you deal with. We can't afford to get caught by using faulty merchandise"
"Fine" replies Urchon,
With a huff, running off down the hallway towards the market.

<u>Chapter 11</u>

Nyah stares at the letter from her mother running
scenarios in her mind,
"If you're worried about Kayla, why don't you go &
see her" Nadaur calls,
From the other room.
"How did you know I was worried?" Nyah calls
back,
Nadaur just sticks his head out from around the
corner giving her a knowing look to which she
responds with a smile,
"Yes, you're right, I'll be back in a while" she says,
Jumping from the cosy couch.

Kayla sits on the floor of Luma & Ravas small
apartment, her fingers playing with the bracelet that
has been the cause of such worry, but also a sense
of strength that she has come to appreciate.
"I must admit to being a little bit jealous," Luma
says,
As she pours herself a big bowl of cereal.
Kayla only heard that her friend had spoken, she
didn't register what she had said at all,
"Beg pardon?" she said
"Your bracelet, I kinda wish I'd found it, does that
make me sound bad?" she asks timidly.

"No, not at all, I can understand how cool it is, even though it's somewhat terrifying a lot of the time" Kayla admits.
"Have you been able to control it consciously at all yet?"
"Nup, it just seems to still be reacting to my heightened emotional state like Nyah said it would.
I still don't really feel as if I'm in charge if that makes sense"
"Yeah, it's like my hunger for cereal" Luma says,
Plopping down beside her with a smile.
Kayla bursts out laughing,
"I think that might be the most powerful magic of all" she says,
In between laughs.
"You wanna share?" Luma asks,
Putting the large bowl out in front of Kayla,
"No, thank you I'm good" Kayla said,
With a little grin.
She had barely refused the kind offer, Luma started munching down on the grainy bowl of cereal & there was three short sharp knocks on the door which break their conversation. Kayla gets up while Luma says with a mouth full of cereal,
"I'm not home",
Receiving an understanding nod from Kayla. She opened the door a small amount to see Nyah standing there, her natural beauty taking Kayla off balance.
"Hi" she says,
Nervously, blushing bright red.
"Hello you two" says Nyah,

Seeing Luma peeking from around the side of the
couch,
"I need to have a word with you Kayla, ok?"
Kayla looks back at Luma who still has the
reminisce of the milk dribbling on her chin.
"Yes, yes come in" invites Luma,
Standing up, taking the bowl back to the tiny
kitchen.
Nyah walks in taking a seat on the couch, moving
Luma's scattered clothes out of the way, while as
Luma is coming back she is intercepted by Kayla
who wipes the excess milk from her little friend's
face saving her from the embarrassment.
Kayla sits down on the chair opposite Nyah, while
Luma sits right next to Nyah as close as she can
without sitting in her lap. Nyah looks down at the
happy little face of Luma smiling up at her giving
her a little wink, which only serves to broaden her
smile.
"Kayla, I don't want you to be alarmed, but news of
your discovery has reached the capitol & the high
council of Imps is aware the accoutrement is one of
the lost Maylar Venets"
Kayla immediately stood up & began to pace
around the small room,
"What does that mean? Will they try to take it back?
because you & Halcyon said that once the blood tie
has taken effect it's a bond till death & sometimes
after"
Nyah walks calmly across the room standing
directly in front of Kayla taking her hands,

"I promise you that I will not let anyone hurt you"
she said,
In such a way that immediately put Kayla to ease,
The look on Nyah's face was truly sincere.
"But you should be aware that there are elements
within the high council that hold the belief that all
lost items are the property of the Imps, more
specifically the High houses & they are not above
trying to take them for themselves, but my mother
is highly respected in those circles & she will do her
best to make us aware of any such attempts or
plans that are in the works" she explains
"Plus, if anyone tries to take it from you the bracelet
will take them apart" Luma butts in, Prompting a
sharp look from Nyah.
"Yes, that might be the case but it would be more
advantageous if we can avoid placing young Kayla
in that situation in the first place, Luma" Nyah says,
Causing Luma to shrink to an even smaller size.
"So, they know who I am?" Kayla asks.
"Yes, they are aware of who & what you are,
meaning not being a native of our realm, but there
are many amongst then high born Imps that believe
as my mother & I do, that there is no claim of
ownership over such objects that have an obvious
will of their own"
"So, what should I do?" Kayla asks.
"Just be aware of your surroundings & those that
populate them, simple as that & If you see
something out of the ordinary or somebody gives
you a bad vibe take note of it & come find either

me, Nadaur, Halcyon or Sikes & we will investigate
it from there"
"What about Tallie?" smiles Luma,
Receiving another sharp look from Nyah.
"While I love Tallie, she can be a little over zealous
when it comes to some matters that might be better
dealt with by a calmer approach"
Nyah stands up to leave taking Kayla by the hand
once again,
"You'll be fine, I'll make sure of that" she says,
Then turns to Luma,
 "& You, don't freak her out any more than she
already is"
 "Ok, I promise!" Says Luma,
Walking right next to her to the door closing it
behind her.
"She so cool" Luma says,
With a huge smile.

Stinal paces around the outer gate of the city a foul
look on his face, clearly fighting with the fact that he
will have to strike out on his own against Cocker &
although family his brother is not the most reliable
second in command, plus by his association with
Cocker he has unwillingly burnt bridges with groups
he would now find a common ground.
"I've got it!"
A voice breaks his concentration, looking up to see
Urchon running towards him holding the box clearly
marked with the symbol for a larklen.
"Put that away you fool" he scolds,

His younger brother,
"If you're executing a plan, no one outside those
who need to know should even be aware that there
is a plan afoot"
Urchon tucks the box under his jacket,
"I'm sorry brother" he says,
With a bowed head.
"You really need to think before you act, one
mistake can cost you more than you might be
willing to pay" Stinal chastises.
"Are we going to place it now? Urchon asks timidly,
Attempting not to anger his brother further.
"No, we must be sure Cocker is out of his hole for
at least twenty minutes to properly calibrate the
larklen. You take it back to our place & wait there &
Urchon don't do anything without discussing it with
me first" he says firmly,
Leading his brother through the gates of the city.

Tallie walks forcefully into the barracks seeing
Faucon & Dabn sitting down the end of the long
room.
Dabn was laying back relaxing eating a blue apple
while Faucon sat across from him tossing thin
stiletto daggers into the apple every time he takes a
bite & every time Dabn would pull them out with a
smile firing them back, expertly missing Faucon
embedding them in the wooden bedframe
millimetres from her head, often catching pieces of
her hair in the impact.
Tallie silently took two blades from her hips sending
them flying simultaneously at a terrifying speed one

hitting the knife out of Faucon's hand just as she
was about to release it sending it to the floor with a
ting, her blade continued straight on lodging itself in
the bed head, while the other found its mark in the
apple in Dabns mouth. He removed the apple from
his mouth seeing Tallies blade had pierced the
apple completely & was protruding half an inch out
the other side drawing a drop of blood from his
tongue.
"You two up for a little fun?" Tallie asked
"What exactly do you have in mind? Your games
can be a little rough" quired Dabn,
Spitting the blood out the window.
Faucon pulled the beautiful blade from the wooden
bedframe tossing it back to Tallie who caught it &
slipped it back into its sheath in one fluid motion.
Dabn taking the opportunity for a little revenge,
throwing the other blade back while her head was
turned, but without even turning her head she
caught the incoming blade twirling it in between her
fingers then returning it to the simple leather sheath
on the other side of her hip.
"Sikes & I have found ourselves on the wrong side
of an Alimana death contract, which apparently we
can challenge but knowing how deceitful those
scummy little shits are I'd prefer to have two of my
best friends & some of the finest warriors I know
watching our back"
"You flatter us my dear, but of course we'll be of
any assistance we can" Faucon says,
Taking an overly dramatic bow to punctuate her
sentence prying another rare smile from Tallie.

"& you?"
She turns to Dabn
"Definitely I hate those slimy creatures & to be
honest I'm bored out of my mind waiting around
here for something to happen" he says,
Jumping over the bed.
"Ok I'll let you know when I have some more
details, thank you both" Tallie says.
Dabn tosses an apple into the air & Faucon pins it
to the wall with a blade.

Rava slinks along the long hallways that lead
toward the Highaster tree, he avoids the eye
contact of everyone he passes, even though his
large stature doesn't really lend itself to being
inconspicuous.
Finding his way to the arch leading out to the
Highaster tree he looks up to see the stars
blanketing the sky with light & the red moon high in
the sky.
He makes his way up the hill to the base of the
majestic tree, then looking down the hill to find his
path.
The light from the moon bathing the whole area in a
beautiful red glow, until he reaches the edge of the
forest where the thick canopy blocks most of the
light save a few moon beams that find their way
through the small gaps in the foliage. He takes one
of Luma's crystals that he is wearing on a chain
around his neck blowing on it to activate the light
within, holding it out in front of himself he carefully
picks his path through the overgrown undergrowth

trying to remember his way back to the secret
passage. The forest is a very different place at
night & definitely not a safe one even for someone
as large & intimidating as Rava. Strange eyes
shone in the darkness tracking his steps. As he
walked things scurried in the darkness that could
not be seen the only indication of their presents
was the rustling of the leaves as they moved.
The deeper he went the more apparent it became
that he was in their world not the other way around,
he felt things landing on him & then jumping off as
soon as he looked to see what it was it was,
beginning to unnerve him quite a lot. He had also
noticed random sounds behind him tracking him
through the undergrowth but every time he turned
to look, he couldn't make out the difference
between the shapes in the dark. By now his heart
was beating incredibly quickly it was starting to
match his quickening stride. He turned his head
because something moved in his peripheral, he
spotted the long thick black tail with a red tuft at the
end disappear up a tree. He turned the light to see
& shone the light on the tree realising that it had a
mark on the trunk & as he moved closer, he saw
that it was the carving that Luma had left which
gave him the confidence to forge onward, he had
found his bearings. He held the light closer to the
ground finding the first of the three trees that form
the lock,
“Now, what was that sequence?” he muttered,
To himself trying to replay the events of their earlier
discovery in his mind.

"Ah I've got it!" he yelled,
A little louder than he had intended,
Sending a wave of unseen things scurrying away in
the dark. He went from one tree to the next,
finishing with the tree that hid the secret tunnel. As
the tree moved, he looked up to see multiple large
black shapes take flight from the canopy their huge
wings beating against the air sending sound waves
through the night sky.
Rava lent forward dangling the gem down into the
darkness of the tunnel, illuminating only the top few
stairs, the rest of the path still obscured by the inky
black of night.
Rava looked around one last time then, not wanting
the tunnel to close, took his first steps down the
spiral staircase that had been cut from the black
stone.
The deeper he ventured the path behind him
became as dark as the path ahead leaving him
stuck in a ball of light, he had no idea what was
hiding just out of sight. He reached out his hand
feeling along the surprisingly smooth walls, there
were no marks, furrows or groves in the rock from
the creation of the tunnel just a smooth glass like
blackness that swallowed the light.
Rava was starting to get more & more concerned
when the tree above closed behind him, the noise
making him jump as he had travelled deep enough
that he could no longer see the opening at the top
& the sound of the mechanism travelled down the
tunnel passing him & continuing into the abyss.
Turning to look back he was suddenly stopped as

his path was blocked at the bottom of the staircase, lowering the glowing gem he was surprised to see that there was no lock just a long handle that curved up at the end, he placed his hand on the handle pushing down gently but the handle actively resisted, he lent his weight down & the handle started to move, after much more effort than he thought was necessary the dull thud of the bolt echoed up the narrow stairway. He pulled on the handle & the door opened with a smoothness that shocked him, it was clean & made not a single sound.

Rava opened the door just enough so he could peer around the edge to see what lay ahead, outside the door he saw a long tunnel carved in the same fashion as the staircase yet this tunnel had balls of white light at identical intervals along the ceiling that only illuminated one small area causing bands of light & shadow all the way down the long tunnel, at the very end he could see the outline of a door.

The tiny gap round the door shone brightly, much brighter than the lights illuminating the path & it was also a much whiter light that those, the light was almost pure & it seemed to actively push back the darkness. Just as he was about to venture out into the tunnel for a better look, he heard footsteps in the distance, a confident stride coming ever closer in the darkness. Rava pulled the door almost closed shaking the gem to extinguish the light, he stood in practically complete darkness listening to the footsteps coming ever closer until they are right outside the door, through the tiny gap he can see a tall figure holding a lamp out in front of them striding down the tunnel, once they had passed & have travelled enough distance from the door he gently pulls the door open, just enough that he can peek out to observe, but he doesn't even need to see the face of the individual to recognize them. The regal ornate robes inform him of their identity, it was The Regent & he was heading with purpose towards the door that was emitting the strange light. He stopped in front of the door, the complete silence had Rava worried, every little noise that he made was amplified in his head. He watched as The Regent fumbled around with something on the door then he took something from the wall right next to the door putting whatever it was on his head & putting on a thick black robe complete with gloves & a hooded mask. The more Rava watched the more he became unnerved by what he was witnessing until finally The Regent began to open the door.

The wider he opened it the further the intensely bright light spilled out into the tunnel filling it up as though the light had actual substance to it & the more light the more Rava leaned out of his hiding spot trying to get a better vantage point not even realising he was doing it. Then as The Regent had completely opened the door the light flooded the tunnel & upon reaching Rava it instantly burnt his skin like white hot fire, he fell back pushing the door closed with his foot as he fell trying with all his might not to cry out in pain, but the pain was so intense that he let a few whimpers slip laying there in the dark. His skin still burning but what had him more concerned was the fact that even in the darkness his eyes felt strangely numb, there was nothing. He frantically felt around searching for the lighting gem finding the chain & following it to the end to find the gem he brought it up to his lips sitting in the complete blackness he blew on the gem illuminating the area, but alas he was still trapped in darkness, the light had scorched his eyes leaving him completely blind.

He sat at the bottom of the stairs for what seemed like ages yet it was only a few minutes, then realising that he needed to get himself out of there knowing that the likelihood that he would be discovered by someone unfriendly was far more likely than Luma & the others.

He remembered the walk down the stairs, knowing that it was a singular path he started up the stairs using the smooth wall as a guide, having no gauge of distance in his sightless state he just took his time trying not to focus on what he could feel were quite severe burns on much of his body. His touch on the wall was muted which told him that his nerve endings on his fingertips had been burnt to a point of sealing them shut.

He took another step finding himself up against the entrance to the tunnel feeling around in the dark his fingers found a small inconsistency in the smooth stone, it was a latch which he pressed down then hearing the churn of the mechanism he knew he

had found his way to freedom, yet he knew he was
not out of the woods yet in both senses of the term.
The tree slid back allowing the night air to flood the
sealed tunnel, drops of rain landing on Rava's head
as he emerged into the dark forest.
The cold rain & cold night air soothing his
traumatised flesh as he felt his way through the
forest by going from tree to tree. Among the sounds
of the forest at night & the rain falling on the leaves
his acute hearing could barely make out the very
faint sounds of the city, he pushed through the pain
& the terror created by his blindness until he
reached the edge of the forest, he knew he must be
close to the Highaster tree & he fell forward
collapsing on the grassy hill.

Cocker looked around, being alone outside the city
always made him nervous because he knew his
father was not well liked among the people &
creatures that resided on the fringes of his rule.
He huddled under an outcropping of rock as the
rain fell around him running down the stone walls.
Cocker looked away for a moment distracted by the
rain, when he looked back there were two rather
scruffy Alimanas standing next to him dripping from
the rain which served to elevated their terrible
odour to a point that caused Cocker to move as far
as he dare, without disrespecting them, as he knew
he would be asking for more than just his normal
level of assistance.

"We were given word that you had some work you
wanna hire us for" said the bigger of the two
Alimanas,
His teeth had gone past yellow & were almost
green.
"Yes, I would like to hire you to act as security in
the retrieval a package for me & aid in its transport"
Cocker said,
Taking his handkerchief from his pocket pretending
to wipe his nose but he was really trying to block
the stench.
"Hmm, sounds important, we want double our usual
fee" said the slimy leader of the duo,
with a sickly grin.
"I am willing to meet those demands, as long as
you do a second favour for me. I need you to issue
a challenge to a contract you've issued on a couple
of good friends of mine" Cocker bargained.
"Who exactly? The Alimana asked,
Widening his beady little eyes.
"Tallie & Sikes," He replied simply.
The two Alimanas turned to each other whispering
& smiling to one another,
"That's a little more than a favour, we would have to
take it up with the leader of our faction, we think
that should be worth a little extra…say three times
our usual rate?"
The lead Alimana suggested,
Cocker wiped his nose putting the handkerchief
back in his jacket pocket looking at the two grinning
Alimanas in the eye as he did, when he removed
his hand from his pocket, he had a heavy knuckle

duster with which he smashed the second Alimana
in the face sending him bleeding & unconscious
into the rain & in the same motion grabbing the
other by his rain soaked coat lifting him up to meet
his eye level,
"I do not negotiate with errand boys! You will relay
my message & for this insult I will pay one & a half
times my usual rate" Cocker commanded,
To which the Alimana gave him a dirty look, in an
attempt to conceal his fear.
Cocker brought his weapon clad fist up to the side
of the Alimana face & with a press of a button that
was on the side, a shiny silver blade shot from the
top of the device stopping millimetres from his
eyeball.
Cocker pressed the blade into the flesh of the
whimpering Alimana's cheek until its green blood
began to flow.
"Now you go back & let your boss know my terms &
have no illusions that the next time I see him I will
be bringing up your insolence" Cocker said,
In his most commanding & threatening tone.
He could see the terror in the Alimanas eyes,
bargaining with someone of Cocker's standing is
reserved for the Bosses of the factions & he would
be in serious danger if he was found out to have
insulted someone who gives them such legitimacy
just by association.
"Please, I beg you! I was only joking, I will relay
your requests to the boss"
Cocker stared into his eyes for a long moment then
dropped him in a puddle & casually washed the

weapon under a waterfall caused by the walls of
the city before putting it back in his pocket.
"I will expect to hear from your boss presently" he
said,
Pulling up his collar & walking out into the heavy
falling rain, leaving the Alimana to collect his
unconscious associate then slinking off down a little
dark alleyway.

Sapere walked the massive shelves of the library
that towered over him. He had exhausted his small
stash of literature pertaining to obsidian, fallen stars
& any reference to the shadow realm, so he had
decided to see what had slipped through the cracks
of the obvious kull of knowledge that had taken
place sometime in the past.
He had been gifted many keys over the years, keys
that gave him access to hidden shelves containing
forbidden & restricted texts. Unfortunately, his
memory for locations was not the greatest of his
attributes, but he had a fair idea where to start. He
found his way to the section containing the books
on laws, which he knew would be a good place to
begin his search as many of his peers enjoyed
breaking the rules so much it would track to their
sense of humour to hide some of the volumes there
& if he was lucky, it would give him some idea of
where to look next.
He searched along the shelves not seeing anything
that could point to a clue, but then he came across
the books on restricting & altering behaviour, he ran
his fingers along the shelf until he felt a knot in the

wood underneath one of the books, stopping &
looking around to make sure the library staff were
nowhere around. He craned his neck seeing that
the knot had a small symbol imprinted around its
circumference, it was the mark of his long lost
friend Brodrick, an adventurer whose main goal
was the acquisition of knowledge.
He would travel to any & all societies he heard
stories about bringing back their sciences, tales &
legends transcribing them into volumes that some
in the higher intellectual & ruling parties often hid
then co-opted the information for their own selfish
intentions, including a few lost volumes on their
very own city.
Sapere fished through his pockets finding one ring
of keys then another, until he finally stumbled
across a ring at the end of one of his older chains
that contained five keys, all marked with a different
symbol.
Sapere held the tarnished old keys up to the light
searching for his friend's mark, which was a quill
hovering over a horizon, containing both of his
loves writing & travel.
He found one that had the faint outline, spitting on
the top of the key & whipping the years of
accumulated gunk on the sleeve of his grubby
jacket, adding just one more stain to its well worn
appearance.
Sapere stood with his back to the shelf feeling
around the knot with his fingers, his presence had
been noticed by some of the librarians who were
now taking a bit more of an interest in his activities.

He felt a keyhole which he then attempted to insert the key into.

Sapere was a widely regarded intellect & had many talents but dexterity was another of the skills that he was found to be lacking in. After some struggling & a few muttered swear words under his breath the key finally slid into the lock, he turned the key one full rotation & felt the lock engage turning around to see what the result was. He saw that the books in the middle of the shelf were sliding apart so he casually strolled toward the gap, upon getting there noticed that the top of the shelf itself had dropped away yet the body of the shelf was still very much present.

Sapere remembered tales his old friend had told him regarding the best hiding places being with in something that people would walk past in their everyday life without giving it a second look. So, he reached his hand into the newly revealed hiding place & he was surprised to see that even though his hand was reaching far into the shelf it was not visible on the underside of the wooden panel.

Poor Sapere was not nearly as tall as Brodrick, so he was high on his tiptoes & almost to his shoulder when he finally felt the familiar texture of the cover of a leather bound volume, but just then he heard the footsteps of one of the Librarians coming his way, he stepped up on the bottom shelf giving him just enough extra length so he could grab the large book pulling it from its hiding place he tucked it under his jacket then quickly slid down to relock the compartment & restore the shelf to its former position just as the librarian rounded the edge of the shelf.

The Librarian attempted to address Sapere but he just rushed past with one of his trademark angry expressions, grumbling to himself under his breath in a way that put the young librarian on the back foot allowing Sapere to push past & on out the doors.

Chapter 12

Halcyon sits attempting to scrape the mysterious box that sat on her workbench, strewn around her were the remnants of her previous failed attempts, a pile of broken & bent tools that had come up short.
She pressed a tool which she had used many times before to cut samples of crystals that she uses as a prism to grow certain plants that require a specific spectrum of light, but yet again the tool failed fracturing at the tip sending Halcyon stumbling across the room.
She circled the object clicking her tongue with crossed arms, then an idea stuck her,
"It's worth a try" she proclaimed,
Loudly to no one in particular,
Looking around but there was no one to share her idea with so she took off her dirty work apron chucking it over the box in a somewhat lacklustre attempt to hide it from the prying eyes of anyone that might find their way into her arboretum, then leaving through the door.

Tallie & Nyah stood at either ends of one of the training rooms holding long staffs.
In the centre stood a quite determined looking Kayla. All were silent.
"Wooohooo!"

Came a shout from Luma, Sitting on the sidelines
with Vincent, Nadaur & Sikes.
Sikes put his huge hairy arm around her shoulder
covering her mouth.
"Shhh!" he quietly growled,
"Kayla must concentrate"
Luma pulled at his hand but the feeble effort only
made Sikes chuckle, he removed his hand giving
Luma a cuddle.
Tallie & Nyah both raised their staffs above their
heads bringing them down with a crack of impact
on the hard stone floor. Kayla stood side on so she
was not facing either of them directly, which
allowed her to keep both targets in her peripheral
vision, which prompted a little grin of
acknowledgement from Nyah.
Nadaur then began the count,
"One, two, three…GO!"
With which both girls took off running at Kayla at full
speed.
Tallie & Nyah were fairly evenly matched for speed
& reached Kayla at about the same time, Tallie
striking directly at her head while Nyah went in for a
sweep, Kayla jumped clearing Nyah's half speed
strike, while putting her arm above her head, she
had come to realise from Nyah's lessons that the
Maylar Venets felt intent as much as it did
emotional state, so her plan was to think as hard as
she could about blocking the blow & nothing else.
Tallies staff came hurtling down at a little more than
half strength, it met Kayla's arm now covered from

knuckles to elbow with a form fitting shield, Tallies
staff shattered into splinters.
"Yeah!" yelled Sikes,
Receiving an elbow in the ribs from Luma in protest
of his double standard which they then shared a
laugh about.
"That was great Kayla" Nyah congratulated,
"You're really starting to get a feel for it"
Tallie gave her a punch in the shoulder,
"Not bad kiddo" she said,
Trying to be supportive,
Which for her did not come naturally.
"I just concentrated like you said & it worked" Kayla
said excitedly.
"Shall we go again? She asked,
Now getting a taste for the new found strength she
was feeling.
Nyah was about to reset for a different challenge
when Halcyon ran into the room quite out of breath.
"Maybe you should do some training to get your
fitness up" laughed Sikes,
To which he received a red faced angry look that
only served to make the others join in on the
laughter.
"Luma, I've been looking everywhere for you, you
said that your uncle was a fabricator of unusual
metals & stones did you not?" she asks,
In between pants.
"Yes, what can I do to help?"
"I've been trying to take a sample of the box but I'm
unable to because none of my tools are able to
even make a mark on the obsidian"

"That's not surprising, most of the tools my uncle
uses are very specific to the type of medium he is
working with. If memory serves, you'll need a blade
made from white ore hardened by ice fire & cured
for over twenty years"
"Really, where am I going to find something that
specific, maybe your uncle would be kind enough to
furnish me with some tools?" Halcyon asked
hopefully.
"No need for that" Nyah chimed in,
"I'll bet that Tallie could help you out, she has an
impressive array of rare weapons"
Everyone stopped, looking over at Tallie who was
completely focused on spinning her new staff at
great speed with high precision.
Tallie finally looked up realising that everyone was
staring at her,
"What?!" she barked
"Tallie, have you got anything…um what was it
Luma?"
"A blade made from white ore & hardened by ice
fire & cured for over twenty years"
Tallie without skipping a beat immediately knew
what she had that could do the job,
"I've got a dagger that was crafted for the war
against the rock trolls that was crafted by those
processes, it's in my weapons chest in my quarters"
"See, I knew Tallie would know, she has an
incredible knowledge of her weapons" says Nyah.
Halcyon having finally caught her breath thanks
Tallie, asking,

"Would it be possible for me to borrow said dagger
Tallie?"
"I don't see why not, I'll bring it down to your place"
says Tallie,
As she walks from the room she tosses the staff
from an impressive distance with perfect accuracy,
sending it straight into its spot on the weapons
rack.
Halcyon looked around noticing Vincent,
"Ah yes, the other person I was looking for, Vincent,
do you think you could draw the symbols you saw
on the box?"
"I'm Sorry, but I don't remember anything from
when the shadow takes hold, but I am willing to try
and relay them as I see them if I can. I would really
like to know what is happening to me" he offers,
Looking quite defeated.
Nadaur, feeling some sort of kinship with Vincent's
lack of control, volunteers some assistance.
"I know a few techniques that can be very helpful
for keeping yourself grounded in a stressful
situation, I'll teach you some things I've learned
over the years"
"Thank you that would be most helpful" Halcyon
says,
Truly happy for his help on the matter.
"I'm coming too" shouts Luma,
Much louder than was necessary.
"I was in no doubt of that fact" Halcyon said,
With a serious look but a little glint of fun in her eye,
she couldn't help but admire Luma's unending
positivity.

"If you don't mind Nyah, I'd like to get a little more practice in" Kayla asks hopefully.
"Of course, you all go, we'll catch up with you later".
The others leave Nyah & Kayla to their training.

A loud knock echoes out in Cocker's den, he stumbles from the back room still half asleep, walking towards the door, so annoyed being roused from his slumber he begins to chastise the visitor before he even fully opens the door,
"You'd better have a good reason for disturbing me!" He scolds,
When he finally opens the door, he sees Stinal standing there holding a scrapy piece of parchment. Cocker can see by the leather ties that bind the letter that the letter is from the Alimanas, hopefully a timely response to his inquiries. Cocker snatches the letter before turning away from his underling leaving him standing in the open doorway to enter & close the door behind him.
Cocker pulls the leather string, which is there more for decoration rather than any real security measure. He quickly scans the correspondence,
"I was handed it by one Alimana down the market, he said it came with an apology for the disrespect that was shown to you by the first two messengers, who as I understand were severely punished for their impudence" Stinal explained.
A smile spread across Cockers face, not from what Stinal had said, he barely heard a word, but the contents of the letter pleased him greatly. He had managed to successfully accomplish both tasks he

was issued by the two people he really wanted to impress & gain some modicum of respect from more than anyone else.
He folded the letter sliding it into his pocket, just before he left the room he stopped turning to his closest version of a friend,
"I'll be back in a few hours if you wanna stay & have a drink?"
Stinal, shocked into silence, Cocker was never that nice all he could respond with was,
"Ah ok"
Receiving a nod of acknowledgement from Cocker as he left the room closing the door behind him.
Stinal stood in the centre of the room, the strange interaction had thrown him for a loop, but regaining his composure he went over to the door opening it slowly to make sure Cocker was out of sight, then he whistled a three octave tune to which Urchon answered by emerging from his hiding place a little way down the hall, caring a small box with him he ran into the room.
"Where are we gonna set this thing up?" Urchon asked,
In a slight panic,
But Stinal was still distracted by the odd behaviour of Cocker, he soon remembered all the other days where he had been treated like dirt, so his commitment to the current plan was rekindled.
"Over here" he directed,
His younger brother.
"We need a clear view of the safe, it's behind this painting"

Stinal stood next to the large portrait of Cocker
looking for the best vantage point.
"Over there"
He pointed to a large bookshelf that was on the
opposite side of the room.
"How exactly do these things work?" Urchon asked,
Opening the box & staring at its contents.
"I've heard of them but I must admit this is my first
time actually using one"
Stinal reaches into the box, which had two
compartments separated by a metal partition
"The Larklen are a completely manufactured
species, they have been bred for a singular
purpose for hundreds of years, but their abilities
have become more refined over time to a point that
they don't actually bear any resemblance to the
creature they once were. See you take one" he
said,
As he pulled the creature from the box.
It was round & about the size of his palm, with
many little feet all around its circumference. Its skin
was made up of tiny scales that camouflaged taking
on the appearance of his skin as soon as it had
settled in place on his hand.
Urchon looked on in shock
"It disappeared!" he gasped
"No, it's just a sort of camouflage, it mimics the
background of whatever it's placed on, plus it will
move if necessary to stay concealed.
Stinal looked at the rows of books, investigating the
levels of dust, he deduced that Cocker was unlikely
to read any of them, so he looked across the room

finding a good eyeline that gave a good view of the
painting. Stinal took the interesting little creature off
his hand placing it on the spine if one of the books,
they both watched as the creature settled into place
then adopting a perfect likeness of the books
leather cover beneath it.
"But how do you see what it sees?" Urchon asked
"Ah that's the interesting part" says Stinal,
He takes the second Larklen from the box &
gestures for his brother to come closer.
"Hold still" Stinal says,
Grabbing his brother by the chin to hold him steady,
then he places the Larklen over one of his eyes like
an eye patch. The tiny feet have microscopic
suction cups that stick fast to his skin.
"It feels so weird, I don't like it" Urchon whines,
Starting to freak out.
"Just give it a moment"
Stinal reassures him.
As the creature settles into place it begins to take
on the appearance of his eye & skin beneath
creating the illusion that it is not there at all
"But I still can't see" Complained Urchon
"That's because I've not connected them yet" says
Stinal.
He walked over to the first Larklen tapping it at its
centre three times, a slit became visible & opened
revealing a large eyeball, it had no white like yours
or mine, just a ring of red surrounding a yellow pupil
which blinked independently of the other set of lids.
"Ok, close your other eye" commanded Stinal,

His brother was significantly freaked out but he
complied begrudgingly. Once he had shut his eye
the Larklen opened its eye,
"Oh, this is so strange" Urchon said,
Holding his hand in front of his face,
"I can see from the perspective of the other one on
the book" he said,
Amazed with a big grin.
"Pretty cool right" said Stinal
"Ok, now we need to set its focal point, hold still &
focus on the painting on the wall & its surrounding
area" Stinal said
"Ok I've got it"
"Now repeat after me Setra Mae" Stinal instructed
"Setra Mae" said Urchon,
As clearly as he could.
Stinal watched the Larklen on the book, its pupil
had changed from yellow to a light purple.
"Ok, we're good to go" he said,
Tapping with his index finger on Larken Covering
his brother's eye three times, it closed its eye &
released, sliding down Urchon cheek leaving a
slimy trail until Stinal grabbed it, returning it to the
box.
"So, all we have to do is place this one over our eye
& we can scrub through until we find the desired
place" he explained.
"Now let's get out of here" Stinal said,
Directing his brother out through the side door.

A young elf ran down the hall towards Otto's
surgery. Otto had only been up and around for a

few days having very little memory of his ordeal in the shadows, say a few scars & frightful nightmares.
The tiny young elf came tearing into the room pale faced & wide eyed, Otto was seated at his apothecary cabinet muttering under his breath about the perceived disarray that Halcyon had left while filling in for him.
"Please sir…"
The distraught little one squeaked.
"A moment" snapped Otto.
The little child danced around in distress, after a moment Otto turned around looking over his glasses,
"Well, how can I help you?" he asked,
Calmly but with a touch of impatience.
The little elf child rushed forward,
"We've found someone, he is really hurt, you have to come!" he said,
At high speed,
Grabbing Otto by the arm in an attempt to hurry him along,
"Now, now young one, give me a second to gather my requirements" Otto said,
Walking over & retrieving a large leather bag that sat next to his desk.
"You said he was hurt, can you be more specific little one?" he inquired gently,
Placing a few extra bottles into the bag.
"Um, well he wasn't moving but his skin was all red & bumpy"
"Like he had been burnt?" Otto asked,

"Maybe, I don't know I'm not a doctor, we need to
go!" yelled the young child,
Who was obviously becoming quite agitated.
"Show me the way" said Otto.
The child took off running down the hallway
towards the arch that leads to the Highaster tree,
Otto walked, but his stride was quick with some
urgency behind it.
The child ran forward then stopped at every corner
looking back to make sure Otto was still behind
him. When Otto finally made through the arch & up
to the trunk of the mighty tree, he looked down the
hill & he could see quite a large crowd of youngins
gathered around, he hurried down the hill as fast as
he was able not being particularly gifted in that
department,
"Clear the way!" he yelled,
As he drew closer,
The group of children parted allowing Otto to see
the large hulking body of Rava lying in the wet
grass, Otto knelt down next to him assessing his
condition, he immediately realised that there was
not much that he could do for the young man here,
he looked around for the eldest of the children
seeing a young Centaur,
"You!" he said,
Pointing to the half beast,
"I need you to run as fast as you can & bring back a
couple of the guards that are posted in the
travelling orb room, Quick as you can!"
The half horse, half boy galloped up the hill with
great pace & disappeared over the crest of the hill.

Otto had a worried look on his face, he could see how laboured Ravas breathing was becoming, he took the same pain killing syringe that had been used on him by Halcyon from his bag putting the tip into Ravas nostril & depressing the plunger, he then took a small vial of clear liquid from his bag shaking it vigorously until the liquid turned a dark blue then administered a few drops onto Ravas tongue.
"Will that help him?" Squeaked the Little elf,
Otto looked around with a serious look on his face, but upon seeing that it was the same young one said,
"It will hopefully help him to breathe a little better & bring his heart rate down"
Then in a rare sign of sympathy he added,
"You did a very good job coming to find me as quickly as you did" patting the child on the head.
Just then the Centaur came barrelling down the hill followed by two of the guards, sliding to a halt next to the crowd.
"Clear the area!"
The guards commanded,
The children moved to the side but not too far as this was far too exciting.
"You two, I've barely stabilised him but we need to get him back to my surgery as quickly as possible, pick him up & mind his wounds!"
The guards gently lifted Rava up, following closely behind Otto as he moved with substantial pace up the hill.

Looking over his shoulder he noticed that the entire
group of children was following them
"No, you all stay here!" he barked,
Loud enough that it stopped the procession of the
city's young inhabitants in their tracks.
Arriving back at his surgery he yelled over his
shoulder as he opened his cabinet,
"Lay him down on the bed & be gentle about it"
Otto put all manner of vials, bottles & jars onto a
wheeled cart pushing it over next to Rava on the
bed. Otto switched his glasses for a second thicker
pair of glasses. He thoroughly examined the
wounds before him,
"What could have done this?" he said,
To himself,
As he noticed that the skin on his arm was still
bubbling, it was continuing to burn long after the
original stimulus had been removed.
He turned to his medical cart, taking a mixing bowl
he picked up a large jar that contained three
massive worms that had filled the jar with a slimy
secretion, Otto took a small amount on the tip of his
finger dripping it onto the wounds & waited a few
seconds to see if it had the desired effect, the skin
still inflamed had begun to calm down.
"It's not a cure but at least it should mitigate some
of this damage" he said,
Taking the worms from the jar with tongs & putting
them into the bowl, he began to slather the pungent
slime over any part of Rava that had been burnt.
"You" he said,
To one of the guards

"Just outside that door in the garden there is a plant
with large orange leaves, I need you to go & pick
me as many of them as there are on the tree, quick
as you can!"
The guard ran outside & the other followed not
knowing what else to do, they stripped the entire
small tree of leaves bringing them back to Otto.
"Over here on the cart" he snapped.
No sooner had they deposited them on the cart
Otto started to lay them over the affected areas.
"These should help to mitigate any infection".
Otto kept working but looked up,
"I have no further use for you two" he said,
 Dismissing them & went back to the task at hand.

There was a cold wind blowing in through the large
windows that line the pathways through the city.
Cocker made his way down the hallway but he
didn't even feel the chill in the air. He was
completely preoccupied with the choice of who to
go & inform of his success first, his disapproving
father or his unrequited crush Tallie.
Going over the pros & cons in his head as he
walked, he finally decided to attend to his father
first & get it out of the way. Cocker's mood was
high as he approached his father's chambers,
stopping outside the door to gather himself he
knocked three times on the heavy door & waited for
a response, after a moment the large door opened
with a satisfying creak.
Cocker looked down to see one of his fathers
cloaked minions standing in the doorway.

Cocker walked past him without any resistance,
striding confidently towards his father who was
seated at the beautiful wooden table at the end of
the room.
"Yes?" The Regent said,
Without even looking up from his book.
"I've organised the security for that task you
requested" he proclaimed proudly,
"Good... Details?"
His father asked simply,
Still not looking up from his book.
"I've set up a crew of ten to work as the guards & to
move whatever you require, plus I've also taken
care of the payment so you don't have to concern
yourself with anything" he explained,
Hoping for at least some kind of praise or at the
very least eye contact.
"Very well, I will send one of my servants with the
details of time & place" he said abruptly,
Continuing to paw over his book.
Cocker stood there for a moment until he realised
that in his father's mind the conversation was
already concluded, without the praise he was
hoping for he left the room.
Cocker in a decidedly more annoyed mood than
before walked towards the barracks to find Tallie,
he was not surprised with his father's lack of praise
but it did nonetheless deflate his confidence
slightly.
As he entered the barracks, he could see Faucon &
Dabn at the end of the room cleaning their armour.

Tallie was knelt by a large chest at the end of her bed searching for something, as he approached, he cleared his throat in an attempt to get her attention but to no avail.

When he ended up standing next to her, she was still shoulder deep in the massive wooden chest surrounded by weapons that she had displaced in her search.

"Excuse me" Cocker said,

In his nicest voice.

Tallie jumped up banging her head on the top of the chest.

"Ouch fuck!" she yelled,

Rubbing her head looking up to see who had startled her.

"Oh, are you alright?" Cocker asked,

With a level of sincerity, she was not expecting.

"Yeah, I'm fine, just wound a little tight" she answered,

Getting to her feet while still rubbing the expanding bump on her head.

"I was able to get you a challenge hearing in five days, I hope that's enough time?" he said rather timidly.

"Oh, that's great, thanks a lot!" Tallie exclaimed,

"Thank you for handling it so quickly, I hope it wasn't too much trouble" she added.

Her reply spiked his mood considerably,

"Oh, it was no trouble at all, I was happy to help. If you would like me to accompany you, I'd be more than happy to, the Alimana are not exactly trustworthy" he asked,

Hopefully.
"Thanks, but I'll have Sikes with me so I think we'll be fine" Tallie answered.
"Right, yes of course, just let me know if I can be any more help" he said,
Walking away as to not push his luck, when from behind him he heard,
"Thanks for helping us out" she said,
With one of her rare smiles then turning & returning to her search.
Cocker strode from the room, his mood lifted & the benefits of doing something nice for someone else just to be helpful were not lost on him, just as he reached the doorway, he heard Tallie yell,
"Yes!"
He looked back to see her holding a dagger with a distinctive white blade.

Chapter 13

The rain fell on the glass roof of Halcyons
Conservatory, Luma fidgets with one of Halcyons
tools while Vincent stares at the covered box on the
workbench.
"Are you sure this is safe to be messing around
with?" he asks,
Remembering the loss of control he had
experienced in the past.
"I will do my very best to ensure your safety young
man" Halcyon said,
In a comforting manner.
"I've got your back" Luma said,
Jumping up from her chair, Halcyon looking down
at her with a serious face but there is a kindness in
her eyes.
Halcyon snatched the tool from Luma,
"That is not a toy little miss" she said,
Putting it back in its place on the rack of tools.
Halcyon walked over to the work bench,
"All right dear let's see what you can see, but to try
& mitigate the boxes ability to cast any influence
over you how about we try this from a distance first,
Here" she said,
Taking a notebook from the shelf & placing it & a
silver pen on the table on the opposite side of the
room.

"Luma sweetheart, I'll be relying on you to keep a
constant eye on Vincent, any sign of bewitchment I
want you to cover his eyes, do you think you can do
that?"
"No worries, Hally" Luma chirped,
"I've asked you not to call me that" Halcyon said,
With an annoyed look, prompting a cheeky little grin
from the young elf.
"Are you ready Vincent?" Halcyon asked,
Standing by the box.
Vincent took a moment to steady himself & after a
deep breath said,
"Yes, I think I'm good"
Halcyon pulled the cover from the black box that
sat on the table, Vincent looked over at the box as
Luma sat on the table top next to him, looking
vigilantly at his eyes.
"Anything?" she asked,
Only receiving a,
"Shhh!" from Halcyon.
Vincent was about to suggest that he should try
moving a little closer when the consciousness
drained from his face.
Luma made a tiny noise of excitement but
managed to hold herself together, but she waved
her hand to alert Halcyon who nodded in
acknowledgement.
Luma looked down to see Vincents hands were
moving which gave her an idea, she took the
notepad & pen from the table placing the pen into
his hand while she held the notepad under it.
Vincent's face was a complete blank but as the pen

moved across the paper an image started to take
shape.
The first was a sun complete with rays stretching
out across the page with a sword plunged into its
heart.
The second seemed to be a wave of black that his
hand furiously scribbled inside, filling in the white
page with the black ink.
Luma was so distracted watching the drawings
taking shape that she almost didn't notice Vincent's
eyes roll over black, but her momentary lapse was
broken with a shriek as she jumped up covering her
friend's eyes as she yelled,
"Cover the box!"
Halcyon flung the piece of fabric over the box &
Vincent immediately dropped the pen, knocking the
pad to the floor.
"Did anything happen?" he asked,
Looking surprised at Luma who was sprawled out
on the table still with her hands on his face,
"I'll take that as a yes"
He continued as Luma collapsed in a heap.
Halcyon walked across the room & picked up the
notepad
"Hmm"
She rubbed her chin as she analysed the drawings,
"What does it mean?" asked Luma
"I'm not sure" answered Halcyon
"That one looks like a crest or something," Luma
proposed.
"Yes, that's a good thought, we should take it to
Sapere. He's much more knowledgeable about the

crests of the ancient families. Vincent how do you feel?" she asked,
"Physically I feel fine, but it is really disconcerting that when I'm under the thrall of the shadows I retain no memory of what has transpired" he said, With a very concerned look on his face.
"Hally will figure it out" said Luma,
Throwing her arm around his shoulder, Halcyon did not react as she could see the little elf was doing an excellent job at keeping the trauma from overwhelming Vincent.
A loud knock at the door made all three of them jump,
"Enter" called Halcyon
The door swung open to reveal Tallie,
"I've brought that dagger you wanted" she said,
Sliding the blade from the scabbard on her hip.
"Ooh, it's so pretty!" exclaimed Luma,
Running over,
Tallie handed the black handled dagger, its white blade almost seemed to glow when exposed to the light to Halcyon.
"Get it back to me whenever you're finished, I don't really have much use for it lately. Is that all you need from me? I really need to find Sikes & get some training in?" she asks.
"Yes, thank you for the loan, I'll take good care of it"
"That's not really necessary, that blade is one of the strongest I've ever come across, I'd be shocked if you could break it" Tallie said,
As she closed the door behind her.

Vincent stood up but his legs instantly gave way,
Luma caught him the best she could & helped him
back on the chair,
"Wow, there's something about that whole process
that really takes it out of me" he says, trying to
regain his composure.
"Luma sweetheart be a dear & help Vincent down
to the dining hall & get him something to eat & I'll
go & inquire with Sapere about these symbols"
Halcyon instructs.
"Can do miss" Luma says,
Putting her arm around Vincent's waist helping him
to the door & as they open it, they see Kayla
standing there with her hand raised as though she
was about to knock.
"Hey, Kayla grab a side, we're gonna get
something to eat" chirped Luma
"What happened to you?" she asks,
Looking at Vincent's less than stellar state.
"I'll fill you in on the way" he says,
As they all pile out of the room.

There is a fresh breeze wafting in through the open
balcony doors of Nyah & Nadaur's cosy abode.
Nadaur is laying on the couch staring off into space
when Nyah comes bouncing through the door, she
barely has time to close it when a knock alerts her
to a visitor, it is one of The Regents little minions.
"Yes?' she says,
Not wanting her pleasant mood to be spoilt by a
visit to The Regent,

"I've been asked to relay a request to you from my
lord, miss Nyah" said the snivelling little creature,
Holding a sealed envelope out in front of him.
Nyah takes the correspondence & immediately
closes the door, she stands in the little alcove by
the door debating whether to open the letter or just
toss it in the bin, when she is startled enough that
she leaps into the air by a voice.
"Who was that?"
"Holy shit, you scared the crap out of me Nadaur, I
didn't see you there!" she yells
"I'm sorry my love" he replies,
Trying to hold back the laughter but failing.
"So, who was it?"
"Oh, it was one of The Regents little helpers
delivering this" she says,
Tossing the letter to him.
Nadaur looks at the fancy envelope complete with a
wax seal & The Regents crest pressed into it.
"He's such a show pony" he says,
Tearing the end of the letter to retrieve the
contents.
He quickly scans the letter,
"Ah ok, he wants you to pick up a very urgent
package from the marketplace"
Nyah groaned,
"Oh, I don't know why he can't have one of his
lackeys do it or his lay about son"
"It says here that it's of the most vital importance,
how about I go with you, I'm not doing anything & to
tell you the truth a little trip to the market might be a
bit of fun"

Nyah rolls her eyes, Nadaur jumps up & over the
couch coming up to her & giving her a cuddle,
"I'll buy you a fairy cake" he says,
Giving her a little kiss.
A little smile starts in the corners of her mouth,
"That's not fair, you know all my weaknesses" she
says,
Returning his kiss.
"All right let's go" she says begrudgingly,
In a slightly lacklustre fashion & they exit arm in
arm.

In a dank little corner of the upper levels of the city,
Stinal & his brother plot their plans for the
mysterious seeds & wonder about their origins.
"Do you think he stole them?" Urchon asks,
"It's not out of the realms of possibility, I mean he
does have access to the high falutin folk, but
there's something about them that seems different
to his normal scams & thievery" Stinal suggests.
"What should we do with them when we get them?
Urchon asks.
"I've been thinking about that, from what we saw
we know that they give the user a massive hike in
strength & speed but it's only for a limited time &
once it's gone you're pretty much screwed for the
foreseeable future without another dose I'm
assuming.
So, what we can do with them will be restricted by
the amount that there are to steal, but something
I've been thinking about is the fights put on by the
goblins.

If we work it right, we can make a tidy sum, I mean
the purse alone on one of their main events could
be enough to get you & me a nice little place on the
middle levels, not to mention the betting side &
most of those fights only last a few minutes if that
anyway" Stinal muses.
"Yeah, but brother they are a fight to the death,
what if something goes wrong, not to mention if the
goblins even think we're cheating they'll gut us &
feed us to their hounds" Urchon says, shaking his
head.
"Well, brother we've been working for Cocker for
eight years now & we're no better off than when we
started, if we are ever gonna get ahead in this
world it's looking like were going to have to do it
ourselves & this is the first real opportunity we've
had, so I'm going to take it & dear brother I'm taking
you with me, even if I have to drag you kicking &
screaming"
"No, no I'm in brother I'm just worried we're getting
in over our heads" Urchon says.
"It's sink or swim time brother" Stinal says,
Putting his hands on his brother's shoulders.

The market is busy this evening, the little stalls built
into the walls one on top of another with makeshift
stairways climbing up to the multiple layers of
catwalks that crisscross the sky.
The open air is filled with the scents of the
businesses that have been corralled into sections.
Right by the entrance are the little stalls selling
knick knacks & souvenirs of the city, mostly of poor

quality. The shopkeepers are loud and always trying to swindle the unaware, most of the inhabitants of the city know to walk through this section quickly, not only to avoid the annoyance of having to deal with these shopkeepers, but there are also a lot of sprite pick pockets that will pick your pockets & fly up into the catwalks where it is pretty much impossible to catch them.
The centre of the market is where the smells become much more inviting with all manner of food, beverages & a wide assortment of sweet treats. Followed by where the necessities of life in the city are found, if you require anything to adorn your home or yourself you can find it here, this is where the majority of the patrons end their excursions, but there are many businesses tucked away in the dark alleyways at the back of the market, which many an elicit item can be procured, but many who enter there on a whim are not likely to find their way out in one piece.
Cocker strides past the food stalls stealing a piece of fruit as he walks, he is focused on his task & is oblivious to the shopkeepers attempts to corral & entice him to enter or check out their wares. His goal is at the back of the market, a place where his presence is well known & he can command an effective amount of respect.
At the other end of the market Nadaur & Nyah stroll through the large doors, the sights & sounds of the market put an instant smile on Nyah's face as she looks around at the many wonders on show.
Nadaur sees the happiness it gives her which in

turn puts a smile on his face. She takes his hand &
they walk into the market. Nyah pulls on Nadaur's
arm making a Beeline for her favourite area, the
central shopping district, she adores finding little
trinkets to decorate their home. Brightly coloured
pots to house her huge collection of plants that she
brings home from the boundaries of the city or
some lovey fabric that has been sourced from
some far off place.
"Ah miss Nyah, we have some real treasures in
today"
A little voice calls from a side street,
Causing Nyah to light up, turning down the street
pulling Nadaur as she goes.
The front of the store is covered in every manner of
vessel you could house a plant in, many
repurposed everyday objects that have been
discarded that have found a new reason for being.
A little woman barley up to their waists wearing
clothes patched together from off cuts & scraps
fashioned into a kaleidoscope of colours,
"Hello Miko" Nyah says with a smile,
"Hello Nyah my dear" the tiny woman replies,
In a gruff voice,
"What are we after today?"
"I was just given a very thoughtful gift by my
mother, four death blossom seeds & I was
wondering if you could help me with some tips with
how to grow them?"
"Ah, yes that was very nice of your mother. The
death blossoms are incredibly hard to procure, in

fact I've only ever had one seed in my many years
of working around the botanical arts"
"Yeah, I asked Halcyon about them too & her
response was pretty much the same"
"Yes, I'm not surprised, on that note would you let
her know that her wandering willow cuttings have
arrived?"
"Of course," Nyah replied
"Now, from what I can recall the death blossoms
require a living pot to survive" Miko says,
Her eye's already searching her shelves.
"A living pot?" asks Nadaur
"Yes, young man, a living pot. It is a very rare style
of ceramic that is created by the woodland pixies,
they infuse the clay with elements of the living
moss that continues to grow along with the plant
that is placed within, some plants like the death
blossoms require this special type of vessel
because they will actively drain the life from the
moss augmenting the nutrients in the soil to fuel the
plant" Miko explained,
"And as luck would have it, I do have a few friends
within the pixie community, it might take me a few
days but I would be happy to acquire some for you"
she offers.
"Well, I'll tell you what, if you can organise that for
me, once I've got one growing, I'd be happy to
bring you a cutting for you to attempt to grow a
mother plant" suggests Nyah,
"Oh, that would be brilliant, thank you so much. I'll
send word when I've got those for you" says Miko,
holding Nyah's hand in appreciation

"For now, I'll just take a few of your beautiful
hanging trellis pots of our balcony…& a couple of
those super cute little ones for my book shelf"
As Nyah paid, she asked,
"Can you just hold on to them for me & I'll pick them
up later? I've got other business to attend to first?"
"No worries my love, whenever you're ready"
Nyah bent down, giving the tiny woman a kiss on
the cheek before walking out arm in arm with
Nadaur.

Walking through the back of the market was not for
the faint of heart, it was not just the content of the
stores that was murky but the content of the minds
of the inhabitants, it was a decidedly unfriendly
place. Cocker knew enough to walk with purpose,
this was not a place for dillydallying. Eyes followed
his movements with dark intent. Cocker's mind was
set on a specific type of dagger that might aid Tallie
in her fight against the Alimana.
The glass on the storefront is obscured by the
darkness that seems to cloak the whole area. The
path, only lit by gas lamps that line the street which
many have been extinguished or disabled by those
that would much rather conduct their activities in
the shadows. Cocker pushes the stores door open
with a loud creak that serves as much to alert the
owner of a customer as anything else. As Cocker
approached the counter a tall slim man rises from
his black leather chair behind the chipped &
cracked wooden counter.

"Young master Cocker, how may I be of
assistance?" he inquires,
The words fall from his mouth in hushed tones that
always send shivers down Cocker's spine each
time they interact.
"I am after a blade infused with venom of the gloom
spider" he announces,
In his most confident tone.
The man behind the counter stands frozen, his tiny
eyes intensely focused on Cocker's eyes for a
moment, then he asks,
"Hmm, trouble with the Alimana have you?"
His eyes locked on Cocker's, a pinpoint of white
light at their centre that begins to brighten as his
interest is heightened.
"It is just a gift for a friend" Cocker replies,
Trying to control the situation but the confidence
becoming less apparent in his voice as the
interaction continues.
The off putting shopkeeper tucks a few strands of
his long black hair behind his pointed ear as he
turns around maintaining eye contact till the very
last moment then disappearing behind a flowing
black curtain into a back room without speaking a
word.
Cocker stands alone in the foreboding environment,
he is constantly hearing little noises behind him but
when he turns, he cannot determine their cause.
His eyes search the shadows of the shelves
investigating the many strange items that make up
the merchandise of the eerie store.

Cocker turns his attention back to the counter to
see the man is already standing there staring at his
with those blinkless eyes, Cocker attempts to hide
his fright but as he is in the process of regaining his
composure the man slams a dagger into the wood
of the counter, the loud bang causes Cocker to
jump,
"I believe this will intrigue the young lady" the man
whispers,
Cocker was quite alarmed by this having not told
the man whom the gift was for, but he pressed on
as he wanted the encounter over as quickly as
possible, he extended his hand to remove the
dagger from the wood,
"Careful, the venom is exceedingly potent, a small
slice will debilitate most beings rendering them
paralysed, but its effects on the Alimana is far more
pronounced. The longer the blade is inserted under
the skin the more pervasive its effects will be, to the
point where if the blade is plunged into one for
merely a moment too long, they will become a
prisoner inside their own body unable to move not
even a twitch until their demise, which will be after
a long and severely painful torment of years" The
man says,
With a pleasure that reinforces what gives him joy.
Cocker retracts his hand, now rethinking his
purchase. With his eyes still fixed on Cocker the
sinister man took hold of the black bone handle of
the dagger prying it from the counter & sliding it into
a shiny black sheath & placing it back gently onto

the wooden counter, sliding it towards Cocker with
his long thin fingers.
Cocker put his hand into his pocket retrieving a
small leather pouch, he tips the contents onto his
hand, a myriad of beautiful sparkling stones. The
eyes of the man shone brighter than ever as he
leant forward over the counter until he was
unsettlingly close to Cockers face, he extended his
thin boney fingers picking one singular stone from
Cockers palm with his long jagged nails,
"This will suffice" he whispered,
In Cocker's ear, then slowly recoiling back behind
the counter.
Cocker grabbed the dagger & moved quickly to the
door, but just as he had opened it the man's voice
sailed across the room,
"Have a lovely day"
Cocker looked back but all he could see was the
man's eyes shining in the dark.

The smell of the old leather filled Sapere's nose, it
was a smell he'd begun to crave over the years if it
was absent in his life for more than a few days.
He knew his old friend Brodrick was one for making
the search for knowledge a challenge, he believed
that knowledge should be freely available but some
knowledge shouldn't be stumbled on by mistake.
His volumes always had a trick to them &
sometimes more than one.
Sapere looked down at the beautiful but weathered
book on top of his table, blowing on the gem
fastened within the lamp & bending it over his work

space to illuminate it, as he did his eyes caught a glint within the gold leaf of the stars that decorated the books cover. He sat back to take in the covers art as a whole to try to discern his friends first challenge.

The image on the front of the book was of a starry sky over a calm sea, Brodrick often used to illustrate his volumes with the memories that most affected him from his travels, not necessarily ones that had any correlation with the contents of the book.

Sapere opened the large book, the spine creaked & cracked as it had been in its hiding place for many, many years. He looked over the pages & it became apparent that the books contents made little sense, the words had been jumbled into a word soup,

"Ah Brodrick" he thought,

With a wry little smile. He knew of his friends' little tricks & that if he focused & took his time, he could discover the solution. Sapere closed the book again, he remembered how the stars on the cover stood out to him. He pulled the lamp closer & he noticed that not only did the stars twinkle in the light but there were iridescent particles laid into the water that when he moved his head the water seemed to rise & fall. Sapere sat there moving his head from side to side trying to catch the tail of his friends thought, when it struck him that the main factor of the cover art was reflection. His eyes danced over the beautiful vista searching for something that was out of place, then he shouted "Of course, the stars!"

The night sky was full of beautiful golden stars some mere pin pricks but there were a few much larger than the rest. Sapere counted, there were eight in all that stood apart from the others, he placed his finger on one furthest to the left & as he touched it, he could feel a slight electric pulse travelling up his arm. Using the tip of his finger he guided the star down to where its respective reflection would reside in the water & to his amazement the stars reflection did in fact follow his finger, but when he released his pressure, the star resumed its regular place at the top of the image.
"Hmm" Sapere thought,
Sitting back in his chair.
"Maybe there is some kind of pattern or sequence" he mumbled to himself,
But then he thought about what his old friend had said,
"That a lock should be just enough to discourage those who need not enter"
He leaned forward placing one finger on each of the eight stars, now the combined pulse was bordering on painful & as Sapere dragged the stars down the leather he could feel that there was a lot more resistance, again his friends' words echoed in his head,
"Some knowledge should take work to obtain"
Sapere braced his legs against his old leather chair & continued to drag the stars into place, just as his pinky fingers were about to give out the stars snapped into place. The image of a night sky over the ocean turned to a beautiful daytime visage of

the same scene. The night sky full of stars was replaced with a beautiful blue sky scattered with clouds that seemed to stretch far into the distance drawing him in. The stars had been replaced by lovely white gulls that danced on the breeze in an enticing illusion.

Sapere stared into the horizon, he noticed a small mark on the sea, he reached into his pocket taking out a piece of leather that housed a small lens placing it over the intriguing mark. A smile filled his face, the insignificant little smudged that would be overlooked by most was his friend Brodrick sailing in his small boat on his way to another adventure. Sapere opened the book, now seeing that not only had the words rearranged but each page had an intricate painting that boarded every one, it was filled with plants & animals from far off lands that spilled out onto the sides of the book that when the book was closed created an image of a lush landscape filled with life & colour.

<u>Chapter 14</u>

The day was almost over, Kaya was standing in the grass outside Halcyons botanical sanctuary moving around practising the movements that Nyah & Tallie had taught her, when an out of breath & clearly panicked Luma came rushing out of the archway.
"You haven't seen Rava have you?" she asked,
Trying to hide the tears in her eyes,
"No, not in a few days" she answered.
"He will usually spend the odd night out near forest to reconnect with his natural side but he's always back the next morning & it's been two days" Luma said,
With a worried look.
"Ok, we'll go & have a look around for him & we'll find Vincent along the way to help" Kayla replied,
Giving Luma a hug.
They ran off down the hallway passing Otto's surgery when they heard a familiar voice,
"Hey there missy"
The two turned around looking in through the door & upon seeing Rava laid out on the bed Luma & Kayla rushed in,
"What the hell happened to you?" Luma asked,
Her panic replaced with curiosity,
Looking at his one side all covered in bandages,
"He received a very serious burn" Announced Otto,

From behind them,
"But the obstinate young man refuses to tell me the source of the injury, even though it impedes my ability to properly treat him in a timely manner" Otto continued,
Grumpily shuffling around.
Luma & Kalya held their injured friend by the hand, Luma peaked over her shoulder checking to see that Otto had returned to his back office.
"What the hell happened to you?" she forcefully whispered.
"I was just trying to do a little recon on the tunnels when I stumbled across The Regent, he's got something stashed down there that is like pure light that burns as soon as it comes in contact with your skin" Rava explained,
Contorting his face as the memory of the pain washes over him.
"It was like the door was holding it back, but as soon as it breached that barrier it was unstoppable, it filled up every ounce of space until there was no darkness to be found"
Luma examined the damage done to her friend's skin,
"How was The Regent not affected?" she asked,
Playing with Ravas bandages.
"He had this whole little outfit by the door for protection that covered his entire body" Rava said.
"But you're alright?" Luma asked,
"Yes, yes according to Otto if I'd been exposed to the energy for a moment longer, I could've been

blinded permanently, not to mention the damage to
my skin, but yes Luma I'll be ok"
Luma then punched him surprisingly hard in the
arm,
"Don't scare me like that you big idiot"
"I think we should tell Nyah about this, she'll know
what to do & I don't think she'll get as furious as
Halcyon would that we didn't tell them immediately.
How long do you have to say here?" Luma asked
"About another week or so Otto said"
"Ok you rest up & we'll go tell Nyah about what we
found out" Luma says.
"Oh, Luma…!" Rava begins
"Yes, Rava I'll bring you some of my chocolate puff
cereal" she quickly answers,
"You know me so well"
Luma gives him a little kiss on the cheek then they
run from the surgery.
Otto had overheard enough that he looked up from
his desk in the back with a concern on his face.

The loud footsteps of Cocker echo against the
stone walls as he moves quickly toward his den
carrying the newly acquired blade wrapped in a
black shroud. He rounded the corner & almost
bumped straight into Stinal & his brother coming
the other way,
"What are you two up too?" he asked,
Still being in a good mood which totally threw off
the brothers. Stinal paused attempting to concoct a
believable lie but he decided to use a little truth
instead,

"We were just coming to find you, we've heard
some interesting news about Tallie's trial with the
Alimana"
Cockers' eyes widened,
"Follow me" he commanded,
& started walking quickly towards his den with the
brothers in tow, Urchon pulling at his brother's
sleeve to ask him what was the plan, but he was
shrugged off.
No sooner had the door closed Cocker grabbed
Stinal by the collar,
"What did you hear?"
"We heard from one of our sources, that the
Alimana intend to kill Sikes & take Tallie hostage to
try to force Nyah to use her influence over her
mother to repeal their banishment from all of The
Regent run cities"
Cocker released Stinal & began pacing across the
room,
"Going into their areas without a solid plan would
be suicide" says Urchon,
Prompting a fierce look from his brother.
Cocker returns to where the two brothers are
standing placing his hands on each of their
shoulders walking them to the door.
"Thank you for this information, I'll look into it" he
said calmly,
Ushering them out & closing the door behind them.
Stinal turns to his brother as they walk away,
"You have to learn when to keep quiet, Cocker isn't
stupid, in fact far from it, if he even gets the
slightest inkling that we're working for our own

purposes it won't be some big thing, we'll just disappear & no one will even notice".

Halcyon looks at the small crystal lens that lay on her table, then across to the much larger mysterious box that has taken up residence on her work bench. Holding the smooth lens in her hand she opens the box seeing that there is a carved inset in the side of the box that seems to be the exact size & shape of the lens, she slips it into place,
"Hmm, I wonder what the rest of this space is for?" she thought,
Looking at the base of the box there was two cut out sections, one wide, cut deep into the obsidian the other a raised section to the left, she runs her fingers around the smooth surface searching for some kind of hidden clue but finding nothing, finally she thinks,
"I have to inquire about these symbols with Sapere".
Halcyon closes the box & begins to walk from the room when she stops, turning around & removing the lens from the box,
"Where shall we hide you?" She says,
Looking around the room,
Spotting a stack of pots on a high shelf she places the lens in the top pot out of sight.
"Best not to leave things like that together" she says,
As she closes the door behind her.

Without a plan, Cocker knew that his best hope to assist Tallie was to get her the dagger & warn her of the intended deception of the Alimana. He had searched the city but to no avail deciding that she would no doubt need to retrieve some weaponry from her chest in the barracks, he made the choice to leave the gloom spider infused blade with a small signatureless note on top of her chest wrapped in the black shroud, he did not want to leave such a perilous tool without some sort of warning of its dangers.

A loud knock breaks Sapere's concentration, nearly sending him tumbling from his chair, he has been enthralled pawing over the immense amount of knowledge his friend had put into this hidden volume but none of it seems to be in any particular order, he knew Brodrick was never the most linear of thinkers but the lack of organisation was frustrating Sapere to put it mildly.
"Come in!" he shouted,
His lack of patience becoming audible,
Rubbing his eyes under his thick glasses,
"Is there any way to greet a guest?" asks Halcyon playfully,
Sapere releasing her attempt at levity replied,
"Sorry, Broadrick's scattered thoughts are doing my head in"
"Well, maybe this can be a welcome distraction" she said,
Placing Vincent's drawing on top of the book.
"Where did these come from?" Sapere inquired,

Putting one pair of glasses away only to fish
another from his pocket at the end of a chain,
"When I exposed Vincent to the Obsidian box again
his trance took hold & he was able to make a
rendering of hidden images that adorn the box"
Halcyon explained.
"Really? how fascinating," Sapere said,
Examining the drawings closely.
"Luma thought they looked like one of the ancient
crests of the high families"
"Yes, there is something decidedly familiar about
them" Sapere said,
Jumping down from his chair disappearing off into a
back room, still looking down at the page.
"There were many ancient houses & families that
were purposely removed from the records for
imagined slights at the powers that be & others for
more nefarious reasons" Sapere yelled,
From the back room over the rummaging noises.
Halcyon starts being noisy, looking through the
papers strewn about Sapere's desk until she is
startled by an exclamation from the back room,
"Ah Ha!"
Sapere emerged from the poorly lit room shaking
the dust & cobwebs from his scraggly hair.
"You might have been right about the dust in here, I
might need to enlist an assistant to tidy up around
here" he said,
As a spider ran across his shoulders.
Sapere climbed the small set of stairs that he had
next to his chair, setting the large leather bound

book on the table with a thud that sent more dust flying causing Halcyon to sneeze repeatedly.
"Now this is a volume that was passed down to me by the private genealogist of an ancient royal family that was wiped out many years ago, she knew that the dissolution of the royal family in favour of a council system would mean that most of knowledge accumulated by the crown was in danger of falling into private hands or worse still being destroyed & reimagined by whom ever found themselves in power. So, she took what she could get her hands on & distributed it to a chosen few that she knew to be trustworthy" Sapere explained.
"Hmm, let me see those drawings again"
Halcyon passed the paper to Sapere who held it up to the light,
"This sun motif is somewhat familiar, but it is also quite a common addition to a family crest, but this black wave is unlike anything I've come across before" Sapere said,
Flipping through the pages of the book.
"Here we go, we might have a little better luck here. This is the section devoted to conflicts between houses"
As he turned the page a beautifully illustrated version of the sun & sword which filled the entire page.
"That's it!" yelled Halcyon.
"Yes, but it's not a sun but a fallen star & according to this the sword represents..." Sapere pauses,
Running his lens over the words,
"The protectors of the light"

"Fascinating" says Halcyon,
Looking over his shoulder.
"Does it mention anything about a feud or an
enemy?"
Sapere ran his finger along the lines of text, until
the look on his face became more serious,
"It appears that they were charged with the
protection of the royals from those who dwell in the
shadows. Their ability to safely maintain the fallen
stars was one of the only defences against their
encroachment into our realm, it also makes
reference to a deal once struck with the corrupt, but
it doesn't go into any more detail" he says,
Sitting back in his chair pondering their discovery.
"Well at least that's something to go on" Adds
Halcyon optimistically.
"Yes & it also ties into that depiction in that portrait
over there of a meeting between the shadow
dwellers & another group who could have been
parts of the royal families" Sapere concludes.
"I'll look further into this, while you go & see if there
are any more secrets to be uncovered within that
box"
"There was something that I noticed" says Halcyon,
"When the box was left for me all it contained was
the lens, but the interior has places designed to
hold two other things, what they are I know not"
"Hmm, very interesting, if you can get a sample of
the material of the box maybe its composition can
shed some light, pardon the pun on its origin &
better still its purpose"

"That is what I was thinking. I've obtained a dagger
that is supposed to be strong enough to take a
sample & Little Luma has family ties to some of the
best artisans when it comes to the manipulation of
rare materials" Halcyon explains.
Sapere climbs down from his chair disappearing
into the shelves of books,
"Keep me in the loop" he calls back,
To Halcyon, who takes one last look at the image
on the page before leaving.

The warm sun shines down on the Highaster tree,
Luma, Kayla & Vincent lay on the grass watching
the wind dance through the leaves. They listen to
the lovely relaxing sound like the crashing of waves
on a distant shore, until their serenity is broken by,
"Hey you three!"
Luma looks up, her eyes still affected by the bright
sun she blinks & squints to see who it is.
"You know that's not the best for your eyes" says
Nyah,
Luma gets a silly grin on her face, Kayla jumps up,
"Hi, Nyah" she says,
Walking toward her trying her best not to trip as she
does.
"I thought you might like to watch some expert
training, Tallie, Sikes, Faucon & Dabn are getting
ready for their trial with the Alimana" suggests Nyah
"What's an Alimana?" asks Kayla
"Ooo they're a nasty stinky group of individuals"
Luma Butts in,

With a cute little scowl on her face that just serves
to make Nyah smile, finding it adorable rather than
any kind of intimidating.
"To put it simply they're involved in all things illicit,
it's best all of you stay far away from them"
instructs Nyah.
Luma speeds up to be walking right next to Nyah,
"Are Tallie & Sikes in some kind of trouble?" she
asks.
"They aren't in a great position, but they are both
on their own quite formidable & together…, Well I
wouldn't want to be their opposition" she says,
Putting her arms around Luma & Kayla as they
pass through the arch.
The large training room has been separated by
thick stone tablets that jut from the floor & walls.
"It's a bit of a tight squeeze" says Sikes,
Forcing his way through one of the gaps,
"That's kinda the point big fella" says Tallie
"Those Alimana are such treacherous little
bastards, they will use every opportunity to their
advantage, especially since in a fair fight they
would have little to no chance"
Faucon pops her head over one of the high
petitions,
"And there is no guarantee that your trial will look
anything like this, this is just the closest
representation of one that I've heard has been used
before" she says.
Dabn seated against the wall stands up,
"I don't know why you're even entertaining this
whole situation. You know they are never going to

fight fair & let's just say we win to a point that it is
impossible for them to argue, What kind of
guarantee do we have that they won't just turn
around & stab us in the back?"
Tallie walks across to him,
"Come on big guy, I know you hate them but if we
can get even a flimsy agreement with them it's
worth the effort, since they have such a presence in
the other realms, they could make it very difficult for
us to do our jobs, such as they are"
"I mean I certainly don't want those sneaky pricks
jumping out at me everywhere I go trying to stab
me" says Sikes,
"Those little knives that they carry really hurt, not to
mention how filthy they keep them on purpose to
cause as nasty an infection on every cut"
"That is a pretty good point, Sikes" Dabn admits,
Begrudgingly.
"All right let's get started" Tallie orders
"Oh good, we didn't miss anything" Nyah says,
Walking in with Luma, Kayla & Vincent.
"I brought these youngins along to watch how some
real warriors train, if you don't mind that is"
Tallie answers her with a little wink.
"Ok, you can just sit up there on the balcony,
unless you wanna join in, that is?" she said
cheekily,
Nyah returns her a little wink & leads the others up
some stairs to a platform that overlooks the training
area.
Luma runs to the edge sitting down dangling her
legs off in the air,

"I'll never get use to how comfortable you all are
with heights" Vincent says,
Sitting down as far back from the edge as he can
while still being able to see.
Kayla & Nyah sit down on either side of Luma.
"So, what are they gonna do?" Kayla asks,
Nyah puts her fingers in her mouth letting out a
piercing whistle,
"Ok, Dabn & Faucon opposite end, you two will be
our dastardly Alimana"
Dabn grumbles,
"I know Dabn, but it's just for the exercise, humour
me ok"
"Only cuz it's you" he says with a grin.
"& Tallie, you & Sikes have one goal for this first
run, just make it to the other side without being
grabbed, if you're grabbed the Alimana will swam &
you will lose" Nyah instructs.
Tallie gets set against the wall with a fairly terrifying
look on her face, with Sikes right next to her, He
leans down & whispers something to her & she
responds with a nod.
Nyah turns to Kayla,
"You wanna do the honours?"
Kayla nods nervously,
"Ready, Set, GO!" she yells,
Sikes takes off with surprising agility & speed for
such a big monster, Dabn cautiously enters the
maze as Faucon skilfully climbs up one of the
higher panels to get a better vantage point.
Tallie waits for a moment then chargers forward
leaping into the air & placing one foot out which

Sikes catches in his mighty paw & with a little flick he sends her sailing through the air in a beautiful spiral prompting an audible gasp from Luma,
"She's amazing" she says to Kayla.
Tallie lands hands first on one of the narrow beams, then executing a perfect handspring landing in a crouched position looking straight at Faucon whom she spotted as she was in flight. With a little grin on both sides, they take off at a staggering pace. Their feet skipping across the narrow tops of the maze. As Tallie closes the distance she looks down seeing Dabn closing on Sikes, she flips off one foot & while she's upside down she lets out a high pitched whistle that causes him to look up just as Skies rounds the corner at full speed completely bowling him over & leaving him in a heap in the corner.
Tallie lands not five feet from Faucon who takes a step then dives forward to grab her but she pivots flipping backward & blindly, but perfectly places one hand on her head as she passes beneath her propelling herself through the air landing in a seated position above Sikes at the other end.
Kayla & Luma let out a loud cheer,
"Wooo hoooo!"
"Go Sikey" says Kayla,
"You're Amazing Tallie" Luma shrieks.
Nyah gives a round of applause,
"Great work, it's obvious your agility is on point, now how about we switch to some close quarters combat?"

Nyah jumps down from the high viewing platform without a second thought, casually walking over to a group of levers on the wall.
Nyah pulls the top lever causing all of the walls causing the maze to withdraw into the floor & walls, then with a pull of a second a hexagon emerges from the floor.
"Who's first?" Nyah asked,
"Well, you look like you could use a little exercise" Tallie proposes,
With a smile Nyah took off her jacket revealing her muscular arms & shoulders, tossing it up to Luma who immediately put it on & hopped over the fence of the arena.
Tallie cracked her neck rather loudly & joined her,
"Let's see what you've got" Nyah said,
With a smile that fell away to a much more serious expression.
Tallie just stared back at her with her trademark scowl, Nyah called up to Luma,
"Give us a three count Luma"
To which Luma jumped up, taking it very seriously,
"Ready ladies, One, two… Three!" she cried,
The two hardened warriors approached each other with caution, each well aware of the other's skill.
Nyah could tell from the look in Tallie's eyes that she was finally taking the threat posed by the Alimana as seriously as it deserved, both women had been through many battles yet the untrustworthy nature of the Alimana made this more of an unknown challenge.

Tallie tested Nyah's reactions with a few quick strikes, changing levels as she did.
Nyah expertly blocking the first few then ending with a counter that barely missed Tallie as she flipped backwards out of reach. The mood had become much more intense in the room, Luma sat close to Kayla holding her hand tightly in shocked silence which was incredibly rare for her.
Tallie again began her assault this time with a series of well placed kicks changing levels from low to high the final strike held such force that Nyah was knocked off balance but quickly regained her footing. Nyah knew Tallie needed her abilities challenged but also did not wish to affect her confidence before the trial, So she used the unorthodox stance that she had found herself in to propel herself forward off the side of the arena grabbing Tallie around the waist taking her down to the ground.
Tallie, having been raised as a warrior since childhood, pivoted instinctively, ending up on top of Nyah. Nyah's skills coming from a more natural place put her feet on Tallie's hips restricting her ability to advance the position.
Both had years of skill, training & natural ability,
"This could go on all day" said Dabn,
With a little snark.
Kayla watched fixated on the skill on display in front of her, fidgeting with the bracelet on the wrist, wondering if she would become something akin to these two impressive specimens.

Nyah twisted in the wrong direction for less than a
second, but that was all the opening Tallie required,
rotating around & taking her back slipping her arm
in around her neck as she had done thousands of
times before forcing Nyah to submit,
"You really are a weapon Tallie" Nyah said,
Rubbing her neck.
"That's high praise coming from you, even if you
weren't going all out" she answered,
Giving her a little punch in the shoulder.
Vincent looked over at Luma sitting next to him who
was completely engrossed in the conflict,
"That was pretty impressive" he said
"Pretty?" she replied
"I don't think I breathed for the last few minutes"
"Well, it looks like you're in incredible fighting form
& I have no doubts you'll both be victorious" Nyah
praised,
"I'm going to go & find Nadaur & get something to
eat, I'll catch up with you later" Nyah says Jumping
over the rail,
"Hey Luma" she calls,
Looking up to see her practising her fighting
manoeuvres on Kayla,
"Huh?" she replied
"My Jacket"
"Oh yes, sorry" she said,
Taking it off & tossing it down to Nyah who caught it
as she left, Luma going bright red in the process.
"I'm gonna check my weaponry, just to make sure
everything is nice & sharp" Tallie said.
"We'll come to" said Dabn & Faucon

"Yes, I need to restring my bow if I'm going to cover
you from a height"
"Ok then I guess that just leaves us, you guys
wanna go get a little snack?" Sikes asks the young
trio,
"Yes please" smiles Luma,
Jumping off the high platform & being caught by
Sikes huge hairy arm.
Vincent & Kayla climbed down & they all set off
down the hallway.

Cocker paced around his dark dwelling trying to
come up with a solution, he wanted to be of
assistance to Tallie but he knew he would never get
anywhere near the Alimanas court while the trial
was in process, finally he stopped dead looking
around the room,
"Are you there? He asked,
Waiting for a reply but none was forthcoming.
"Please, if you're there I need your help"
Again, he waited but to no avail. Eventually he
walked over to his safe pressing the stones to
trigger the mechanism, he stood there holding the
powerful seeds in his hands & then he heard,
"Were you seeking our assistance?"
That distinct haunting voice that sent shivers down
his spine echoed in his head, he quickly tossed the
seeds back in the safe, closing the door, his eyes
searched the room for the telltale shadow until he
saw it undulating in the corner of the room.
"Yes, I need to get somewhere that is restricted & I
need to remain hidden" he asked

"Ah this is an easy task," said the voice.
"I also need something to help with the side effects
of those seeds" Cocker added.
"Now that is more costly, the potions from my world
are not to be shared lightly with outsiders, the price
may be too high"
"I'll pay whatever you require, can you help?"
The slender pale fingers began to emerge from the
shadow,
"Bring me your hand" the voice commanded,
Cocker reached up to shake the menacing hand
but instead with a lighting fast slice of its razor
sharp talons Galbaial opened his palm, Cocker
cried in shock as the wound was inflicted so quickly
there was no pain. His blood finally made it to the
surface spilling out onto the floor.
"What was that!" he yelled,
"Words & gestures are not a binding agreement, we
require the promise of flesh & blood to seal our
bargain for the blood can carry not only your
lineage but a debt or a promise though time"
The hand disappears back into the darkness &
emergers holding a small vial crafted from bone,
"You must fill this to show your willingness to
comply. Remember, this is stronger than your word,
this will be attached to a part of you until you fulfil
your part of the bargain"
Cocker took the vial, snatching it quickly not being
a stupid individual, he held it under the free flowing
blood that ran from his hand filling the vile until the
blood spilled over the sides then he handed it back

to the disembodied hand that protruded from the
shadows.
"The deal is struck" Galbaial's voice announced,
As its arm retracted into the abyss.
Cocker stood there for a moment, just as he was
about to inquire about their side of the bargain the
hand emerged in a fist, Cocker stepped closer as
the hand rotated & began to open, in the centre of
the large but slender hands pale palm was a
whistle that although it looked like metal its surface
moves & changed with the light as if it was opposed
to the very presence of it. Cocker reached out to
take the curious item & as his fingers touched the
cold skin of the stranger he began to speak which
startled Cocker & made him jump,
"This is the silent scream, blow into it three times &
it will summon me to your presence & I will escort
you to your desired location, but after the fourth use
it will become toxic & I warn you not to use it a fifth
time lest it sap the life from your very bones"
Cocker stared at the strange item in his hand lost in
the hypnotic swirls that made up its form, he was
not paying attention when the hand slid from the
darkness again stopping mire inches from his face,
when he finally noticed the proximity made him fall
backwards onto the floor,
"I envy you your fear, the burst you feel that drives
you to have such extreme reactions" the voice
poured from the darkness.
"It does not feel nice" Cocker said,
Getting back to his feet,

"Things extreme in nature can be most pleasurable,
it just requires the correct palette to understand the
sensations" Explained Galbaial.
His hand turned over & somehow standing in the
very centre of his palm defying gravity was a bottle
of viscus red liquid that escaped from the top
turning to vapour on contact with the air even
though the top looked tightly sealed with a black
substance that ran down the sides of the bottle into
hardened drops.
"What is it?" Cocker asked,
Looking closely at the mysterious substance,
"This is the Lacks taper, all you have to do is place
a few drops on your tongue at the same moment as
one of the seeds I gifted you & their effects will be
greatly improved, yet as with any gift of this nature
there is a price that must be paid, for each time you
partake in their advancement you will suffer a
decline in your final years"
Galbaial relays the foreboding warning.
"What does that mean?" asks Cocker,
With a worried look.
"It is different for all inhabitants of the realms
outside our own, just know the effects will advance
more the more you indulge"
Galbaial voice trails off into the distance,
Cocker looks up he sees that the shadow has
receded back into nothingness.

The sleepless nights have begun to take their toll
on Sapere, he relaxes back in his chair rubbing his
tired eyes, he has been trying to make some sense

of his friend Brodick's writings for three days &
nights but the jumbled nature is making it much
more difficult. Searching for hidden knowledge is
hard enough without having to wade through his
friends chaotic writing style. He takes off his
glasses & tosses them onto the page & just as he is
about to turn in for the night, he notices that the
word shadow is framed & magnified by his glasses,
putting his glasses back on to examine the excerpt,
"The course was laid for the meeting to take place
between the Shadow dwellers & the five ruling
families to discuss the potential use of the shadows
as a feasible way of virtually instantaneous travel
without the limitations & negative side effects of
some others" He read
"That tracks with what we know from the portrait"
Sapere thought to himself,
Then as had happened many times before the topic
switched to a hunting party Brodrick took with a
family of ogres to celebrate the changing of the
seasons.
Sapere had a new burst of energy at least now he
knew he was on the right track & that Brodrick did
in fact have some interactions with the whole
mysterious situation.

The chime of the ether rang out in The Regents
chambers, The Regent sat, a worried & angry look
covered his face, the chime which was melodious &
consistent became louder & more pervasive the
more he tried to ignore it, finally he knew he had to
answer, peeling himself out of the grand leather

chair he inhabited shuffling across the room to the altar that held the ether placing his finger in the centre of the pool of liquid to end that horrible chime,

"How dare you keep me waiting" An angry voice scolded,

"Do not let your position on the outskirts give you some false confidence that you are out of my reach" the voice continued.

"I do apologise Grand Regent, I would never want to give you the impression that I did not respect your position & authority, although I do have important things to deal with as you rightly know" The Regent said,

Attempting to hide his disdain.

"That's all very well, but do you even fathom how much having the shadow travel system down has brought our ability for trade to a crawl, you know the other methods of instant travel are not fit for moving large quantities of supplies as they tend to spoil the goods, not to mention our waning influence over some of our outlying areas that we have had to let fend for themselves during this time. Our circle of influence is diminishing & I & the other members of the High Regents court are less than impressed with the action or lack thereof with which you have handled this situation" The High Regent said impatiently.

"I must remind you that I am not the only one to have control over the outcome of this situation, there are four other keepers of the text that will

need to be a part of any feasible outcome"
reminded The Regent.
"You tell me this because why? You think I'm
unaware of the history of the situation we find
ourselves in? Let me remind you that my family
was in attendance at the original meeting all those
years ago.
This is not only about position & power for me, this
is about my family's legacy & I will not let anyone
sully it, either find a way out of this darkness or I
will appoint someone who will" The High Regent
said,
Angrily, severing his connection.
The Regent took a swipe at the glass of wine that
he had sat on the railing sending it crashing in to
wall,
"I will need to move up my time table if I'm going to
retain control of this situation," he said,
As he hurried out the back door of his chambers.

Nyah & Nadaur walk casually up the steps to their
cosy little abode hand in hand,
"I love these afternoon walks we take, it's a great
way to decompress" Nyah says,
With a calm smile.
"It is very relaxing" replies Nadaur,
As they turn the corner to the hallway containing
their apartment, they see the very same Imp
messenger standing at attention in all his finery.
"This can't be good" says Nyah
"Hmm?" questions Nadaur

"My mother hates to use resources wastefully, so
the arrival of another letter that requires a
messenger to hand deliver is a telling sign"
Nadaur let a slight smile slip as he rather enjoyed it
when Nyah had to deal with things that pertain to
her high born status. There is an elegance to it that
he appreciates & admittedly is also amused by.
As soon as they get within speaking distance the
messenger drops to his knee, presenting another
gilded letter to Nyah.
"You may stand" she says,
With a little more authority than usual.
"Is there some kind of problem in the Royal city?"
she asks,
"Forgive me Miss Nyah, but I am not privy to those
details" He replied,
Holding the envelope out in front of him.
Nyah accepts the letter dismissing the nervous
young Imp messenger who disappears down the
stairs. Nyah wastes no time opening the envelope
while Nadaur opens the door.
Nyah walks in, eyes down reading the letter &
Nadaur closes the door behind her.
She sits down on the couch completely focused on
the contents of the letter, Nadaur knowing that she
will fill him in as soon as she finishes, takes two
beautiful crystal glasses from the shelf filling them
with the most sparkling clear water & places one on
the table for Nyah, while he sips his while relaxing
back on the couch.
"I knew it!" Nyah exclaimed,
"That bastard!"

Nadaur leaned forward in anticipation, Nyah saw
him in her peripheral vision.
"Oh, sorry, yes, it's from my mum again, she
wanted to warn me about some troubling news she
had heard about The Regent. She doesn't know too
much, but from what she was able to find out The
Regents high council is somehow involved with the
lockdown of the shadow travel & there has been
more than just the instances of unseen violence
that we knew about, involving much larger groups,
which is what prompted the lockdown in the first
place" Nyah says,
An angry look spreading across her face.
"So does your mum know what roll The Regent is
playing in this whole saga?" Nadaur asks,
Nyah completes scanning through the letter,
"No, but apparently he is very integral part its
resolution" says Nyah,
A little smile forms on her face wiping away the
scowl.
Nadaur looks around at her face as she looks up,
"Oh, my mum just ended the letter asking about if I
liked the death blossom seeds, it's alright I'll write
her back later, right now we need to inform Sapere
& Halcyon about this & see if they have been able
to discover what the hell is going on" says Nyah.

Chapter 15

In a high dark & dank section of the city far
removed for the fresh air of the central living
quarters, Urchon lay sleeping on a mattress on the
floor covered in makeshift blankets sewn together
from scraps of others discarded bedding.
Everything about this place was moist & the
constant dripping of water ate away at the psyche
all that inhabited in this part of the city.
"It happened!" Shouted Stinal,
Startling his brother out of his slumber.
"What?" his brother replied,
Still half asleep.
"Cocker finally used the safe," Stinal said.
"That's great," Urchon yawned.
"But that's not all, it would seem that our boss has
made a new friend" Stinal said,
"What do you mean?" his brother asked,
"That's for later, right now we need to figure out
how to get Cocker out of his chambers so we can
get our hands on those seeds" Stinal says,
Looking around in thought.
"What about Tallie? We could leave a note saying
she wants to meet him somewhere" Urchon
suggests,

"You know what, that's actually a pretty good idea,
see when you use your brain & think you can come
up with good ideas, let's go" says Stinal,
Pushing his brother out of the room.

Halcyon's long robes swept the floor as she moved
through the city on her way to see an old friend who
had just retired to the city after years of travel.
Halcyon was hopeful that she would be able to
shed some light on the ailment that plagued poor
Vincent.
Her friend had taken up residence in one of the
coveted towers that in ancient times were used to
house dangerous criminals, but in recent years
have become fancy tri level apartments with a
balcony that looks out over the entire forest.
Halcyon climbed the stairs carrying a beautiful
example of her botanical prowess as a small
housewarming gift for her old friend.
Her ascent up the narrow spiral staircase was
hampered but the vast number of boxes that lined
the stairs,
"Eyes up below!" a voice bellowed,
As a remarkably large man came down the stairs at
what Halcyon thought was a dangerous pace, she
pressed herself to the wall as best she could as he
passed her by with a,
"Thank ya mam",
Which in & of itself annoyed her as she despised
being called mam.
Finally arriving at the door which was a beautiful
blue, she was just reaching up to use the brass

knocker that hung prominently from the centre of
the door when she heard a familiar voice,
"Just a moment"
& then the door flung open, Calinton immediately
embraced her old friend,
"It's so good to see you, I truly have missed you"
she said warmly,
"I must remove that knocker" she said,
Lifting it up,
"Look what those terrible moving men have done,
they've left great dents in my beautiful blue door"
she said,
With an angry look.
Calinton was a bright sprite of a woman, her mother
was a woodland sprite & her father was an
adventurer & she retained the best parts of both.
She was older than Halcyon by a few years, but
she was as vibrant & athletic as they come, lifting
piles of books out of the way as she led Halcyon
out to the balcony where an ornate little table sat
with three chairs.
"Have a seat my love, can I interest you in a
beverage?" she asked.
"I'd love a cup of tea, if one is going" answered
Halcyon,
Calinton disappeared into the upstairs half kitchen.
"That's lovely, is it for me?" she called,
From the other room,
"Yes, it's a hidden rose, I thought it would bring
back fond memories of your time living in the south"
Halcyon called back.

Calinton returned carrying a large silver tray that had very delicate engraving on it & it looked much too fancy to be just a tea tray, but Calinton disliked too much pomp & ceremony in her mind it's a tray so I'll use it as such.
"That's pretty, where did it come from?" Halcyon asked.
"Oh, it was a reward of sorts for some work I did for a rich family whose land was being invaded by giants & I managed to broker a deal between the two parties…Cake?" Calinton asked,
Changing the topic.
"Yes please" Halcyon said,
Licking her lips, because among Calinton's many careers over the years she worked in the royal kitchen as the pastry chef.
Calinton cut Halcyon a slice of the most delicate cake she had ever seen filled with layers of jam & cream,
"It's been pretty interesting around her of late" Calinton said,
Flashing her friend a knowing look,
"The birds still keeping you informed," said Halcyon.
Calinton replied with a wink,
"Is this a purely social visit or may I be of some assistance?" Calinton asked.
Halcyons brow furrowed,
"I've got a mystery with a young Disin, Vincent is his name, who is plagued by something I've never come across before. He seems to have a second

creature inhabiting his body that he was unaware of & unable to control" Halcyon said.

"Fascinating, does he become this other entity or does it split off from his physical form?" Calinton inquires.

"It splits off leaving him helpless & he is always unaware that anything has transpired" says Halcyon.

"What form does it manifest itself in?" Calinton asks already fascinated.

"It starts with a deep black that takes over his eyes, that black abyss then spreads outward consuming his body until then & only then does it leave his body in the shape of a massive black wolf, but not a regular black it is a hollow black, every moment you look into it, it draws you ever deeper, but it never completely separates there is always a tether connecting the two" Halcyon recounts.

"A black as deep as the ocean & as far reaching as the night sky" Calinton mumbles,
As her gaze drifts into a memory.

"Does it sound familiar?" Halcyon asks,
Leaning closer,

"I will have to do some research, but it bears a striking resemblance to a blood curse that I came across in my youth. Vincent, you said this boy's name was? What family was he hidden from, what was the threat?" Calinton asks,
Becoming more concerned.

"He has no memory of anything to do with our world" Halcyon answers.

Calinton stands from the table,

"I must go & look into something"
She stops, taking her old friend but the hand,
"You must keep him away from the shadows, if I'm
right & I hope I'm not, this could be catastrophic.
Stay safe my love" she says,
Leaving out the door & down the stairs.

Stinal pressed his ear against the wood of Cocker's
chambers, listening closely,
"Can you hear anything?" his brother asked.
"I'm not sure, come over here" Stinal said,
Leading his brother to a corner of to the side, he
took the box containing the Larklen turning towards
the wall,
"Keep a lookout"
He placed the strange little creature over his eye,
his vision being transferred to the one already in
place in Cockers chambers.
Stinal looks around, limited by the viewing angle of
the Larklen, he waits for a moment then just at the
edge of his peripheral he sees Cocker walk behind
the bar,
"He's in there" says Stinal,
Prying the stubborn creature off his face,
"That really does hurt" he admits,
Rubbing his face where the odd little creature has
removed a few layers of skin.
"Have you got the note?" Stinal asks,
Holding out his hand,
"Yes, yes, here it is" says Urchon,
Passing his brother the envelope which they had
stolen from Tallies chest. At the centre of the

envelope is the crossed daggers of Tallies warrior clan who had evolved into a highly regarded political power as they bring a great deal of battle tactics to the table.

Stinal takes the letter & slips it under Cocker's door knocking three times with a firm hand then he & his brother run off down the hall concealing themselves around a corner to make sure Cocker retrieves the note.

After a moment or three Cocker opens the door holding the envelope & looking left & right for whoever left it before retreating back to his chambers.

Cocker held the pristine envelope in his hands staring at the crest at its centre, Cocker immediately recognised the insignia as Tallies, after all he had had lessons on the crests & family regalia of the many houses of his world since he was old enough to understand.

He took a small dagger from the table running the sharp blade under the folded seal cleanly slicing it away & removing the folded letter, upon opening it he found that there was a clean outer sheet that held a second sheet containing the correspondence.

Cocker opened the second sheet seeing that it was only a few lines, but he was not even expecting this so he was not put off but the curtness of the letter. The letter simply stated Tallies appreciation for the assistance he had provided with her Alimana situation as she put it, signed with a simple letter T.

A smile found its way to his face as he reread the
letter a second time before placing it back into the
envelope, he took the letter over to a tall shelf that
had lots of interesting odds & ends curated on it &
placed the letter in between a crystal goblet & a
small figurine of a dragon. Then the thought
occurred to him that he might be able to explain the
uses & the dangers of the gloom spider infused
dagger which he had left for her which sent him
hurrying from the room.
Stinal & Urchon ducked back behind the wall as
Cocker emerged disappearing down the hall in the
opposite direction. Urchon let out a squawk of
excitement which was met with a strike to the back
of the head from his brother,
“We haven't succeeded yet!” he said angrily,
Leading his brother around the corner & back to
Cocker's door.
”Quick & quiet” Stinal instructs,
Looking into his brothers’ eyes waiting for an
acknowledgement. Urchon nods & they enter
Cockers chambers, both brothers make a b-line for
the back wall which holds the painting that conceals
the safe. Stinal stands in front of the portrait with
the Larklens box in his hands taking the creature
from its compartment he places it on his left eye, he
focuses on the point where Cocker opens the safe,
the slightly telepathic nature of the Larklen finds
exactly what he is looking for, keeping his right eye
open he watches Cocker move through the
sequence unlocking the safe finding reference
points on the wall as he watches. After a couple of

views, he is confident pressing the first stone in the
sequence feeling the satisfying click, then the next
& the next until the paintings latch releases
revealing the safe.
"What the hell!" Urchon exclaims,
"There's no dials"
"Shit, I was afraid of this, it's a blood seal"
complains Stinal,
Shaking his head,
"Let's get out of here, we need to regroup & come
back later" he says,
Returning the painting to its original position.

A gentle breeze blows through the garden outside
Halcyons little nook where Kayla, Luma, Vincent &
Rava lay in the grass looking up at the sky,
"I think we need help" Kayla admits,
"As the person who experienced what's down there
alone, I wholeheartedly agree" responds Rava,
"& telling Halcyon will definitely result in us getting
in less trouble than if we told Sapere" adds Luma,
Forever trying to limit the amount she gets in
trouble, even if it never goes to plan.
"Did I hear my name?",
A voice comes from behind them. They all crane
their necks to see that it is Halcyon, who had just
entered through the arch,
"We've discovered something important" says
Kayla in earnest,
"Does it have something to do with the state that
young Rava finds himself in?" asks Halcyon
knowingly,

Luma looks down at her feet,
"It wasn't his fault, it wasn't what he expected" she
says bashfully.
"Things rarely are," Halcyon says,
Taking a seat on one of the stone benches that line
the garden.
"Now, what exactly happened?" she asks calmly,
The four youngsters gather around her sitting on
the ground.
Kayla looks over at Luma, who nods at her to tell
the story,
"Well, we were mucking about up in the high parts
of the city when we stumbled across Cocker & his
friends talking" Kayla recounts,
"You should stay as far away from those three as
you can" interrupts Halcyon,
"You are not wrong" replies Kayla,
While Luma & Rava nod in agreement,
"We overheard them scheming about some kind of
secret tunnels that start in the forest & lead back
into the city" Kayla explains,
"There are lots of hidden passageways that have
been lost to the years, many that lead outside the
city, they were meant as an escape route in the
event of a siege in the city, but I'm unaware of any
that end up in the forest" Halcyon interjects.
"Through sheer genius we figured out the location
& how to open the entrance" Luma blurts out with a
big smile,
Halcyon looks down at the happy little elf over her
glasses doing her best to hide how impressed she
was.

"We decided it was not the best idea to venture down into the dark passage, but Rava took it upon himself to do a bit of recon, just to see the lay of the land as it were" Kayla continues,
"Rava, do you want to tell this part?" Kayla asks, Rava nods & sits up,
"The way it appeared to be set up is that there are a bunch of small tunnels that lead to a much larger main tunnel. The walls are smooth like glass but they are jet black" Rava recounts,
"Hmm, like glass" Halcyon mumbles to herself, Rava looks up at her but she gestures for him to continue.
"When I came to the bottom of the slim staircase there was a door leading out into a bigger hallway, but before I could venture out, I heard someone coming, it was The Regent, he made his way to a door at the end of the hall, I watched through a crack in the door.
The door that he approached was rimmed in white light, you could see it bleeding out through any gap no matter how small"
Ravas voice begins to slow as the trauma of his situation moves to the forefront of his memory,
Seeing the visible distress that has taken over his face Luma jumped in & took over the story.
"Rava said that The Regent had to cover his entire body to protect it from the light which had a force & substance to it, so much so that when The Regent opened the door rushed forward like water filling up every inch of available space leaving no darkness behind" explained Luma.

"This light, is that what caused your injuries?"
Halcyon inquired,
"Yes" Rava answered,
"I was only exposed for a moment but the power of
the light was beyond intense"
Halcyon leaned back on the bench processing what
they had told her,
"Thank you all for bringing this to my attention, it
does answer some questions. But as is usually the
case, it raises all new ones. Do you think you can
show me where exactly this entrance is?" she
asked
"Yes, that place is burnt into my brain" Rava
answers.
"Ok, well I need to consult with Sapere & I'll need
help from Nyah & Nadaur, So I'll come & find you
all when I'm ready" Halcyon says,
Getting to her feet brushing the stone dust from her
skirt, she is about to cross the threshold of the
archway leading back into the city when she stops
turning around,
"Now I need you all to promise me that you will stay
far away from there until we sort this out"
"We promise"
The four say in unison with enough honesty in their
voices that Halcyon was satisfied that they were
telling the truth & continued on her way.

The light streamed through the evenly spaced
windows that lined the barracks, Tallie strode
forward with her usual speed & purpose, her mind
focused on the task that lay in front of her, in truth

she relished the challenge. Since she had been
assigned to the city with Nyah, she had grown to
miss their days as elite warriors moving from battle
to battle never staying in the same place for too
long.
Her mind travels back into her past, reliving
moments in time that she is now so far removed
from that it seems like someone else's life until her
daydream is broken when something catches her
eye.
She is still at the other end of the massive room
which houses the barracks but she can see
something laying on the top of her weapons chest,
her eyes narrow & her pace quickens as she does
not like people touching her things especially her
weapons.
Tallie picks up the black shroud that covers the
object & as she does a note flutters to the floor, she
picks up the paper scanning the few lines of text
that inform her,
"This dagger is specially hardened & prepared with
the venom of the Gloom spider, which makes it
dangerous for most but incredibly potent for use on
Alimanas"
Tallie flips the note over looking for some inkling
that might point to who left her such a gift but
finding nothing. She places the note down on her
weapons chest & unwraps the mysterious dagger.
It's simple but beautifully crafted sheath informed
her immediately of its quality, she carefully
removed the blade feeling the cold black bone of
the handle against her skin, she could see just by

looking how sharp the blade was, she holds up the black shroud that once concealed the blade & with the gentlest of pressure drags the dagger's edge across the hanging cloth slicing it in two.

Tallies pupils dilate as she examines the dagger as the piece of severed cloth floats to the floor.

Tallie loves all manner of weapons but her favourite are knives. She returns the blade to its sheath tucking it into the back of her belt then picking up the note & the two pieces of black cloth tossing them onto her bed.

Tallie crouched down in front of her cache of weaponry all meticulously maintained & housed in their own little compartments, she had great pride in her possessions. Tallie took the choosing of weapons for any sort of engagement very seriously as the wrong choice could be devastating if not fatal for her or worse someone she cared about.

Tallie thought about it for a second while perusing the impressive arsenal,

"I'm definitely going to need a range weapon" she said to herself,

Taking two leather straps from the box that she processed to fasten across her body in the shape of an X. Then opening one of the many draws she took out a set of throwing daggers all very thin & coated in a black substance so they didn't catch the light, Tallie slid these lethal little weapons into slits in the leather holster she had just put across her chest, then taking one of her favourites, a belt that on one side held the scabbard for a short sword & on the other a sheath for a curved blade whose entire design was to aid in the clean removal of heads & other limbs. Tallie then straps a small device to her forearm that with a flick of her wrist propels a stiletto style blade from under the sleeve of her jacket which she puts on over the top. Her jacket is a weapon in and of itself, clad with metal spikes in varying lengths down the arms & across the back in case anyone should attempt to grab her.

Finally, Tallie take a small axe that is attached by leather straps to the underside of the lid of the chest, as soon as she has the axe free, she effortlessly spun the weapon first one way then the other, her comfort was such that the axe became an extension of her own arm, this she slid the handle first into a compartment built in to the back of her jacket.

The last item Tallie equipped herself with was a pair of black leather gloves that had dwarf forged metal sewn into compartments to add weight & spikes across the knuckles with which she closed her chest & confidently exited ready for war.

Sapere sat at his desk his head lay on the piles of books he grumbled to himself as he slept between snores, he had been working on deciphering Brodrick's manic writings with every waking minute but the lack of sleep had finally overtaken him, when suddenly he was awoken by a loud knock on his door.

"You'd better have a good reason for pounding on my door!" he yelled,

As he stumbled out of his chair half asleep to open
the door, before the door is even completely open,
he hears,
"You're really leaning into the whole grumpy old
man stereotype aren't you"
Sapere turned not even opening the door
completely,
"Let yourself in Halcyon" he said,
Without even needing to see her.
"I assume by your urgency that you've discovered
something of substance?" Sapere grumbles,
"More interesting than decisive" replied Halcyon
"I had a visit from the young ones, they seem to
have unwittingly stumbled into something that might
allude to the source of our troubles" Halcyon
explains.
Sapere climbs back into his chair while Halcyon
takes a large mass of papers from the only other
chair, shifting closer to Sapere.
"You really should get some more chairs in here,"
she said,
As she did.
"More chairs invites more people, why would I want
that?" he said,
With a scowl to which Halcyon just smiled.
"You said you had some insight?" he asked,
More ill tempered than usual from lack of sleep.
"Well, our young friend Rava stumbled into one of
The Regents many nefarious activities"
"No doubt a very long list" interrupts Sapere,
Receiving a nod of agreement from Halcyon.

"Anyway, apparently young master Rava saw The
Regent enter a clandestine room, hidden away in
some secret tunnels that from his account of the
situation The Regent might have in his possession
a fallen star, the purpose he is using it for is less
apparent" Halcyon says.
"Hmm" Sapere says,
Taking off his glasses, laying them on the book in
front of him.
"It must have something to do with who or what
resides in the shadows, but what he is protecting is
still a mystery, but I would hazard a guess the light
from a fallen star would make an almost perfect
weapon against the shadow dwellers & it may have
once been the contents of a certain box that now
resides in your possession" Sapere surmises.
"Oh yes, I think you might be right, I've also a lead
on Vincent & his wolf troubles" says Halcyon.
"Forward motion that's all we can do" replies
Sapere.
Just then another knock echoed through Sapere's
chambers making Halcyon jump,
"Yes!" he yelled,
"Oh, good you're both here" said Nyah,
Entering followed by Nadaur,
"I was just going to come & find you" said Sapere,
"Looks like we saved you the trouble" Nadaur
responds,
With a cheeky grin,
"I just received this letter from my mother & from
what she has been able to discern The Regent &

The High council of Regents are at the centre of
this whole messy affair" said Nyah,
As she hops up, taking a seat on one of the many
tables scattered around Sapere's cluttered abode.
"Well, that lines up with what we've figured out so
far too, it looks like The Regent is hiding a
secret in some hidden tunnels just outside the city"
says Sapere,
"What kind of secret?" ask's Nadaur,
"Our best guess is something that is being
safeguarded by the use of a fallen star" adds
Halcyon,
"Do we know how to access these tunnels?" ask's
Nyah,
"We, do not but apparently our young friends
stumbled upon the information whilst
eavesdropping on Cocker & his associates & poor
Rava suffered the consequences of being a little
over zealous in learning its secrets" Halcyon
explains.
"Wait a minute, that box you have with the shadow
lens, wasn't that made of obsidian? Now my
knowledge on the topic isn't the best but I seem to
remember hearing that a fallen star's energy can be
contained by obsidian" recalls Nadaur.
"Yes, young Miss Luma led us in the same direction
too," says Halcyon.
"So, let's just go down there & neutralise the star
with the box & see what he's hiding" suggests
Nyah.
"That was my first thought too, but knowing The
Regent & from something that Rava said in his

recounting of the events I wouldn't be surprised if
The Regent has a blood seal on the door at the
very least, which we will need to contend with" says
Halcyon.
Nyah slumps against the wall nodding,
"Otto!" snaps Sapere,
Making Halcyon jump again, to her annoyance,
"What did that troublemaker do now?" ask's
Halcyon.
"No, not what he did but what he can do, I'm sure
he would have a sample of The Regents blood that
we could borrow." Sapere posits.
"Will that work? I thought the blood had to be living
to trigger the blood seal?" asked Nadaur.
"You are not wrong, you can't just wipe a blood
stained rag across the door but there is a process
that Otto uses to maintain the blood so it is still
viable for medical purposes that might just work"
says Sapere.
"I think that one is going to be your job Sapere, I
think you have the best chance to have a
favourable result with any kind of request to Otto"
says Halcyon,
With a grin.
"Yeah, you're probably right" grumbles Sapere.
"OK you take care of that, we have to go to see
Tallie & Sikes off to deal with their little Alimana
problem" says Nyah.
"Oh, that's now? Give them my best, those Alimana
can be a treacherous bunch" says Sapere,
Shaking his head.

"That's why they are taking Dabn & Faucon as
overwatch just in case" Nyah explains,
As she jumps casually off the table.

Tallie glides through the city completely at ease,
the impending battle has centred her more than
anything. Her upbringing had been brutal & any
sign of weakness was chastised. Without a drive or
as much of a purpose in the city she had begun to
feel scattered which made her more anxious than
she is used to, but the lead up to this impending
battle had washed all that away & helped to focus
her mind & body, not to mention her confidence
had returned.
She knew her skills & what she was truly capable
of. Sikes on the other hand was happy with his new
life of leisure since his ability to be incredibly
ferocious was based on instinct more than a drive
for & talent violence like Tallie, but his drive to help
& protect his friends was much stronger than any
for a quiet life.
Sikes attached the segmented armour that allowed
him to retain as much movement as possible while
still protecting his vital areas from attack, the many
battles of the past returned, each dent or abrasion
on the metal & leather a point where he was
acutely aware that someone had tried to end his
life, although he had very little memory of these
events because in the throes of battle he becomes
quite feral only conscious enough to aim his
aggression in the right direction.

"I'm sorry I dragged you into this" Tallies voice
says,
From behind him,
Without even turning around he replies,
"I would have done the same thing, you can't trust
an Alimana as far as Sapere could throw one,
besides not going with you was never an idea that
even occurred to me, you are like family to me"
Tallie hugged his giant hairy arm in a rare display of
tenderness.
"So how does this work?" Sikes asked,
"From what I understand we will be meet by an
escort who will use a snap to take us to the location
where the trial will be held" says Tallie,
"But if they are using a snap, how will Dabn &
Faucon know where to follow?"
"With this"
A voice calls from around the corner,
Tallie & Sikes look up to see Dabn & Faucon
casually walking in looking ready for battle in their
well worn regalia. Faucon holds out her hand
revealing four tiny metal orbs,
"What are they?" Tallie asks,
"They are Kaliton which roughly translated means
link in Impish, I borrowed them from Nadaur. How
he explained it there are two that send & two that
receive, indicated by the different colours, they
were created to give a tactical advantage by
allowing a backup team to use a snap, the orb or in
those days the shadows to be staggered in their
approach & instead of arriving at the same spot the
second team will be placed at a safe distance for

ingress & it will give the back up the knowledge of where the first are engaged in the conflict without letting the enemy know that they are not alone & apparently they are completely undetectable to all known scans " Faucon explains.
"Are they safe?" asks Dabn,
Faucon gets a weird look.
"Nadaur said they were, but Imp magic always takes a toll, he also mentioned that if you don't pass them within a few days, you'd better consult with Otto" he says,
Receiving a worried look from the rest of the group.
"Ok then" says Tallie,
Putting out her hand.
Faucon takes the two silver spheres, giving them to Tallie & Sikes who both proceed to swallow them, while he & Dabn swallow the golden ones.
"Do you have any idea where this trial thing will take place?" Dabn asks,
His obvious disdain for Alimana right there on the surface.
"No, not really but from what I understand there are a few places in the underworld that the Alimanas occupy that they frequently use, but then again as you well know they can't be trusted & will change details last minute to throw their competitors off their game" says Tallie.
Sikes brings his giant fist up bumping knuckles with Tallie, Dabn & Faucon then growling in a low tone that makes their ribs vibrate within their chests.
"We are the victors because the alternative is unacceptable" he growled,

With a calm resolve.
Tallie just says simply,
"See you there"
Waving over her shoulder as Sikes & her walk
towards the gates of the city to meet their escort.
Outside the gates stands a unassuming thin man in
a long brown coat & hat. He is stands with his feet
together bolt upright with incredibly strict posture,
as soon as Tallie & Sikes emerge through the door
he doffs his hat & bows bending at the waist almost
touching his head to the ground.
"Lady Tallie & Mr Sikes, I am here to escort you to
your trial, my name is Calaponis, I am a member of
the guild of requirements, we assist in the
completion of contracts in all forms"
The man explains.
Sikes & Tallie look at each other,
"This is much more formal than I was expecting"
Sikes whispers,
To Tallie who raises her eyebrows in agreement.
"We offer our services to keep all to keep a level of
honesty…at least until the trial begins, Mr Sikes"
The man says,
Shocking both Sikes & Tallie with his hearing.
"In our line of work, it tends to be advantageous to
pay close attention to everything our charges say"
he explains,
With a remarkably creepy little grin.
"First, before we depart, I must insist upon checking
you for any devices that go against the terms of the
agreement, you two after all will be the only
opposition" The man says,

Walking toward them in a strangely stiff fashion.
Both Tallie & Sikes look at each other hoping that
Faucon was right & Nadaurs links were truly
undetectable.
The man stops uncomfortably close to them placing
his hand in his pocket to retrieve a small device
which he held out in front of him in the palm of his
hand. Tallie & Sikes looked down at the strange
object, it was a golden circle that had been
stretched into points at each end, at its centre lay a
beautiful red gem that seemed to float not attached
at all, the odd man then closed his eyes as the gem
began to spin in all directions, Tallie moved her
hand very calmly to the blade that rested on her hip
just in case, the gem got faster & faster until the
bright red turned clear.
"Thank you" the man said,
Placing the device back in his pocket while Tallie &
Sikes did their best to hold their composure.
"Are we ready to depart?" he asked,
Raising his hand high into the air, on his thumb &
forefinger two gilded thimbles,
"Yes" Tallie & Sikes replied in unison,
The man snapped his fingers & the three of them
disappeared in a swirl of red, black & green smoke.
Moments after the smoke dissipated Cocker burst
through the city gates, he inhaled deeply, the
telltale sweet smell of a snap filled his nose, the
smell of overripe fruit.
"Damn it, just missed them" he says,
To himself retreating back through the city gates.

The dining hall is almost at capacity as the weather
outside has been very erratic of late with more
storms than usual, not that that bothers Luma who
professes her love for the dark & stormy weather at
every chance she gets,
"Are you guys really hungry?" she asks,
"It's so busy in here, are you sure you don't wanna
go & run around in the wind & rain?" Luma
continues,
"I'm up for that a little later, but I find the food here
doesn't fill me up for as long as back home, or I'm
just much hungrier here" Kayla admits.
"Oh good, I thought it was only me" adds Vincent,
"I'm starving all the time"
Rava grabs a table for the group at the back of the
hall, while the others pile their trays high with an
assortment of tasty treats & find a seat at the table,
"How has your training been going?" Rava asks
Kayla,
"Nyah & Tallie are incredible teachers, they've
taught me how to gain a little more control over my
emotional state but it is starting to follow my desires
to a degree" She explains,
Picking up a roll from the plate in front of her &
tossing it into the air, she thrusts her fist forward
firing a barbed point attached to a chain from the
bracelet skewering the bread in mid air & with a
little flick of the wrist retracting the chain till she can
catch the roll in her hand.
"That was so cool!" yells Luma,
Grabbing Kayla's arm to examine the fantastical
bracelet.

Up high in the rafters of the dining hall among the spiderwebs, dust & other shadows a deeper shadow begins to spread in a corner, nothing emerges from the darkness say one word, "Feast"

The others being completely distracted by Kayla's new found skills do not notice Vincent has begun to blink his eyelids getting heavier with each one until he finally slumps back in his chair, his arm left to dangle, as it sways his finger tip becomes black as though he had dipped it into a pool of ink, but this blackness is not without intent it drops & pools for a moment before moving off towards the closest table. By now Vincents whole hand has become engulfed in the absence of colour as the puddle becomes larger feeding the strand that is on the hunt.

The tendril wraps quietly around the leg of an unsuspecting young elf seated at the table next to theirs & in a moment of terror the black wolf emerges from the ever growing pool under Vincent, catapulting itself forward viciously attacking the young elf eviscerating him in seconds sending the rest of the table's occupants fleeing in shock & fear. Luma runs up to the unconscious Vincent slapping him across the face but the only response she received was the attention of the massive beast who turned in an instinctual fashion to protect its host, the very same impulse that Kayla felt when the wolf lunged at Luma. She put herself in between them to protect her friend.

The wolf led with its razor sharp claws leaping
across the room with startling speed & ferocity,
Kayla now having more confidence in her newly
discovered power but still retaining a healthy
amount of fear thrust her arm forward, the only
thought in her head being to shield her friends, but
instead of a shield the bracelet shot a battering ram
from her wrist, shooting a second spike into the
ground between her legs to brace the impact, the
other end impacting the wolf as it sailed through the
air sending it crashing out the windows that line the
back wall of the dining hall.
Kayla stood her ground as the huge beast jumped
through the shattered remains of the window,
"Kayla!" Yelled Luma,
Tossing her the multiple crystal pendants from
around her neck, Kayla caught them as Luma
yelled,
"Blow on them, use the light!"
Kayla activated the bright lights that lay dormant in
the heart of the crystals with a deep breath holding
them to the bracelet visualising her goal.
The wolf attacked once again this time leading with
its snarling jaws lined with jagged sharp teeth,
Kayla tried her hardest to be brave but in that final
moment she closed her eyes, all she could hear
was the unearthly noise produced by the wolf,
awaiting the impact but it never came. She opened
her eyes she saw that the bracelet had driven the
illuminated crystals down the wolves snarling throat
causing it great pain, so much so that it retreated

back into the safety of Vincent's unresponsive body.

"Holy shit!" yelled Luma,

Kayla still in a battle mindset cautiously approached Vincent looking for any signs of the wolf, but all she saw was the pile of glowing crystals laying on the stone floor. Rava & Luma ran as fast as they can to see if there is anything they can do for the young elf boy but the carnage that was left it was very apparent the boy was beyond help.

Vincent started to stir as his awareness returned to him, Nyah & Nadaur came through the doors at great speed followed by Halcyon doing her best to keep up with the two spritely Imps. Nyah went immediately over to the remains of the young elf, the ferocity shocked even her a seasoned warrior, while Nadaur split off too secure Vincent.

"What happened here?" Halcyon asked,

With a great deal of concern,

"We saw everyone fleeing but most gave conflicting reports"

"It was the wolf" said Luma,

Still visibly shaking.

"There was no warning or reason to any of it" added Rava,

Nyah walked over to Kayla who was still in a state of shock holding her arm outstretched, with a sharp,

"Kayla!"

She snapped her out of her state,

"It looks like you did everything you could" she said,
To her calmly,

Looking into her eyes that had begun to fill with tears. Nyah put her arm around her shoulders to comfort her, Nadaur looked over to Halcyon,
"We are going to have to confine Vincent, we can't have this kind of threat freely roaming around the city, especially since we have no idea what is triggering these attacks or how to remove this peril from him.
"You can't just lock him up" Rava protests,
But as he stands up Vincent grabs his arm,
"They're right, regardless of intent I'm responsible for that young boy's death, it's not safe for anyone to leave me unrestrained" he said,
As he hung his head.
"No, this was not your fault, you were a weapon wielded by someone else, you are no more responsible than the sword in the hands soldier" said Halcyon,
Placing her hand on his shoulder,
"Don't give up hope Vincent, we are all still putting great effort into removing this shadow from over your head" she continued.
Just then The Regent followed by a group of soldiers burst into the dining hall,
"Take him into custody" he commanded,
Nyah stepped forward to interject knowing she was more likely to obtain a positive result,
"May we be allowed to handle this Please your grace?" she asked,
Playing to his vanity.
The Regent beckoned for her to follow him out of earshot of the others.

"There are lots of eyes on the city at the present, we can't afford these types of incidents, especially not in such a public forum" he forcefully whispered, "We have already made inroads into the problem & we are quite sure we are getting close to the main cause" Nyah said,
Trying not to tip her hand about their knowledge of The Regents involvement.
"But Vincent will be contained until we can rid him of this parasite, please let us take care of this for you" Nyah said leaning closer,
The Regent thought for a beat,
"At ease men, Nyah & her compatriots have the matter in hand" The Regent said.
But as he & the soldiers turn to leave, he added, "He must remain in custody or I will have no alternative but to remove this threat from my city by whichever means I deem necessary"
Nyah walks back to the group, her disdain for The Regent clear for her friends to see,
"Where are we going to put Vincent up?" asked Nadaur,
"It needs to be somewhere secure & as far from The Regent as possible" suggested Nyah,
"I've got just the place" said Halcyon,
"Around the side of my garden is a cellar that has been dug into the earth & walled in stone, it has a thick wooden door that should keep young Mr Vincent or anyone else from harm". Vincent nodded in agreement,
"I promise we will figure this out" said Nyah.
"I'll take him down & get him settled" said Halcyon,

"Can we go with him?" asked Kayla,
Receiving a smile & nod from Halcyon who then led
the youngsters out towards her garden.

Cocker made haste through the city heading back
to his chambers when he heard his father's voice
behind him,
"Cocker!"
Cocker had the briefest of thoughts that he could
get away with ignoring his father's address but it
passed as quickly as it came.
"Yes father" he replied,
Deflated on the inside but doing his best to hide it
he held his head up & walked to greet his father.
"My commission has been completed, I need you to
escort its delivery" The Regent said.
"Is that really necessary?" Cocker asked hopefully.
"Yes, it is time you took on more responsibility" his
father replied coldly,
"The fabricator has a domesticated ogre who will
carry the object for you as it is extremely heavy, but
you must chaperone it as they are not usually
permitted inside the city gates. This should take
priority over any of your silly little antics, I need this
taken care of immediately" The Regent said,
Turning & walking away without even waiting for a
reply.
Cocker turned towards the city gates to head down
to the market when he heard,
"Son, do not let me down, this is of the utmost
importance"

Before striding away followed by his personal guard.

Cocker could not understand his father's insistence, he had never included him in the inner workings of the city, in fact he barely interacted with him at all outside of public events, but he had to hurry since Tallies trial would be beginning any time now & he wanted to be there to assist her even if she was unaware of his presence. He ran out the gates & down towards the market, as he entered the usual spruiking took place but he forced his way through the overly aggressive vendors who populated the entrance of the market.

The fabricators workshop was stuffy, things burned & bubbled sending foul smells into the air. Cocker could hear the impact of a hammer pounding in the back so he proceeded into the working part of the store.

"No manners, any of you!" an angry voice yelled.

"Excuse me?" Cocker replied,

"You are not excused, none of you high born have any respect for other people's spaces. When you enter someone's shop you wait to be addressed, you don't just take it upon yourself to go wherever you please!"

The muscular man with a long white beard yelled constantly, his hearing had been permanently damaged by the hammer strikes over the years, he untucked his long beard from behind his heavy leather apron,

"Beards & forges don't mix, learnt that the hard way!" he said loudly,

"I guess you're here for your father's box then"
"Box? Um, yes" Cocker replied.
"Ok, now you may come through" the fabricator
invited,
"Hurry up, I have other people's jobs to finish" he
grumbled impatiently.
He led Cocker into a back room & sitting on a
remarkably sturdy wooden table made from a huge
single piece of tree trunk sat a large black box.
Cocker stared at the shimmering object running his
fingers over the smooth surface, the black was like
the ocean at night, little twinkles of light reflections
of the fire in the forge that were there one moment
& gone the next the obsidian actively swallowing
the light.
"It is some of my best work" the man said proudly,
"I don't have much call for the manipulation of
obsidian anymore"
"Obsidian?" queries Cocker,
"That's Obsidian" the man said impatiently,
Pointing to the box,
"That's why you require Beroris to get it back to
your beloved city" the man said,
"Beroris! He bellowed,
Cocker felt a hot breath on his neck turning to see
the belly button of a massive hulking ogre. Cocker
startled he fell back against the table which made
the old man laugh out loud.
"Where did it come from?" Cocker yelled,
In a higher register than he expected.
"Amazing isn't it, that something so big can move
so silently, you wouldn't think it to look at them but

in the wild ogres are ambush hunters, they can
move through the undergrowth & you would never
even know they were there until they crushed your
head in their palm" the man explained,
Revelling in the fear he was creating in Cocker.
"Is it safe to have in the city?" Cocker asked,
"Safe is a relative term & it's a He" said the man.
"Beg your pardon?" said Cocker,
In a dismissive way.
"He is not an it!" scolded the man,
"Beroris take this and follow master Cocker & leave
it where he tells you" The man instructs, Tossing
something up into the Ogres mouth,
"& when you come back you can have another
treat"
Cocker raised his eyebrows in curiosity,
"Ogres love candy" said the man,
Anticipating his question, walking back through to
the front of the workshop.
Beroris picked up the box with both hands as the
table creaked in gratitude at having the weight
removed from it & lumbered towards the door
following Cocker.
Cocker opened the door and the man said with a
smile,
"I'd stay to the eastern side of the market on your
way out as the western side is where the candy
shops are found"
Cocker looked up at the stone faced creature &
ventured out into the market & back to the city.

Chapter 16

Smoke swirled making seeing impossible, it burned
Tallies eyes & throat, she could feel
Sikes' hairy body behind her. She now falls victim
to the side effects of travelling by snap, her
equilibrium is completely disturbed & distorted.
Tallie closes her eyes to try & regain her
composure using the sturdiness of Sikes to ground
herself.
She can feel Sikes heartbeat slow & steady, the
pulsing helps her relax & get back to her base of
control, his deep breaths end with a little growl that
reverberates through her entire body & as much
self confidence she has, it is calming to be fortified
by such a formidable friend.
In a flash the smoke burned off leaving Tallie &
Sikes blinded momentarily.
Tallie immediately grabbed one of the knives from
her hip grasping the handle of the blade tightly with
her thumb over the end of the handle bracing her
grip. Once her eyes have finally cleared Tallie could
see that they weren't in some secret ceremonial
space held sacred by the Alimana, but instead they
had returned to the nightclub where the whole
incident had started.

The air had finally cleared apart from the potent &
pungent smell of the gaggle of Alimana that line the
circumference of the room. Seated in one of the
VIP sections is the leader of this clan,
"So, you are the one that killed my cousin in the
tunnel" The larger Alimana hissed,
The stench clung to his words as they travelled
across the room to Tallie & Sikes, the smell was
overwhelming & was starting to aggravate Sikes'
calm demeanour.
"Can we just get this over with!" snapped Sikes
"Now, now we are here because of your infractions,
so we will dictate the terms of the trial" The leader
states, with more intelligence than any Alimana
they've ever interacted with.
Out of the corner of her eye Tallie sees one
particularly slimy Alimana reaching its fingers out to
try to relive her of whatever it can grab, Tallie
maintains eye contact with the addressing Alimana
leader, but as soon as the opportunistic hand
enters her space, she grabs it along the knuckles
crushing many of the small bones in its hand
causing a cry in pain from the Alimana.
The leader rises from his chair & screams,
"Not until the Trial is underway!"
Pointing to the culprit who is immediately
swallowed into the writhing mass of bodies that
seems to be growing in number.
"Allow me to introduce myself, my name is
Wrathbone & I am the leader of this clan, after the
death of my cousin at your hand, I absorbed his
clan into my own & in doing so not only acquired

his responsibilities but this clan became the largest & most powerful among our brethren" Wrathbone explained.

Sikes panned the room making sure to stay aware of the ever growing numbers that now surrounded them & as he did, he noticed Dabn & Faucon hidden but watching them from the skylight, he leaned forward & whispered,

"Seconds are here"

Tallie kept her focus on Wrathbone but gave enough of a twitch that Sikes knew she had understood.

Tallie had dealt with the Alimana many times but this clan leader was somehow different, more controlled & far more eloquent which gave her pause. The Alimana were always seen as a nuisance but just by sheer numbers alone with proper leadership they could become a formidable problem.

"There are many forms of resolution trials that have been used over the years, but I've always thought the trial should be equivalent to the transgression" said Wrathbone,

"So, keeping that I mind I've decided to implement the Gauntlet of Three" he continued,

At the mention of this the crowd cackled & screamed in joyous agreement, Wrathbone raised his hands & the wild noise died down.

"It's quite simple, all you have to do is make it to the other end of the room & severe the head of the Rolpheran" Wrathbone said,

He walked over to a cage that sat on the ground
opening the small latched door on the top & as
soon as his hand entered the cage it began
violently shaking, while savage growing & gnashing
escaped through the thick wire mesh of the cage.
Wrathbone held the creature high above his head
as it writhed & twisted trying to take chunks from
his hand with its sharp teeth.
The creature was long & skinny with short fine
brown hair that bristled with aggression as it tried to
escape its captor, to the cheers of the crowd.
"But first the rules" he said,
Forcing the wild creature back into the cage,
"The rules are quite simple, all you two must do is
make it to the other end of the room & as I said in
the beginning severe the head of the Rolpheran,
simple enough right" Wrathbone says,
With a little wink to the boisterous onlookers, but as
the name suggests your opponents will be threefold
& three strong, although since there are two of you
it only seems fair that your opposition is multiplied
by two as well" Wrathbone says,
With an evil grin.
"The room will be separated into five sections, the
first is your starting position, followed by three rows
of six handpicked Alimana"
The crowd cheers again at this announcement,
Wrathbone holds his hand aloft to quite the
jubilation,
"The final section holds the Rolpheran & your
freedom from future attempts on your safety, if you
disable all opponents in a row, you may move

forward to the next, but be aware if you attempt to move on while the chosen Alimana are still able to challenge they are allowed to rejoin the skirmish" Wrathbone explains,
"Now the trial will only end when either of you sever the head of the Rolpheran, after all death is an end for us all!" Shouts Wrathbone,
Causing the other Alimanas to begin a chant of,
"Death is the only end" over & over again.
Tallie looks back at Sikes with a confident tone & a glint in her eye says,
"Let's show em what real warriors are big guy"
Sikes nods, an intense look fell across his face that even gave Tallie a moment's pause. Wrathbone casually walks back to the cage that is being held down by two Alimana on either side, the feral creatures moving with such vigour that the metal cage is starting to break at the seams. Wrathbone opens the latched door taking out one then the other holding the two savage little creatures above his head to the boisterous cheers of the unsavoury crowd. He calls over an Alimana who attempts to take one of the creatures from him but in the process the Rolpheran's jaws snap shut on his finger, the Alimana screams in pain as his finger falls to the floor, the crowd cackles at his misfortune as he moves to the other end of the room spilling his foul blood as he goes.
Holding the Rolpheran down he places a metal collar around its neck & jumps back as he releases his grip, the Rolpheran launches wildly at him only being stopped by a thick metal chain attached to

the wall. Wrathbone walks over to the small elevated platform of the VIP section holding his hand out to his side, one of the other Alimana moves forward kneeling down holding a curved blade that is caked in blood & other unidentifiable substances, he holds it above his head & the crowd falls quite aside from the occasional hiss,
"For one hundred & fifty years the edge of this blade has signalled the start of the trial, so shall it be" Wrathbone says,
The response quickly followed,
"Death to the unworthy!" cry the Alimana. Wrathbone brings the blade down, cleaving the head of the Rolpheran from its body, sending it bouncing down the stairs of the platform still snapping its teeth the whole way down until it finally fell still.
Tallie immediately went on the attack pulling three blades from the holsters that crossed her chest firing them with incredible speed & unrivalled precision, hitting three of the fast approaching Alimana in the knee. The blades penetrating deep into the bone & cartilage dropping them to the ground screaming in pain, all three trying to pull the blade out but the sharp edge was stuck fast in the bone of their legs.
Tallie then turned her attention to the three others who had closed the distance with impressive speed. Tallie looked to be heading straight for them but at the last second ducked down sliding across the floor & with a flick of her wrist launched a blade with frightening intent into the back of the lead

attackers knee sending him crumbling to the ground followed by one of the others who could not stop in time who ended up in a tangled pile on the floor. The other managed to stop just in time turning to face Tallie but just as he was about to take off towards her Sikes grabbed him by the back of the neck flinging him with such force that when he hit the wall his bones pierced his skin, the onlooking crowd stand shocked at the carnage that lay at their feet.

Tallie turned her attention to the as yet uninjured Alimana that is attempting to untangle himself from the limbs of his cohort when Tallie zips past reducing him to an unconscious bloody mess with an expertly placed elbow to the side of the head. One of the Alimanas standing off to the side in a long floor length black robe lined with dark green strikes a large brass gong, the raucous noise signifying the passing of the first level of the engagement.

The look on Tallies face is a mix between rage & pleasure, the conflict reigniting a fire for combat inside her that she has had to quench living in the city for the past few years. As she moved forward to engage with the second & more formidable group of assailants lined up in front of her, something whizzes past her, from high above Faucon tracks the secondary threats, her big hyper focused eyes spotting an Alimana who was launching projectiles at Tallie & Sikes. Faucon reaches into a quiver strapped to her leg taking a single ultra fine translucent spine that she loads into a beautifully carved blowpipe, her aim & lock in on the target was almost instantaneous, with a short sharp breath the practically invisible projectile slices through the air embedding itself deep into the flesh of the Alimanas shoulder, it went so deep as to have no external presents at all only the excruciating pain felt by the treacherous cheating Alimana. He was unaware of what had happened outside the pain he now felt & as he moved the barb shattered into tiny pieces tearing his flesh internally as they shifted & moved.

Tallie saw the difference in the second row immediately, they didn't rush in as the first row had, instead they moved out & away in an attempt to flank her, but they had an error in their strategy as they focused on Tallie as their main antagonist, Sikes with great skill and agility flanked them attacking from the side with frightening aggression. He hit one with his massive paw sending him tumbling into the crowd causing them to topple to the ground. He then took the next in line by the leg in his impressively sharp teeth slinging him back & forth shredding his flesh to the bone & with one last swing he used that disabled Alimana to bludgeon the third in the head, the impact of their skulls hitting each other was enough to shatter their bones leaving them an unresponsive mess of blood & flesh on the ground.

Tallie meanwhile had set her sights on the other three, she pushed forward as they attempted to utilise the same tactic of flanking & surrounding her. The Alimana immediately behind her lunged

forward with a long straight blade attempting to skewer her in the back, but a millisecond before the blade made contact Tallie spun to her left moving out of the way & using the Alimana's momentum sent him careening out of control until his blade inevitably found its way into the eye socket of one of his fellow combatants. Tallie using the momentum from the spin drove her spiked elbow into the cheek of the remaining assailant. Tallie turned back to check on the danger posed by these opponents & she was somewhat surprised to see all three were still in the fight. The two that had clashed had made their way back to their feet, one holding the other by the hair & pulling the blade from his eye leaving a viscous stream of blood & aqueous humor running down his cheek.
Sikes charged forward & as he passed Tallie she noticed that he had multiple small daggers imbedded in his back further evidence of the untrustworthy nature of the Alimana. These Alimana weren't going to be as easy to dispatch as the previous Tallie concluded as they actively drew Sikes forward in an attempt to flank him again. Sikes was a feral fighter but he was not without his wits, he had incredible battle field awareness & as soon as the Alimana got into his position behind Sikes he planted his arms on the ground kicking back with his powerful hindquarters sending the Alimana through the air towards Tallie who leapt meeting him half way driving her knee deep into the soft tissue if his torso inflicting untold damage to his internal organs. The two remaining Alimana both

attacked Sikes simultaneously, Sikes caught one by the face, his enormous paw engulfing his entire head. Sikes drove it into the nightclubs wooden floor splintering the wood, but in that moment the other caught Sikes off guard plunging his blade into his shoulder. The blade had barely penetrated Sikes thick skin when Tallie moved passed him, The Alimana stumbled backwards thinking he had gotten away with the manoeuvre but as he looked up at Sikes, He could see his hand still holding the handle of the knife still lodged in Sikes muscle, looking down he realised that Tallie had cleanly removed his hand above the wrist leaving an open wound that pumped his life blood all over the floor. The gongs aggressive clang echoed out into the nightclub again, Tallie backed up to be in line with Sikes plucking the daggers from his back flinging them into the crowd. Their final six challengers moved from the darkness into the light, these were no normal Alimanas they stood at least twice the height & held themselves quite differently, they did not attack like their brethren, instead they carefully spread out across the floor, Tallie switch the curved blade for the mysterious black dagger that had been left for her.

In a corner of a back room a shadow began to grow spreading out into the hidden space. Each of the more formidable Alimana produced a weapon, ranging from long staffs with a blade on each end, duelling daggers to a length of barbed chain that at its end was tipped with a heavy metal sphere adorned with spikes that cut into the floor as its

wielder advanced, with a flick of his arm the chain
pulled taught the weight of the ball keeping it
tethered to the wood floor, then with surprising
athleticism he leapt into the air whipping the chain
sending the spiked ball in a horizontal arch that
caused Tallie & Sikes to drop to the ground to
avoid. The spiked ball impacted on a group of the
bystanding Alimana almost decapitating one as the
chain's barbs tore into the skin of another three.
The large Alimana moved across the room his eyes
never leaving his targets, a sinister grin spreading
across his face as he stalked. The other five just
hanging back happy to watch the carnage. As he
nonchalantly walked across the room he again
pulled the chain taught flinging the weighted ball
from the other side of the room this time, but
neither Tallie or Sikes are new to the world of battle
strategies & as the chain sails through the air Tallie
tosses Sikes her axe just before she ducks, Sikes
catches the axe ducking just enough to avoid the
chains path but holding the thick hardened wooden
handle up to block the chain which wraps around
the axes handle & once the danger of the spiked
ball had been neutralised Sikes gave a mighty tug
on the axe sending the Alimana flying through the
air, Tallie then ran up Sikes' back & upon feeling
her first footstep Sikes pulled the chain taught
again, Tallie with incredible balance & grace ran
down the length of the chain driving the black blade
into his skull dropping him instantly to the ground.
Sikes gave the chain a little flick which Tallie used

to flip majestically through the air landing back at Sikes side.

One of the remaining Alimana cried out,

"Brother!"

Rushing forward to check on his fallen sibling, who was far from help. The distraught Alimana let out a blood curdling scream, he swung his double sided axe into the floor sending splinters of wood into the air. Tallie crouched ready to move in any direction, Sikes on the other hand returned the Alimanas war cry with one of his own a deep roar that shook the stage lights that hung from the ceiling. The two huge creatures ran at each other while the others following a nod from their leader Wrathbone also entered the fray.

Tallie moved to the left putting the brawling Sikes between her & two of the others leaving her with two to deal with, Dabn looked down,

"I need to get down there & help her!" he said to Faucon,

"We must stay out of sight, we don't want to give those slimy bastards any reason to nullify the trial" she replied.

Dabn begrudgingly backed down as Faucon fired two more bolts into the hands of Alimanas in the crowd as they produced daggers to throw.

The two approached Tallie crisscrossing as they twirled their staffs, the blades on either end catching the light as they spun creating a very effective distraction, but Tallie was in her element, her love of combat had been reinvigorated & her confidence was unmatched. Sikes & the Alimana

were fairly evenly matched in size but Sikes had staggering power & ferocity, and despite the motivation of the death of his sibling the Alimana was no match for Sikes, but he was tricky.
Sikes hit him full force in the face knocking him to the ground but as Sikes moved in for the kill he spat a mouth full of rancid blood into Sikes eyes, Sikes managed to close his eyes just in time but just having the blood in vicinity of his eyes was enough that the potent fumes made his eyes burn, he winced in pain as the Alimana made his way back to his feet & began to approach the impaired Sikes.Faucon not being a fan of such behaviour waited until the cheating Alimana got within striking distance of Sikes & sent an expertly aimed bolt into his left eye relieving him of his advantage, unfortunately this was noticed by Wrathbone who quietly lent over to a group of decidedly nasty looking Alimanas dispatching them to investigate the intruders on the roof.
Sikes seeing through blurry eyes saw the approach of his enemy & led with his head driving one of his long horns up through the base of the Alimanas jaw exiting out the back of his head, his body fell lifeless. Sikes gave his enormous head a shake flinging the corpse into the path of two remaining Alimana forcing them to scatter out of the way.
The two Alimana moved toward Tallie, their movements were a lot more elegant than the brute force of the others, they keep their staffs in motion creating an oddly mesmerising spectacle. Tallie noticed herself becoming slightly hypnotised by the

light being reflected by the silver blades, she backed off shaking her head which was the exact thing the Alimana were waiting for, they shot forward with amazing grace.

Tallie was just able to regain her composure when the blade of a staff impacted the floor at her feet, using the staff as a volt the Alimana flew at Tallie, as she moved out of the way she was caught on the cheek by the toe of the Alimanas shoe that was bordered with a razor sharp blade that sliced cleanly into the flesh of Tallies face. With no time to worry about such a small wound Tallie landed a strike of her own slicing deep into the hamstring of the Alimana as its leg sailed past with her small dagger, the Alimana landed but the wound that would have been enough to subdue most attackers seemed only to mildly inconvenience the much more agile Alimana, who just utilises their staff as a second point of balance to replace their immobile limb.

The other staff wielding Alimana had advanced & engaged with Tallie, Driving her back with the range of its weapon, but Tallie knew that if she held his focus long enough Sikes would strike & as she allowed it to close the distance Sikes bounded in from the side causing the Alimana to retreat slightly, at this moment an Alimana in the crowd flung a blade at Tallie but as he followed its path through the air it disappeared, it didn't impact on Tallie nor did it fall to the floor.

Faucon focused on the battle below did not hear the group of particularly nasty Alimana exit through

the backdoor but Dabn was more aware hearing
the movement in the alley below, his ears pricked
up, he heard them moving toward the fire escape to
make their way to the roof.
Dabn peeked over the edge seeing that three of the
five had already started their ascent prompting
Dabn to act, he leapt over the edge catching the
ladder as he went, he slid down with his feet &
hands on the outside of the ladder, his mass & bulk
caught the Alimana by surprise knocking them off
the ladder one by one until there was just a pile of
bodies lying in the muck & grime of the ally, but
Dabn did not cease his attack because he knew
that if even one of those Alimana made it back
inside not only would Tallie & Sikes' participation in
the Trial be for nought, but he & Faucon would be
in danger from the rather large numbers of Alimana
that remained inside.
He made sure to put his body in between the
injured assailants & the club, his size made it an
impossibility that any of them could get past him &
back into the clubs back door, but he also knew
that being as quiet as possible would be to his
advantage, so rather than utilising his strength by
hitting them with a dumpster which would be his
first instinct in a normal situation, he took hold of
the writhing creature on the top of the pile by the
back of the neck easily crushing the vertebrae
tossing his body to the side repeating the same
process twice more leaving only two Alimana
standing in challenge to him, one took a deep
breath as if he was about to cry out to his brethren

for assistance, when he & the other just stopped, the consciousness left their eyes & they fell silently to the ground, Dabn looked around & as he looked up he was a little annoyed to see Faucon with her head over the edge with her blow pipe, she had shot two spines straight down into the Alimanas brains killing them instantly & silently,

"I had everything under control" Dabn grumbled to himself,

As he concealed the bodies in a nearby dumpster then made his way back up the ladder to the roof. The two Alimana moved back into a well trained formation as did Tallie & Sikes. Tallie switched her smaller blade for the larger gifted blade that sat at the small of her back, the two Alimana seemed to recognize the style of blade & became more cautious.

Sikes in his amped up state attacked but even though he was incredibly quick he could not hope to match the agility of the Alimana he was challenging who waited till the last second before moving out of the way both striking at Sikes' sides, their blades piercing him in the ribs which caused him great pain but was not life threatening, Sikes grabbed the shaft of one of the spears pulling it from his side, the wound had slowed him down slightly but more than that it had annoyed him, Sikes pulled the spear bringing its wielder within reach & with one mighty strike of his paw crumpled the Alimana to the ground like paper.

Tallie & the last Alimana had not broken eye contact, they circled each other, both aware of the other's prowess in battle, Sikes moved to the side watching the intense battle, he knew that Tallie would not be impressed if he intervened in a one on one scenario.

The Alimana stuck first firing the spear through his hands at amazing speed, Tallie with intense focus dodged each incoming attack by the narrowest of margins, Sikes watched the battle & saw an Alimana on the sidelines toss a knife at Tallie, but just as he was about to run across the room & flatten him he saw the knife disappear in midair inches from Tallies back, he thought it must have been Faucon yet he did not know or understand how it had been accomplished.

The Alimana lunged at Tallie his blade impacting at her feet, Tallie took two steps launching herself into the air flipping over her surprised foe slicing him down the middle of the scalp, the black blade making a clean incision sending his toxic blood streaming down his face, his eyes widen as he becomes aware that he is paralysed but just as he has this realisation Tallie lands & using her curved blade severs his head from his shoulders, his eyes still wide as his head rolls across the floor.

Tallie staring down Wrathbone walks over to the tethered Rolpheran whose feral nature had caused the metal collar to cut into is neck & with a swift blow it fell still. Tallie picked up the mass of hair & blood, closely followed by Sikes, she carried the head dripping blood the whole way until she was face to face with Wrathbone, who while angry still had a little glimmer in his eyes, Tallie with blood

running down her cheek tossed the severed head
into his lap, causing the crowd to hiss & cry,
Wrathbone raised his hand to quite the crowd,
"It would seem you are the victor, you are both free
to go & the bounty is lifted"
Tallie, still in the mind state of a warrior, began to
approach only to feel Sikes' large hand on her
shoulder. The two of them walked to the exit of the
club making sure to keep their distance from the
rest of the furious crowd before slipping out the
door.
Wrathbone sits back down in his chair,
"Why did you let them leave? we could've just
overwhelmed them & claimed victory" a little
Alimana squawked,
Wrathbone snatched him by the throat bringing him
close to his face,
"Soon we will return to the Cities then all who
wronged us will be held to account, but we must be
more calculating in where & how we display our
true power" Wrathbone said,
Tossing him to the floor.

<u>Chapter 17</u>

Kayla paced up & down Luma & Ravas small home
still furious the fate that had befallen their friend,
"We can't just leave Vincent alone, locked away,
we need to figure out what this wolf really is" she
said,
Quite beside herself,
"Try to relax" Rava encouraged,
"Nyah, Nadaur, Halcyon & Sapere are on the task,
what we need to do is keep Vincent calm, we
should go see & sit with him" he continued,
"What do you think Luma?" asked Kayla,
Luma thought for a moment,
"You know what I'm really curious about is,
What exactly is The Regent up to,
Something tells me he's at the centre of this whole
mess" she proposed,
Kayla fell into the sofa in between her two friends,
"I am just so stressed" Kayla admitted,
"While I do believe I was meant to find my way here
& this city has become my home,
The intensity of the stakes here are very different
than what I'm used to dealing with,
Not to mention the responsibilities of the Maylar
Venets" Kayla added,
Fidgeting with the bracelet.
All of a sudden, they heard a commotion down in
the orb room, the trio ran out onto the balcony to

see Tallie, Sikes, Dabn & Faucon had returned, Luma & Kayla noticed that Sikes was laboured in his movement & that was enough to prompt them to hurry from the apartment to make sure he was alright.

The two girls ran down the spiral stairs closely followed by Rava who was still slightly hampered by own his injuries as the scar tissue pulled as he walked down the stairs. By the time they had made it to the orb room Sikes was already being tended to by Otto while Tallie was recounting the day's events to Nyah & Nadaur.

Kayla & Luma made a B-line for Sikes who was sitting against the wall to give Otto easier access to his wounds.

"Are you having any trouble breathing?" Otto asked,

While examining the puncher wounds on Sikes' sides.

"No, it's just painful, now that my back to my wits" said Sikes wincing,

"Are you ok?" Kayla asked timidly

"He'll be fine, I just need to clean his wounds because those sewer dwellers are a filthy bunch & so are their weapons, but Sikes here is lucky because his species does not have lungs like you & Luma, his body has a double lined diaphragm which allows him to exert himself to a much higher level than most, but it can be devastating if the outer is punctured but luckily the big guy seems fine. You'll need to follow me down to my surgery & I'll irrigate those wounds" explained Otto.

He then tried to examine Tallie who brushed him off
immediately,
"I'm fine, leave me alone" she said,
Grumpily & returned to her tale,
"It was odd" she said,
"I was expecting more of a challenge to be honest,
but between Sikes & I we made pretty short work of
most of their challengers, but…" her voice changed,
"Have you ever come across this Wrathbone
character?" she asked,
Nyah turned to Nadaur who mirrored her response
with a shake of the head,
"He's something different than the other rabble, he
was calculated & seemed like he had plans far
beyond some petty squabble about the death of a
couple of underlings" Tallie said,
"How do you mean?" asked Nadaur,
"Well although he was involved in the trial, he really
didn't seem too fussed or invested in the outcome,
it was like he had already moved on to something
else & was only going through the motions of the
trial to appease those who held some meaning in
the old ways" Tallie continued,
"Maybe I should go & ask Cocker…nicely about it"
suggested Nadaur,
Tallie & Nyah gave him the same look,
"& what exactly do you mean by Nicely my love?"
asked Nyah,
Nadaur just smiled,
"No, I don't think that will be necessary" said Tallie,
"I can ask him about it, besides I believe I have
something of his that I need to return"

"Fine but if he gives you any trouble, I'm more than willing to question the spoilt little brat" scoffed Nadaur,
Which provoked a little grin from Tallie, she did not require his protection but she appreciated his offer.
Kayla & Luma attempted to help Sikes to his feet, but were just engulfed under his arms, but they did their best & walked with him to Otto's surgery,
While Nyah & Nadaur walked hand in hand towards the dining hall leaving Tallie to make her way to Cocker's den.

A shadow spread over the corner of Cockers chambers, Cocker stumbled out of the darkness the effects of the potion had now worn off leaving him drained & although he had managed to catch the first knife that was thrown, he had misjudged the timing on the second overshooting it & the result was the blade was lodged between his shoulder blades, he turned to ask assistance of his new associate but the shadow had disappeared as quickly as it had appeared.
Cocker looked around the room trying to figure out how to solve the problem himself, he moved over to the door leading to his back room, he wrapped his belt around the handle of the door & moved over to the door jamb wedging the knife's handle in the small gap wincing as he inadvertently pushed the knife deeper into is back. He then pulled the belt which closed the door causing the handle to be held between the door & its frame falling forward

the 6 inch blade slid from is flesh leaving a bloody wound.

Cocker released his grip in the belt causing the blade to fall to the floor, he lay there face down on the cold stone floor unable to move, the pain pulsed but his body had succumbed to the fatigue.

"It was worth it" he thought,

The cold floor calmed his breathing until he heard a loud knock at his door.

Lying there barely able to move, Cocker was not really concerned about who was at the door until he heard Tallie's voice call out,

"Is anybody there?"

He heard the door handle begin to turn.

Cocker tried to will his body to get up but the after effects of the potion were still too prevalent, so he did the only thing he could think of, he used every ounce of remaining strength to retrieve the whistle from his jacket pocket blowing it releasing the silent scream,

"Please Galbaial hide me" he begged,

He heard the click of the bolt & the door slips the lock & the creak of the door being opened slowly,

"Hello?" Tallie called out again,

Cocker noticed a black haze fall over his eyes & he was now looking up from several feet below the stone floor of his chambers.

Tallie wandered through the room looking around but she couldn't see anyone & no one returned her calls. She walked over to the table searching around she found a blank scrap of paper, Cocker

watched as she scribbled something on the paper placing it on the table.
Tallie then turned to leave but as she was walking out, she noticed the bloody knife laying on the floor, she crouched down picking up the cheap blade, she immediately recognised the manufacturing style as that of the Alimana, she dipped her finger in to the blood & she saw that the blood was red not the horrid green puss like blood of the Alimana. Tallie looked around again her brain coming to the conclusion that Cocker must've had some kind of encounter with some Alimana at the very least. She left the blade & the blood as she had found them & left the chambers. Cocker then realised he was raising up until he was again lying on the cold stone floor, unfortunately still quite paralysed all he could do was stare up at the table making up musings of what the note would say.

Halcyon walked leisurely towards her botanical habitat, when her friend Calinton hurried passed her,
"Scuse me" she said,
As she passed holding armfuls of books & papers, she hurried down the long hallway.
"Cali!" Halcyon call after her,
She stopped looking around,
"Oh, I was just coming to see you" she said,
Happy at the coincidence,
"I have found some very interesting information about your young man & his pet wolf" Calinton said,
Motioning towards her stacks of documents,

"Let's go to your beautiful little garden & I'll fill you
in on what I've found…perhaps over some tea &
cakes" Calinton said,
With a hopeful look.
"The dining hall is on the way, we can pick up a
tasty assortment as we pass," Halcyon said.
Passing through the arch that leads to her both
meticulously curated & slightly wild little garden,
Halcyon directed her friend over to a lovely little
round table. The top made from a single piece of
stone & the base appeared to be the trunk of a tree
that had been altered to halt the growing process
but it gave the appearance of a huge ancient tree
only in a much smaller form.
Halcyon pulled out the miss matched chairs for her
friend & placed the tray of cakes on a small stone
bench that ran alongside the table.
"I'll just fetch the tea, are you alright with one of my
special blends?" she asked,
"That sounds wonderful," Calinton answered,
Looking around in awe at the serenity that her
friend had created for herself.
"It's a very interesting case you've stumbled into
with your young man, what was his name?"
"Vincent!" shouted Halcyon from inside,
"Ah yes" Calinton mumbled,
As she tried to organise her papers & her thoughts.
Halcyon returned placing the tea tray next to the
tray of treats & as she poured them both a cup she
asked,
"So, you've made some headway into our little
mystery?"

"Yes, it's quite a fascinating story once you make it
passed all the misinformation & straight cover up"
Calinton said,
She pulled a piece of parchment that had a
beautiful depiction of the same image that adorns
Sapere's wall,
"This image shows the meeting between members
of royal families & the dwellers from the shadows"
she explained,
"Long ago a bargain was struck for the use of the
shadow realm for virtually immediate travel from
one place to another as time & space work
differently there" Calinton recounted.
"Yes, that's about where we've gotten to, but it
seems that someone has done a very good job of
hiding anything further on the topic, just one reason
I was so grateful to have my knowledgeable old
friend back" says Halcyon.
Calinton shoots her a little smile,
"Luckily there are still a few of us out there that are
actively trying to preserve knowledge & the truth of
the past & how we made it to this point, between
you & me we're pretty sneaky about it too".
Calinton adds a couple more cakes to her plate as
she sips her cup of tea.
Halcyon is looking at the pile of papers & the cover
of one of the books catches her eye, she pulls it
from the stack trying her best not to knock the rest
off the table onto the grass. She holds up the thick
leather bound book that was frayed on every
corner, what had caught her eye was on the front

cover was a painted image of a black wolf rising from a black abyss,

"What is this?" she inquired.

"Ah, I thought you might be interested in that one after hearing about your young charge. That is the catalogued works of a writer whose musings are widely regarded as fiction, most of his stories revolve around a mysterious black wolf that emerges from the darkness controlled by the will of a hidden group of pale skinned entities that are imprisoned in their realm by a powerful faction within the ruling classes" Calinton explained.

"Does it say anything about how we might sever the bond between someone & one of these wolves?" Halcyon asked hopefully,

"Sadly no, most of the stories are told from the second & third hand perspective but as the book nears its end it becomes more apparent that the author is having a more personal experience with these encounters, but with the more firsthand knowledge comes a level of insanity that makes deciphering reality from fiction increasingly difficult, it's as though something had taken a hold on his psyche pushing him further & further into madness" Halcyon ran her fingers over the tarnished leather,

"Thank you so much, I'm sure Sapere will relish the challenge of deciphering the hidden meanings" she said.

"Ah but that's not all I found" Calinton said,

With a mouthful of cake,

"Ummm" she said,

Trying to find the offending scriptures,

"Ah ha, here we go!"
Handing Halcyon a bundle of papers that were all at odds & ends with each other.
Halcyon tried to organise the mess slightly as Calinton explained their significance,
"These are the documents that were kept by a family who brokered deals for the ruling classes. They were very fastidious & kept multiple copies of any agreement they were involved in as insurance against any fallout from disgruntled parties whom they had represented, as they knew that the powerful don't always like to be forced into a deal even if they receive the better side of that deal" she said.
Halcyon scanned through the pages & as she got to the final page under the signatures was a crest. It was something she had seen before, it was a pen that morphed into a sword halfway being stabbed into a document causing it to spill a mix of blood & ink.
"I've seen this before, yet I cannot recall where exactly" Halcyon said,
Racking her brain as she took a sip of her tea.
"Yes, that is the crest of the family, it represents the switch from war to get a result to democracy. The blood & ink harkens back to a time where bargains were sealed in blood rather than ink" said Calinton.
"That is where your young man Vincent come in to the story" she continued,
Rummaging through the mess she had created on Halcyon's lovely table.

"Here we go, this is an excerpt from a folk tale which tells the story of a family who was cursed for their role in a bargain struck between two parties. The curse was such that all of their descendants would be cursed to be taken over by the will of the wronged party in the form of an ethereal black wolf" Calinton read,
"Does that not sound like your young man?" she asked,
Halcyon, fascinated, nodded,
"You really are an incredible researcher, this is outstanding. Does it mention anywhere on how the curse can be broken?" Halcyon asked,
"Well, that's a little trickier," Calinton said,
Shaking her head.
"From what I was able to put together the curse cannot be broken, but I did come across a story of a young girl who garnered a level of control over this parasitic entity by breaking the outside influence over the wolf, which came with its own issues because freeing her & the wolf gave her influence on the wolf but the wolf gained a personality & will of its own in the process" Calinton explained.
"That sounds somewhat better than his current situation, even if it's not a complete success. It doesn't happen to give a detailed description of the process, does it?" Halcyon asked,
Already knowing the answer.
"As most tales go it is more of a fable rather than a how to guide" Calinton said,

With a chuckle picking up the tattered old
parchment scanning though until she found the
relevant passages.
"It just says though meditation & communing with
the beast within a kinship was formed"
Halcyon sat back in her seat & sipped her tea
looking out into her pretty little garden,
"You really are a gift & a good friend" she said,
Picking one of the wild flowers that grew next to
her, putting it into the eyelet of Calinton's
buttonhole.
"I'll keep looking into this in my spare time but I
must get back to organising my new place. You
may keep all that I've found so far & hopefully you
& that old grump Sapere can find something to help
your friend" Calinton said,
Standing up & giving Halcyon a warm hug before
leaving.

The winds found their way into the city & seemed to
gain a life of their own gently travelling the halls
with a subtle moan that was unnerving & sent
shivers down Kayla's spine as she sat on Lumas
balcony looking down into the darkness of the
sleeping city. She had gained enough control over
the bracelet that she could form it into a small blade
then back to the snake, which she did speedily over
& over again as she sat there.
While her sleeping had become much better since
she had arrived in the city, the stress of the last few
days had caused her insomnia to return. Her lack of

sleep had left her exhausted & the strange events of her new reality had become like a waking dream. As she watched the iridescent fairies flitting up into the night sky, she heard the voices of people down below. Moving back into the shadows she watched to see who the disembodied voices belonged to.
"What are we supposed to do now brother?" one asked.
"You must be more resilient than this" the other said,
"Not every plan will be a success & all you can do is use the knowledge & skill you acquire along the way to come up with a new plan" he continued.
Kayla could now see that it was Stinal & his brother skulking around. The two walked in circles while arguing. Kayla picked up a small pebble from one of Lumas plant pots tossing it as lightly as she could to try to wake the sleeping Luma, who had passed out on the tiny but comfy couch just inside the balcony door with her legs & arms akimbo. After the first few failed to rouse her Kayla tried three at once, this did the trick waking Luna up with such a sudden start that she rolled right off the couch & onto the floor, popping her head up from behind the coffee table with a confused look on her face.
"What, What the hell is going on?" she asked, Blinking her big eyes.
"Shhh!" Kayla hushed,
Beckoning to her friend to come closer. Luma crawled under the table & out to see what Kayla

was so fascinated with, laying on her stomach she peered over the edge of the balcony.

"Oh, it's those two boneheads again, have they said anything interesting this time?" Luna asked, "I didn't hear much, but they definitely said something about a plan they had which went awry" Kaya replied.

The two watched as the unsavoury duo moved through the large open area arguing back & forth until they disappeared down one of the many hallways that led off from the atrium.

Kayla & Luna rolled over laying on their backs looking up at the stars, watching the iridescent fairies playing in the wind that rose up into the starry sky.

The air in Cockers chambers had become unnaturally icy, Cocker lay in his bed his breath visible in the air but the sudden drop in temperature did not rouse him from his slumber as the effects of the potion he used to elevate his abilities had such a taxing after effect that his sleep is much deeper than natural rest. Above his unresponsive body on the cold stone ceiling a shadow grows once again, bleeding out into the room like a cut that has never quite healed correctly.

Something began to breach the inky black abyss, Galbaial's porcelain pale skin seemed to glow against the colourless black, his red eyes fixed & unblinking on Cocker as he breathed slowly in & out, the only sound in the cold dead room.

"Let's discover your fathers secrets" Galbaial's
voice whispered,
Yet there was no heat to his breath, he was as cold
as the stone which he protruded from.
Galbaial extended his tongue, piercing it with one of
his pointed fangs which line his smile, letting a
single drop of deep purple blood drip from its tip
landing on the forehead of the sleeping Cocker.
The drop acting under its own power split in two
each entering one of Cockers closed eyes. With a
snap his eyes opened, but these were not his
normal eyes they had been coated in the dark
purple of the demonic blood. Galbaial's form slid
down the wall the shadow moving smoothly over
the stone until he was beside Cockers bed.
"Time for you to rise" he whispered.
Cocker sat bolt upright in bed tuning to the side &
without flinching placed his bare feet on the cold
floor.
His movement was brutal & sharp, the substance
controlling him was just triggering points in his brain
to achieve the actions. Cocker stood face to face
with Galbaial's menacing smile his blood still
coating his teeth with a purple tinge. With a look
Galbaial commanded Cockers actions, he extended
his hand before Galbaial who's own hand breached
the darkness placing a small spider like creature,
black with flecks of red all down its body onto his
outstretched hand. Galbaial's long fingers gently
brushing Cockers palm as it disappeared back into
the darkness.

The creature disappeared up Cockers sleeve as
Galbaial's unblinking red eyes relayed his
commands. Cocker blinked & the purple instead of
his whole eye now only filled in his usual colour. He
walked somewhat mechanically towards the side
door of his chambers,
"We will have your secrets, Regent" Galbaial
whispered,
As he returned to the shadows.

Sapere's brain had become as muddled as his
friend Brodrick's trying to decipher his musings into
tangible facts. He lay sleeping with his head on the
open volume Brodrick had hidden away.
His sleep as restless as his waking life had been of
late. As he slept the words on the page began to
stir, first with just a small vibration until eventually
they all began to work their way towards Sapere's
ear. His eyes darted back & forth under his eyelids
as his breathing became quite rapid, then with a jolt
the entire contents of the pages disappeared into
Sapere's head.
Sapere was not much for dreaming, he had often
stated that in his hundreds of years of life he could
only recall a handful of dreams & those made little
sense & were rather unhelpful, but his head was
now full of images that seemed to fall from the air.
He walked through a forest he didn't recognize yet
he was not alarmed & felt quite at peace. As he
walked he noticed that things were not as he would
assume, he let his hand fall to his side to run it
through the leaves of the plants that grew alongside

the path but they did not behave correctly instead of his palm moving the leaves to one side they spread & swirled like a layer of oil atop water. Fascinated he looked down at the beautiful display but when he returned his attention to the path, he noticed it was no longer a path in a forest but a bridge over a stream which seemed odd to him but only for a moment.

Sapere kept walking onto the bridge, he felt an unseen force driving him onward. The landscape began to resemble somewhere familiar to him yet he could not place it.

As he reached the other side of the bridge the terrain had changed once again & yet again his mind acknowledged the change but it did not unnerve him at all in fact, he felt quite safe. Then something caught his attention, it sounded like soft singing but the words were not something he recognised. He pushed his way through the dense undergrowth, it moved out of the way much easier than it should've coming to an opening in the forest, it was a large circle & at its centre was a huge piece of flat stone, he recognised it immediately, it was the location of the portrait on his wall. As he stood off to the side beings began to arrive, their voices were the source of the strange singing, they were talking between themselves but Sapere was unable to understand what exactly they were saying, to his ear it just sounded like ethereal music.

The individuals in attendance seemed to be am mix of many creatures that were familiar to him, even if

it was only from books or ancient stories. They
seem to be milling around talking amongst
themselves, all Sapere could hear is the same
musical chimes. All of a sudden, the music stopped
a group all dressed in the finest of garments
approach the stone slab. The smaller creatures find
places amongst the tree branches to sit & watch
the events while the larger beasts create a
perimeter around the clearing.
The regal looking individuals had separated into
five groups each taking up their respective position
with their underlings falling into place behind them
in perfectly rehearsed, precise positions.
Sapere stood there on the side lines admiring the
pageantry of it all when an audible change fell over
the woodland creatures. The tone of their song
shifted to a much more foreboding level that left
him immediately unnerved & uncomfortable, the
hairs on the back of his neck stood on end & he
had an overwhelming feeling of sadness & dread.
The five regal individuals seemed to adjust their
posture slightly to appear more imposing. While
Sapere's focus was on them he failed to notice the
very air around him was becoming darker by the
second. When he finally looked around, he noticed
the fear in the woodland creatures' eyes all looking
in his direction. Sapere began moving backward &
as he did, he inadvertently moved into the same
space occupied by a large minotaur, but instead of
colliding with it he moved straight through the
mighty beast. After the shock of this wore off, he
saw that a shadow had formed in front of the men &

women in their finery, but these shadows were not natural.

They were not the result of the light being blocked nor were they being cast on a surface instead they just hung in the air like smoke fraying at the edges but as dense as stone.

One of the royals stepped forward & began to speak, Sapere pricked up his pointed little ears but alas the same tonal song flowed from his mouth. He spoke for a moment then dipped his head ever so slightly in some half hearted of show of respect. Then from each of the floating black pools of nothingness a white face broke the surface. The faces had an elegance to them, such fine features, they almost looked as though they had been carved from the finest white stone. The faces all were different yet all the same with bright red eyes that held such menace Sapere could not look directly in them for more than a few seconds.

The forest had fallen silent, the pleasant tone of the others had dissipated completely, when one of the menacing strangers began to speak. The noise that reached Sapere's ears was no more than a whisper, but there was nothing pleasant about it, it was sharp & biting like the far off cries of an animal being slaughtered. Sapere was so affected by the noise he had to fight his impulse to run as far from there as fast as his little legs could take him, but he closed his eyes & took a deep breath telling himself,

"This is just a dream, it cannot hurt you",

Trying to convince himself more than anything.

Each of the royals then sent forward a young boy or girl holding a scroll which they placed before the shadows before returning to the safety of the other side of the stone slab.

The same highborn again began to speak, his dulcet tones were almost like a lullaby putting Sapere into a relaxed state. While he spoke the shadow dwellers reached their long thin hands from the abyss, each of their arms clad in a flowing black sleeve that hung almost to the forest floor, their hands moving forward like a snake in the grass sliding effortlessly forward picking up the scroll returning it to the shadows. All while keeping those red unblinking eyes fixed on their opposites on the other side of the ceremonial slab.

Then from the shadows five black books were produced but unlike the gentle gathering of the scrolls these were released upon the stone slab & even though they only fell mere inches the impact created a sound that made all in attendance jump. Even the highborn were startled though they did their best to hide the fact.

Each of the five placed their pale hand atop the black book onto a spike that adorned the cover, slowly & without breaking eye contact or a reaction of any kind they pressed their palms onto the beautifully fine edge of the spike allowing their dark purple blood to flow onto the books cover. All the creatures in attendance including Sapere watched in shock & amazement. All were again startled when they lifted their hands & the book sprang open with a deafening thud that echoed through the forest.

The whispers again flowed through the forest as the mysterious creature read from the book. The words were a mystery to Sapere but the way it made him feel was immediate & visceral, every fibre in his being was screaming at him to run as fast & far as her could but he remained & watched as the shadow dweller completed his sinister verse. A shadow porthole opened in the centre of the stone slab, with a singular chime from one of the highborn a small faun child stepped forward climbing up on to the stone. The fear was evident in its eyes as it stepped closer to the black abyss, its surface shimmered but no reflection was cast in fact although the shadow was opaque its very appearance pulled you in & you became lost in the cavernous void.

Sapere noticed that the edges of the porthole seemed to be at physical odds with the natural world it now inhabits, actively fighting against the light.

The small faun closed his eyes & stepped forward into the darkness, the porthole faded into smoke & mist. The onlooking creatures gasped wide eyed & frightened by what they saw, then with another passage from the shadows a second porthole appeared in the same position & the youngster stepped back into the light caring an armful of fruit. Sapere moved closer & he recognized the fruit, it came from the frozen isles many weeks travel from any forest resembling this one.

The highborn gathered together looking over the offering talking in hushed tones that had more than a passing resemblance to the tone of those from the shadows. Then after a brief conversation they turned back, the obvious leader stepped forward taking a beautiful silver blade from his side running it across his palm letting the blood run free, the ruby red drops landing on the stone turning to almost black. He held his hand out in front of him & just as he had done the presumed leader on the other side extended his hand out of the shadowy darkness followed by his other holding a small black dagger that came to such a fine point that one hair would have covered it completely. He ran the tip across his palm but this blade was viciously sharp & unlike the highborn his wound was deep & opened wide enough that it took a moment for the deep purple blood to reach the surface, when he reached out to shake the highborn's hand the blood fell onto the stone, the purple mixing & overtaking the red, but not in drops but an open faucet it splashed from the stone leaving spots of purple all down the immaculate robes which inducing grimaces from most in attendance.
Sapere stood fascinated but as he looked around the creatures in the trees & those gathered around the perimeter were simply gone, then in a blink the highborn also vanished leaving the swirling black shadow portholes hanging in the air in complete silence, he heard the whisper, that deep visceral feeling took him over again.

Sapere sat bolt upright in his chair falling backwards onto the floor, he jumped up a little confused trying to regain his bearings & realised he was back at his desk in his office, moving forward he looked at the book that lay open on his desk, the lines of words had moved to create an image of the meeting he had just witnessed but as he watched they reorganised back into the normal layout of a page & when Sapere looked closer he noticed the passages made no reference to what he had seen.

<u>Chapter 18</u>

Kayla had been training with Nyah & Nadaur all afternoon while Luma sat on the platform above gleefully cheering all three of them on. Kayla's confidence had been growing over time, partially due to her incredible adaption to her situation but also because of the belief that all around her have with her ability to become more than she thought she could. She had also gained a level of understanding & control over the Maylar Venet & that her emotions are a benefit to her rather than a hindrance. She had actually begun to relish these training sessions because she was very aware of her abilities growing with every session, not to mention Luma's unending energy to give positive reinforcement & her wonder at the feats they all could achieve.

Nyah & Nadaur moved across the training floor in such perfect unison, they read each other's faints perfectly, Luma watched them enthralled but it is apparent to both her & Kayla that they're only using a very small amount of their skills & if they so wish to, they could easily overwhelm Kayla.

Nyah moved towards Kayla, Nadaur mirrored her approach perfectly, Kayla did her best to stay calm & move with purpose. As the two came just outside Kayla reach she raised her arm then drove it down

towards the floor the Maylar Venet sprang into
action firing a spike into the ground that continued
to extend lifting Kayla high into the air to the
surprise of all three that witnessed it, Nyah &
Nadaur impressed at the level of control & Luma
cheered & squealed at the spectacle of it all.
As impressed as they all where they had noticed
that Kayla was still perched precariously high in the
air,
"Kayla, relax & concentrate" Nyah said calmly,
Kayla closed her eyes, regulated her breathing &
by the time she had opened her eyes again she
was descending to the floor.
"You're doing really well" Nadaur praised,
As she planted her feet back on the ground letting
the Maylar Venet return to its passive state.
"Thank you so much, but you two are something
else, your physical control & knowledge are really
awe inspiring" Kayla gushed,
Enamoured by the impressive duo.
"Don't tell him that, he already has an abundance of
confidence" Nyah responds,
With a laugh,
"That was so cool!" Luma said with glee,
Running up from behind causing Kayla to blush.
Luma squeezes her tightly in a congratulatory hug.
As they are all walking towards the exit Cocker
passes the archway,
"I wonder what he's up to?" Nadaur asks curiously,
They just miss crossing paths, Nyah looks down
the hall seeing Cocker captured in one of the giant

mirrors that are speckled around the city, she catches his eyes for a split second,
"What the hell!" she exclaimed,
But Cocker disappeared around the corner.
"What is it?" Nadaur asked
"I don't know, but I could've sworn there was something wrong with his eyes, but it may have just been a trick of the light" Nyah explained
"Come on, I need to wash off, I'm far too sweaty to deal with his rubbish today, anyway we'll see you two later" Nyah says.
Giving both Kayla & Luma a tap on the shoulder, to Luma's delight.

Cocker moved quickly but rigidly through the halls driven forward by a purpose that was not his own, moving passed & not acknowledging any & all in his way, but that was not out of the ordinary so the other occupants of the city paid him little mind. Cocker approached his father's chambers where he had led the ogre to leave his fathers handcrafted consignment, he paused by the wall peering around the corner only bending at the waist which looked quite foreign, his purple rimmed eyes as unblinking as the one who controlled his movements. Cocker's knowledge was still present even if his will was not. His pupils enlarged while the same unflinching look remained on his face. He saw the lack of soldiers on guard at his father's door which alluded to the fact that he was not presently in attendance.

Cocker moved quickly, his body stiff as if he was being forced & somewhere inside, he was aware & attempting to halt his progress but was being overpowered.

He twisted the large brass handle on the wooden door opening it quickly unaffected by the loud creak made by the hinges that usually make him cringe. Closing the door behind him he scanned the room seeing the newly crafted black obsidian box sitting on the huge wooden table that occupied the middle of the room. Cocker approached, he placed his hand on the top of the beautiful box, the spider emerged from his sleeve moving to the centre of the box's lid, Cocker stood silently watching the sinister little creature do its work. It stopped then with its back legs began to produce an extremely fine red filament from its spinnerets, the same red which adorned its abdomen, attaching it to the top of the box in a perfect triangle. Once it had added multiple layers of the bright red tendril Cocker watched as it flashed a vivid red then completely disappeared to the naked eye, but to Cockers enhanced sight it still glowed a vibrant red. The spider then repeated this process on every side of the box save the base which it could not access. Then as if it had given some type of unseen signal Cocker turned & left the room as the spider moved across the table, its sharp black legs moving in an unsettling choreography. The spider disappeared to the underside of the table securing itself where it would not be found.

Cocker returned to his chambers, his movements still mechanical & severe, he moved into the back room first sitting then laying on the bed his eyes still wide open. As his head sank into the pillow above him on the wall a shadow crept back into the room, Cockers eyes blinked once & his eyes were again completely covered in the viscus purple blood, he lay there still & quite as the purple blood ran down his cheeks like tears leaving no remnant on his face, it moved across his pillow up the wall & disappeared into the shadow which also dispersed leaving no trace.

The air was stuffy in Vincent's new accommodation baring a slight breeze the crept under the door blowing the leaves & flower petals that had been tracked in by his visitors of which he had daily across the floor. Halcyon checked on him as often as she could, not to mention Kayla, Luma & Rava who kept him in daily companionship & treats from the dining hall. Luma even letting him borrow some of her prized comic books.
He sat on the bed that Halcyon had moved in for him reading Spawn Vs Batman when there was a knock at the door,
"Vincent, is it alright if I come in?" Halcyon's voice called through the wood.
"Of course," he replied,
Putting a leaf in the comic as a bookmark. The fresh air filled the room & the smell of the garden brightened Vincent's afternoon,
"We'll just leave this open for a while" Halcyon said,

Placing a rock decorated with paint against the
door to keep it ajar. Vincent looked very tired,
"You're still having bad dreams?" Halcyon asked
"Yeah, it's always the same, I'm being chased by
something I cannot see but I can just feel it's there"
He admits,
Bowing his head,
"Well, you don't need to be an expert in dreams to
understand that now do you?" she smiled,
"Has the meditation & relaxation exercises helped?"
she asked.
"Well, I've not had any incidents" he said,
"But the ferocity of the chasing creature in my
dreams has become...um...more urgent if that
makes sense, like it's trapped & it doesn't like it"
Vincent explained.
"Hmm, yes well like Miss Kayla learning to
understand your impediment is helpful in gaining a
modicum of control, even if it's just learning to aim it
in a productive direction" Halcyon said calmly with a
soft smile,
"Do you have everything you need?" she asked.
"Yes, I'm all taken care of" Vincent said,
Gesturing to the table full of comics & snacks
brought by his friends.
As Halcyon approached the door Vincent said,
"I just wanna thank you for taking the time & trouble
to try to help me, I mean Nyah, Nadaur, Sikes,
Sapere & even Tallie have put themselves in a
precarious position with The Regent & who knows
whoever else by helping me, so I just wanted to say
that I appreciate it"

"Of course, sweetheart," Halcyon said.

"Everything is healing up nicely" Otto said,
in his usual slightly annoyed tone,
"It's so itchy" Sikes complained.
"Don't scratch at it you big oaf" Otto chastised,
Receiving a little growl from Sikes in return.
"You were stabbed with an Alimanas blade, you
know how vile those things are, the wound must be
properly irrigated, sterilised & the correct antibiotics
administered, luckily for you I'm an excellent
physician & Halcyon keeps a healthy stock of
sparrow thistle, which does itch but that's how you
know it's killing something" Otto said with a humph.
"How's he doing doc?" Tallie asked,
Noticing Sikes as she walked past,
"& how's your wound healing?" Otto asked,
Grabbing her head tilting it to get a better look,
which only seemed to amplify her bad mood.
"Hmm, I don't like the look of these green specks,
pulling his glasses down to examine her."
Have you been using the sparrow thistle cream I
gave you?" Otto asked,
Looking over the top of his glasses, already
knowing the answer.
"That stuff smells terrible" Tallie says,
Making a face.
"Well, if you would like to be able to keep making
faces like that at me, you'll use the treatment I've
assigned" Otto said, shortly
"Fine" Tallie snapped
"I'll see you later" she said,

To Sikes as she left, quickly to get away from Otto.

The bright sun shone down on the city creating
patterns on the walls as it found its way through the
tiny gaps in the stone. Sapere walked at a brisk
pace through the halls towards Halcyons Garden,
the other occupants of the city darting out of his
way as he muttered at them under his breath
organising his thoughts. He was carrying Brodrick's
book in his arms, the book was bigger than his
torso but he still managed to move at quite quickly.
Sapere turned the corner & walked through the
arch into Halcyon's garden, not looking around he
went straight over to her door & realising his hands
were full began to kick the bottom of the door,
"Hey, now is that really necessary?" A familiar voice
called out,
Sapere looked around in a huff seeing Halcyon
relaxing at her little table enjoying the sunshine & a
cup of tea. Sapere walked over laying the large
book on the spare chair & slumped in the other,
"You look exhausted" Halcyon said,
"Would you like a cuppa?"
"Thank you, having your dreams invaded is a taxing
experience" he replied,
As Halcyon poured him a cup,
"Are you going to elaborate? or am I supposed to
guess" she said,
With a playful smile.
Sapere began to add spoon after spoon of sugar to
his tea to the amusement of Halcyon,

"I found this hidden in the library, it was stashed away by an old friend of mine named Brodrick. He was a self appointed documentarian of sorts. He believed it was his duty to travel as far & wide as he could collecting stories, tales & documenting the things he witnessed on his travels so they wouldn't be lost to time" Sapere explained,
"He believed that these could be used not only to entertain, but to teach, so the same mistakes would not be made over & over again, but because of the nature of his relationships with some very important & influential people & creatures, some of what he archived with his writing was dismissed as fable or in the more severe cases were banned on penalty of death, mostly by those who didn't wish their misdeeds to be written down for all to see"
Halcyon looked over the table at the large leather bound book that lay on the chair wondering what kinds of wondrous stories resided within its pages.
"Now, I was well aware that Brodrick had a…we'll say interesting brain, what I wasn't aware of was how much his scattered thoughts created a unique style in his writing, especially when he knew the material needed protection. Plus because of his travels he gained access to some rather interesting security measures to say the least" said Sapere, Shaking his head.
"The dream invasion?" asked Halcyon,
To which Sapere nodded in response,
"What did you see?" she probed,
Sapere sat back in his seat felling the gentle breeze on his skin,

"Seeing doesn't quite cover it" he said,
"It actually gave me situational anxiety, like I was
actually present for the event, or I had inhabited
Brodick's consciousness as he witnessed the
event, it was more than a little off putting" Sapere
admitted,
Just by the look that had spread across his face
Halcyon knew that he was not exaggerating.
"Though I could not understand a word of what was
said, I understood everything that happened" he
said,
Taking a sip from his cup, his hand shook as he
brought it to his lips.
"It was some of what we already suspected, the
meeting in the forest between the two parties, but
they were not the only ones in attendance, it was a
packed affair & it seems this meeting was not a
closely guarded secret but more of a bargain of
sorts" Sapere continued,
"Between those who dwell in the shadows & some
very regal looking highborn, but the most
interesting part was that although the shadow
dwellers seemed to be the more sinister of the two,
the highborn shared their tone when they spoke
among themselves & the deal was struck. The fact
that we were completely unaware of the mysterious
shadow dwellers existence it's safe to say that
somewhere along the way they were betrayed."
Halcyon perked up almost choking on her tea, after
coughing for a second, she said,
"Oh, yes that completely tracks with something that
Calinton discovered in her research into our poor

Master Vincent's troubles. Apparently, his affliction
has more than a passing resemblance to a story of
a curse that was inflicted upon a family for their role
in a bargain that was not honoured, in fact the
second party had no intention of honouring the
deal, but said family was cursed to have their
descendants to pay the price for their role in the
deception" Halcyon explained
"Was there anything else that stood out to you in
this dream?" she asked,
Sapere took a second cake taking a large bite
thinking for a moment & before he had quite
finished chewing, he said,
Sending crumbs down his already grubby vest,
"Now that you ask, the books" he said,
With a thoughtful look.
"Books?" she asked,
"Yes, each of the shadow dwellers had a very
interesting book that they placed in front of them on
the stone slab, they were defiantly a major part of
the bargain seeing as the highborn only agreed to
the deal after seeing a demonstration of the
contents of one of these volumes" Sapere
recounted,
"But they had some kind of seal or lock on them
that was only released once the purple blood of
their owners flowed onto the cover.
The books themselves had a presence & power to
them that made my hair stand on end" Sapere said
seriously.
Halcyon got up from her chair & began to pace
around the garden causing Sapere to spill his tea

all down his front. She mumbled to herself as she walked trying to grab the end of an idea that had sparked a thought in her brain. Finally she walked back to the table placing her hands on the table top & looking Sapere dead in the eye,
"I'll bet you my favourite pruning shears that that's what The Regent is hiding in the tunnels that the young ones found" she said,
With a huge grin.
"That would make a lot of sense & would explain the blinding light that scorched young Ravas skin so brutally, A fallen star, because none from the shadows could get anywhere near it to retrieve it & it would also explain The Regents queries about the movement of said fallen star after the first incident that caused the suspension of shadow travel" theorised Sapere,
"Now what we need to discover is what exactly The Regent plans to do with said artefacts & if we can somehow relieve him of it safely, because we know scarily little about these shadow dwellers or their true motivations for attempting to reacquire the book" said Halcyon, as she sat back down sipping her tea,
"I will go & talk with Luma, hopefully her family connections can give us a little insight into what protocols we need to abide by in the process of moving or extinguishing the star if worst comes to worst" she said.
"Ok, while you do that, I'll venture deeper into Brodrick's writings to see if there is any other helpful information to be gleaned" Sapere said,

Picking up two cakes shoving them into whichever pocket had enough room.

The air in the basement room that Vincent had been sequestered in had a chill, the cold air moved easily under the door blowing across the room giving him a gentle breeze on his face as he slept. He had only been there for a week but this movement of air had become his white noise that calmed his brain, at least a little. His sleep was still somewhat fragmented, although that was nothing new, his sleep had been broken for as long as he could remember.
On this night like all of the others preceding it Vincent had had his small meal brought to him by Luma & Kayla, then he had done his breathing exercises & one hour of meditation to try to control his unconscious mind, which he had been taught this by Halcyons friend Calinton who seemed to know a great deal about a great deal & a few from Nadaur, then to bed.
Vincent had no ill feelings about having to be held in this place, in fact it had given him a level of control however imagined that control was.
Every night he listened to the whooshing of the wind under the door & across the floor, causing the leaves & remnants of flowers to rustle as they moved. But on this night as he slept the noises in the small room changed.
Vincent was sound asleep when a different type of air was all of a sudden moving around the room. The strange noise didn't affect Vincents slumber at

first but the prolonged change triggered him to wake slightly. Still half asleep & not quite sure he wasn't still dreaming, he lay there with his eyes still closed as a deep consistent noise repeated over & over again. Finally he very cautiously opened one eye. The room was dark except for the streams of moonlight that snuck through the cracks in the large wooden door. As his eyes became more accustomed to the lack of light he could see that the noise that had roused him was the wolf, sound asleep on the floor by his bed. Vincent stayed as still as he could, his fear amplifying every noise or movement he made. He lay there terrified listening to the deep repetitive rumble of the massive creature.

Vincent saw that the moon rays which were more visible because of the dust that filled the air disappeared as they touched the wolf, the light was not powerful enough to illuminate the creature. Vincent lay there as still as he could manage & at some point he must've slipped back into a dream, because all of a sudden, he was awoken by the movements of Halcyon walking above him, the floorboards creaked & cracked as she moved around.

Vincent peeked over the edge of the bed, but there was nothing out of the ordinary. He lay back on the pillow running the night's events over in his head, was he dreaming. After a little while of going over it in his head he had almost convinced himself that it was a dream.

He put his legs over the side of the bed, sitting there stretching his tired body, he looked down & to his alarm he could see the outline of a shape left in the dust on the floor, the more he looked the more he was convinced he could make out the shape of the body of the great beast & while most were messy one paw print remained crisp & clear. Vincent was just about to get up to knock on the ceiling to gain Halcyons attention when the door sprung open & with it a strong breeze that blew across the floor displacing the dust & dirt,
"Morning sleepy head" Said Luma with a smile,
Vincent just stood there staring at the floor & his missing proof, he could hear Luma & Kayla prompting him for an answer but he just stood shocked,
"Vincent!" Kayla shouted,
Which snapped him back to reality,
"Huh?" he said,
Looking up somewhat bemused,
"Now I don't want you to think I'm going crazy, but I'm almost positive that the wolf was in here last night" he said,
Luma & Kayla looked around for any sign of the destruction they had witnessed when the wolf had separated from Vincent in the past,
"Are you sure you weren't dreaming?" Luma suggested,
As kindly as she could,
"That's what I thought too, because the wolf wasn't behaving as it normally had, it was just sleeping on

the floor by the bed as I slept. There was nothing
vicious or scary about it" he said,
"So why don't you think it was a dream?" asked
Kayla,
"Because I could have sworn that it had left imprints
in the dust on the floor, but they were blown away
by the wind when you opened the door" Vincent
said,
As the two girls examine the floor for any sign,
Vincent sat back down on the edge of the bed,
"It's really hard to keep everything straight in my
head, but I really think it happened," he said, trying
to hold on to some measure of certainty.
Kayla & Luma sat down on either side of him,
"We believe you" said Luma,
Laying her head on his shoulder,
"Yeah, after all of the other strange goings on
around here, this doesn't sound too out of the
realms of possibility" Kayla said,
With a smile, holding out her wrist to reveal her
bracelet,
"But this is a good thing…right?" asked Luma,
"What do you mean?" Vincent replies
"Yes, she's right, doesn't this mean that your
control is growing slightly. I mean going from a
snarling beast to a sleeping one seems to be a step
in the right direction, no?" posits Kayla.
"We'll tell Halcyon as we go past. Do you have any
requests for breakfast?" Luma asked,
"Perhaps some cereal?" she continued,
With a cheeky gleeful grin,
Which caused the other two to burst out laughing,

"Whatever you decide is fine with me" says Vincent,
Beginning to calm down a little bit,
"See you soon" sang Luma,
As they disappeared through the door, leaving
Vincent to run hypotheticals in head as he lay
sideways in bed.

Up in the mostly uninhabited highest parts of the
city, Stinal headed back to his little corner of the
world. He & his brother had taken over an old
storage space that had been left to ruin, since the
ability to bring in whatever was needed via the
shadows had made the need to stockpile supplies
become less necessary, at least to The Regents.
Stinal turned the dark tunnels that even in the
daylight remained dark & gloomy, the stale smell of
abandonment filled the air making even breathing a
chore.
Stinal had been out all night trying to strike a
bargain with Wrathbone, he had heard about the
upheaval in the leadership of the Alimana & was
trying to ingratiate himself to the new power that be.
The door to their space can be locked from both the
outside & in, but once locked from the inside it
cannot be unlocked from the exterior. Stinal turned
the handle but the satisfying click of the lock was
not forthcoming, he had already had an incredibly
frustrating night & this was just one more
annoyance, he pounded on the large metal door
sending noise reverberating through the empty
tunnels. The tunnels were cut into the stone &
insulated the area from the rest of the city. Stinal

stopped placing his ear up to the door to see if he had roused his slumbering brother, but there was no sign. Now in no mood to be patient Stinal took a small crystal marble from his pocket, he crouched down & just before rolling the marble under the small gap at the bottom of the door he twisted the top & bottom in opposite directions causing an audible snap, then he stood back & waited, counting to himself,
"One, two, three…"
A bright blinding flash of yellow light followed by a series of bangs & pops like fireworks going off came from under the door. Stinal stood there patiently as he could now hear Urchon moving about the room falling over & swearing as this was not the most optimal way to be woken from ones slumber. The metal door opened halfway as the hinges were in a state of disrepair & the door caught on the stone floor,
"Was that really necessary?" asked Urchon,
He blinked his eyes attempting to regain his vision.
"I'm in no mood" Stinal snapped,
"Huh?" his brother replied,
As his hearing had not yet returned.
Stinal pushed past going over to the sink that hung from the wall in the corner of the room. He turned the tap which caused the pipes to shake & howl before not quite clear, but not entirely brown water spilled from the faucet. Stinal washed the sweat & grime of his face & the back of his neck, then plugged the sink with a rag that hung next to the sink & once full he dunked his face under the water

blowing bubbles from his nose with some force. He lifted his head from the water brushing his hair back with his hand,

"Their stink gets so deep in your nose" he said,
Using the wet rag to blow his nose several times.
Urchon sat on the old mattress that lay on the floor against the wall,

"Where'd you go?" he asked,
Stinal sat on a chair that he had stolen from the dining hall a few weeks earlier, he sat with his head against the wall letting the water drip from his chin,

"I was trying to figure out what our next move should be. After the debacle with Cockers safe I was thinking we should venture out from the city, there is a big world out there & money & power for those who are willing to go out & find it" he mused,

"& if Wrathbone's attempt at unification is successful the Alimana could become a very powerful force, they already have a presence in most populated areas & the only reason that I can see that they are not more of a threat is that by their very nature they are disorganised & spend most of their time dealing with petty internal squabbles, but I see a great deal of promise in Wrathbone. From our limited interactions he seems to be more intelligent & much more focused than the rest" Stinal said,

Getting up from the chair & walking over to the cupboard that was barely clinging to the wall with a few random screws.

"Have you eaten all the cakes again?" he snapped,
"No, I left one in the back" Urchon said,

Softly attempting to placate his short tempered brother,
"You really are inconsiderate aren't you" Stinal said,
Not really looking for an answer just stating that fact,
"I'm going to sneak down into the kitchen to get some food, don't lock the door behind me" Stinal said as he left.

The morning sun shone down through the atrium causing all the plants that grow from the balconies to turn their leaves to the sky. A cat jumped from a substantial height attempting to catch a rasp for its breakfast, the shimmering little creature evaded the attempt on its life by the narrowest of margins, the cat landed on Nyah's balcony with ease despite the distance being far greater than a cat should have been able to, its fur strobed with a plethora of colours as it impacted,
"Nearly had it" said Nyah,
Giving it a little scratch on the head to the pleasure of the feline.
Nyah was tending to her little garden she had set up on the balcony for those plants that appreciated a little more sun, one in particular her death blossom which needs lots of sun to sprout then must be kept in a very controlled environment. Nadaur had cleaned out a small space for it in the spare room after he did some reading about it in the library.
Nyah had placed it in the special pot she had bought from her friend at the market, The death

blossom requires specialised soil made from the ground bones of goblins as it mostly grew on the battlefields after a particularly brutal battle hence the name Death blossom. The soil has a dark brown colour with specks of green from the goblin bone. Nyah had been checking the pot every day since she had planted it, but to no avail, but today the soil was slightly disturbed & Nyah could see a tiny black shoot had broken the surface,
"Nadaur, come see!" she yelled.
A half asleep Nadaur stumbled from the bedroom,
"What is it my love?" he asked,
Fighting to keep his eyes open,
"It's sprouted" she announced,
With a big smile.
Nadaur looked down at the barely visible sprout,
"That's so cool" he said,
While stretching in the sunlight.
"We have to go & see Sapere, apparently he & Halcyon have discovered some interesting things about The Regent & the shadow dwellers & what this mess might be about" Nadaur said,
"Would you like a cup of tea before we go?" he asked
"Yes please, thank you sweetheart".

Cocker woke from the unnatural slumber, the last few nights he had been experiencing a sort of fog & most days he didn't remember going to sleep yet he woke up in his bed all the same. He sat on the edge of the bed trying to piece together the last few days from the fragments he could remember, but

his memories didn't make sense, he could recall his
travels through the city but he couldn't recall the
reason or the destination of any of those outings.
His dreams were also disturbed to the point that
any sleep that he was able to get was not restful, it
was actually the opposite, he awoke drained like
little pieces of himself were being stripped away. All
of this had left his brain muddled, so the obvious
was not immediately apparent to him, he was
existing in a fugue state. He had flashes of himself
in locations & one that stood out to him more than
most was his father's chambers, so as fatigued as
he was that was his idea for somewhere where he
might be able to begin to piece together what is
happening to him, as he left the room the red eyes
tracked his egress from the shadows.

Chapter 19

Halcyon had been looking for Kayla, Luma & Rava all day, she wanted to question them about the tunnels & hidden the entrance. She knew she could have asked Vincent but she did not wish to burden him with anything more than what he was already dealing with. As she passed the training room, she heard the distinctive laugh of Luma, it was like the happy little trill of a bird in the morning. She poked her head in through the arch to see both Luma & Rava clad in the training armour that was used to help warriors become accustomed to the weight & how much extra fatigue is caused by just the simplest of tasks. Halcyon watched in amazement as Kayla moved around the room effortlessly using the Maylar Venet to vault high into the air any time either Luma or Rava came within striking distance, which was the cause of the boisterous laughter.
"There you are" Halcyon said,
Announcing herself as to not startle Kayla, she did not wish to experience the effects of the bracelet herself.
The young trio moved to greet her & the sight of Luma & Rava attempting to walk casually in the bulky oversized armour actually provoked an audible chuckle from Halcyon,

"I know they look a bit silly, but I'll take silly for safety" Kayla said,
"I'm gaining more control over the Maylar Venet as Nyah said I would, but I wouldn't be able to forgive myself if I accidentally hurt one of my friends, but they still insist on helping me train" admitted Kayla,
"Sounds like a very intelligent idea to me" Halcyon said,
With a little smile,
"The reason I came looking for you three was I need you to show me where those tunnels are & the means to open the secret passage"
Luma stepped forward almost toppling over, Halcyon grabbing the large helmet that had fallen over her eyes lifting it off,
"Thanks, I don't think this is exactly my size" she said,
With sweat running down her bright red face,
"We can definitely help, but why now, have you discovered what The Regent is doing down there?" asked Kayla,
"Let's just say we've had some light shone on the issue"
Rava was standing behind the others, from the look on his face Halcyon could see that his thoughts were racing,
"Rava you do not have to go" she said gently,
"No, no I need to get it out of my head & the best way to do that is to face it head on"
The moment was broken by a loud crash of Luma dropping most of her armour to the floor
"Sorry" she said,

Her little face still flushed with the effort of the whole engagement,
"You three go & wash up & I'll meet you…where?" Halcyon asked.
"At the Highaster Tree, it's the easiest place to begin" suggests Rava
"In an hour then?" proposes Halcyon,
The others nod in agreement.

The chimes from the ether again ring out in The Regents chambers, & again The Regent knowing full well who & why they are calling chooses to assert his control over the situation in the only way he has, by making them wait for him. After he was satisfied with his petty accomplishment he slowly strolled across the room to the raised platform, where he again pauses before placing his finger into the ripples of silver liquid,
"Your childish games are not amusing & will have much more severe repercussions the more you utilise them as a tactic" a stern voice berates.
The Regent doesn't dignify the chastising with a response.
"Are the arrangements complete for the transition?" the voice inquired,
"I have organised everything & the process will be taking place promptly" The Regent said curtly,
"See that it is, we cannot afford any more delays, we have much more at stake than just the loss of our ability to use the shadows to move goods around" said the voice angrily,

The Regent paused as he registered the slight
panic in the High Regents voice,
"Has a new stronghold been secured" The Regent
inquired,
"You don't need to know that, all you need to do is
pass the item on to the High guard as soon as
possible" the voice said,
Sharply & severed the connection.
The Regent walked back to his chair,
"This is my power & if those old fools think I'm
going to give it up that easily they truly are out of
their tiny minds" he said to himself.

The sunset over the Highaster Tree was awe
inspiring & always drew the artists of the city
seeking inspiration for their works. Kayla, Luma &
Rava sat in the grass waiting for Halcyon to show
up. Kayla & Luma sat mucking about with a half
black half white cat that was play hunting them,
using the hills to leap out in an ambush & upon
landing its colours switched & rippled down its body
to the girl's delight. Rava sat behind them trying to
get his head around going back to a place which
nearly cost him his life, he was giving himself a little
internal pep talk when Halcyon walked up followed
by Nyah & Nadaur,
"Are we ready to embark?" asked Halcyon,
To which the three youngins jumped to their feet,
"Ready to go" said Luma,
Trying to be serious, just at that moment the cat
jumped from a high hill knocking her back to the

ground causing everyone to burst out laughing to her embarrassment.
Nyah & Kayla helped her back to her feet & they all began to walk towards the edge of the forest. Rava was hanging towards the back of the group & Nadaur fell back to walk alongside him,
"It takes a lot more courage than people think" he said,
Rava looked up,
"I'll be fine" Rava said,
Trying to convince himself as much as Nadaur,
Nadaur looked up at the sunset,
"Sometimes experiences change our perspective for the better, they make us more aware of the consequences & that helps us make more intelligent decisions." He said,
Always keeping his eyes fixed on the sunset,
"The first battle I was in I was about your age" Nadaur continued,
Rava looked over at him,
"Really, I couldn't even imagine doing that," Rava replied.
"I went into it with reckless abandon & a complete lack of fear" he said,
With a wry smile,
"But the second battle I was terrified because I now understood not only what could happen but what was expected of me" Nadaur explained.
"You were scared? That is hard to picture" said Rava,
Embarrassed & looking at the ground.

"I'll let you in on a little secret, being scared can be useful. It shows that you can be honest with yourself & that honesty can keep you & the others that look to you for support safe" said Nadaur.
"How do you move past it?" asked Rava,
Nadaur took a deep breath looking over at Nyah & with a little smile he said,
"It's not so much about moving past it, it's about learning that just because something happened once it doesn't mean the same thing will happen again, but even if it does your experience gives you better ability to deal with it to greater effect" Nadaur explains,
Rava nods,
Appreciating the insight.
"You know that actually does help, Thank you"
Nadaur gives him a pat on his wide back,
"Just remember to stop, think & breath if you get overwhelmed"
The rest of the group wait at the border of the forest for Rava & Nadaur to catch up & once they are all together Halcyon asks,
"Ok, which way now?"
But just as Luma & Kayla are about to answer Rava walks to the front of the group,
"Follow me, it's this way"
Taking point.
Nadaur gave a little smile,
"That was very sweet" says Nyah,
Putting her arm around him & giving him a kiss on the cheek.

”What do you think that sneaky Regent is doing
down in the tunnels?” Luma asked,
Looking up at Halcyon. Halcyon paused stepping
over a fallen log,
“Nothing good my dear" she answered,
“This is odd” said Luma,
“What is it?” asked Nyah
“The forest is too quiet”
Nyah stopped looking around & Luma was right,
usually the forest would be alive with the rustling of
unseen creatures scurrying around the
undergrowth & the tree tops would be full of birds &
other assorted flying creatures but something
seems to have chased them away, a faint smell
wafts through the trees that both Nyah & Nadaur
instantly recognize,
“There's nothing else that smells like that” Nadaur
said,
Putting his hand on his dagger,
“But what would Alimana be doing this close to the
city?” asked Nyah
"Keep your eyes open” Nyah said to the group,
“It's over here!” called Rava,
Leading them towards the three trees. Luma, Kayla
& Rava took up their positions in front of the trees,
”Do you remember the sequence?” Kayla asked,
“Um, don't tell me” Said Luma,
Looking up into the sky trying to recall the order,
“Oh, yes, it was Rock, Knot then Root, right!”
screaked Luma in excitement,
Halcyon, Nyah & Nadaur watched closely seeing
the three switches,

"Ok, first its Rock" Says Luma,
Jumping hard on the rock & hearing the audible
click,
"Then the Knot" says Rava,
As he too pushes the switch & is rewarded with the
second satisfying click, followed by Kayla who
activates the final switch, stepping back as the tree
moves to reveal the entrance to the tunnel & again
as the air rushes from the stale tunnel, that same
foul smell fills their noses, But much more potent
this time. Nyah & Nadaur look at Halcyon with slight
concern, maybe you three should wait up here"
suggests Nadaur,
"No, I wanna see what's down there, we promise
we will stay behind you" pleads Luma,
"Ok but you must follow our lead," said Halcyon
begrudgingly.
Nyah takes the small crystal from around her neck,
holding it in her hand she blows across its surface
causing it to glow brightly. Nadaur rummages
around in his pocket retrieving three small crystal
marbles, two bright red & a green one with black
spots, he put the two red ones back in his pocket &
crushed the green one in his palm releasing a
green vapour that he inhaled deeply with his eyes
closed. Luma & Kayla fascinated peaked around
from the side, seeing that when he opened his eyes
again, they had changed to the same green &
vapour trailed from his eyes into the darkness of
forest.
Nyah & Nadaur stepped down into the thin spiral
staircase, the smooth black walls reflecting the

white light of Nyah's crystal for but a moment, while the green emitted by Nadaur's seemed to be swallowed by the darkness. Nadaur's crystal had given him perfect vision in the darkness, Halcyon's eyes were incredibly precise which helped her with the fine detail work with plants but they weren't the best in the darkened environment, luckily Nyah's crystal was bright enough she could make out the outline of the staircase & the narrowness of the tunnel kept her on track.

Luma had given Kayla a necklace that matched her own with a much smaller & less powerful version of the crystal wielded by Nyah. Kayla held hers high to give Rava as much light as possible so he didn't freak out.

"At the base of these stairs there is a door which leads to another hallway & at the end of that is where The Regent kept whatever caused my injuries" Rava called ahead.

The smell of the Alimana was strong but had dispersed enough that both Nyah & Nadaur knew the likelihood of them being behind that door was minimal but not knowing the level of seal on the doors it was still a distinct possibility. Nyah pressed her sensitive ear to the smooth polished black stone of the door, while everyone stood as silently as they could manage. Nyah unable to hear anything looked back to the glowing green eyes in the darkness of Nadaur,

"It sounds clear" she whispered,

She pressed her shoulder against the door & it moved just as smoothly as it had for Rava who

stood at the back of the group trying to stamp down
the impulse to run back up the stairs & disappear
into the forest, while Luma & Kayla peak from
around Halcyons sides. As the doors seal is broken
the strong smell of the Alimana filled the cramped
tunnel,
"What is that?" Kayla whispered to Luma,
As the foul smell crinkled their noses.
"Some Alimana have been down here" she replied,
With enough concern on her face that Kalya had no
follow up questions.
Nyah & Nadaur moved out into the adjoining larger
hallway & as Halcyon went to follow Nadaur held
his hand up to halt her progress until they had
made sure it was secure.
The door at the end of the hall was left slightly ajar
& as the others moved into the hallway Rava
informed them,
"That's the room with the light",
Pointing to the door. Nyah & Nadaur hugged the
walls as they moved towards the mysterious door,
their focus unmatched. Nyah pushed the door
letting it swing smoothly open but aside from a
pedestal at the end of the room it was noticeably
empty. Both of their postures changed to a more
relaxed stance as they looked around the room,
"Eww!" squealed Luma,
Causing everyone to be on guard & rush to her.
Halcyon looked at the little elf scraping mud & other
unidentified substances off her boot,
"What happened?" Nyah asked,
"Oh, I just stepped in something" she said,

Nyah held her light down illuminating the tracks on the smooth floor,

"Halcyon, take a look at this" she said,

Holding her crystal above the mud, it was a huge footprint, much larger than any of theirs even Rava's would be dwarfed by is immense size.

Luma & Kayla hold their crystals high in the air & the light is enough that they are able to see that the footprints lead off down the hall into the darkness. Halcyon crouched down,

"Just judging by the sheer size & the flatness of the sole I'd say that this is the footprint of an Ogre"

Luma grabbed Kayla's hand in terror,

"Are you alright?" Kayla asked,

"Ogres are monsters" Luma said,

With a quiver in her voice.

Halcyon looked back at her with a knowing look, remembering that it was ogres who massacred many of the dark & forest elves when attempting to gain dominance over the forests, but Kayla distracted her by walking forward still holding her hand.

"Let's go have a look in that room" she suggested,

Ushering her frightened friend forward they both entered the room. The smell was quite different, it had a burnt tinge to it that got stuck in their noses. Nyah was standing next to the pedestal that rose from the centre of the room, the clean black stone had layers of caked on dark purple muck that wasn't familiar to either her or Nadaur. Nadaur's attention was on a cage that hung from the centre of the ceiling immediately above the pedestal. The construction of the cage was what he found more intriguing than its position, it was charred but this looked to be its natural state rather than something that had happened to it over time,

"I don't know what that could possibly be crafted from" he said allowed,

Halcyon gestured to Kayla to prompt her to involve Luma,

"Has your family ever worked with something like that?" Kayla asked,

Luma, who was still somewhat distracted by the possibility of an Ogre in the nearby vicinity, barely heard the question but Kayla followed it up with a little,

"Hmm?"

Which gained Luma attention,

"Oh, I'm sorry, I was miles away, what was the question?"

"The cage sweetheart, do you have any idea what it could be crafted from?" Nadaur asked calmly,

Luma walked closer as Nyah held her crystal high in the air to give her a little more light which illuminated some bright shiny golden fragments embedded within the actual bars of the cage itself & as soon as Luma saw that she knew immediately what it was,

"It's dragon bone" she said with certainty,

"Do you see the golden flecks within the bone, that happens because most dragons will consume their treasure to keep it from being discovered, but they will first melt it into a liquid with their breath to make it easier to swallow" Luma explained,

"& you can see that those pieces must've come from the throat of the dragon, all the bones in front of the dragon's ignition chamber become blackened & incredibly strong".

As she is explaining Kayla steps backwards to get a better look at the cage when something crunches under her feet, the room is pristine with smooth glossy surfaces so something being on the floor made little sense but she just assumed it was more mud. She held her glowing crystal down towards the ground & as she illuminated the substance, she let out a scream,

"What is the matter?" Halcyon asked in a panic, Seeing the colour had drained from her face. Kayla stood there shocked until Nadaur walked around the pedestal to see what had caused such a reaction, his glowing green eyes cut through the darkness & he saw three charred bodies lying in the corner. Kayla had inadvertently stepped on one of these creatures' hand's that had crumbled to nothing with the weight of her foot.

"It's hard to make out, but I'm pretty sure they are Alimanas" he said,

"See here you can just make out their pointed yellow teeth" Nadaur continued

"But what were they doing down here in the first place?" wondered Nyah.

"Judging by the lock on the door, they must've been brought down here by The Regent, but for what purpose?" pondered Halcyon

"They appear to have been exposed to the same fallen star as young Master Rava, but came to a grizzly end" said Nadaur

Nyah looked up seeing that Luma, Kayla & Rava where all standing by the wall looking quite distressed,

"Maybe we should move on, it would seem that we missed what ever happened here" Nyah suggested,

Nadaur took point, followed by Nyah & Halcyon surrounded herself with the young ones & they all ventured down the dark tunnel.

"Are you alright?" Halcyon asked.

"Yeah, I think so, I just got startled" said Kayla,

Luma had forgotten her fear & become more interested in the why of the whole situation, she didn't even hear the question,

"So, The Regent was using a fallen star to what, secure something?" posited Luma,

"But what would warrant something so rare & powerful, not to mention the amount of power that is emitted by a fallen star is gargantuan & using it as a security system seems like a very poor use of such power" Luma continued,

Nadaur looked over at Nyah, giving her a little nod,

"We think it has something to do with a creature that lives & controls the shadow realm" Nyah explained,

"Wait, there are beings in the shadows, I was always told it was an empty space & that was why we used it for travel" Rava butted in.

"That was what we were all told, but it seems from what we've discovered recently that is not the case" added Halcyon,
"So, what you're saying is that The Regent was using the fallen stars light to prevent the creation of any shadows within that room, why?" asked Luma,
"Yes, we believe it was because of a book. Long ago a bargain was struck between the highborn & those who dwell in the shadows for access to the shadows as a form of travel, but somewhere along the way the Highborn betrayed the Shadow dwellers & stole the books giving them access to the shadows & trapping them within the darkness" Halcyon explained.

The Regent followed by only one of his minions opened a door on the side of the city, the hinges were rusty from lack of use, yet the three locks that are in the shape of a triangle in the centre of the door are much newer & well maintained. The reason he had brought only one minion was soon clear as he grasped two of the dials & with a,
"Humph"
He directed the small waddling underling to take hold of the third,
"Counter clockwise" The Regent stated,
With authority.
"Three, two, one" The Regent counted,
Then simultaneously they twisted their respective dials in varying degrees until there was three audible clicks that pulled the dials into the door with a satisfying thud.

The Regent stepped back as he had no intentions of using any effort he did not have to, leaving the small hooded creature to use every ounce of strength it possessed wrenching open the heavy door. The rust fell away from the hinges as the door slowly lurched open. When the seal was broken the terrible smell wafted in & a myriad of snarls & cackles became louder, as the creature used the last of its strength.

A group of the most despicable looking Alimana stood in the overgrowth that ran along the side of the city bickering between themselves. Behind them stood a giant chained Ogre, his chains not held by the Alimana, the chains where his own. One around his neck that ran down his front connected to each of his wrists, these where a sign of ownership rather than actually any attempt to contain him in any way as he could have easily broken his bonds at any time if he had the urge.

The Regent stepped forward, without a word he took a stiletto dagger from his waist he stood behind the weakened minion & drove the dagger slowly through its head, as he did, he maintained unflinching eye contact with the Alimana. Once the creature had fallen still, he tossed the lifeless carcass out the door into the long grass. He stood there in the doorway silent & stoic as the rabble caused by the Alimana became broken then nothing at all, the only sound was the deep laboured breathing of the Ogre.

Once The Regent had gained some measure of control, without a word he turned & walked with purpose sticking to the walkways that run alongside the mighty city walls as they are much less travelled than the inner paths of the city. The Regent's long coat swept the dusty floor as he walked. Behind him the Alimana chopped & changed position as they moved along the overgrown path. Growing up the walls the ivy & vines had used each other to climb the walls on the outside allowing them to cascade over the other side into the narrow paths that surrounded the city. The Ogre despite its size seemed to be able to move through the tangle of foliage without becoming snagged or taking a large portion of it with him as he moved, the only sign that he had been there at all were large muddy footprints on the stone floor. All of a sudden, The Regent stopped causing the Alimana to bump into each other prompting spite & snapping among them, while the ogre just sighed at the commotion.

The Regent had stopped in front of a wall which had four small pots carved from the same stone as the wall, in fact they looked as though they were as much a part of the wall as any other part. The Regent fished a bottle from the pocket of his long coat, The Alimana gathered together paying close attention, thinking they might learn some secret they could later relay to Wrathbone.

The pots looked solid & built into the wall but The Regent took hold of the one on the top right of the square moving it across the slab of stone along a track that could not be seen by the naked eye. Then he took hold of the one on the bottom left moving it into position directly under the first, then the lower right & finally the upper left until he had manoeuvred them into a line down the wall. He then picked up the bottle he had placed on the ground, tipping the contents, which appeared to be plain water into the top pot until it overflowed into the second, third & the final each one filling the one below. The Regent used the entire bottle to the very last drop & as that final drip fell from the mouth of the bottle behind the wall a whole rigmarole of mechanisms sprang into life, finally resulting in the wall pulling back along a seam that was truly invisible & sliding into place leaving a gaping opening in the wall.

The shocking contrast between the rough weathered stone of the city walls & the smooth black glass like texture of the hidden tunnels shocked the Alimana,

"What is this?" one cried

"I'm not going in there!" another yelled,

To which The Regent simply stopped & turned on the spot looking down at the shorter Alimana & said calmly,

"You have been paid for, so either you'll go or you have shown yourself to be useless to me & you've seen what I do with unnecessary items"

Which caused the Alimana to shrink & huddle together. A little glint appeared in the eye of the ogre showing a level of understanding not often attributed to such large beasts. The Regent entered the tunnel, a metre or so in there is a small shelf cut into the wall with beautifully razor sharp edges.

Sitting on the smooth surface is a metal canister with harsh dwarfish letters carved into the silver. The Regent took a passing look over to the door seeing the Ogre had just past the threshold & placed his finger on a seamless bump on the shelf which when depressed resulted in the door effortlessly swinging closed with incredible precision blocking all light from entering the tunnel. Neither the Alimana nor the Ogre react to this as they both had more than efficient low light sight, but The Regent did not, this was the purpose of the Dwarven object. He lifted the small silver tube above his head, using more effort than such a small object should require, he then flicked open the lid with his thumb causing a bright spark to be released from the tube which floated up into the air growing in size as it grew in height until it neared the ceiling it began contracting into a swirling orb of fire that settled above his head.

Accustomed to this procedure The Regent began to walk as soon as the flaming orb settled, moving at a quick but steady pace causing the Alimana to move much faster than they were used to but not being familiar with these tunnels & The Regents utter disregard for their safety they needed to keep him in sight.

The tunnels twisted, turned & turned back on themselves again so much so that it was almost impossible to recall which direction they had entered the labyrinth of confusion. After what seemed like much longer than it actually was The Regent stopped in one of the longer tunnels, it

looked as though there were no doors anywhere along the path, there were no corners visible but given the nature of the glass like material it was often impossible to see a corner before you were in the middle of it. Once the rabble behind him had caught up he pushed on a point on the wall which silently opened revealing a small room, The Regent simply ordered,
"In"
There was barely enough room for them all, let alone having an Ogre in tow, but with some effort they all fit somewhat snuggly.
"You must not leave this room until I return to retrieve you" The Regent commanded,
pulling the door & leaving it to close on its own disappearing down the tunnel & around an unseen corner.
Just as the door what about to close one of the Alimana wedged a worn, chipped & dirty blade in the door jamb stopping it from closing all the way,
"We need to keep an eye on him to see where he's going" one snapped,
"But we will never find our way around here" snarled another,
"Imagine how Wrathbone will reward us with if we can learn his secrets" schemed another,
"I'm going" crowed another,
The Alimana with the blade wedged the door jamb pulled the door open, two others joined him & they scuttled off down the tunnel feeling their way along the wall as the door closed.

Their eyesight was above average in the low light environment but although smooth and reflective the black walls seemed to swallow the little light that remained. They turned a corner at the end of the tunnel seeing The Regent, he was putting on a coat that the Alimana just assumed was somehow part of his pomp & ceremony, they watched & waited in silence as The Regent covered himself from head to toe & once he was ready, he began a sequence to open the door. The Alimana listened closely & upon hearing the lock on the door click they rushed forward pushing passed The Regent, who surprisingly made no effort to halt their progress, he merely stepped out of the way. They pushed the door open to claim their prize. The light immediately became overwhelming turning their skin to cinders in the blink of an eye.

The Regent watched silently as their bodies crashed to the floor like dry leaves, he walked in behind them casually using his foot he pushed their charred corpses into a corner behind the pedestal which held an obsidian box, a book & a severed hand dripping purple blood, which still seemed to be holding on to life despite being disembodied & left the inhospitable environment.

It had taken The Regents minions two weeks to drag the obsidian box from his chambers to the hidden room. The Regent pressed a switch that sat next to the pedestal with his foot that would be easy to miss if you didn't know what you were looking for, which caused the cage that held the viciously bright burning star to begin to lower via a substantial chain which was crafted from the same material as the cage. Once the cage had disappeared inside the box The Regent pressed a second switch on the other side of the pedestal, which released the star into the box & when he lifted his foot from the switch the cage retracted & returned to its original position. He then closed a secondary lid built within the box to separate the monumental heat & light of the fallen star from the other two items, this lid had one hole completely invisible to the naked eye but enough to allow some of the light to leak through.

Once the brutal light had been contained the black & red spider poked its head from the lining of The Regents long coat quickly disappearing back into the safety of the shadows.

The Regent reached into his pocket taking out the dwarven torch striking the lid to create the sparks & once the flaming ball had ascended into place The Regent then placed first the book, facing the spiked cover down, the spike sliding into a readymade slot, then the disembodied hand on top, as he lifted the hand the fingers twitched startling him momentarily & causing him to drop the hand into the box & close the lid quickly.

Then rather than walk back to where he had left the others, The Regent simply walked over to the door & called,

"Come!"

The Alimana opened the door falling out into the tunnel,

"They say we smell bad" one whined,

"Let's get moving, I don't trust this Regent" snapped
another,
Rushing down the tunnel towards the ominous glow
coming from around the corner, followed by the
lumbering Ogre whose movements had become
impaired after being trapped in such a confined
space.
Once they entered the room, they saw The Regent
standing next to a black box, the swirling flames
hanging in the air above them,
"Hey where'd the others go?" one of the Alimana
asked,
The Regent simply replied,
"They are gone."
The Alimana looked to each other, they knew no
further explanation would be forthcoming.
The Regent looked toward the Ogre, then gestured
to the box,
"Pick it up" he ordered,
Not thinking engaging any of them in any form of
conversational niceties was remotely necessary, he
had paid for the ogre & in his mind it was his as
much as any other possession.
The Ogre lumbered across to the box, on either
side were squired off knobs just big enough to give
some purchase for someone attempting to lift it.
The Ogre tried to lift the box but it was far heavier
than it realised, it tilted its head in an attempt to
understand but he was met with,
"Pick it Up!" from The Regent,
The huge creature braced itself & tried once again,
this time with a mammoth effort the box gradually

lifted from the pedestal, A tiny amount of pleasure crept onto The Regents face only for an instant before leaving the room followed by the Alimana then the Ogre moving even slower as it beared the tremendous weight.

Chapter 20

"Hey big fella" yelled Tallie,
As she ran down the hall, Sikes looked around
giving her a little toothy smile as he caught her eye.
She darted down the hallway to catch up to him,
"Where is everybody?" she asked,
"Since the shadows have been down a lot of the
city's inhabitants have had to open small stalls
down at the market just to barter for the bare
necessities" Sikes explained.
"Where ya going?" she asked,
Being somewhat at a loose end,
"I'm on my way to see Sapere, your welcome to join
me, If you'd like" he replied,
With a wink of his massive green eye.
Tallie fell in walking next to the huge walking mass
of hair, they had become quite close, well as close
as it is possible with someone as guarded as Tallie.
They walked in silence down the hall passing the
massive portraits of past battles & those who
apparently turned the tide of events of history in
one way or another. Most of their names lost to the
ages even though their visage were still quite
familiar to the present inhabitants of the city.
Sikes finally broke the silence saying,
"That's an interesting blade"

Trying to use something that he knew Tallie
enjoyed to jumpstart the conversation.
Tallie pulled the scabbard from her belt,
"Yeah, I don't know quite where it fits in, but it did
come in handy" she said,
With a slightly puzzled look.
As they were approaching Sapere's door they could
hear muffled musings coming from his office,
before knocking Sikes leaned his huge head
against the door in an attempt to decipher these
wild noises. Tallie watched the little smile that crept
across his mischievous face, which gave her the
overwhelming want to join him. As she presses her
ear to the cold wood, she felt a playfulness that was
quite foreign to her but she had begun to rather
enjoy. They both looked at each other to see if they
could understand anything, but they could only
make out high cries & barely audible mumbling, So
they both stood back from the door.
Sikes knocked on the door with much more force
than he had intended, sending echoes down the
hallway, which embarrassed him slightly but Tallie
found it quite amusing. Sapere flung open the door
red faced & annoyed,
"Oh, it's you two" he barked,
"If you break my door I am not going to be
impressed" he said,
With an angry look, craning his neck as he
struggled to make eye contact with Sikes.
"Come, come, I've just discovered something really
intriguing"

For someone much smaller his presence was such
that even Sikes hurried when Sapere urged him in.
The air was thick with dust which got caught in the
light that found its way in between the stacks of
books & scrolled papers, it shone through creating
beams of light that crisscrossed the room.
Sapere climbed up into his well worn chair,
"Look here" he directed handing them each a lens,
Pointing to the large portrait on the wall. Tallie &
Sikes stood before the incredible piece of art,
"You'll notice that this depicts the meeting between
those who we now know dwell in the shadow realm
& a mysterious group of Highborn who we are yet
to identify, but what does warrant further
investigation are those five books & what I've just
discovered in an old friend's musings is quite
troubling"
Tallie & Sikes both leaned in trying to get a better
look at these mysterious books, when they are both
startled by Sapere opening the heavy leather
covered book letting it slam on the desk.
"Hidden within this parable about the stars in the
night sky there is a concealed text which explains
that each of these five books hold the key to one
aspect of the shadow world, you may try but it
mightn't be revealed to you" Sapere explained,
Tallie & Sikes with their wildly different sized heads
pressed together stared into the page, after a
minute or so they both lost a little hope & Tallie let
out a little sigh, but just as they were about to give
up their eyes widened as they both saw a slight
twitch of a few letters around the page. Sapere

watched them closely with an almost imperceptible smile. The words began to spread out across the page taking up positions like stars in the night sky. Sikes & Tallie stood mesmerised as the words fell into the background, But as they looked closer the stars began to create shapes, each cluster joining together to form the outline of a book, five in total, each fell into an ascending order from the bottom to the top of the page. When the books had settled into place the stars again began to twinkle.
Tallie & Sikes watched in awe as the stars moved across the page, they were both reminded of watching shooting stars on a clear night. The stars fell from all corners of the page finding their place on the cover of a book, the first of the five, the stars swirled on the cover until for the briefest of moments a word was visible through the chaos,
"Pathway!"
Sike & Tallie yelled at the same time,
Looking across to Sapere, who just responded with a little nod. But when they both looked back to the page to see what the other books had to offer the page had returned to normal,
"What happened?" asked Tallie,
Sapere looked at their confused faces & said calmly,
"You don't need to know everything at once, sometimes a little push in the right direction is much more helpful for you to discover the truth for yourself"
Tallie & Sikes leaned against the desk, their minds swimming trying to decipher the clue,

"But wait, do we know where any of these books
are?" asked Sikes,
Scratching his head,
"That is more complicated, but we have surmised
that The Regent is hiding something in secret
tunnels that run beneath the city & from the security
measures he has put in place we can only assume
he is in possession of at least one of those stolen
volumes" guessed Sapere.

Vincent had become quite use to his solitude over
the last few weeks, not that he was alone all the
time, It was impossible to keep either Luma, Kayla
or Rava away on a daily basis. While he had told
them about the strange interaction with the wolf he
had not informed Halcyon or any of the other adults
& truthfully he had not been completely forthcoming
with his friends either, as over the last little while
since he had woken to the wolf asleep on the floor
he had had many interactions with the creature, not
only in the waking world but in his dreams. He had
found himself on more than one occasion walking
alongside the massive beast, its breath like the
puffing of a steam train as they walked to nowhere
in particular, its presence had become somehow
comforting rather than the terrifying ordeal that it
once was, in fact he had noticed that as he
scanned the environment on these nocturnal
wanders the wolves eyes tracked the same shapes
in the darkness as he did.
These dreams had been consistent for the last few
days, but each time he woke although there were

signs that the wolf had been present in the waking
world Vincent hadn't seen its actual presence since
it occurred that night.
Vincent lay in bed awake but with his eyes closed
going over the significance of such dreams when
that same sound filled the room, in & out like a
piston pushing air into the room. At first Vincent
thought he was still dreaming but the noise wasn't
static, it moved about the room. Vincent froze, he
knew he should have been terrified but his
heartbeat was steady & his breathing had fallen
into rhythm with the wolf, he had been taught to
control his breathing in the meditation sessions with
Calinton.
Vincent turned his head to the side & counted to
three then opened his eyes to see the red eyes of
the wolf staring back at him, but again he felt no
fear or malice from the situation, he slowly sat up in
bed dangling his legs over the side, he noticed that
unlike what he had been told about the previous
encounters with the wolf there was no tether
between them, he could feel that the wolf was
conscious of him as he was of it but the wolf was as
calm as he.
Vincent sat watching the massive beast walk
around the small room like he was watching it
through a lens, almost removed from the situation &
the wolf did the same looking back at him from time
to time.
But then Vincent's heart skipped a beat as he
heard the familiar sound of someone approaching
the door in a panic, he wanted to yell out but

instead something inside him told him to relax &
take control of the situation, he closed his eyes &
concentrated on recalling the wolf into himself,
"Return" he said,
Over & over again in his head until he heard the
latch on the door click & he felt the fresh air from
outside,
"I've brought you some breakfast, young master
Vincent" a familiar voice said,
Vincent opened his eyes to see the wolf had
vanished & standing in the doorway holding a tray
of food was Calinton, she calmly walked across the
room taking note of the large prints that circled the
floor, she placed the tray on the table & said simply,
"I see the meditation is having the desired effect"
with a little smile.
Vincent sat there still somewhat in shock, until he
was able to muster up the confidence to speak,
"I always thought Meditation & stuff like that was
spurious & practised by people who didn't know
better"
Calinton took the chair from under the table moving
it closer to where Vincent sat, she sat down with
one of the scones with jam & cream that she had
brought, after a few bites she wiped the cream from
her mouth & said,
"I find It's more about discovering what works for
you, everyone is different & what works for one
person might not work for someone else, it's just
about being open & trying until you find what helps
you gain a little control within the chaos"
She stood & as she was leaving, she turned back,

"I might just steal one more of those?"
Picking up another scone,
"You don't mind, do you?" she asked,
Having already taken a bite,
"Not at all, help yourself" replied Vincent,
Calinton had just disappeared around the
doorframe when Vincent said out loud but still quite
quietly,
"Thank you"
Calinton popped her head back around the door,
"You are most welcome" she replied,
Having excellent hearing.

"It is time"
Galbaial's voice spilled soft & smooth into Cocker's
chambers. Cocker didn't understand why but he
had been sleeping more & more, he constantly felt
drained, like a sickness was taking hold, but he had
no one to talk to as his underlings Stinal & his
brother seemed to have abandoned him.
Cocker lay in his palatial bed but all the comfort had
little effect. He would pass out & awaken hours
later but felt more & more tired as the days trudged
on. His mind had become confused, the days bled
into one another & his life had become a
monotonous cycle he could not escape.
Galbaial's hand pierced the veil between his world
& Cockers once again,
"Time to awaken" he whispered,
Pressing his nail into his palm until the purple blood
dripped from the open wound onto Cocker's
forehead, then with malicious intent the blood crept

into Cocker's closed eyes. Nothing happened for a moment then his eyes snapped open wide but there was no consciousness behind them, he sat bolt upright moving to the edge of the large bed. Cocker stood facing the shadow that rippled on the wall, its glossy blackness seemed somehow inviting & terrible at the same time.
"Your father believes he can outwit us, but he is sorely mistaken" Galbaial said,
His voice never changed from the singular tone, barely a fluctuation, calm but sinister.
"The stalker spider will guide you to his location" Cocker blinked once & the purple again retreated to the iris, leaving him to appear normal at a glance. Cocker left his quarters & headed for The Regents chambers.

Stinal returned to the hovel he shared with his brother,
"Get up, we've gotta move quickly!" he yelled.
"What, what's going on?" his brother asked,
Having only just woken up,
"There's something big going on in the city & we've gotta take our chance" Stinal said,
With urgency,
"Here" he said,
Tossing his brother a poorly kept blade that landed on the stone floor with a sharp clang.
Urchon got up from the piled blankets & other rags that were his makeshift mattress putting on the same clothes he had worn for months,

"What exactly has you so riled up brother?" Urchon asked.
"The Alimana are in on something, but we're being left out in the cold again!" Stinal answered furiously, "We have to push ourselves into the mix, if we don't this will be as far as we ever get & I want more for myself…much more" said Stinal.
Stinal moved the large box that he had been using as storage & crouched down running the broken tip of his knife into the groove around a piece of stone that jutted out from the wall, he removed the stone putting his whole arm past the elbow into the wall, he felt around, then emerged holding something wrapped in a piece of filthy cloth. He unwrapped it on the floor, inside was a black bladed dagger quite small but somewhat familiar & some random coins, crystals & jewels.
In the centre a black leather case with golden symbols embossed into its top,
"What's that?" asked Urchon,
Slightly getting on his brothers' nerves,
"This" his brother said,
With a huff
"Is how we are going to find those filthy Alimanas in the city"
Stinal held the small case out, it was no bigger than a glasses case, opening it the old hinges creaked & snapped into position. Urchon looked into the case, inside was what looked like a pair of glasses but instead of lenses it had a brass piece in the centre that fitted over the wearers nose, it had very fine detailed flowers carved into the metal,

"I stole it from Halcyon's Conservatory many years ago, I knew someday it would come in handy, she used it to distinguish fine notes in the scents of certain plant species, but it amplifies smells to such an extent when adjusted properly that I should be able to track the Alimana's vile odour & find them anywhere in the city".

Kayla & Luma had become so intrigued with the mystery they had somehow found themselves a part of that their focus had shifted, from the danger of the situation to the solution that they knew was just outside of their knowledge but with every little clue the picture became clearer.
Nyah & Nadaur had both fallen into their protective mindsets, they had been in many places like this & those circumstances were usually caused by someone in a high position of power behaving badly & not wanting to give up whatever power they had accrued through their misdeeds.
While Halcyon had become more concerned about what they didn't know & the depths of The Regents involvement or his knowledge of the true motives behind the events, outside of his tiny role in them. They moved down the tunnels turning this way & that, Nadaur was an excellent tracker but this was putting even his expert skills to the test. He crouched down looking for any sign, the smooth nature of the tunnels left very little in way of discernible evidence of The Regent & those who followed him.

Nyah crouched down next to him, the green vapour
still vibrantly being expelled by his eyes, Nyah
looked past that to the love of her life & asked,
"Is there still any sign of them?"
Nadaur took her hand placing it onto the ground,
"Close your eyes" he said,
Nyah closed her eyes as Nadaur moved her
fingertips over the floor, her eyes opened wide
"There are tiny little scrapes in whatever these
tunnels are made from" she said excitedly.
"Yes, they must've been made by the ogre, it would
take something of incredible weight to scratch such
a hard substance" Nadaur surmised,
The smell emitted by the Alimana's had also been
getting progressively stronger, which they all had
noticed making the closed quarters of the tunnels
much less hospitable,
"This stench is making my eyes water" Luma
complained,
Night elves such as her have very sensitive eyes
because they are usually only active after dark. As
they rounded another corner they came upon a
tunnel cut into the wall leading up, like the one that
had led them down there in the first place, Nyah
sprinted up the stairs at an incredible pace. She
made it to the top of the spiralling staircase & found
herself at a door, like the other the locking
mechanism was very simple on the inside as
opposed to the complexity of the outside. Nyah
shook her crystal to douse the light then carefully
pressed the latch releasing the door, she pushed
the door very gently only opening it a tiny crack, as

the air rushed in the stench of the Alimanas was replaced with a musty smell, that while still unpleasant was somehow familiar as are the muffled voices she hears.

Nyah pushes the door a touch more peeking out through the small opening, she was amazed & pleasantly surprised by the fact that even though they had been walking for hours the door had opened up into one of the cities smaller libraries, the constant twisting & turning of the tunnels no doubt used as a mechanism to trap anyone who found themselves down there unawares. Nyah pulled the door closed before running back down the stairs to find the others.

"Where does it lead?" asked Halcyon,

"One of the small libraries at the back of the city from what I could tell" she replied.

"Oh good, why don't you take the young ones back up into the city" Nadaur suggested to Halcyon,

"Nyah & I will press on"

"No!" Luma protested,

"We want to see this through to the end" she exclaimed,

Nyah came over to the furious little elf,

"We need to let the others know what's going on down here, it is vitally important to relay this information & where we are" Nyah explained,

"Plus, I don't know about you but I would rather not turn one of these corners & find an ogre standing in front of me" Rava chimed in,

"I didn't think about that" admitted Luma,

She immediately got an image of her in front of an ogre in her mind which terrified her,
"We will find Tallie, Sikes & Sapere & fill them in & show them how to get into the tunnel where we got out" said Halcyon,
As she moved the children up the stairs,
"Be careful"
Kayla turned back & said,
As she ascended the spiralling climb.
Once the others were out of sight Nyah & Nadaur began moving down the tunnel this time at a greatly accelerated pace.

"If anyone knows about what's going on it'll be Cocker" said Stinal,
While he & his brother moved past the dining hall.
"Couldn't we stop for a little bite, I didn't have breakfast?" complained Urchon,
His brother stopped dead, turning around & grabbing his brother by the throat,
"If we don't figure something out, there won't be any Breakfast, Lunch or dinner cuz we'll find ourselves out in the cold or with an Alimana dagger in our ribs!" Stinal threatened,
"Look!" Urchon said,
Pointing over his brother's shoulder, Stinal released his grip & turned to see Cocker stoically marching down the hallway towards the orb room. Both Stinal & Urchon began following him hugging the walls & holding at each corner to make sure Cocker didn't notice them. They lingered behind him & never got to see his face, because if they had they would

have noticed the blank expression painted across
his face.

The fresh air filled their lungs as Luma, Kayla, Rava
& Halcyon left the library,
"We need to inform Sapere about what has
transpired" Halcyon announced,
Walking with purpose towards his office with the
three youngsters in tow.
"Where do you think The Regent is heading?"
Kayla asked,
"I don't know, but he must be trying to get the star
out of the city" guessed Luma,
"He has to be going to use some form of instant
travel, since not even The Regent would be
arrogant enough to attempt to travel with such a
dangerous item, especially since we know what the
shadow dwellers are capable of" added Rava.
"I wouldn't begin to guess the heights of that man's
arrogance" scoffed Halcyon,
quickly followed by,
"Oh, I didn't mean to say that out loud"
With a slightly embarrassed look on her face, which
caused her three companions to laugh.
They turned a corner & were almost bowled over by
Cocker,
"Hey watch where you're going!" Luma yelled,
But there was no acknowledgement from him at all,
he just kept on marching down the hallway. Once
they reached Sapere's door Kayla got a big grin on
her face,
"What is it?" asked Rava

"Sikes is in there" she said happily,
"Oh, I love Sikesy, he's so cute" said Luma,
Jumping up & down. Rava looked at them both with
a puzzled look as he found it strange to call a giant
beast such as Sikes Cute, in fact he was quite
intimidated by him.
Halcyon knocked on the door & heard an angry
Sapere command Tallie to,
"See who that is!"
Tallie pulled the door open but before she could
even tell him who it was Sapere pushed his way
around her,
"Oh, it's you, you've got good news I hope" he
barked
"Charming as ever" Halcyon replied,
"I don't know if it's good per se, but it does fill in a
few gaps & moreover it requires us to act quickly"
she explained.
Sapere looked over his glasses with a sigh said,
"Now what's happened?"
"Well, there's a secret tunnel & an ogre & a whole
bunch of Alimana in the city, plus The Regent has a
magical book & a fallen star" Luma blurted out,
To the shock of all the adults, who stood there
staring at her until Tallie forcefully questioned,
"There are Alimanas inside the city walls right
now?"
"Yup," Luma answered simply.
"We've gotta get out there!" yelled Tallie,
But as she was halfway out the door Sapere called
her back,

"We mustn't just rush off without even knowing where we are going" he said calmly,
"First, is anyone following The Regent?" Sapere asked,
"Yes, both Nyah & Nadaur are on his trail in the tunnels" Halcyon answered,
Which relaxed both Tallie & Sikes,
"You mentioned some Tunnels, where exactly are they?" Sapere continued,
"We used the entrance you already know about in the forest past the Highaster Tree but we had no idea the extent of the tunnels, they stretch under the entire city & much further into the surrounding area I'd wager" Halcyon said,
Which surprised Sapere.
"They twist & turn so much under our feet that I wouldn't be surprised if there wasn't an entrance somewhere in here, but the exit we found was in the old Library by the city walls" mentioned Kayla.
"Tallie, you go get Dabn & Faucon, head down there & back up Nyah & Nadaur" ordered Sapere,
"I'll show them where the entrance is" offered Rava,
"Are you sure?" Halcyon asked,
"Yes, I'd like to be helpful, if I can" he answered.
Luma & Kayla gave him a big hug,
"You Be careful, or a bunch of stinky Alimanas will be the least of your worries" said Luma, Looking surprisingly scary.
As they left Halcyon turned to Sikes,
"I've got need of your muscles" she said,
"Anything I can do to help" Sikes replied,

"So, I'll take these two & Sikes, you see what else
you can decipher from Brodrick's books" Halcyon
said,
Leading the others from the room. Luma & Kayla
took up positions on either a side of Sikes, Kayla
felt a sense of safety walking in close proximity to
the hulking beast, which surprised her since she
had always had a slight fear of large animals but for
some reason since she had gotten to know him,
she never had the slightest inkling that she was
anything but safe in his presence. Luma on the
other hand was so comfortable around Sikes that
she would pull at his arm to lead him without
thinking about the fact that he was so much larger
than herself.
"So, what exactly are we doing?" Sikes growled,
Both Luma & Kayla felt the resonance of his voice
pass through them,
"In our investigation we've discovered that the
fallen star, which The Regent has co-opted for his
own means, was actually brought here long ago &
the means in which it was originally contained was
discarded by those who manipulated their way into
leadership as nothing more than a box containing
the power they sort" Halcyon explained,
"Those dummies" chirped Luma,
Looking up at Sikes' shaggy face with a big smile,
to which Halcyon cleared her throat in minor
annoyance & to regain the focus.
"So, with that luck, we actually have something
capable of containing such an object, but alas given
its purpose it is far too heavy for any of us mere

weaklings to lift, let alone move it with any speed over distance"
"It almost crushed me twice!" announced Luma,
Receiving a wide eyed look from Sikes & a smile from Kayla who was thoroughly amused by her friends' antics & an almost audible roll of the eyes from Halcyon.
"But how are we going to get the box away from The Regent?" asked Kayla,
Halcyon shrugged & replied,
"Yet to be solved".
The section of the city where Halcyon's lovey little oasis was located was definitely not made with someone of Sikes proportions in mind, but little of the city really was. He could move through most areas without much trouble, but some of the archways in this part gave him little room to manoeuvre. He was somewhat jealous watching Luma dart around.
Halcyon opened her door as Sikes stretched his back as he stood in her idyllic garden, Kayla & Luma moved around looking at all the beautiful wild flowers that fill the empty spaces.
The creak of the door called them all back to attention before Halcyon could summon them.
In the centre of the room the obsidian box still sat on Halcyon's heavy duty workbench. The top of the structure was made from a huge dense slab of well worn wood with chips & scratches abound & little bits of whatever she was working on in the moment imbedded within the grain of the wood. As they surrounded the box, they could see that just sitting

stagnant had allowed the weight of the box to sink
into the wood by at least an inch,
"This is the object in question, do you think it's
possible for you to move without hurting yourself?"
Halcyon asked,
Sikes looked at the relatively small object & had a
little confident smile on his face as he grasped the
box, but that confidence was quickly tested as the
box caused him to strain more than he liked. Sikes
took a second to make sure his grip was as secure
as it could be on a square box & just with brute
strength, he lifted the box leaving a perfect indent in
the wooden benchtop. Having lifted the object, he
placed it back on the bench & said with a little huff,
"I think we should be ok, do you know where we
have to take it?"
"Hopefully Nyah & Nadaur will discover that
information for us shortly" Halcyon answered,
optimistically.
Halcyon walked over to a little side shelf
rummaging around for a while until she cried,
"Ah ha!"
Holding out the crystal lens that had originally
occupied the box,
"I put it over here so I would know where to find it,
but unfortunately everything gets somewhat
consumed by the mess that surrounds me. I swear
it has a mind & will of its own"
"What does it do?" Sikes asked,
Looking at the small object curiously.
"Its true purpose? that's a mystery but we have had
some success using it as a small measure of

control over the shadow being's ability to remain in
our world".

The city had lost the life that lended to its carefree
nature, the inhabitants seemed to know something
was happening by just the strange feeling that hung
in the air. They had all retreated to their various
domiciles scattered around the city, but you could
see them peeking out from windows & cracks of
doors all curious about the mysterious goings on.
Stinal kept Cocker in sight as he stiffly marched
towards his destination, he passed his father's
chambers but then stopped dead in his tracks, he
lifted his chin turning his head as if someone was
talking to him, guiding him where to go.
"What the hells he doing" Urchon asked,
A little loud for his brother's liking who quickly
covered his mouth, but as he watched Cocker
didn't look around or even seem to notice the
outburst.
Cocker opened the door to The Regents chambers,
but only let it swing closed behind him rather than
actually closing it himself. Stinal darted from his
hiding spot at the end of the hall & just caught the
door before the lock snapped closed, he peeked
through the tiny gap watching Cocker. He moved
into the centre of the room then turned one way &
then another, holding for a second in each position
almost as though he was listening to see which
direction a noise was loudest. After a few of these
pivots Stinal watched him go over to one of the
many bookshelves & after a little movement that he

couldn't quite see as Cockers body was in the way, the bookshelf opened up & Cocker disappeared down a darkened passageway. Stinal saw the bookshelf returning to its original position & he pushed open the heavy door running as fast as he could across the large room & just before the shelf closed in line with the others Stinal lunged forward & thrust his knife into the gap barely stopping the secret passage from closing. As he gently pushed it open the familiar smell of the Alimana filled his nostrils, Stinal turned to speak to his brother & saw that he was still waiting in the open doorway,
"Get over here & keep your eyes open!" he said, Through his teeth becoming more exhausted by him,
Neither of them had any kind of light, Stinal looked around seeing an antique lamp hanging on the wall. He gave it a shake not really expecting it to have any fuel but he had a tiny bit of hope, He looked behind The Regents bar for something, finding a bottle of dragon's breath, an extremely potent form of intoxicant that was outlawed in most places, but as is usually the way the rich don't live by those rules. He filled the lamp tipping it upside down to soak the wick, then with a quick strike of a match that he found behind the bar, putting the box in his pocket, the lamp flashed brightly into life with an audible pop. The vibrant blue flame quite a bit larger than he assumed at first causing him to jump backwards. Then just before he & his brother ventured down the cramped spiral staircase into the unknown, he took the case from his pocket, he

removed the strange object putting it on his face as though it were a pair of glasses but instead of lenses it had an ornate piece that fit over his nose.

The Green hue that had allowed Nadaur to see so efficiently had long since faded away & he was experiencing one of the many side effects of that particular assistance of the imp's cradle. As with many things the necessity for most people will outweigh the unpleasant after effects, although the thumping headache only hampered him slightly & in truth his anger at the pain made him more dangerous to The Regent & his recruited cronies. Nyah saw the discomfort on his face & took a small silver box from her pocket she stopped causing him to stop as well. Nyah opened the box which had a few delicate pink petals that were speckled with green dots, she took one tearing in half & placed it under his tongue,
"This is a solace petal, it should give you some relief from the side effects" she said,
Nadaur gave her a little kiss,
"Thank you, my love,"
As they continued, they began to realise the tunnel had begun to ascend becoming steeper. Where the floor was completely smooth before it now had small stairs which became more pronounced as the gradient grew. The stench of the Alimanas was much stronger as well letting them know they were getting close to their quarry.
Nadaur reached the crest of the slope finding himself at another door, Nyah joined him, both

silent they gently pushed on the door. It was much thicker than the previous ones, it opened just enough that they could see that they were just outside the massive orb room. Far on the other side of the room they could see The Regent standing at a distance from the ogre & the Alimanas, the room was otherwise completely deserted, Nyah whispered,
"What is he waiting for?"
Even from that distance they could see The Regent was looking impatiently at something in his hand. The tremendous room was very poorly lit, which made the addition of many shadows forming among the many that naturally occurred all around the room go unnoticed.

Vincent sat at his small table eating the snacks that had been left for him when a sensation of dread fell over him, the feeling was strange & terrifying but it tickled a long lost place in the back of his memory, then he felt it, that same deep & controlled breathing, the instant the hot breath hit the back of his neck he had no doubt.

The seriousness of his task was not lost on him, Rava led Tallie, Dabn & Faucon into the old library,
"How many Alimana did you say there were?" asked Dabn,
Already furious that his city had been violated by such filth, but before Rava could answer Faucon butted in,

"Did you miss the part where he said they had an ogre big guy? I think that should be our main concern"
Tallie on the other hand was feeding on the adrenaline that came as a precursor to battle, it was a feeling she had felt thousands of times throughout the years & as a small child had been taught to feel & focus it making her much more aware & much more lethal.
"Over here!" Rava said loudly,
Causing the tall slim librarian to look over with a disapproving glare that seemed very at home on her face. The door still had the book wedged in the gap to hold it open, Rava pulled it open being careful to not open it all the way, the foul smell of their prey flooded out into the library.
"You head back & tell the others we've entered the tunnels" Tallie said,
With a serious but somewhat gleeful look, she pulled a round object from her pocket,
"Here give this to Sikes" she said,
Opening the object holding it out, inside it had a dial decorated with beautiful engraved vines,
"This will lead him to us, this is its other half" she said,
Holding out a small golden leaf that hung on a leather strap around her neck. The trio disappeared into the darkness led by Faucon with her far superior eyesight, leaving Rava to wedge the book back into position in case they needed a quick escape route & then he took off running to find the others.

<u>Chapter 21</u>

Sapere found himself at the last few pages of Brodrick's book, he was still holding out hope that there would be some sort of clue about the shadow dwellers true motivations, but he only found fragmented musings & fractured thoughts. Sapere turned the last page & he was left with the back cover of the book which had been decorated with many colours that swirled into each other. The beautiful artwork was slightly ruined however by a large unsightly drop of ink in the lower right corner, which annoyed Sapere enough that he took his hanky out & with the aid of a little spit he attempted to remove it but had little success. In fact, the more he scrubbed the farther the stain spread. Sapere was so focused on the spot, when all of a sudden, he found himself high above an unfamiliar forest, beautiful & vibrant the forest brimmed with life, but something caught his eye, something that ruined the pristine beauty, a small black spot. He tried to focus on the abundance of pleasant natural beauty but every time his eye was drawn back to the singular black spot & every time, he looked back the spot had enveloped a little more of the forest. Sapere looked closer & to his shock the spreading darkness was more than just an absence of light, it seemed to be replacing the forest itself with a void that had its own substance. Its growth was timid & gradual at first but as it consumed more of the forest it appeared to gain an appetite for spreading out. Each time it took a little more & each time it became a little more aggressive, until without him actually noticing the shadow had engulfed most of the forest, leaving a void but not a lifeless one. Sapere strained his eyes peering into the darkness, he could see movement but he was unable to identify its source. Then from behind him a bright light appeared burning back the abyss until it receded into nothingness, but its impact was not. The bright vibrant forest had been drained, the once loud abundance of life now fell silent, the trees broke & splintered under their own weight, the fragile leaves blew away with the slightest breeze. Sapere was thrust back into his chair in complete shock he touched his face realising he had tears streaming down his cheeks at the true terror & obliteration of what he had witnessed, he knew he had to inform the others & hurried from the room so quickly he left the door wide open.

Nyah & Nadaur stood watching The Regent, he was becoming more & more agitated as the time ticked away, both of their pointed ears pricked up as they heard someone in the distance of the

tunnel. Because of the twists & turns the noise
became dissipated as it bounced from wall to wall,
but Imps are known for their stellar hearing, they
both closed their eyes & in an instant they both
remarked,
"It's Tallie"
As they recognised her cadence & the faint rattle of
her many blades.
Tallie, Dabn & Faucon reached their companions in
short order moving with incredible speed, they
addressed each other in hushed tones,
"What's happening?" Tallie whispered,
Seeing the serious look on both Nyah & Nadaur's
faces, Nadaur guided her to the sliver of a gap in
the door. Tallie's pupils dilated as she saw the
wretched group standing in a place she walked
through every day. Tallie's temper almost got the
better of her, her instinct for violence welled up
inside her once again, clutching the scaled handle
of her blade,
"We need a plan, they will scatter if we just try to
rush out & attack them & we don't want a rabble of
Alimana lose in the city" whispered Nadaur,
Dabn growled at the mere mention of the Alimana,
his hatred rising to the surface.
Tallie pulled the leather lanyard from her neck, she
held the beautiful little leaf in her palm & with the tip
of one of her smaller daggers sliced the tip of her
finger letting a single drop of blood fall on the metal
leaf. The others watched as the blood travelled
along the veins of the leaf until the leaf let out a tiny

but noticeable pulse. Tallie returned the amulet to her neck & remarked,
"The others should be here soon".

Rava burst through the door of Halcyons sanctuary huffing & puffing, startling both Luma & Kayla & funnily enough even Sikes jumped which Luma found endlessly amusing,
"Here, it just pulsed" Rava said,
Handing the device to Sikes, his large hands struggled to open the delicate clasp, but as soon as it popped open the vines had transformed into a representation of the city & within what looked like a solid wall was a tiny leaf, not green like the others but blood red & slowly blinking,
"That looks like it's just off the Orb room" said Halcyon,
Examining the device.
"Sikes you'd better get moving, you don't know how much the weight of that box will slow you down" she said,
Guiding the much larger creature around the room. Sikes heaved the box from the bench leaving the room as fast as he was able but definitely hampered by the immense weight. Halcyon looked at the youngsters,
"You three stay here where it's safe, I have to go & see what's happening"
Leaving & locking the door behind her before they could protest.
Luma, still with her mouth open as she was about to cry foul, realised quickly that they had all the

information they required & immediately went over
to look at the lock,
"Do either of you know anything about locks?" she
asked,
Peering into the lock's mechanism, before she
could even answer Kayla looked down as she felt
her bracelet move. The bracelet had formed a thin
talon extending out from the band. Without a word
Kayla walked over to the door crouching down &
inserted the shard into the lock, they all stood in
silence as they heard tiny clicks until the lock
snapped open.
Luma reached out & turned the handle & the door
swung open,
"Huh, that's handy" said Rava in amazement.
"There's a small hallway behind the Orb statue that
we should be able to use without being spotted"
schemed Luma,
Kayla looked down once again at the bracelet that
had given her a choice, whether to be afraid or take
action,
"Let's go" she answered,
With a new found resolve.

The overwhelming foul stench of the Alimana had
filled the orb room & hung thick in the air, but that
was only one of the objectionable things about the
Alimana when gathered in a group. Small bickering
arguments had begun to pop up, at first a simple
glare from The Regent was enough to quash the
aggressive nature, but the longer they waited his
control was waning. A blinding flash filled the room

460

& when they had regained their vision a squad of the elite high guard stood in front of them in full regalia,
"I wasn't informed of your arrival!" The Regent said angrily,
To which he received no response. His confidence was clearly shaken & he was very aware that this was not what had been discussed,
"You there! Bring that over here!"
The lead soldier commanded to the ogre,
The ogre began to lumber across the room, but just as the Ogre passed The Regent a flood of Alimana appeared from every hallway. The Elite high guard immediately closed ranks around the Ogre who was becoming fairly agitated by the sudden influx. Nadaur pushed the door open running into the fray closely followed by the rest of the group,
"Don't spread out, stick together!" he yelled,
As he knew that against such a larger force it would be incredibly easy to be flanked & surrounded & once that happened, they would be hopelessly overwhelmed.
The Regent drew a long sword swiping expertly at anything that came close. Within the rabble he saw Wrathbone enter the room, he sat atop a dwarven mole, a vicious creature with skin like iron & rows of teeth that could chew through the densest stone. They were used by the dwarfs to not only dig tunnels but clear any & all that may occupy areas that held wealth which the dwarfs converted above all else.

The Alimana bit & sliced at anything they got near including Wrathbones vile steed which responded by removing any limb that came within reach of its rows of razor sharp teeth.

Dabn charged in crashing into the writhing mess of bodies first, sending squealing Alimana flying through the air. Having trained together since they relocated to the city they functioned incredibly efficiently as a group, not to mention Nyah, Nadaur & Tallie had fought in countless battles together during the war.

Even with their incredible skills the odds were not remotely in their favour, Nadaur pulled the two red marbles from his pocket passing one to Nyah who promptly crushed it inhaling the vapour, within a millisecond her muscles bulged & she let out a chilling war cry which was scary enough that the Alimanas who were in her close proximity had second & third thoughts about getting anywhere near her. Nadaur absorbed the second, his reaction being far less aggressive as he was no stranger to the effects of the imp's cradle, with a squeeze his concealed blades jutted from his forearms, clean & shiny but with traces of his blood dripping from the point. Tallie drew the mysterious black blade, she had witnessed its effectiveness first hand as a potent weapon against Alimana & was eager to dispatch as many as she was able.

Faucon moved with lighting speed staying just outside the reach of the snarling horde, she moved with purpose & precision, she knew her talents lay in overseeing the battlefield from above, her target was the massive Orb statue. As she began the climb, she caught sight of an Alimana out of the corner of her eye, she fired two barbed quills that drove themselves deep into her pursuer's eyes, causing it to crash to the floor & be engulfed by the mass of bodies.

The stench in the room was almost overpowering, The Regent was brutal & efficient with his strikes leaving a trail of disabled victims in his wake, some dead but most just severed in such a way that left them to be trampled by their brethren. His eyes were trained on his target, Wrathbone,

"How did you breach my city?!" he yelled,

Wrathbone laughed,

"The people you see as below you are as good as invisible, so if one of the group breaks off to open the same door you let them in, it goes unnoticed by your highness"

Wrathbone rears back on his ghastly steed but as it went in for the attack The Regent moved putting the Elite guard in between them.

The Elite guard had surrounded the Ogre who was becoming increasingly agitated using the obsidian box to cave in the skulls of any Alimana that managed to slip through the Guards formation.

Tallie, Nadaur & Nyah were working incredibly efficiently cutting small groups from the horde & dispatching them with brutal precision,

"We need to get that box out of here!" yelled Nyah,

Over the song of battle,

"Sikes will be here!" Tallie yelled back,

As she drove her blade into the face of an Alimana.
Dabn had become surrounded & was being
overwhelmed by the sheer numbers, the Alimana
would attack & retreat slicing at him with toxic
blades that were coated in all manner of filth.
Faucon spotted her friends dire situation & pulled
two arrows from her quiver & with astounding
accuracy placed the arrows in the ground in front &
behind the trapped beast,
"Dabn, Flash!" she yelled,
Dabn immediately covered his face as the two
arrows unleashed a blinding white light that
scorched the skin of the Alimana & cauterised their
eyes leaving them blind & writhing in pain on the
ground. Dabn's thick skin protected him somewhat
from the intensity of the blast & he was able to
break away from the perilous position.
A group of Alimana had banded together & begun
targeting Tallie, she didn't take a backward step
facing them with a gleeful brutal resolve. Her blade
cut deep into their putrid flesh leaving the black
blade dripping in green blood, but one had snuck
around behind her, it slinked closer raising its
gnarled blade to strike at her back. Tallie turned but
just as the blade was thrust forward the Alimana
was hit with such force its bones splinted &
protruded from its vile flesh, Tallie looked up to see
Sikes' furry but furious face surveying the battle,
"Halcyon told me you would need this" he said,
Holding out the second box.
The vile stench had permeated the entire city as
the Alimana insides smelled infinitely worse than

their outsides. Luma, Kayla & Rava found their way
to the battle their eyes burned with the foul odour.
They reached the end of the hallway & Kayla let out
a terrified cry, Luma looked to her thinking it was
the carnage that was unfolding before them but
Kayla said,
"I can see them, they are everywhere!"
"The Alimana?" Luma asked,
"The shadows, they have opened all over the room"
Kayla could see the portholes vividly even though
they were obscured by the darkness & they were
closing in on their friends.
Kayla stood frozen, she felt her bracelet shift. She
& Luma watched as the Maylar Venet formed into a
robust gauntlet with spiked knuckles, it continued to
grow spreading up her arm & sending out straps
that lashed across her chest & forming into a sturdy
chest plate
"Woah, that's so cool!" said Luma in amazement,
A little loud attracting the attention of a few
scattered Alimana. They immediately began
running toward her, the noises they made were
equally as disturbing as the odour & the frenzied
nature of their movement which put Luma on her
back foot, but Kayla steadied herself simply saying
to herself,
"This is what all the training was for, concentrate"
She adjusted her stance bending her knees & then
as one Alimana came into reach she struck him low
in the abdomen sending him crashing to the floor.
Some of the others could not stop in time tripping
over his body, resulting in a heap of snarling flesh.

Kayla turned her attention to the other two Alimana
that had avoided the collision, Luma meanwhile
was watching the muddled mess of limbs quickly
getting back to their feet. Rava looked around
seeing a large & rather regal looking wooden chair
by the wall, he easily broke one of the longer
pieces of turned wood from the frame of the chair,
"Luma, eyes up!" he yelled,
Tossing her the post.
Luma had quite a bit a practice with the simple
weapon, learning how to efficiently utilise the bow
staff was a staple part of the forest dwelling elves
schooling. Luma stuck hard & with brutal precision
on the most delicate points of her incoming foes,
shattering collarbones & noses as she went. While
Rava was just utilising his brute strength tossing
anyone he managed to get his hands on against
the hard stone walls. Kayla was pushing forward
trying to get to somebody to tell them about the
gateways opening all over the room, but the chaos
of battle was something she wasn't prepared for.
The incredible noise blended together & she was
finding it difficult to do much more than survive. She
whacked an Alimana in the jaw with the point of her
elbow from which a sharp edge had formed, in a
barely controlled frenzy she felt a large presence
behind her, she turned to strike but was pleasantly
surprised to find herself face to belly with Sikes, he
had spotted her & had been moving across the
carnage to make sure she was alright & remove her
from the fray,
"The Shadows are open everywhere!" she yelled,

The concern on her face alone was enough for
Sikes to take her at her word as he had no reason
to doubt her.
Sikes crouched slightly,
"Jump on!" he growled,
Gesturing with his massive head. Kayla climbed
aboard with no hesitation holding on to the long hair
on his Sholders. Sikes yelled,
"Can you see Nyah or Nadaur?"
Kayla climbed as high as she could on the mighty
beasts back scanning the battlefield for their
friends. After a frantic search she caught a glimpse
of the bright red vapour being emitted by their eyes
caused by the Imps cradle.
Kayla yelled but Sikes was too distracted by the
onslaught of enemies as he was one of the largest
targets, Kayla used her weaponized hand to thump
three times on his immense head finally gaining his
attention, Sikes looked up & Kayla pointed,
"Over there!" she shouted,
Sikes bounded towards their comrades, Kayla
clung on for dear life swiping at any of the Alimana
who tried to follow her ascent. Sikes slid to a stop
taking out another few combatance giving Nyah &
Nadaur a brief respite,
"This is not the only fight!" snarled Sikes,
"What?" Nadaur yelled back,
His head still in the midst of the battle,
"The shadow dwellers they've opened portholes all
over the room" Kayla asserted,
Both he & Nyah scanned the room & although they
were unable to see the pathways from the different

realms, they were obscured by darkness, they did however notice that random Alimanas were disappearing, being snatched into nothingness.
"We need to get that box out of here!" Nyah yelled, Making a beeline for The Regent followed closely by Nadaur.

The Regent was still engaged in conflict with Wrathbone, both seemingly unable to gain the upper hand on the other, but both had inflicted significant damage.
Wrathbone had sacrificed his steed in the attempt to land the death blow rushing at The Regent in the fashion of a joust but was unsuccessful.
The Regent had been trained since birth in many of the deadly arts but his true passion was the sword, it allowed him to strike while staying at a safe distance. Wrathbone on the other hand preferred wielding dual short swords which allowed him to strike & perry at the same time, he may not of had the highborn tutelage but his will was immense & his practice brutal. The two circled each other, The Regent limping from a deep gash to his thigh, his blood ran down his leg spilling onto his feet causing him to constantly slip in his own exsanguinated vital fluid. One of Wrathbones arms hung by his side lifeless, The Regent had relieved him of one of his weapons by flaying the flesh from along his bicep severing the tendons & rendering that arm useless. They both were not ones for giving praise or believing that anyone else was truly their equal but it was abundantly apparent to both of them that the

other was more than formidable & by that merit
they both believed the other needed to be removed
from their path if they were to succeed.

The Elite guard had been whittled down, only a
handful stood guard around their prize, the box.
Some found their end at the hands of the feral
rabble & a few unlucky individuals strayed a little
too close to the unnerved Oger meeting a quick but
sticky end.

Halcyon & Sapere entered behind Luma & Rava
who had wisely stuck to the outer edge of the
conflict. Halcyon approached Luma & was almost
stuck in the face with her staff as she had become
quite manic trying to stay ahead of the seemingly
unending horde. Luma's eyes widened,
"Oh, shit Hally, I nearly took your head off!" she
said in shock,
"I'm well aware" Halcyon replied,
Retreating against the wall.
Sikes bounded up with Kayla still clinging to his
back, he spun around quite gracefully & Kayla
jumped landing inches from her friends. Kayla was
breathing heavy but she had a look, A new found
steely resolve in her eyes. Kayla stood in front of
Sapere & Halcyon but still faced the fray,
"They're here, the shadow dwellers, all around us!"
She said frantically,
Both Halcyon & Sapere examined the room not
seeing any obvious sign, but they took her at her

word as they knew she had the ability to see what others could not.

"They must be after the book" Sapere said

"And that gross Hand!"

Yelled an over-stimulated Luma,

"Where exactly is the box in question?" inquired Halcyon,

"There!"

Luma pointed to the diminishing Elite guard with her staff,

Then cold-cocking a menacing little Alimana.

Sapere looked at the situation for a moment trying to assess & come up with a plan,

"Ah!" he cried,

"Took me a minute"

"What!" yelled Halcyon,

Somewhat uncharacteristically, but given the circumstances completely understandable. "Ogres hate fire" Sapere informed them,

"If we can get the Ogre to drop the Box, maybe with a distraction Sikes can switch them"

Nyah still in the midst of the battle & quite a substantial distance from the conversation heard the suggestion, Imps having extremely stellar hearing. She whistled to Nadaur & with only a gesture & look in the direction conveyed her intention. He began moving towards her as she grabbed the closest Alimana using it as a shield slamming it into anyone in her path. Once she got close enough, she kicked the back of its knees & ran up its back leaping high into the air, she sored

gracefully & had no doubt her love would be exactly where she needed him to be. Nadaur cut a bloody path, letting nothing get between him & his heart. Nyah flipped & Nadaur was there with raised arms. Nyah landed on his outstretched hands & he summoned as much strength as he could muster letting out a scream at the excursion as he flung her towards the statue of the Orb & Faucon.
Nyah landed with elegance on the thin struts of the statue exactly where she had intended.
"We need you to encapsulate the Ogre in fire!" she commanded.
Meanwhile Nadaur who had also heard the plan headed straight for the Elite guard. Now while he had no love for the high born or their pretentious royal guard he knew if they were to be killed in result of any action of Nyah the consequences could be dire & possibly something her mother would struggle to protect her from.
Nyah had Faucon draw her bow but told her to hold as she understood what Nadaur was attempting. He fought his way through the remaining skirmish till reached the guard & knowing that they would never bow to his request he removed a barbed chain from around his waist while he closed the distance.
Although their numbers had been almost depleted there was still five large strong individuals surrounding the ogre. Nadaur whipped the chain into the closest, the barbed end cutting deep into his flesh. Nadaur then ran around the remaining guard pulling the chain taught as he did imbedding

the barbs into each of them. When he reached the
last two, he looked up catching Sikes eye,
"Sikes, over here!" he yelled,
Sikes heeding his friends call forced his way
through the remaining Alimana with singular intent.
Nadaur attached the final two just in time for Sikes
to grab the end of the chain, his immense power
easily tearing the guard from their feet leaving the
ogre unguarded.
Faucon fired three arrows at once, then a fourth.
The first volley released a bright green gaseous
substance & second ignited it encompassing the
ogre in green fire.

Stinal & his brother follow as closely as they dare,
but Stinal has become very aware that their
presence seems to have little to no effect on
Cocker. He is being pulled toward something & that
motivating force is not his own. Stinal's temper is
being sorely tested by his brothers constant
questions to the point where he held him against
the wall covering his mouth with his hand, when he
turned back Cocker was standing dead still in the
middle of the slick black tunnel, he turned & turned
again, Stinal watched, it looked as though Cocker
was being pulled towards something but he wasn't
quite sure where it was.
Cockers purple tinged eyes scanned the seemingly
barren wall, he reached out his hand holding in
place against the cold stone. Then as Stinal
watched Cocker's gaze snap he had discovered
something unseen that had caught his mind's eye.

Cocker took his hand off the wall, holding his palm up he took the dagger from his belt & with no reaction pushed the blade through the centre of his hand. Stinal watched as Cockers blood ran down his arm & dripped onto the ground. Cocker pulled the blade from his hand in the same unflinching fashion, there was something about the way his blood flowed that gave Stinal pause, but truthfully the whole situation had put him on edge. Cocker once again stretched forth his hand to the wall, Stinal & his brother watched in awe as his hand passed through the wall, there was a strange appearance to the place where his hand penetrated the stone, a different deeper shade of black that attracted Stinal's eyes in the more he stared. Cocker's hand emerged from the strange black abyss holding a deep red stone set in a jagged black setting, Cocker turned again facing the wall stone, a pale white hand passed into the light, Cocker placed the dazzling object into the palm of the disembodied arm & began again with his military style march down the tunnel.

Stinal with Urchon clinging to his side moved towards the place of activity & they were shocked to see there was nothing there, no rhyme or reason why Cocker had been drawn to this place, Stinal bent down dipping his finger in the spilt blood, "Hmm" he said,

Feeling the oddly congealed blood between his fingers & he noticed the odd purple tinge.

The battle had changed & changed again & our heroes had pivoted expertly with everything that had been thrown their way but they were also aware that there was a party who had not shown their hand. Sikes quickly binded the Elite guard leaving them in a corralled in the corner out of danger. The Ogre thrashed wildly dropping the box which hit the ground with a tremendous thud taking a large chunk from the stone floor. The Ogre was completely out of control, Nadaur saw his chance, he took off running at an astounding pace leaping over the flames impacting the off balance beast sending it careening out of control through the fire until it found itself far enough away from the torment of the flames. The Ogre looked up, Nadaur saw in its eyes that it had consciousness & a tinge of understanding but it was trapped by its own ignorance & the bad intentions of others. The Ogre disappeared down one of the adjoining hallways, on any other day an Ogre roaming the city would be a huge problem but they had far greater things to deal with.

"Get the box!" commanded Wrathbone,

To any of his scrappy soldiers that remained. The feral creatures flung one another over the green flames but found themselves thwarted by the incredible weight of the Obsidian box.

The small area circled by flame was soon full of Wrathbones minions, they pushed & squabbled as they always did pushing each other closer to the fire until one ventured a little to close & woosh it went up in flames, in a panic & writhing in pain it

ran into the others & in their attempt to avoid it they found themselves alight. Wrathbone watched as the vast majority of his remaining forces burned to cinders leaving only the box remaining.
The Regent smiled at Wrathbone,
"You cannot win" he said,
Gleefully, he didn't care how many had to die in his attempt to hold onto his imagined control or the circumstances of their death.
Wrathbone was furious but he calmly smiled back,
"This was but a skirmish" he replied,
Turning & slinking off towards the city's main gate, his wounds beginning to overwhelm him. The Regent walked over to the Box sitting in the middle of the room turning to face the others,
"Your presents is no longer required" he said,
Addressing them as little more than hired help.
"You have no idea the true nature of what resides in that box!" said Sapere sternly,
The Regent glared at Sapere who was not intimidated in the slightest,
"They are already here!" Sapere said with conviction,
"The Danger has passed" The Regent scoffed.
A singular voice filled the room, not because of its volume but because its origin was all around them,
"You stole something far beyond your comprehension"
The words had weight, they pressed into their brains invoking a physical response.

The colour drained from The Regents face while he
frantically scanned the room, the once hidden
gateways now visible all around the room.
Kayla watched as the shimmering light that she
saw was swallowed by an endless black. A shadow
opened behind The Regent, Nadaur without
thinking ran leaping & knocking The Regent to the
ground just before a pale hand swiped at his back,
"Your evil is contained, you can't breach the
shadows!" The Regent yelled,
With a diminished confidence,
"Evil" the voice chastised,
"Evil is just a word, something those in power
constructed as a means of control, a guideline
which they themselves had no intention or ability to
abide by & little understanding of its true nature"
The voice stated,
"You assign this term to us, we never agreed to
behave or live within an arbitrary set of rules you've
concocted"
The voices' words fall into the room with pointed
aggression but an underlying truth & nature that
inflicts a sense of dread to all who hear them.

At the far end of the room out of sight, a panel on
the floor slides back, Cocker emerges walking up
the final few stairs, his blank expression remains as
he backs up to the wall into shadow awaiting
instruction from his master.
"We need to contain the box" said Halcyon,
Trying to remain calm but obviously panicked.

"But with the star inside we dare not open it in here or we will suffer the same fate as those slimy creatures in the hidden chamber!" Luma yelled, Halcyon turned to find her bag lying against the wall, she ran over pulling the heavy coat & gloves that she had taken from outside The Regents secret room,

"Nadaur this will help to subdue the star's destructive power!" Halcyon called.

The green flames still surrounded the box keeping it just out of reach of everyone. Luma & Kayla began to shiver,

"What's going on?" asked Luma,

Kayla looked up at the gateways that had opened above them, while her gaze was still drawn deep into the unending abyss the edge of the gateway shimmered like a mirage in the desert, something was moving outward. The green flame didn't flicker as quickly or violently anymore, it was not being extinguished but in fact it is beginning to freeze in place. The tips of the flames that once danced among one another now frozen into pointed shards, delicate & razor sharp. The Regent seeing his opportunity to remove the tether that restrained the Elite guard, with little care for their wellbeing he grabs the end of Nadaurs chain tearing the barbs from their flesh,

"If you wish to earn the favour of your masters, this is your opportunity" he said,

Pointing his sword at the coveted box.

The Elite soldiers stood, instantly forming into a precise formation moving forward without

hesitation. The lead soldier reached out to attempt to part the frozen flame but as soon as his hand made contact the chill began to spread into his fingers and into his hand, his visceral cry of pain was so out of character his fellow soldiers seemed trapped in place, reactionless. Tallie not being as easily disturbed moved quickly across the room & with one swift & clean strike severed the man's arm just above the wrist. His hand clad within the Elite guards armoured gauntlet fell to the floor continuing to be taken by the frost as it fell shattering into pieces on the cold stone ground.
"Get back you indoctrinated fools!" yelled Nyah,
As she & Nadaur join Tallie in between the soldiers & their quarry.

Cocker stood still against the wall obscured by the darkness, the familiar voice began again to coerce his actions,
"She has the means" the voice stated,
Cocker's head turning, until his gaze was fixed on Halcyon,
"Use the cloak & remove the star"
The words not spoken aloud, they pressed themselves into Cockers brain, deeper & deeper like a recurring thought until he could no longer resist,
"Move with the shadows" the voice instructed,
The darkness that concealed him began to grow creeping along the wall towards Halcyon, His movements were much more meticulous no longer stiff & wooden more akin to the stalker spider.

Halcyon stood holding The Regents protective robe but she was unable to give it to anyone that she considered in the position to utilise it.

The Elite guard did not stop to attend to their injured brethren, their only thought was the acquisition of the box for their masters, but having seen the only one able to lift the box being the ogre they had quickly realised they needed to rethink their plan. The lead solder turned & said to his immediate subordinate,

"Use a snap & return with the might"

The soldier immediately took a snap from his belt triggering it disappearing with the loud concussive snap.

Nyah, Nadaur & Tallie served as an incredibly formidable deterrent & although The Elite guard held a certain level of respect within the highborn hierarchy, they did not compare with the battle experience of the three who stood between them & their prize.

Across the room Stinal & his brother popped their heads from the tunnel & immediately Stinal knew they were in well over their depth, so rather than enter the fray they stayed in the safety of their current position.

Kayla & Luma stood behind Halcyon, they could see the predicament that she had found herself in, having the solution to a problem but being unable to put said solution into practice. But Kayla had a new found belief in her own abilities & Luma was the perfect partner in that belief. Kayla grabbed the two thick black gloves that were sticking out of the

top of Halcyons leather satchel tucking them into her belt,
"We need to get past them"
Kayla told Luma leaning in close,
Kayla looked around Halcyon catching Nyah's eye, Kayla having learnt the merit of a simple gesture from watching them train raised her chin trying to get the point of the assisted vault which they had done countless times in their training sessions of late. With the smallest shifts in her body weight Nyah made both Nadaur & Tallie aware of Kayla & with the slightest peek around The Elite guard made eye contact with Kayla & were all alert & ready.
All that was left was for Kayla & Luma to build up their courage.
The others had not noticed, but The Regent was hyper aware that those who dwell within the shadows had been remarkably silent for too long, scanning around the vast room, he could barely make out two huge objects moving stealthily within the darkness.
Sapere stood toe to toe with The Regent, his newly discovered knowledge making him unwilling to let a glorified figurehead destroy not only his home but the entire world.
"You have brought this on yourself, thinking you had the ability to control or contain a power of this magnitude" Sapere said furiously,
But The Regent was unmoved, his eyes barely fell to meet Sapere's gaze. Sapere watched tracking

his eyes & as he turned, he too saw the movement
in the shadows,
"Sikes!" he yelled,
Trying to alert the others of the impending danger.
Luma took the heavy robe from Halcyon,
"Be careful you two" Halcyon said,
As she handed the protective garb.
"Follow me & stay close!" Kayla instructed,
with a level of confidence that reassures Luma.
Holding her best friend's hand they both had a
steely look fall across their faces.
Nyah looks up to catching the eye of Faucon who
was ready & waiting to offer any assistance
required of her. From her vantage point high above
the battleground she could read the situation
quickly, she saw Kayla & Luma readying
themselves, Faucon drew an arrow from her quiver,
a black shaft with a bright white arrowhead. She
took a full draw holding for the optimal moment.
With the slightest nod Nyah signals Kayla & Nyah
leaps from the orb. Kayla & Luma take of running
with all their might both knowing this was not a time
for anything less than every ounce of effort. Faucon
releases the bolt sending it sailing past Kayla &
Lumas heads with precise aim, the arrow skewers
one of The Elite guard with such force he just stood
in the formation with the arrows white payload
jutting from his chest, his brethren have just enough
time to turn when the arrowhead ignites releasing a
blinding light that renders the soldiers blind.
Nadaur & Tallie grab the nearest soldier pushing
them out of the way while the remaining suffer the

impact of a full speed Sikes sending them crashing across the floor, their armour creating an awful racket but protecting them from true harm.

Kalya & Luma close the distance but just as they cross the halfway mark one of the massive objects' fires from the secrecy of the shadows launching into the air, it was one of the giant wolves, its red eyes burning bright against its absence of colour, its jaws snapping wildly driving it forward with even more aggression.

Halcyon screamed in terror & in an attempt to warn her young friends of the imminent danger. Luma turned her head just in time to see the giant animal impacted from the side, she turned her head back continuing on her task thinking it was one of her cohorts that removed the danger.

The wolf slid across the floor fighting to regain its footing, snarling its white teeth biting into the darkness of another wolf, Halcyon turned her head to see Vincent, his face twisted with the concentration of the immense effort of influencing the will of the wolf that had become a part of him.

Kalya leapt into the air closely followed by Luma, Kayla's foot found Nyah's hand vaulting her high over the frozen flames, while Luma was launched by Nadaur, Kayla landed but her momentum caused her to roll stopping millimetres from the razor sharp static inferno & turning back just in time to catch the slightly out of control Elf that followed,

"You will not deny us what is ours!"

The bone chilling voice announced from the shadows a tinge of anger now very evident,

"You can't just open the box!" Sapere yelled,
"The star's power will kill you"
"You dare impede my will!" The Regent snapped,
with vitriol swiping at Sapere with his sword.
Sapere only avoiding being mortally wounded by
the skin of his teeth, Nyah put herself in between
them blocking a second strike,
"How dare you!" The Regent scolded,
"I dare because you have no reason in you!" she
replied,
The Regent reached forward grabbing Nyah by the
collar,
"You all work for me, I own you!" he screamed,
Losing his veneer of control.
Nyah grasped his wrist pushing The Regent
backward until he was directly in front of one of the
Shadow gateways,
"A little closer"
The disembodied voice requested,
The Regent releasing his peril began to panic
attempting to push back against Nyah but her
strength like her resolve was far greater than his.
A pale hand slid from the darkness taking hold of
The Regents throat,
"But we were meant to be" The Regent pleaded,
Nyah leaned in,
"You knew nothing of me" she said,
Realising her grip.
The Regent was lifted off his feet,
"Plea…!"
His cry was cut short as he disappeared into the
black abyss.

Cocker willed forward made a mad dash towards
the box, Tallie saw him out of the corner of her eye,
taking the black dagger she carefully sliced into his
cheek, her skill with the blade was such that she
barely broke the skin but it was enough to render
him paralysed, Cocker fell to the floor his body
frozen but otherwise uninjured, left with his
hypnotised purple eyes staring at the ceiling.
Luma's pointy ears twitched, she turned to Kayla,
"I know what to do" she said,
With a big smile & wide eyes. She grabbed the
gloves from Kaylas belt putting them on, then
looking up she sure she made eye contact with
Sikes,
"Run!" she mouthed with no sound,
Sikes pivoted turning around he took off bounding
away from the two girls on his way he scooped up
Tallie & clutched the immobile Cocker's leg
dragging along until he lifted him off the ground.
Nyah & Nadaur saw & followed suit, Faucon shot
an arrow at Dabns feet alerting him & they both
disappeared down one of the adjoining hallways.
Sapere & Halcyon had already taken refuge in the
hallway behind the Orb statue.
Luma placed her glove clad hands on the boxes lid
& Kayla pulled the heavy robe over both of them,
once they were completely entombed in the
protective nature of the garb, Luma with a mighty
heave flung open the lid releasing the immense
power of the star,
"We cannot be destroyed, only suppressed!" the
voice announced,

As the blinding white light filled every corner of the room, Stinal ducked just in time but his brother was too shocked to move & his body burned to ash that rained down on Stinal as he cowered in the tunnel closing the door just in time.
The light filled the room overtaking the shadows, the unending darkness replaced by the light.
"Luma!" Sapere screamed,
She used what was left of her strength to close the box, the light was instantly extinguished. Kayla flung back the robe & the two looked around the room, the fire which had once encompassed them was completely gone. They clambered to their feet letting the robe fall to the floor mostly covering the box. Kayla looked shocked until the silence was broken by a loud exclamation of pure excitement from Luma, who still wearing the oversized gloves threw her arms around her friend,
"We pretty much saved the world" Luma said with a cheesy grin,
The others emerged from their sanctuaries assessing the damage left in the wake of the stars power. The huge metal statue of the orb was reduced to a puddle of bubbling liquid on the floor. They approached the two saviours as they embraced in victory,
"That was among the bravest things I've ever witnessed" said Nadaur,
"We are all in your debt" added Nyah,
Placing her hand on each of their shoulders, which Luma took as permission to give her a mighty hug, which with a little smile Nyah responded in kind.

"What are we gonna do with that?" Tallie asked,
Kicking the box with her boot, Sapere looked over
at Halcyon & with a wink said,
"I think we can come up with a safe place for it"
Just then two Elite Guards appeared in a snap, the
loud bright noise echoed in the vast empty room,
then with another much louder snap a huge hulking
creature appeared wearing a bastardised version of
the Elite armour,
"What exactly can I help you with?" Sapere
inquired,
Somewhat playfully,
"Don't be needlessly obtuse, you know why we're
here sir, the box"
Sapere maintained eye contact, then as an idea
occurred to him the slightest of smiles virtually
imperceptible to those unfamiliar with his trademark
scowl,
"I'll be happy to have this thing out of my city after
all the trouble it's caused" he said,
The others watched on not quite sure of his plan
but confident in their trust in him.
Sapere turned & with an open hand pointed to the
box Sikes had brought from Halcyons chambers
still lying on the ground,
"It is remarkably heavy" Sapere quipped,
The Elite guard looked down his nose at Sapere &
ordered the young giant to obtain the coveted item.
Luma looked on squeezing Kayla's hand tightly in
an attempt to keep her glee at Sapere's trickery
from spreading to her face.

The box sat on the stone floor in a chipped crater of its own creation, the lumbering behemoth crouched down lifting one side then the other slipping thick chains under the box, he placed the chains over his shoulders standing up slowly groaning under the immense weight.

The other guards stood heads high, chests up barely acknowledging the others presence in the room, once the towering being had returned to his place behind the others with no further words exchanged between them, they activated their snaps & vanished in a loud concussive bang.

"You sneaky little bugger!" Luma blurted out with glee,

To which Sapere responded with an extravagant bow.

Halcyon turned to Sikes,

"We'll need to get this box to Calinton, she will know a safe place for it to reside, I'll take you to her"

Sikes walked over to the box passing Tallie as he went, he tussled her hair with his giant hand,

"Oi, knock it off," she yelled,

With a playful tinge.

Kayla & Luma ran over to Vincent who was sitting against the wall, the wolf had retreated back into him but the effort required to enforce his will upon the great beast was immense.

"Thank you, you saved us" Kayla said,

Sitting down next to him followed by Luma on his other side,

"It looks like you two were instrumental yourselves"
he replied,
"Yes, we were pretty amazing" Luma added,
with well placed pride in their actions,
Sikes walked past with Halcyon,
"You three deserve a nice meal, meet me later in
my garden & we'll have a lovely barbeque.
"Oh yes please" Luma said,
"Hally is a great cook"
She told the others.
Nyah & Nadaur walked over with Tallie to where
Cocker had been deposited by Sikes, Sapere was
already examining him as he lay paralysed on the
cold stone floor, his eyes still wide open the purple
tint still visible,
"He's being puppeteered by those we just
banished, it looks to be some variant of blood
hypnosis, Otto should be able to drain the offending
substance from his system" Sapere explained,
"I'll drop him off with Otto on my way past" offered
Tallie,
"Mmm" replied Sapere,
Still deep in thought,
Tallie hiked him over her shoulder with ease & as
she walked past,
Kalya said,
"Tallie, Halcyon is having a meal later in her
garden, if you wanna come?"
Tallie nodded,
Neither agreeing or dismissing the offer outright,
"I know we're going to eat later but I could really go
for a bowl of cereal" Luma announced,

"Let's be off then" Vincent said,
Holding out his arms, Kayla & Luma pulled him to
his feet, Leaving Nyah & Nadaur talking with
Sapere. A loud snap rung out which immediately
put all three of them back on guard but as they
looked, they saw the traveller was the same
messenger that had visited Nyah with
correspondence previously. Nyah darted across &
the royal messenger dropped to one knee holding a
familiar white envelope with her family crest pushed
into wax sealing in the contents. Nyah took the
letter but she didn't open it because she saw
Sapere & Nadaur were walking towards the largest
hallway,
"You are dismissed" she said,
Already running to join her friends.
The messenger stood bowed by simply dropping
his chin then disappeared in a second snap. Nyah
stuffed the pristine letter into her back pocket & ran
to catch the others yelling,
"Hey, wait for me!"

<u>Chapter 22</u>

The warm night air moved with a lovely soft wind that made the patches of wild flowers dance & sway. Halcyon had already set up a large half dome that she had filled with wood that had burnt down creating a perfect fire for cooking. Luma, Kayla, Vincent & Rava were sitting in the grass enjoying the idyllic evening, filling each other in on the parts of their adventure they might've missed.
"Make yourselves useful"
Halcyon broke into their conversation,
"Grab that grill & the tripod with the spit that are over there by the wall"
Luma groaned, but the others dragged her to her feet. Sapere sat off to the side puffing on an old pipe that appeared to be crafted from a single piece of bone, staring up at the waxing red moon that hung among the stars. Although the current danger had been thwarted the looming threat still occupied his mind. As the four young ones enjoyed the task of trying to figure out how to assemble the cooking accoutrements, Rava purposely making Luma's life difficult amusing the others. Halcyon sat next to Sapere taking a beautifully carved wooden pipe from her pocket packing the bowl with a blue mix from a small leather pouch.
"Just one evening" she said,
Breaking Sapere's train of thought,

"Scuse me?" he replied.
"Taking a moment to breath & relax is vital to your ability to function at your highest when it is required" she suggested gently,
Sapere took a deep breath letting it out & trying to release some of the tension that made his shoulders stiff & sore,
"I do envy the ability of the young to pivot & change" he said,
As they watched the young ones finding such fun within a simple task.
"I was just wondering if those tunnels were the result of the presence of the book & the hand beneath the city, somehow bleeding outward" he mused.
"Sikesy!" yelled Luma,
Seeing him squeeze through the archway, Kayla & Luma ran over each giving one of his huge furry arms a hug, Sikes lifted them both off the ground and returned their cuddle, squishing Luma a little more than was comfortable but they both entirely enjoyed the interaction.

Tallie placed Cockers unresponsive body on the bed closest to the door of Otto's small ward, she turned to leave & she heard from the poorly lit office,
"That's an interesting blade"
Otto walked out & began examining Cocker, peering into his eyes with a remarkably thick pair of glasses. Tallie pulled the black blade from her belt,

"It definitely came in handy that's for sure" she
admitted
"Well then it served its purpose" Otto replied,
Looking up with his eyes magnified to a comical
degree, Tallie fought the urge to burst out laughing.
"Will you let me know?" she asked,
Looking towards the unconscious Cocker,
"Mmmm" Otto replied,
Already engrossed in the mystery that had landed
on his doorstep. Tallie left finding herself
unintentionally walking towards Halcyon's little
garden refuge. She turned the corner seeing Nyah
& Nadaur walking with an arm around each other's
waist in the same direction, she snuck up behind
them & just as she was about to scare them Nyah
turned around yelling,
"Ahhhh!" scaring her first.
"Heading to Hallie's?" Nyah asked.
"Apparently" Tallie replied,
As she was very new to socialising in any fashion
outside combat focused events, Nyah did not press
the point as she could see that Tallie was trying her
best. They walked chatting until they passed
through the arch into Halcyon's Garden seeing
Luma & Kayla playing a version of tag with Sikes &
the boys. Tallie immediately headed to the little
makeshift bar that Halcyon had set up on a bench
by the door to the basement room Vincent had
been occupying, pouring herself a drink she
understood why people seek out the mundaneness
of a normal life. Nyah & Nadaur sat at the back of

the garden on a bench leaning back watching the shooting stars fly across the night sky,

"Are you gonna open that?" Nadaur asked, Looking at the letter still protruding from Nyah's pocket, Nyah knew that his curiosity had been peaked enough that he wouldn't be able to truly relax until she read the correspondence, so she pulled the letter out to the joy of Nadaur. Nadaur attempted to read over her shoulder by to no avail, it was written in the regal Impish calligraphy. Nyah's brow furrowed as she scanned the letter. Nadaur went over & fixed them both a drink while she continued to read, when he returned, he handed her the glass & she informed him,

"Apparently the Wolves are interested in recruiting Vincent"

"That intense little strike force that uses the trained wolves?" asks Nadaur

"Mmmm" Nyah replies,

As she continues to read her face changed again, "My mother has invited Kayla to the capital to try to establish to the other powers that be that she has now gained enough of a measure of control over the Maylar Venet that it would be more advantageous for everyone involved to utilise her rather than dismiss" Nyah explained.

She continued to read while Nadaur watched Halcyon with the aid of the youngsters cooking large steaks & an assortment of veggies over the fire, the wonderful smells igniting his appetite. As he turned to Nyah to inquire if she would like some food, she let out an audible groan,

"Bad news?" he asked
"Oh, not really, it seems my reprobate brother has
gotten himself in trouble again" she replied,
"But that's a problem for tomorrow, fancy a little
dinner?" she asked.
Nadaur nodded & they walked over to join the
others seeing Luma trying her darndest to get Tallie
to join in their silly games under the beautiful night
sky.

Thank you very much for reading my book, I really hope you enjoyed yourself. I'm currently working on the next instalment & I hope you will continue to enjoy the ongoing adventures.

<u>T.E.V.JUPP</u>